A Distant Dream

By Pamela Evans and available from Headline

A Barrow in the Broadway
Lamplight on the Thames
Maggie of Moss Street
Star Quality
Diamonds in Danby Walk
A Fashionable Address
Tea-Blender's Daughter
The Willow Girls
Part of the Family
Town Belles
Yesterday's Friends
Near and Dear
A Song in Your Heart
The Carousel Keeps Turning
A Smile for All Seasons
Where We Belong
Close to Home
Always There
The Pride of Park Street
Second Chance of Sunshine
The Sparrows of Sycamore Road
In the Dark Street Shining
When the Boys Come Home
Under an Amber Sky
The Tideway Girls
Harvest Nights
The Other Side of Happiness
Whispers in the Town
A Distant Dream

Pam
EVANS
A Distant Dream

headline

First published in Great Britain in 2013 by
HEADLINE PUBLISHING GROUP

1

Cataloguing in Publication Data is available from the British Library

ISBN 978 0 7553 9428 9

Typeset in Bembo by Palimpsest Book Production Limited,
Falkirk, Stirlingshire

Printed and bound in Great Britain by
Clays Ltd, St Ives plc

Headline's policy is to use papers that are natural, renewable and
recyclable products and made from wood grown in sustainable forests.
The logging and manufacturing processes are expected to conform
to the environmental regulations of the country of origin.

HEADLINE PUBLISHING GROUP
An Hachette UK Company
338 Euston Road
London NW1 3BH

www.headline.co.uk
www.hachette.co.uk

To my dear friend Alma Cassell for her warm-hearted
interest in and enthusiasm for my career

Acknowledgements

Many thanks to Clare Foss, my lovely editor, who has returned to me after a long gap, and all the team at Headline, including the designers who come up with such stunning jackets year after year. Thanks also to my agent Barbara Levy.

Chapter One

Errand boy George Bailey swung off his delivery bike, propped it up in the kerb and bounded in to the Green Street Pavilion, a white-painted shack adjacent to a children's playground in the back streets of Ealing in west London.

'Morning, Mrs Stubbs,' he greeted the woman behind the counter, a jolly blonde of middle years who was wearing a floral pinafore over a summer frock. 'Lovely day.'

She nodded towards the sunshine outside. 'It certainly is. What can I do for you, George?'

'The usual, please.'

'A cup of tea and a currant bun coming up,' said Flo Stubbs, who had blue eyes and a beaming smile that was genuine now after years of pretence when times were hard. 'As long as you're not behind with your delivery rounds. I don't want your boss coming round here and giving me an earful for encouraging you to skive.'

'I'm sure he wouldn't mind my stopping for a breather

so long as I keep on top of things,' he suggested. 'I'm a fast worker. I don't hang about.'

'What the eye doesn't see, eh?'

'Exactly,' he said, winking at her.

She lifted a large cream-coloured enamel teapot with green edging, poured the tea into the cup through a strainer and added a generous helping of milk from a jug, then took a sticky bun from under the glass cover and put it on a plate.

'Ta very much,' said George, helping himself to sugar from a bowl on the counter and handing her a ha'penny.

'You put your money away, boy,' she urged him. 'Have this one on us.'

George hesitated. He preferred to pay his way, especially with decent people like the Stubbses, who hadn't had things easy in the past. 'It's generous of you to offer,' he began, hoping not to cause offence by seeming ungrateful, 'but you don't want to be giving stuff away, not here at the shop anyway.'

'And we don't as a rule, but I'm in a good mood today and I think we can afford to treat our daughter's pal every now and again,' responded Flo, thinking what a handsome lad George was growing up to be, with his shandy-coloured eyes, curly chestnut hair and cap worn at a jaunty angle. He was the image of his father, God rest him. The boy's cheery demeanour gave no hint of the trauma he'd been through or how tough things had been for him at home these past couple of years. The Stubbs family knew him well because their daughter May had been friendly with him since they'd started school together aged five. Now both fifteen, they were still close friends and George was a regular visitor at the house. Sweethearts? Not as far as Flo knew, but they were far too young for that sort of thing anyway. They both needed to grow up and spread their wings a bit first. 'It won't happen often, so make the most of it and enjoy.'

He thanked her warmly and sat down at a table in the sunshine on the roomy veranda. He was soon joined by other errand boys, to whom this little café and general store was a magnet as a stopping place on their rounds. Having served the lads with tea, Tizer, cheese rolls and seed cake, Flo worked her way through the queue of women wanting sundry provisions they'd run out of or forgotten to get at the Co-op. That was the service they provided here at the Pavilion; people could get things cheaper in the shopping parade, but they came here for convenience and a chat with the locals.

The café was a big attraction, being in a heavily popu-lated residential area and the only one of its kind close at hand. Their menu was limited to light refreshments – sandwiches, cakes and a variety of hot and cold drinks – but they did very well, especially with their seasonal favourites: home-made ice cream in summer and toffee apples in the autumn when the fruit was plentiful.

A trip to the playground next door with the children was less of a chore for adults now that there was some-where they could enjoy a snack while the children played. Crowds of fearless infants clambered on to the witch's hat roundabout and the see-saw, some hurtling head first down the slide and hanging on for dear life to the ends of the swinging horse as it creaked from side to side. On fine weekends the Pavilion was packed out.

Glancing around in a quiet moment at the potted geraniums and pansies on the veranda, a splash of bright colour embellishing the white-painted wooden structure, Flo thanked God for this place, which had come to them unexpectedly four years ago. Not only had it rescued the Stubbs family from abject poverty, it had also given Flo a new sense of purpose and had later helped her to cope with the grief that haunted her even now, though it was three years since they'd lost their beloved ten-year-old son Geoffrey to diphtheria.

It had been a gamble taking on a derelict cricket pavilion that had been empty since the cricket club moved away several years before, especially as neither Flo nor her husband had any experience of shopkeeping or catering. But when one of the gentlemen Flo cleaned for surprised her with a modest sum in his will in recognition of her hard work and kindness, she'd seen an opportunity to get Dick off the dole and herself out of charring, and to build some sort of security for their family.

She had long thought that a commercial venture was what this back-street area next to the recreation ground needed. Fortunately there was plenty of space inside the pavilion, and room on the veranda to add a few tables, while water and electricity had been installed by the previous owners.

Being in such a state of disrepair and a long time on

the market, the shack had been going at a rock-bottom price and there had been just enough money left over from the purchase to do it up and stock it. After a slow start, the place had soon gathered momentum, and Flo believed that it was now a real asset to the community. It didn't earn them a fortune, but it did give them a decent living, and now that May had left school and was working as well, the deprived days were behind them; for good, she hoped.

In theory, Flo and Dick ran the business together, but it was actually Flo who was in charge. Dick was an asset serving behind the counter, being such a popular and gregarious soul, but he had no initiative for shopkeeping and was happy to leave the management to her. His skills lay elsewhere. A qualified metalworker, he'd lost his job during the worst of the depression and had been on the dole for several years before their change in fortune.

Now, in the summer of 1936, things were still very hard for people in parts of the north of England and Wales, but here in the south-east there had been an improvement for some areas these last few years, mostly due to the new industries and an increase in house-building, especially in the London suburbs. Factories producing such things as aircraft and electrical goods had opened in nearby areas and were flourishing and keeping unemployment down. So it had proved to be a good time to start a business.

Dick appeared from the stockroom wearing a brown overall and carrying a carton of tinned peas, which he began stacking on to the shelves. He was a tall, jovial man with greying dark hair, his liking for a sociable pint or two manifest in a sizeable beer belly.

'Can you look after things here, Dick, while I pop home and do a bit indoors?' asked Flo. 'I need to go to the butcher's as well to get something for dinner.'

'Righto, love,' he agreed affably.

She left the Pavilion and walked briskly past the playground and through the serried ranks of red-brick terraced houses with their privet hedges and tiny low-walled front gardens. She was home within minutes. It was very convenient living so close to the job, she thought, as she turned the key in the lock, noticing that the red doorstep needed some polish and deciding that she would deal with that before she tackled the rest of the housework.

Flo was an energetic woman and an avid housekeeper, occupation was her salvation, and with a home and a business to look after, she didn't have time to mope. That wouldn't be fair to her husband or her beautiful daughter May, whose endless exuberance filled the house with light. May and her father had both suffered the loss of Geoffrey too, and Flo made sure she didn't forget that by being self-indulgent in her attitude towards her own grief.

Oh well, let's get cracking, she said to herself as she stepped into the narrow hall, itching to take the broom and floor polish to the lino.

Dick Stubbs cleared some empty tables and stopped for a chat with two elderly men who came to the café every morning for a newspaper and a cup of tea.

'How's your luck, me old mate?' said one of the men, who was wearing a trilby hat and a dark suit despite the warm weather.

'Not so bad,' Dick replied.

'It's a bit better than that, I reckon,' joshed the man. 'This place must be a little gold mine.'

'Hardly that,' said Dick, 'but it keeps the wolf from the door so I'm not complaining.'

'It was a good idea of yours to open up a café here,' remarked the man. 'It's somewhere for us to go out of the way while the missus is cleaning.'

'Not half,' agreed his friend.

'It was my wife's idea actually,' Dick explained.

'Good for her,' the man enthused. 'We don't know what we'd do without it now.'

'Glad you're pleased.'

'Will we see you in the local tonight?' asked the man in the trilby.

Dick nodded, smiling. 'I expect I shall come in for a quick one,' he said, moving away as he saw someone approach the counter. 'I'll see you boys later.'

When he'd finished serving, he fell into reflective mood. All of this, the shop, the café, the satisfied clientele and the fact that he and his family were no longer on the breadline was almost entirely down to Flo. She made everything run like clockwork and it was her kindly nature that had enabled it to happen in the first place. She'd been astonished to receive a legacy from the old man she cleaned for, but knowing her as he did, Dick guessed she'd put more than just housework into the job.

As well as extra favours like shopping and changing his library books she would have taken the trouble to listen if he wanted to chat, no matter how busy she was. Flo had the ability to hide her true feelings from the outside world. She could seem to be cheerful when her life was actually falling apart. Only he knew how much she had suffered when they lost young Geoffrey. Even May had been protected to some degree from her mother's grief because Flo had considered it her duty to be strong for their daughter. Dick was well aware that he was married to a very special woman.

Their standard of living was better than it had been for years and working here was a pleasant enough way of life. But although he would never say as much to Flo after all her efforts, there was something missing for him. His trade! He was good with his hands and missed the satisfaction his work had given him as well as the atmosphere of the workshop and the male company. It had been hard graft compared to this but it was what he'd been trained for and he'd been proud to call himself a tradesman. Most of the time working here didn't feel like work at all, except perhaps when it was his turn to get up at the crack of dawn to sort the newspapers for the rounds.

Still, he was a very lucky man in all other respects and he had no intention of complaining.

'We have something new in that you might like to consider, madam,' said May Stubbs to a customer at Bright Brothers

Department Store where she worked as a junior in the lingerie department. A blond girl with the look of her mother about her, she opened one of the wooden-framed glass-fronted drawers behind the polished mahogany counter, took out a pair of pink satin French knickers with lace edging and spread them out on the counter. 'We have them in white and blue as well. Beautiful, aren't they?'

'Indeed they are,' agreed the customer, who was middle aged, attractive and well dressed though in matronly style like many women of her age. 'But I'm not quite sure if they are right for me.'

'For a special occasion perhaps?' suggested May.

A sharp poke in the back startled her and she turned round quickly to see her superior, Miss Matt, glaring at her.

'The customer has plain white knickers of the larger, comfortable variety,' whispered the older woman. She'd been serving someone with a winceyette nightdress but had left that to flex her senior status muscles over May. 'She's been shopping here for years and that's what she has.'

'But these are so pretty, and new in, so I thought perhaps . . .' began May.

'Plain white interlock cotton with elasticated legs,' hissed Miss Matt. 'You should know that's what older ladies prefer.'

May turned back to the customer. 'I can see that you are doubtful about them, madam,' she said tactfully. 'Perhaps something a little plainer might be more to your taste.'

'These are very nice, though,' remarked the customer, fingering the lace lovingly.

'My assistant is young,' interrupted Miss Matt dismissively. 'She's still learning the job. You can trust us here at Bright Brothers to look after your best interests as always.'

'The French ones are ever so pretty,' began the customer, enthusiasm growing.

'We have something much more appropriate,' Miss Matt cut in speedily. 'Get them, please, Miss Stubbs, and quick about it. You've kept the customer waiting for long enough already.'

May did as she was bid and laid a pair of huge cotton interlock bloomers on the counter, putting the others to one side.

'Mm,' murmured the customer. 'They do seem a little . . . er, heavy in comparison. May I see the others again? The white ones as well, please.'

'Certainly, madam,' said May, leaning down to the drawer, feeling the full blast of Miss Matt's disapproval and crushing her own urge to giggle.

'But the lady purchased several pairs of each type of knickers,' said May defensively, having had a thorough trouncing from Miss Matt as soon as the customer had made her way out of the store, which was all dim lighting and dark polished wood. 'That must be good for business, surely.'

'Personal service is what we pride ourselves on here

at Bright Brothers,' lectured Miss Matt, who was middle aged, plain and very prim. 'We aren't the sort of store to concentrate on a quick sale to boost turnover. We look after our customers so that they will stay with us in the long term.'

'I thought we were also supposed to promote our goods and make recommendations,' remarked May.

'We are, of course, but our suggestions must be right for each individual customer,' said the older woman.

'The lady seemed very pleased with her purchases. I'm sure she'll continue to shop here.'

'If she does come back it may well be with a complaint against us for encouraging her to purchase inappropriate garments.'

May decided to push her luck. 'Please don't think I'm being rude, Miss Matt,' she began with the respect demanded of a junior, 'but why exactly are the pretty ones inappropriate?'

'The customer is a married woman of a certain age, not a Hollywood film star.'

'If she can afford pretty underwear, why shouldn't she have it?' May enquired.

'Because it's the way things are,' insisted Miss Matt, exasperated. 'Why can't you just do as you're told without questioning every darned thing?'

'I'm just naturally curious, I suppose,' replied May, an energetic girl with bright blue eyes and a sunny smile.

'Well you know what curiosity did; it killed the cat, so let's have less of it please.'

'But I thought the management would want us to take an interest in our work,' persisted May.

'That may well be so, but they certainly don't want junior members of staff questioning the decisions of their superiors,' claimed her colleague.

'So are you saying that a woman has to wear hideous drawers for the rest of her life just because she's over forty?'

'She doesn't have to, but most respectable older women do,' Miss Matt explained. 'It's only right and proper. Besides, people like to be comfortable when they get older.'

'Oh, I see,' said May, finding it rather a dull prospect.

'Anyway, that's enough of your questions,' said Miss Matt, bringing the conversation to a swift conclusion. 'We've work to do. There is some new stock to put away and everything needs tidying up in the department.'

'Yes, Miss Matt,' said May politely.

May's best friend Betty thought the French knickers incident was hilarious.

'Oh you never tried to sell them to some old girl,' she said, giggling as they walked home together through busy Ealing Broadway, past the Palladium Cinema and Lyons tea shop, the brightly coloured striped awnings being taken in as the varied assortment of shops closed for the day, the pavements crowded with people queuing for electric trolley buses and hurrying towards the station. 'No wonder old Matty blew her top. You might as well try and sell satin knickers to your mother.'

'The customer bought them anyway,' May pointed out, 'and good luck to her. I hope she enjoys them even if she does have a few grey hairs.'

'At least you get to work with nice things,' said Betty wistfully. A brown-eyed brunette the same age as May, she was employed at Bright Brothers too, in the bedding department. 'All I see is boring old sheets and pillowcases.'

'Come on, you do sell the occasional eiderdown,' said May, teasing her.

'Thanks for reminding me,' retorted Betty, taking it in good part.

'I must say, I do enjoy being in the lingerie department, though Miss Matt is a bit of a pain,' admitted May. 'At least I get to see a bit of glamour, even if I can't afford it myself.'

'Maybe we'll have enough money to buy satin underwear one day,' said Betty.

'We certainly can't at the moment on the wages we get from Bright Brothers,' May responded.

'We'll have to wait and have it for our trousseau then.'

May laughed. 'That's looking a long way ahead,' she said. 'We've got to find someone to marry us first.'

'You'll be all right. You've got George,' Betty pointed out.

'George is just a friend and he'll have lots of girls before he finally settles down, Mum says, and I'll have boyfriends,' added May. 'She says I'm much too young to think about things like that.'

'Mums always say that sort of thing,' Betty remarked.

'Mine is just the same. You're too young for this that and the other . . . especially the other.'

The girls thought this was very funny and erupted into laughter.

'I can't imagine life without George,' said May when they had recovered and were being more serious. 'I've been close friends with him all my life and I know I always will be, whatever happens between us and no matter what Mum says.'

There was rather a long silence.

'Anyway, will I see you after tea?' asked Betty, moving on swiftly rather than linger on the subject of May and George and their special friendship.

'I think I'll go for a bike ride if you fancy coming,' said May.

'No thanks,' replied Betty. 'That's far too much like hard work for me.'

'As you wish,' said May.

Betty nodded. 'Where are you going to cycle to?'

'Wherever the mood takes me,' replied May casually. 'I need the fresh air and exercise.'

'Haven't you had enough exercise, on your feet all day at work?' said Betty.

'Cycling is a different sort of exercise,' said May, who'd had a bicycle from her parents for her fourteenth birthday. 'It makes you feel really good somehow.'

Betty was sometimes in awe of her friend and often very envious of her. May had something that Betty lacked: an independent spirit and opinions of her own, whereas Betty tended to go along with the herd. Cycling to Richmond on her own was nothing to May; she even went all the way to Runnymede on her bike by herself sometimes. Betty didn't do anything without company, but May would do things alone if she had no one to do them with.

The worst thing for Betty was the green-eyed monster with regard to May and George Bailey. Betty actually hated her with a passion over that. George was the best-looking boy around and he only had eyes for May. Always had! The confusing part for Betty was the fact that she loved May as a friend very much. She was great fun and there was no one else Betty would rather spend time with. So why did she hate her so much at times instead of being pleased for her? Betty, May and George had been friends since they were children, but there had always been something special between those two and Betty had always secretly resented it.

'George will probably go for a bike ride with you,' she suggested as reparation for being so ill willed.

'Yeah, he might do,' agreed May. 'I'll call at his house on my way out to ask him, though he may be going to the boxing club, in which case I'll go on my own.'

'No harm in mentioning it to him, is there?' said Betty.

They headed past the train station on the other side of the street, the road crowded with motor vehicles, bicycles and some horse-drawn carts, and walked along by Haven Green alongside the railway line and into the back streets, chatting amiably until they came to Betty's turning, which was the one before May's road.

'I'll see you tomorrow then,' said May.

'Okey-doke,' responded Betty.

★　★　★

'I'm ever so hungry, Mum,' said May, digging a knife into the potatoes bubbling in the saucepan on the gas stove. 'These are done. Shall I drain them?'

'Turn the gas off but better leave the spuds in the saucepan to keep hot while I make the gravy,' Flo suggested. 'The meat pie is ready.'

'I'll set the table,' said May.

'Thanks, dear.'

In the living room at the back of the house where the family had their meals and took their leisure, the front room only coming into use on special occasions, May took the tablecloth and cutlery from a drawer in the sideboard, pausing to look at a framed photograph of her brother and herself in the garden a year or so before he died. She would have been about eleven; he was nine. Every day she looked at this and still got a lump in her throat.

It seemed strange, even now, that Geoffrey wasn't around anywhere, *ever*. They used to argue like mad – as siblings do – but they'd loved each other for all that. Being the elder she'd always felt duty-bound to look out for him, and after he died she'd thought it must be her fault.

She'd come to realise that it wasn't after a while, but she missed having him around even if sometimes he had been her annoying little brother. Now it was just her and Mum and Dad. No other young person in the house to josh with; no childish squabbles, or shouts or giggles or standing united against parental authority. It was as though the youthful spirit of the house had died along with Geoffrey. She loved Mum and Dad dearly – and empathised with them all the time over the loss of their child – but they weren't young. May had become an only child on that terrible day three years ago. There was something awfully lonesome about that.

But she had her two best friends, George and Betty, and they both meant the world to her. She wiped a tear from her eye with the back of her hand and got on with laying the table. Tiddles, the family cat, strutted into the room with his usual proprietorial air and rubbed himself around her legs meowing demandingly. She picked him up and stroked him, loving his shiny black fur, yellow-green eyes and the feel and sound of his vibrating purr. He was a glutton for cuddles and that was fine with May, because she enjoyed making a fuss of him.

Her father came into the room and sat in the armchair by the hearth, unlit at this time of year. As he opened the newspaper she noticed a picture of the American athlete who was doing so well in the much-publicised Berlin Olympic Games that were on at the moment.

'Has Jesse Owens got another medal, Dad?' she asked.

'Yes,' he replied, peering at her over the top of the paper after glancing at the headline.

'The star of the games so they say.'

'He certainly is, and Mr Hitler will be none too pleased about that,' he said.

'Is that because he only wants his own people to win?' she enquired.

'Something like that,' replied her father.

May knew that there was some sort of controversy

about the games in Germany and that it concerned Hitler and the Nazi party. But her interest in the Olympics was purely sporting and everything else went over her head.

'Grub's up,' called Flo from the kitchen, and May went to help her bring the food in.

There was an argument in progress when George Bailey got home from work, which wasn't unusual because his sister and their mother were always at daggers drawn lately.

'Oi oi,' he said, hearing shouting coming from the kitchen. 'Pack it in, the pair of you.'

'Tell your sister that,' said his mother Dot, a sad little woman with dark shadows under her eyes, her once black hair now almost white. 'She started it.'

'What's it all about this time?' he sighed, and turning to his sister added, 'Sheila, what have you been saying to Mum to upset her so much?'

'She's pathetic,' declared Sheila, a feisty thirteen year old. 'Why can't she be like other mothers and do the things they do like shopping and ironing our clothes? Why do I have to go to the butcher's before I go to school every morning and do the household jobs when I get home?'

'It doesn't hurt you to help out,' said George.

'Help out, I'll be doing the bloody lot before long,' declared Sheila, who was similar in colouring to George and had brown hair worn in long plaits. 'All she does is mope about the house all day.'

'That's enough of that sort of language,' admonished George.

'Who are you to tell me what to do?' she shouted. 'You're not my father.'

'No, but seeing as he isn't here, I'm standing in for him,' he said. 'Mum's had a bad time, so go easy on her and treat her with respect.'

'That's right, take her side like you always do.'

'She's our mother,' he reminded her sternly.

'Huh. I thought mothers were supposed to look after their kids,' retorted Sheila.

'She does her best,' said George.

'For what it's worth.'

'I don't know what's got into you, Sheila,' he told her. 'You didn't used to behave like this when Dad was alive.'

'She used to be a proper mum then, didn't she?' she said, her face suffused with red blotches and eyes brimming with angry tears. 'Now all she does is feel sorry for herself.' She looked at her mother, who was standing in the doorway crying silently. 'There she goes, booing her eyes out again. She's not the only one who suffered. We lost our dad.' Sheila's voice broke. 'I'm sorry, Mum, but I just can't stand it, coming home from school every day to your miserable face. Why don't you try to cheer up and give us all a break?'

With that she ran from the room sobbing.

George went over to his mother and put an affectionate arm around her. 'She doesn't mean it, Mum,' he said. 'She's growing up and getting stroppy with it.'

'I try, George, but I can't shake it off,' she said thickly. 'This terrible despair.'

19

'I know,' he said kindly, holding her close. 'But maybe if you were to keep busy it might help somehow. It's two years since Dad died. You've done enough grieving.'

'He didn't just die, he was murdered,' she reminded him.

Hearing it was like a physical blow, but he didn't want her to know how much it hurt because she was in no state to take on anyone else's problems. She needed him to be strong and supportive. 'Yes, I know, Mum,' he said. 'But it's all over now and Dad's murderer has been hanged. It's time for you to start living again.'

'I feel as though I can't do anything because I'm so weak,' she said.

George felt completely unequal to the problem of his mother. Common sense told him that the persistent low spirits that had troubled her for such a long time must surely be something more than just grief. But even if he could find the money to seek medical help he risked having her carted off to the lunatic asylum. That was what they did to people who got sick in the head. So all he could do was be kind to her and encourage her to get back to doing normal things, like going out and looking after the home properly.

'I know,' he said sympathetically. 'Why don't I make you a nice cup of tea and you sit down quietly and drink it.'

'Thank you, son.'

'Have you managed to get a meal ready for us?' he asked hopefully.

'It's in the oven.'

Thank God for that, he said to himself. More often

than not when he got home from work his sister was out with her pals, having rebelled and refused to cook a meal yet again, and he had to go and get fish and chips, which he couldn't afford often on his wages as an errand boy. And his low pay was something else he had to deal with as a matter of urgency.

'I'll put the kettle on,' he said.

'You're so good to me, George,' said Dot.

Filled with guilt for sometimes being irritated by her hopelessness, he said, 'And you've always been good to me, Mum. Together we'll get you through this rough patch, don't worry.'

'I know, son,' she said pitifully, twisting his heart. 'I know.'

'Can't you try to be a bit kinder to her, sis?' asked George, finding his sister sitting on her bed sobbing.

'I do try, but all this misery of hers is driving me mad,' she said. 'I miss Dad and I know you do too but we don't go about like the living dead every day, do we? At first it was understandable for Mum to be upset, but it's just going on and on.'

'We're young, we've got more stamina than she has and our lives ahead of us, as well as friends and outside interests,' he said. 'Whereas Dad was her husband and her whole life.'

'I know I'm awful and I hate myself for being so mean to her,' said Sheila, wiping her eyes. 'But it's all wrong the way she is. My friends think she's loopy; they talk about her behind my back and are always making remarks about my having to do all the shopping. I won't put up with that so I end up defending her and quarrelling with them. And that makes me feel even worse. I'll be glad when I've left school altogether. I wish I could leave home too.'

'Well you're not old enough to do either yet, so how about giving me some support with Mum to help her get back to her old self instead,' he said.

'S'pose I shall have to,' she agreed miserably.

'You can start by telling her that you're sorry for your outburst, and then we'll sit down together and eat our meal and you can try not to lose your temper again.'

'All right, George.'

'Good girl.'

'I don't know how you manage to stay cheerful with Mum the way she is.'

'It must be in my nature,' he said, but he wasn't as happy-go-lucky as he seemed. Unbeknown to anyone else, he suffered from fierce bouts of fury towards the man who had robbed them of their father and broken their mother's heart.

Their dad, Joe Bailey, had been a small-time boxing promoter who had been in the business for the love of the sport, not for the money. Other people in the boxing community were more materialistic, and when Dad had refused to agree to allow a fight to be rigged, he had been attacked by a man called Bill Bikerley outside a pub in Shepherd's Bush and had died of his injuries.

Even though justice had been done and Bikerley had been given the death penalty, the anger remained in George's heart, and when he saw the broken woman his mother had become, it grew almost unbearable. Senseless he knew, since there was no one to direct his rage to now that Bikerley was dead. But still it came, especially when Mum had a bad day as she had today.

'Oh, by the way, George, there's a school trip coming up and I need tuppence to pay for it,' his sister was saying. 'Will that be all right, do you think?'

He hesitated for a moment, then said, 'You'll have your money, I'll make sure of it.'

'Thanks, George,' she said, cheering up.

Following her down the stairs he was thoughtful. Thanks to a persistent insurance agent who had called at the house every week, their father had taken out a life insurance policy, so Mum hadn't been left destitute when he died. She had enough for rent and food and other essentials to keep the house running, but there wasn't much left over for unexpected expenses such as his sister's school trip. Of course he paid for his keep now that he was working, and bought his own clothes, so he was no longer a drain on Mum, but his sister still had a year left at school.

The wages of an errand boy just wasn't enough. It really was time he did something about it.

After all the family tension earlier, George was so delighted to see May when she knocked at the door after they had finished their meal that he wanted to take her in his arms and smother her in kisses. But he didn't have the skill or confidence to smother anyone in kisses yet and she was a decent girl, so he gave her a beaming smile instead.

'Just wondered if you fancy coming for a bike ride with me,' she explained. 'We might as well make the most of the light nights.'

'Yeah, I'd like that, May,' he said. 'I'll just tell them where I'm going and I'll be with you. Won't be a minute.'

While she walked to her bike at the front gate to wait for him, he went back inside.

'Is it May?' asked Sheila.

'Yeah, and we're going for a bike ride, that is if I can trust you two not to kill each other while I'm out.'

'You can relax,' said his sister, seeming calmer. 'Mum is going to undo my plaits and brush my hair for me when we've done the washing-up, and we might listen to the wireless.'

'Thank God for that,' he said, relieved that things seemed to have improved and his mother had finally stopped crying. Mum did seem to be better in the evenings – he'd noticed that before – and Sheila had apologised as she'd promised. So all was well, he thought; for the time being anyway.

May and George sat on a bench by the river at Richmond, watching the river traffic go by, a medley of pleasure craft and working boats, listening to the gentle splash of the oars as the rowing crews practised along this stretch. The wildlife was abundant here; swans and ducks preening and pecking and gliding by in groups. The air was balmy, the orange sun low in the sky behind the trees on the other side of the Thames, the image softened by the beginnings of a pearly mist.

'Sorry I didn't ask you in when you came to the door earlier,' he said.

'It doesn't matter, George,' she assured him. 'Is your mum not too good again?'

'She was a bit dodgy earlier on and there was all-out war between her and Sheila,' he explained. 'I wanted to spare you the atmosphere of the aftermath.'

'I didn't mind, honestly,' she assured him, smiling at him and melting his heart.

'I've decided to try and get another job,' he announced out of the blue.

'Really?' she said, surprised. 'Why is that?'

'Dosh,' he replied candidly. 'I need more of it to put into the pot at home. It's hard for Mum without Dad to support her, and Sheila still being at school.'

'What sort of job are you hoping for?'

'I'm thinking of trying one of the new factories over Acton way,' he replied. 'You can earn good money if you put in the hours, so I've heard.'

She looked doubtful. 'But I thought you liked the freedom of being out delivering.'

'I do, but it pays peanuts and I have to face facts,' he said. 'Anyway, I can't be an errand boy all my life.'

'No, but you are only fifteen,' she pointed out.

'I have family responsibilities.'

'Yeah, I suppose you do.'

She thought it must be hard for George to be burdened at such a young age, and was sad for him too because she knew how much he'd wanted to work with his beloved father in the boxing business. He might have even become a boxer himself when he was old enough if his dad hadn't been struck down as he had.

His father's murder had been a shocking thing at the time; the whole of the neighbourhood had been reeling and everybody had been talking about it. Joe Bailey had been a popular man in the area and the streets had been lined with well-wishers for the funeral procession.

George had been amazingly brave but May knew he'd been devastated because his dad had been his hero and they'd been close. But he'd faced up to it and at thirteen years of age had become the man of the house.

'Anyway, I've heard that one or two of the factories are looking for unskilled labour, so I'll go to the Labour Exchange in my dinner break one day soon.'

'If that's what you think is best, I hope you find something soon,' she said.

'Thanks,' he said, taking her hand and sounding gruff because he found it hard to cope with the strength of his feelings when he touched her these days.

Of course he knew all about the birds and bees. Embarrassingly, his father had given him a rather garbled version and his mates passed on any information they had and it was the subject of much speculation and laughter. You had to pretend you knew as much as the others to avoid mockery. But it was all a bit smutty and on the quiet; no one ever talked openly or seriously about it.

So he had no idea how he was supposed to cope with loving someone as he loved May. Fifteen-year-old boys weren't meant to indulge in such sentimental feelings. It was supposed to be all about biology and restraint. There were times when he wished he was older and had more savvy. At this age he was still in between, neither man nor boy, even though his father's death had made him grow up overnight in some ways.

'I suppose we'd better set off for home soon,' said May. She too had only a basic knowledge of the facts of life but guessed that all these new feelings she was experiencing had something to do with them. As the subject was absolutely taboo, she kept the way she felt when she was with George to herself. She didn't even want to talk to Betty about it. It was far too personal and embarrassing; even a little shameful. 'Before it gets dark.'

'Yeah, you're right,' he agreed, standing up. 'Come on then, let's go.'

They got on to their bikes and cycled along by the river for a while, then through Richmond town with its winding and elegant high street and up the hill and onwards to Kew Bridge, heading home with the scent of a summer evening and wood smoke in the air. Until they passed through the less fragrant Brentford, where the noxious pong of the gasworks prevailed.

Back on home ground, with dusk falling and the amber glow of a London night all around them, May

27

was aware of joy so strong it almost brought tears to her eyes. She and George had spent a lot of time together comfortably for most of their lives, but lately she had noticed a new intensity between them. Now, though, the atmosphere was as warm and soft as the air around them.

When they reached her house they stood under the lamp-post opposite, talking for a long time, not wanting to part but knowing that they must. When the time finally came, he brushed his lips against her cheek briefly, got on his bike and rode away. She stood looking after him until he turned the corner, then went indoors.

Chapter Two

'My mother was in tears after the King's broadcast last night,' May mentioned to Miss Matt one Saturday morning in December as they were preparing for the store to open its doors to the customers for the day's trading.

'I very much doubt if she was the only one,' said the older woman. The King's abdication speech had been broadcast from Windsor Castle the night before and had attracted practically the entire nation to within earshot of a wireless set. 'It's a sad thing indeed for our country.'

'It isn't very nice for him either, is it?' said down-to-earth May, who found the other woman to be quite chatty when she was in the mood and her strong opinions about absolutely everything rather entertaining. 'I don't see why they couldn't have let him marry the woman he loves and carry on being king.'

'The reason you think along those lines, my dear, is because you are a young girl with a head full of romantic notions,' stated Miss Matt unequivocally. 'Mrs Simpson

29

is a divorced woman and therefore not suitable to be the King's consort. Not suitable at all.'

'But he's had to give up the throne so that he can be with her, and that seems very harsh,' May pointed out. 'It also speaks volumes about his feelings for her.'

'His duty is what matters and he's turned his back on that and left it for his brother to do,' stated Miss Matt with cutting disapproval.

'But he doesn't feel able do the job without Mrs Simpson by his side, does he? He said as much,' May reminded her.

'Tosh,' said the authoritative Miss Matt. 'What sort of a world would it be if we all just did what we wanted the whole time? The royal family set an example and it has to be beyond reproach.'

'Seems rather inhuman to me.'

'Look, the man can do exactly what he likes now that he's turned his back on us, so he'll get what he wants anyway. Don't waste your sympathy on him.' Miss Matt checked that the sales pads were all in place, patted her hair as though to make sure it was tidy, stood up straight to correct her posture and smoothed her grey woollen dress over her middle with her hands. 'Anyway, that's quite enough idle gossip. The store is now open, so let business for the day commence. With Christmas almost upon us, our sales should be well up or the management will want to know why not. Put on your best smile, Miss Stubbs, and let's liven this place up and get those overhead wires buzzing.'

Dressed in a black skirt and cardigan over a white blouse,

her blond hair falling loosely to her shoulders, May glanced around the store and thought it would take more than a few Christmas decorations to liven this place up. The powers that be on the management had made some sort of an effort with a few paper chains and a Christmas tree in the entrance hall, but the atmosphere was determinedly tasteful and traditional, which created an air of gloom.

She had little time to brood on it, however, because customers were flooding in and a lot of them were heading her way.

May's favourite moments in the course of a working day were those immediately after a sale when she made out the bill and put that and the payment into a metal container, which she hooked to an overhead wire. Then she pulled a cord, which would ping, and the cylinder would whizz across the shop to the cashier at the other side, who would, eventually, return the capsule containing the receipt and the customer's change. When all the departments in the store were busy, there was a positive fury of activity overhead.

'There you are, madam,' she said now to a woman who had purchased some woollen vests as she handed them to her in a Bright Brothers paper bag. 'A merry Christmas to you.'

'Likewise, I'm sure.'

May turned away to cough discreetly behind her hand before serving the next customer, which was a much more interesting sale, being a satin petticoat with bra and pants to match. That's more like it, she thought.

★ ★ ★

31

The Pavilion was busy that same Saturday morning and there was no lack of Christmas spirit despite the royal goings-on the night before, about which there were mixed opinions, from outrage at the King's dereliction of duty and fury with his lover for stealing him away from his people to those who couldn't care less and some who simply wished him well.

Paper chains garlanded the ceiling, tinsel was in abundance and the paraffin heaters were going full blast. Dick was looking after the café while Flo served at the shop counter and sold raffle tickets for a well-stocked Christmas hamper provided by the management, all proceeds to go to the poor. She hadn't forgotten the misery of that predicament and knew it was still rife, especially in other parts of the country. The recent march of the Jarrow unemployed to London was proof of that.

'So what will be in this Christmas hamper then, Flo?' enquired a regular female customer while Flo weighed up a quarter of tea for her.

'A Christmas pudding and cake made by my own fair hand, a tin of ham, chocolate biscuits, a quarter of tea, a bottle of ginger beer, an assortment of sweets and any other little treats I might decide to put in as a surprise for the winner.'

'Sounds lovely,' said the woman. 'I'll take a couple of tickets please, dear.'

Flo was in her element. There was a queue in the shop and every table in the café was taken, the scones and jam sponges she'd made last night at home had sold out and the sandwiches were going the same way. It

wasn't just the fact that they were taking money, as satis-
fying as that was; it was the warm atmosphere and the
sense of camaraderie, that put a smile on her face. The
weather outside was cold and cloudy – not a soul sitting
on the veranda today – but in here it was positively
glowing.

In a lull between customers that afternoon, Miss Matt
took May aside for a quiet word.

'I think you should get some medicine for that cough
of yours,' she suggested. 'It's getting to be a nuisance.'

'You're telling me,' May responded. 'I must have got
a chill or something. I just can't seem to shake it off.'

'It isn't good for business for you to be coughing while
you're attending to customers,' she lectured.

'I realise that,' said May, though she was taken aback
by Miss Matt's callous attitude.

'I know that might sound heartless, but it's a fact of
life I'm afraid, my dear,' the older woman went on. 'I
realise that it can't be pleasant for you, but people don't
want to be picking up coughs and colds when they go
shopping, do they?'

'Mum did get me a bottle of cough mixture from the
chemist,' May told her, feeling embarrassed and guilty,
'but it doesn't seem to have made any difference at all.'

'Then you must get something else, because you've had
it for quite a while now,' she said. 'Lemon juice with honey
is supposed to be very good. And you must get some cough
lozenges to control it while you are on duty here.'

'I'll do what I can,' May assured her. 'I really am very sorry. I feel terrible about it.'

'It isn't your fault, of course. It's my duty as head of the department to mention it, that's all.' Miss Matt regarded May studiously, her grey eyes softening slightly. 'You look a bit tired. You're not feeling poorly with it, are you?'

'No. I'm fine.'

Miss Matt peered at her. 'That's all right then. We can't have you falling sick at this time of the year. You don't want to miss all the fun, do you?'

'No, of course not,' said May, but suddenly she didn't feel very much like having fun. Her superior had managed to make her feel somehow gauche and inferior.

Christmas passed pleasantly in the Stubbs home, though they all missed Geoffrey terribly at this time of year. May tried to keep her irritating cough at bay with linctus and lozenges and attempted to ignore the fact that she felt a bit off colour.

On New Year's Eve things livened up considerably when George's pal Henry invited him, and anyone he cared to bring with him, to his house to listen to records on the gramophone. As no one else had one of these amazing music machines, George, May, Betty and Sheila – who had begged her brother to let her go with them – were delighted to go along.

'Mum and Dad are out for the evening, or a part of it anyway,' Henry informed them and a few other young people who were there, 'so we've got the place to ourselves.

Let's hope they don't come back too early, though they'll definitely be home before midnight, so everybody out well before then.' He produced a bottle of gin, smiling broadly. 'Look what I've managed to pinch from the sideboard. One drink each so they won't notice we've been at it, especially if I add some water to make up the difference. We'll take turns to wind up the gramophone.'

Everyone agreed, and the evening got under way with Bing Crosby singing 'Pennies from Heaven' and Sheila turning the handle on the side of the gramophone, which was housed in a large polished wooden cabinet with space to store records. Everyone except Sheila, who had been deemed too young for alcohol by her brother, had a glass of gin, and May and Betty, who had learned the basics of the quickstep from an older girl at work who went to dance halls, were trying to pass their knowledge on to George and the others.

It was all quite hilarious and May felt better than she had for ages; the drink had given her a real lift and she was feeling quite giggly and a little daring. Even the fact that Betty was flirting outrageously with George didn't bother her tonight.

They danced to Tommy Dorsey and his orchestra, Fats Waller, and Fred Astaire singing 'The Way You Look Tonight', and the small front room resounded with music and laughter as the young people had what felt like proper grown-up fun.

'Enjoying yourself?' asked George as he and May jigged around the room while it was Betty's turn to rotate the handle.

'I'll say,' she replied. 'It feels good to be out enjoying ourselves with people of our own age, doesn't it?'

'Very good. '

'This is just the beginning, George,' she said excitedly. 'There's more fun to be had for us. It's time we started going to dance halls. Proper glamorous ones like the Hammersmith Palais, not just dances at the town hall. This is our time.'

'I'm game for anything,' said George. He now worked in a factory so was better off financially.

Because they had to leave before midnight they did 'Auld Lang Syne' early. There was a lovely sense of good will in the air and they sang their hearts out. May was with the two friends she loved most in the world and felt happy.

When she started to cough she went outside into the hallway for reasons of courtesy and coughed into her handkerchief until the need subsided. When she came back into the room her mood had changed completely, and she knew that her life would never be the same again.

Her mother was doing her best to be reassuring, but May could tell that she was as frightened as she was herself.

'It'll probably be nothing to worry about,' Flo said, having been shown the bloodstains on May's handkerchief as soon as she got home from the party. May had known she mustn't keep a serious symptom like that to herself.

'We'll take you to the doctor in the morning and let him have a look at you. A bottle of tonic and you'll be as right as rain. Don't upset yourself.'

But Flo was actually in despair. She'd lost one child to illness; now it seemed likely to happen again. Not May as well, she prayed silently. Not our darling May.

It was a cold January day and May was in bed outside on the porch of the isolation ward at Ashburn Sanatorium in the Surrey countryside. Fresh air and bed rest were considered to be the best medicine for what she had, and the air was fresh all right. In fact it was absolutely freezing.

She could still hardly believe how her life had changed the instant she had seen the blood on her handkerchief. It seemed as though one minute she had been enjoying life in the bosom of her friends and family and the next she had been plunged into isolation, low temperatures and strangers.

Here at Ashburn she was a TB patient, a victim of the much-feared consumption, otherwise known as the Great White Plague. She still winced when she actually made herself say the words in her head. It wasn't an easy thing to face up to, because the mortality rate was so high. The family doctor had lost no time in arranging for her to go to this sanatorium, which was funded by the London County Council.

Looking back, perhaps she should have checked with the doctor earlier, but you didn't go rushing to the surgery every time you had what you thought was a cold, especially as it cost money. She could see now that the signs had all been there, the night sweats and the fatigue as well as the cough. But it was only when she'd seen the blood that alarm bells had rung, because she'd heard about that particular symptom and knew what it meant. Maybe things would be easier for future generations, because apparently there were plans to introduce a scheme to test schoolchildren so that the disease could be diagnosed earlier.

As for May, she didn't know exactly what her prognosis was, because you didn't ask questions here; you just did as you were told. It was a huge place with an orchard, large gardens and farmland where some recovering patients worked. The barrack-room-type wards outside the main part of the hospital were set out in rows and seemed endless. Hospital discipline was strict; men were segregated from women even in the grounds where patients could go when they were up and about and feeling well enough.

The treatment was mostly bed rest, lots of nourishing food and fresh air. The family doctor had told her that they would do their very best for her here, but there was no guarantee with this cruel illness for which they had yet to find a definite cure. They had collapsed her lung to rest it and she had to have it inflated twice a week – a painful process in which a needle was inserted under her arm – so she felt that something was being done. But her life and her future were out of her hands and somehow she must accept it. Naturally she was very frightened for herself, but she felt sorry for her mother too. Flo had been absolutely stricken by the diagnosis but had hidden it beneath a barrage of optimism. 'You'll be all right, love; they'll soon put you right in the hospital,' she'd said whilst choking back tears.

One of the worst things for May was not seeing anyone from home. No visitors were allowed here because of the risk of infection and also because it was thought to be unsettling for the patients, who were encouraged to treat Ashburn as their home for the duration of their stay. She didn't know how anyone from London would get here anyway, because this place was miles from anywhere, though even in her grey state of mind she could see that it was in a lovely spot, surrounded by countryside and with a view of rolling hills beautifully bleak at this time of the year.

For the first time in her life she felt utterly alone. The party with the gramophone music and George by her side seemed like another world.

'Cor, it's parky out here,' said the patient in the next bed, a determinedly cheerful girl from Chiswick called Connie. She was a brunette with huge dark eyes and very pale skin, and was about the same age as May. 'If we don't die of TB we'll probably get wiped out by pneumonia.'

May managed a watery smile.

'Missing your family, are you?' Connie asked.

She nodded. 'And my friends.'

'It is hard at first but you'll get used to it. Never say die, eh, girl.'

'That's right,' said May, but the homesickness didn't abate.

★   ★   ★

Dot and Sheila Bailey were at it hammer and tongs when George got home from work.

'Pack it in, you two,' he said wearily.

'Mum's been moping about the place again,' Sheila informed him miserably.

'No I haven't.'

'Yes she has, George, she was—'

'I don't want to hear about it,' he cut in, his voice rising to a shout. 'You can get on and sort it out yourselves. I'm not in the mood for your bickering tonight.'

They both stared at him aghast. Such an outburst from George was almost unheard of.

'Ooh, hark at him,' said Sheila at last.

'He's missing May,' suggested his mother.

'Yeah, that's what it will be,' agreed Sheila.

'Too right I am, and you two should spend less time arguing and more time counting your blessings,' he stated categorically. 'Just think of May being taken away from everything she knows with no idea if she'll come through this illness or not. Why don't you concentrate on being thankful for your good health and each other instead of arguing the whole time?'

There was instant silence.

'Yeah, he does have a point, Mum,' agreed Sheila after a while. 'Let's go and get the dinner and leave George in peace.'

After George had washed away the factory grime at the kitchen sink, he sat in an armchair by the fire lost in thought while his mother and sister were busy in the kitchen. He was still reeling from the shock of May being taken away so suddenly. She'd seemed all right at the party apart from the cough, though she had been a bit quiet towards the end.

As well as missing May personally, the thought of her being ill and among strangers caused him pain, such was the extent of his empathy. It was all a bit hush-hush too, as though May had something to be ashamed of. Consumption was often shrouded in secrecy because it was such a feared illness. He got the impression that Mrs Stubbs had only let him into the secret because he was such a close friend of May's. The news had got around the neighbourhood though; he'd heard people talking about it.

Not being able to visit added to his distress. She must be feeling so lonely out there in the country and there was nothing he could do about it. Except . . . maybe there was one small thing he could do that might cheer her up, and he would do it right away.

'Have we got any writing paper and envelopes, Mum?' he asked, going into the kitchen.

'In the sideboard drawer,' she replied.

'Thanks, Mum.'

He went over to the sideboard, feeling slightly better. He wasn't exactly a master of the written word, but he'd do his best. It wasn't much, but it might help.

Betty was missing May too. Her best friend had been whisked away out of the blue. It had been a huge shock. TB! Blimey, that was the big one. Betty's main worry initially had been that she might have caught it from her, but the doctor had now given her the all-clear, thank goodness.

But she still had the problem of an absent best friend, she thought irritably as she refolded an eiderdown that some nuisance of a customer had looked at lengthily then left the store without buying. Who was she going to go about with now that May was out of the picture? The two of them had always been self-contained, apart from George. Now she had no one to go to the pictures with or spend the lunch hour with, or anything. They had been going to start going to dance halls soon too. Now it was all ruined because May had got ill, damn her. What was Betty supposed to do in her spare time now? She couldn't go out on her own. The whole thing really was most annoying.

Then it came to her. With May out of the picture, maybe she herself would stand a chance with George. He wouldn't look at her while May was around – she'd tried it and he wasn't interested – but who was to say what might happen now if he was given a little encouragement? Some good might come from May's absence after all.

'I'd like to see some double bed sheets please, miss,' said a customer.

'Certainly, madam,' said Betty, recalled to the present with a start but pleased that she had worked out a possible solution to the problem of her depleted social life.

Flo and Dick kept the Pavilion closed until the doctor said there was no further risk of infection to the customers. When they reopened, nobody came; not even for a newspaper. People's fears about TB were sometimes out of proportion.

'It'll pick up,' encouraged Dick, dusting tinned stock on the shelves. 'People will see that there is nothing wrong with either of us.'

'I don't really care, to be honest,' Flo said, rubbing a cloth over the teapot.

'But you love this place.'

'I love May more,' she said. 'I'd sooner be back in poverty and have her alive and well.'

'It isn't a case of choosing one over the other,' he pointed out.

'I know,' she agreed. 'But at the moment there is only one thing on my mind and that is May. If I had to choose I'd go for that every time.'

'Well maybe we can have them both,' he said, putting his arm around her. He knew the depth of her suffering over May's illness. He was upset and worried too, but as her mother, Flo's pain probably went deeper. 'We have to stay positive. At least she's having some treatment.'

'But some people are in those places for months, even years, and they still don't walk out through the front door,' she said. 'They go out the back way feet first.'

'Now, Flo, that sort of talk will upset me as well as you, so let's have no more of it,' he admonished.

'Sorry,' she said, turning to look at him and putting her hand on his. 'I'll be all right, love.'

'Oi oi,' came a voice and a woman walked in. 'Doing a spot of courting, are we?'

They sprang apart, embarrassed, both managing a watery smile.

'How's that girl of yours doing?' the customer asked.

'As well as can be expected is what they tell us when we ring up from the phone box,' said Flo. She was surprised at the question; people were usually too embarrassed to mention TB.

'I suppose they are too busy to say more,' said the customer. 'Still, she's in the best place.'

'We hope so.'

'Anyway,' began the woman, 'I've got a list for you today, so let's start with a pound of sugar.'

Two more customers came in.

'Wotcha, Flo, Dick, I didn't realise you'd opened up again.' It was one of their regulars, an elderly man with his pal. 'We've missed you.'

'Not half,' added his friend.

'Nice to see you, boys,' Dick greeted.

'Hear, hear,' added Flo, exchanging a look with her husband. People were beginning to drift back. It didn't change the situation with May, but it did make Flo feel a little more human again.

One evening in the spring, George had a visitor come to the door.

'Hello, George,' said Betty.

'Wotcha, Bet.' He frowned, fearing that some sort of bad news about May might have brought her here. 'Everything all right?'

'Yeah. Haven't seen you for a while,' she said.

'No, I've been spending a lot of time helping out at the boxing club,' he explained.

'At least you've got something to do,' she said with complaint in her voice. 'I miss May something awful.'

'Me too, but at least I'm keeping in touch by letter. Have you heard from her lately?'

She shook her head. 'I haven't written to her,' she admitted ruefully. 'I'm not a letter-writer.'

'Neither am I usually,' he said, surprised she hadn't made the effort to write to her best friend. 'But it's different when it's May. We don't want her to think we've forgotten about her because we can't visit, do we?'

'Of course not,' said Betty, wanting to please him. 'I'll get around to writing to her sometime. But it's all so weird her going away to that awful place.'

'Who said it was awful?'

'It's bound to be, those kind of places always are,' she said with authority.

'Have you been to one, then?'

'No, but I've heard about them. Terrible places, everyone says so. Poor May, just the thought of that horrible illness makes me feel sick. Mum says I mustn't tell anyone that I have a friend who's got it.'

'I don't see why not,' said George.

'Because it's *that* illness, I suppose,' she suggested. 'If you know someone who has it, you might have it your-self, is what they think.'

'Anyone would think it was leprosy the way people

carry on,' he said disapprovingly. 'Well I'm proud to be May's friend, whatever is the matter with her.'

'Oh yeah. Me too, of course,' Betty said unconvincingly.

Puzzled as to why she had come, he gave her a questioning look. 'Is there any particular reason why you've called?' he asked.

'Er . . . there is, actually,' she began hesitantly. 'I was wondering if you'd like to go out sometime . . . to the pictures or something.'

He stared at her in astonishment and closed the front door behind him because he knew Sheila's ears would be flapping. 'What, you and me . . . ?'

'Not like that, of course,' she was quick to explain, having seen the look of dismay in his eyes. 'It's just that we are both missing May and I don't have anyone to go around with now. I thought perhaps we could keep each other company every now and again.'

This was something of a dilemma for George. He didn't want to hurt Betty's feelings because he guessed she would be lonely without May. But neither did he want to get involved with her. He could see from the look in her eyes now, and from her behaviour on previous occasions, that that was what she had in mind. He was at an age when his hormones were running riot, and he was flattered, of course. Betty was an attractive girl in an ordinary sort of way and she had a good figure, but May was the only girl for him; not her best friend. Besides, even though there was nothing actually binding him to May, it would seem disloyal to her somehow.

'It's kind of you to ask me but I think we'll wait until May comes home and we can all go out together.'

'Oh,' she said, smarting from the rejection and astonished at his optimism, she herself having written May off completely. 'But she'll be away for ages, probably years, and some people never come back from those places.'

'That's something I never even allow myself to consider,' he said sharply. 'I'm not prepared to give up on May yet.'

'No, of course not, me neither,' she blurted out guiltily. 'It's just that you hear such terrible things about that illness and we have to face up to it, George.'

'And I will if I have to,' he assured her. 'But the time for that definitely hasn't come yet. Maybe at some point later on we might be able to go and visit her. I know visitors aren't allowed at the moment but that could change.'

'Oh, I wouldn't go there even if we were allowed,' Betty burst out, looking alarmed at the thought.

'Really?'

'Definitely not,' she stated. 'I'm sorry if that makes me sound awful, but I wouldn't go near one of those places and neither will you if you've got any sense.'

George found her attitude cold hearted in the extreme but knew she wasn't the only one to feel that way. 'That seems a bit hard on May,' he remarked.

'It probably is, but I can't help the way I feel.'

'No, I suppose not.'

'It's a dangerous illness, George.'

'All the more reason for us to give May as much support as we can. '

Betty shrugged in reply.

'Anyway, let's just look forward to the three of us getting together when May comes home,' he said, determined to stay positive and not wanting an argument with Betty, who was obviously more interested in self-preservation than supporting May.

'All right then,' she said, looking downhearted. 'I'll see you around.'

'See you,' he said. He felt rather sorry for Betty even though he knew her to be a very shallow person. He had known her for a long time and had a certain amount of affection for her as he would for any long-term pal. But he knew it wasn't just friendship she wanted from him, so he needed to steer well clear.

Betty was down but definitely not defeated as she walked home. George Bailey had become a challenge and she wasn't going to give up at the first hurdle. After all, there was nothing definite between him and May, so it wasn't as if she was being disloyal to May or anything. It was lonely not having a best friend, and a boyfriend would solve all her problems. Her chance would come, and when it did she was going to grab it with both hands.

'At least we get good food here,' May remarked to Connie one day in May when their beds had been wheeled out on to the porch as usual.

'That's part of the cure; lots of nourishing grub,' said

Connie. 'The rice pudding is much creamier than what we have at home.'

'Home,' May sighed. 'I'd love to be back there.'

'I shouldn't wish too hard for that,' said Connie. 'They sometimes send people home from here to die.'

'Oh Connie,' she said with a wry grin. 'Cheer me up, why don't you?'

The other girl laughed. 'Only teasing,' she said. 'I have heard people say that but it might just be a rumour. Don't worry, it won't happen to you.'

'I flippin' well hope not.'

'Nothing we can do about it anyway, kid, is there?'

'There certainly isn't.'

'Let's talk about what we would like to do when we get out of here,' suggested Connie. 'First thing for me is to find a boyfriend, and while I'm looking for someone I'm going to go to Lyons Corner House for afternoon tea.'

'I'll join you,' enthused May. 'If we can find a job to pay for it, that is.'

'They say it's hard when you come out of here,' Connie mentioned, looking serious. 'Employers don't want to take you on when you've had TB in case you get ill again and don't turn up for work or infect someone. That's why a lot of the patients stay on here to work as groundsmen or nurses.'

'Let's go back to our daydream about what we would like to do after Ashburn,' suggested May. 'Real life is a bit depressing.'

The two girls had become good friends over the past few months; there was nothing so binding as a shared illness. The ward in general was friendly. All the women here were young.

'What do you want to do when you go home?' asked Connie.

'Nothing special, just ordinary things . . . Maybe go out dancing if I'm not too old by the time I get out of here.'

'Give over, May.'

'Well I was fifteen when I came in here. I'm sixteen already and could be here for years yet,' she said.

'You poor old thing,' said a matronly nurse sweeping on to the scene. 'Well, time is moving on and so are you. The doctor wants you shifted to another ward.'

'Does that mean I'm getting better?' she asked.

'I have no idea,' replied the nurse. It was more than her job was worth to give a patient any sort of hope; such were the complications of the disease, it could easily turn out to be false. 'But you will have a little more mobility. You will still be in bed for most of the time but you will be able to go to the canteen for meals and other communal areas.'

'Oh whoopee,' said May, then she looked at her friend and added, 'Is Connie coming?'

'I have only been told to move you,' said the nurse. 'You'll have to do without your pal for the moment.'

'I'll be coming along soon, don't worry,' said Connie, but May found herself to be a bit tearful as the nurse wheeled her out of the ward.

★　★　★

The day of the coronation of King George VI was a public holiday, so George and Henry and some other mates went to the West End to join the crowds and get into the spirit, no one in the least deterred by the cool, cloudy weather. The lads managed to catch a glimpse of the royals on the balcony at Buckingham Palace and joined in the cheering and singing. After a day in this celebratory mood, Henry wanted to finish off with a party of their own.

'We need girls, music and booze,' he declared.

'And how are we going to get any of those things?' asked George. 'Let alone a place to have a party.'

'Let's head home and have a look at the local street parties. There might be some spare girls at one of them,' said Henry. 'I reckon I look old enough to get served in the bottle and jug if we go somewhere they don't know me, and we can make do with the music in the street even if it is only someone on the piano.'

'Let's give it a try,' said one of the group.

'Yeah, all right,' agreed George, and full of youthful exuberance, they headed through the crowds to the tube station en route for home ground.

Betty was sitting on the front wall outside her house, bored stiff and miserable after an afternoon of entertainment aimed at the under tens: races, games and other tedious activities. What was the use of a day off work and a national celebration if you had no one to share it with? This gathering was made up of kids and old codgers; apart from the little ones, there wasn't a soul under about thirty-five. Anyone of her age had gone to the celebrations in the West End or at least somewhere more exciting than a London back street full of children and an old man on a piano playing 'Nellie Dean'; and now to make things even worse, it was starting to rain.

It was at times like this that she missed May more than ever. If she hadn't been carted off to the wilderness the two of them could have gone to a dance to find some boys and excitement. There were lots of special coronation dances on tonight. This street party was the last word in dullness. Some of the small children were getting tired and fretful. Why couldn't their mothers take the little brats indoors to bed, for goodness' sake, instead of inflicting their wretched whining on everyone else?

Finding new friends after you'd left school wasn't easy because there weren't many meeting places, unless you liked churchy types. There were a few girls of her age working at the department store, but she didn't seem to have anything in common with them; there wasn't anyone she wanted to spend time with as she had with May. She and May had been friends for so long she'd never bothered with anyone else. She'd relied on her for company and now there was no one. Why did May have to get ill and leave her all alone? she thought, full of self-pity. It really wasn't fair. Even her plan to go after George Bailey hadn't materialised because she hadn't been able to summon up the courage to go round to his house a second time and she hadn't seen him around anywhere.

'Betty,' called her mother. 'Come and make yourself useful instead of sitting there with a long face. We need some help washing the dishes, and there are sandwiches to be made for people to have with their drinks.'

She sighed irritably. 'All right, Mum. Just coming,' she said, getting up and heading indoors.

George and his pals were decidedly merry as they walked the streets of Ealing, having managed to obtain several bottles of cider from the bottle and jug in a pub in Ealing Broadway where the person serving had turned a blind eye to their youth in the interests of the pub's turnover.

There were several parties in progress in the area, though some seemed to be in the final stages. They had to steer clear of their own particular streets because of family disapproval of their underage drinking, so that narrowed it down, but they found one gathering with a man playing the piano and decided it was worth staying for a while.

'Do you know any modern songs, mate?' asked Henry.

'You tell me how it goes and I'll play it.'

The boys sang 'Is It True What They Say About Dixie?' and the pianist played it and the whole street came to life; people singing along and dancing.

It occurred to George vaguely that this was Betty's street, but she wasn't around so he guessed she was out having fun somewhere else. She didn't know what she was missing; this was a really good shindig . One of the best they'd been to tonight. 'Red sails in the sunset . . .' he sang at the top of his voice after another healthy swig from a cider bottle. For the first time since May had gone away, life seemed like fun and he was having a good time.

Betty was delighted when she went back outside with a plate of sandwiches to see that the party had livened up. Something was apparently happening further down the street beyond the trestle tables; she could see a crowd in the lamplight and hear people singing. She put the sandwiches on the table and hurried towards the action.

'George,' she said, hardly able to believe her luck. 'What are you doing here?'

'Joining in the party and having a good time,' he replied, smiling broadly at her through an alcoholic haze.

'So I can see.'

'We've been all around the town and your street has the best party of the lot.'

'What do you expect when I live here?' she said, catching his mood and becoming flirtatious.

'Thassa point,' he drawled drunkenly.

'Glad you realise it,' she joshed, considering herself to be very witty indeed.

'Come on then, come and have a dance,' he invited. 'Let's have some fun.'

Without a moment's hesitation she went into his arms and held on to him tight.

'But to get you in the party mood,' he said, leading her to a low garden wall behind which the boys had hidden the cider, 'have a swig of this.'

Betty needed no second bidding. She was hungry for excitement, and suddenly here it was right on her doorstep.

They did energetic versions of the conga, the hokey-cokey and 'Knees Up Mother Brown'. Everybody was in the mood and ready to do it all over again.

'Shall we go for a walk, George?' suggested Betty, eager to get him alone, away from his mates and – even more importantly – out of range of her mother's vision. She was never going to get a better chance with George, and she was damned if she was going to let it pass her by.

'What for?' he asked blearily.

'Just to cool down a bit,' she told him, holding on to his hand and loving it.

'All right,' he agreed, feeling very inebriated. 'Let's take a bottle with us.'

They collected a bottle from behind the wall and left without anyone noticing. Betty slipped her arm around him.

'Where are we going?' he asked.

'You'll see.'

George wasn't too drunk to realise what she had in

mind but he wasn't sufficiently in control to resist, especially as the booze was making him amorous. Out of the light in a dark alleyway, she stopped and put her arms around him.

'I've wanted this for so long, George,' she said, overwhelmed by the excitement of it all.

If he'd been sober, this was the last thing in the world he would want. Three sheets to the wind it didn't seem like such a bad idea.

Chapter Three

By the autumn of 1937 May was resigned to her uncertain circumstances, and with acceptance came a certain sense of peace. She'd been through periods of fury and self-pity about her illness, but now she endured her fate with as much patience as she could muster and tried to make the best of things at Ashburn. Because the medical profession were still searching for a reliable cure for tuberculosis, patients were closely monitored and their weight noted regularly, with even the slightest loss causing concern. But the wall of silence about an individual patient's recovery remained.

So May lived from day to day immersed in the Ashburn community and looking forward to letters from home. Her parents and George were her main correspondents, with a very occasional note from Betty.

The regime here was strict, but it wasn't all rules and severity. Occupational therapy was very much encouraged, and recovering patients with a particular skill were asked to pass it on to their fellow patients by means of classes. May learned to knit, and play simple tunes on the piano, and she became a whiz at dominoes and any number of card games. She developed a love of fresh air as it played such a large part in her life here. Now that she wasn't on complete bed rest, she was allowed to stroll in the grounds so long as she didn't overexert herself.

Because most of the patients were young, a great deal of flirting went on at mealtimes in the canteen where the sexes were mixed, even though men and women weren't allowed to sit together. A certain amount of covert communication was possible in the queue for food, and there were all sorts of stories of couples who defied the strict segregation rule by getting through the undergrowth near the boundary fence and meeting up after dark.

There was a strong sense of togetherness here, and May was fond of the other women in the ward, among them Connie, who had been moved here soon after May herself.

When the management relaxed the segregation rules to allow a male patient, an artist, to give art classes in one of the communal areas in the women's section, there was a great deal of laughter and speculation, and a lot of the women suddenly realised that they had artistic tendencies.

'He's a bit of all right, that Doug Sands,' said one woman after they'd been given the news. 'I've noticed him in the canteen and had my eye on him. A tall fella with blondish hair. A bit skinny, but he'll do for me.'

'You'll have to be quick to beat me to him,' joshed another.

'Now now, ladies,' intervened May lightly. 'No falling out over a bloke.'

'What about you, May, are you interested?' asked someone.

'He's too old for me,' said May, having seen the man in question at mealtimes. 'So I'm not in the running. No fighting over him, you lot. He might even be spoken for.'

'While he's stuck in here for years? Don't make me laugh,' said the woman. The rate of broken romances due to this illness was high.

'Some people don't give up on us,' stated May, thinking about George, even though he wasn't actually her boyfriend.

'Plenty do though, May,' said Connie.

'So everyone keeps telling me.'

'It's bound to happen when people are miles away from each other for years,' said Connie.

'Yeah, well don't all of you go after the art teacher at the first class,' May said jokingly. 'You'll frighten him half to death.'

'Since when has a man been afraid of women?' asked Connie lightly. 'It's the other way around.'

'Since when have you been an authority?' asked May.

'All my life. My dad rules the roost in our house and Mum has to do as he says,' she replied. 'She's scared stiff of him.'

'Oh,' said May, a little shocked. There was nothing like that in her family. 'I suppose something like that would make you a bit biased.'

'That and a bossy boyfriend who dropped me as soon as I got sick,' added Connie.

'Mm, well don't tar all men with the same brush, and go easy on the art teacher,' advised May. 'He's just a patient like us, and none of us are in the best of health.'

'We'll bear that in mind, won't we, girls?' agreed Connie with a wicked grin.

The art class proved to be a lot of fun. The teacher, Doug Sands, a quietly spoken, slightly built man was well able to deal with all those who didn't take it seriously.

'This class is meant to be therapeutic for us all, but we are here to learn something and if you muck about the whole time they'll stop me coming over to the women's wards,' he told them in his refined way. 'Let's have some order here, if you please.'

'Do we call you sir?' asked Connie with tongue in cheek.

'I won't bother to answer that,' he said. 'But for those of you who don't already know, my name is Doug.'

The women quietened down after that. May had always known she had no talent for drawing and she told him so. 'I can't even draw a cat,' she informed him.

'There's room for improvement then,' he said optimistically, 'and I like a challenge.'

'I'll be a challenge all right,' she replied.

'We'll see,' he said, smiling at her.

He was a good few years older than her, she thought, probably mid twenties. He wasn't a good-looking man; he was too pale and thin for that, but he did have a certain charisma, a nice smile, clear grey eyes and a lustrous mane of blond hair. In that first lesson he asked them all to draw a bowl of fruit, and there was a lot of hilarity at the results.

'Yours looks like a cross between a lavatory seat and a pile of sprouts, May,' said Connie, laughing.

'I told you I'm hopeless at drawing,' May came back at her. 'I was always the worst in the class at school.'

'That isn't too bad for a first effort,' decided Doug, looking at her painting over her shoulder. 'You'll get better with practice.'

'I enjoyed doing it, which is odd as I'm so bad at it,' said May. 'I'd like to improve, though, so I'll come again.'

'You probably won't have much choice if the nurses have anything to do with it,' Connie piped up. 'You know how keen they are on occupational therapy.'

'Only because it's good for us,' said May.

'And it gets us out of their way,' said one of the more cynical patients.

'I'll see you all next week then,' said Doug, 'and in passing in the canteen.'

'Yes, sir,' said Connie with a cheeky grin.

May was in good spirits when they got back to the ward, something she'd thought in her early days at Ashburn she would never experience again. She yearned for the time when she could leave here and go home, but the homesickness had eased off a little now and was intermittent.

There was a letter for her on her locker. She could tell from the handwriting that it was from George, and her heart rose. Looking forward to reading it, she took it out to the porch and sat down in the shade in the glorious autumn weather, the low sun washing over the trees, which were a blaze of colour as the leaves turned. Opening the letter, she began to read.

Dear May

I hope you are getting better and that you will be coming home soon. Everyone here is missing you. I still call at the Pavilion regularly though not as often as when I was a delivery boy of course. Your mum and dad seem well though they'll be even better when they have you home again.

I have some news that will probably surprise you. I can hardly believe it myself. The thing is, May, Betty and I are getting married. She is in the family way so we have to do it as soon as possible for the sake of her reputation. It isn't what I had planned but it's happened and I have to do right by her. We'll be living at my place as her parents have thrown her out and banned her from the family. Obviously there will be a lot of gossip especially as we are both only sixteen. I expect Betty will write and tell you about it herself but I wanted you to hear it from me personally.

I hope you are not too ashamed of us and very much hope that you'll feel able to stay friends.

Your dear friend,

George

May was too shocked to move. She just sat there staring unseeingly across the gardens, feeling totally betrayed. George and Betty had done that huge, mysterious, unmentionable thing together. May wasn't ashamed of them, or disgusted; just heartbroken that it was Betty and not her. She had always thought it would be her and George. Betty had often flirted with him and they had all taken it to be just a bit of fun, but now it seemed as though it had been more than that. Pregnant at sixteen, though; she wondered how Betty felt about that.

In an isolated place like Ashburn you became institutionalised and distant from the outside world. Now she realised that life beyond these rolling hills was moving on without her. It had to, of course. People didn't stop living and progressing just because she was ill, and why should they take her into account when she wasn't around? One thing was for sure, she had to end any romantic notions about George. He was going to be a married man. Even the thought seemed ludicrous, because he was still just a boy.

A less charitable side of May's nature made her feel spiteful towards Betty for stealing the boy she had known May loved. They had told each other everything, so Betty had been very well aware of May's feelings. Still, that was the stuff of childhood and May felt very grown up suddenly. Of course she wanted to stay friends with George and she would reply to his letter. But not now, not yet. She needed time for the pain to subside.

It was Sunday morning and George was standing at his father's graveside in the autumn sunshine. He often came here when he was confused or miserable, both of which he felt overwhelmingly at the moment.

Whereas his mother was worried by the scandal of his predicament, his dad would have been more likely to understand. He wouldn't have been pleased about George's misdemeanour – in fact he would have given him a thorough trouncing – but he would have listened to what he had to say and somehow helped him through it man to man. As it was, George was living in a house full of women – three now that Betty had moved in – and had no one to talk to about his turmoil. His mates, while intrigued about the act that had led to his current situation, thought he should do a bunk rather than tie himself down at such a young age. Being extremely immature, they were of the view that he shouldn't have sown his wild oats so close to home, but that as he had, he should disappear pronto.

Unfortunately, George didn't have it in him to do such a cowardly thing, as much as he hated the situation he was in. He was sixteen and not ready for marriage to anyone, least of all Betty, who was even less mature than he was and to whom he had never felt even remotely drawn. All of this because of something he could barely remember and that had only happened because he was drunk. He was still reeling from the shock, having not seen Betty since the coronation party until she'd turned up at his door a couple of weeks ago to tell him that she was pregnant and her parents had disowned her.

He felt as though his life was over, which was probably a huge exaggeration, but things were certainly going to change with a wife and child to support. Fortunately his sister had left school and was working at a local greengrocer's now, so that was one fewer financial burden, but he still had to help Mum out when he could. Betty had her job at Bright Brothers, but she would have to stop working after the wedding, as they didn't employ married women.

He didn't earn bad money at the factory, and there was often the chance of overtime. If he was desperate for cash, there was always bare-knuckle fighting to fall back on. It was a last resort but it paid well and he would do it if he had to, strictly on the quiet, of course, as it was illegal and dangerous. His father would turn in his grave if he knew he was even considering it. Dad had been a stickler for the straight and narrow, sadly as it happened, as it had brought about his early death.

As usual when he thought of his father's demise, his murderer came into his mind with blinding fury. In his imagination he saw the inscription on Dad's headstone. Murdered aged forty by Bill Bikerley, a thug and a bully. But no . . . he wouldn't tarnish his father's memory with thoughts of that man. It was a waste of energy. Justice had been done, leave it at that, George. You've enough on your plate. Let it go. But he knew he wasn't able to do that. The anger would torture him for the rest of his life.

He turned away from the grave and began to walk home, half dreading getting there. Betty's endless prattle was very irritating to him now that he was with her so much. His heart twisted as he thought of May. She would have received his letter by now and he knew she would be disappointed in him, both for getting her friend into trouble and also for betraying her.

There had never been anything definite between them, but they had loved each other and he had thought they would be together one day after the growing-up process was complete. He still loved her and always would, but it could never be any other way than as a friend now, and all because of his damned recklessness. He'd been careful not to even hint at his dismay at marrying Betty in his letter to May. It wouldn't be fair and it was best she didn't know. The girls were friends so May would be loyal to her, which was more than Betty had been to May.

One thing he was certain his father would have said to him was to do right by the woman he must now be committed to and make her a good husband. He felt completely inadequate to the task but knew he must do his best and try to be a decent husband and father as his own dad had been.

As he walked home past the pub he saw a group of men going in for the midday session. The pub was sometimes known as the married men's haven. He smiled to himself. He was soon to be a husband and father, yet he wasn't even old enough to have a pint in a pub.

Walking home from work across Haven Green carpeted in fallen leaves, Betty decided it was time she wrote to May about what had happened. Her conscience was trying to bother her but she wasn't going to allow it to spoil things. She hoped May didn't mind about the turn in events. After all, she had no actual claim on George and she couldn't expect other people to stay away from him when she wasn't around. If it hadn't been me it would have been some other girl, Betty told herself, so I'm blowed if I'm going to feel guilty.

She had to admit that she wasn't keen on the pregnancy side of things; she hadn't bargained on that. She had thought it would be all right as it had been the first time for them both and neither had really known what they were doing. It wasn't much fun feeling sick and below par all the time. On the other hand, she had well and truly got her man, which meant she didn't need a girlfriend to go about with and she wouldn't have to work in that dreary store any more after the wedding. In fact she wouldn't have to work anywhere, because George would be keeping her in future. As a married woman she'd have status and people would stop bossing her around.

So pregnancy was a small price to pay for all the benefits. As for the baby, she couldn't even begin to imagine herself as a mother. But that was ages away yet, so there was no need even to think about it. For now, she was going to enjoy her role as George's soon-to-be wife.

Admittedly he hadn't seemed very happy about the prospect, but he was going to do the decent thing, as she'd known he would, so it didn't matter. They hardly knew each other at a personal level, but that would change now that they were living together, and getting better acquainted would be fun.

There was a strong sense of victory in having bagged the best-looking bloke around, though annoyingly, this was coloured slightly by a persistent niggle of conscience about May. But her friend was like a distant memory now, having been away for so long with no talk of her coming back. Betty was determined to forget all about her and enjoy herself.

'Well, George, it's very good of you to come and tell us, but I can't pretend not to be disappointed in you,' said Flo shakily when he visited the Pavilion to tell May's parents what had happened. 'In fact, I really am very shocked indeed.'

'I didn't want you to hear it from anyone else and it'll be all round the neighbourhood soon,' he said, feeling embarrassed and guilty as hell.

'Does May know?'

He nodded. 'I've written to her about it.'

'She'll be, er . . . surprised at the very least,' said Flo. 'I always hoped that you and May might one day . . .'

'It isn't going to happen now, is it,' said Dick quickly, waving a tea towel at a wasp that was hovering near the toffee apples on the counter. 'You've been and gone and done it now, boy. Pleasure usually comes at a price.'

'Dick,' said Flo in a tone of admonition. 'Don't be so crude.'

'All I said was—'

'I know what you said and I want no more of that sort of talk, if you please,' she instructed.

'Look, these things sometimes happen,' Dick pointed out. 'Nature is a very powerful force.'

'You wouldn't be saying that if it was your daughter who is in trouble,' said Flo.

He gave his wife a close look and George could almost feel his pain. 'I'd rather our daughter was in that sort of trouble than the sort she is in; seriously ill and shut away from her family and friends,' said Dick.

George saw his words hit home as Flo's expression saddened and her eyes filled with tears.

'When you look at it like that,' she said thickly, 'I suppose it does put it into perspective.'

'Anyway,' began George quickly, hoping to ease the tension, 'now that you know what a degenerate I am, am I banned from the Pavilion?'

Dick looked at his wife in that way people have when they are very close. George had seen it in his own parents. Then he said, 'Don't be so daft, lad.' He thought George would pay for his misdemeanour many times over in marrying so young and having a wife and child to support when he was just a lad himself. 'What you get up to is none of our business.'

George looked at Flo with a raised eyebrow.

'Of course you're not banned,' she confirmed. 'What sort of snobs do you think we are?'

'It takes two to make a baby,' added Dick.

'Shush,' said Flo as a customer approached the counter.

'In that case, can I have a toffee apple and a *Daily Mirror* please,' said George.

'You big kid,' said Dick, handing him a toffee apple.

'Autumn wouldn't be the same without one of your specials, Mrs Stubbs.'

'Mr Stubbs made these as it happens,' Flo told him.

George nodded approvingly towards the older man, then went to a table on the veranda with the newspaper and the fruity confection. He was glad to have made his peace with the Stubbses. They meant a lot him.

As he sat there in the sunshine, the smoky chill of autumn in the air, he felt as though May was everywhere here, in the breeze that rustled through the trees and in every creak and squeak of the swings in the playground. Even before the Pavilion had opened, they had spent a lot of their time here as children. Happy days.

But all that was well and truly over, and he felt overwhelmed by adulthood. Oh well, enough of nostalgia; onwards and upwards, he said to himself. Glancing through the newspaper, he noticed a face that was becoming increasingly familiar. It was a picture of Adolf Hitler at some demonstration or other in Berlin. That bloke was always in the papers lately spouting his politics, thought George casually, turning to the sports page.

It took May quite a while to get over the shock of George's news, but as soon as she felt able she decided it was time she snapped out of it. She wrote to both George and Betty individually wishing them well. Then she immersed herself in life at Ashburn. Some days she felt reasonably well; others she was tired and listless.

With perseverance she did improve a little at the art

class. While knowing that she would never excel at drawing because she wasn't gifted that way, she did seem to have an eye for colour, and Doug encouraged her to use it to interpret her own thoughts and the things she saw around her. The other patients teased her about her efforts.

'What's that supposed to be?' asked Connie one day in late October when May had produced a colourful piece. 'It looks like nothing on earth.'

'It's Guy Fawkes night,' explained May. 'Can't you see the bonfire and the guy?'

'Not really. It looks more like an accident with a few pots of paint to me,' laughed Connie, who was very outspoken but never in a malicious way.

'It's surreal art,' Doug explained. 'Not everyone expresses what they see in the same way.'

'It's kind of you to make it seem significant, Doug, but I wouldn't know surreal art if it jumped out of the paint pot and landed on my nose,' said May. 'It's just me doing the best I can and having fun with a few colours. I haven't got a clue.'

'At least you're enjoying it,' he said. 'That's the whole idea.'

'You need sunglasses to look at that,' joked Connie, because May had used a lot of red and yellow.

'Let's see what you've done then, clever clogs,' said May. She had to admit that her friend's picture of the view from the window was recognisable.

'I was always pretty good at drawing at school,' Connie said breezily.

'Didn't anyone ever suggest that you take it up?' May enquired.

'Don't make me laugh,' she said. 'I'm one of six kids and I needed to be earning. I went straight into domestic service, cleaning up other people's mess. Being in here is like a holiday for me.'

'Anyway, that's it for this week, ladies, so if you could start clearing up please,' asked Doug.

They did as he said and May was about to follow the others back to the ward when Doug came over to her.

'I hope you'll still come to class despite your friend's derogatory attitude towards your work,' he said.

'Take no notice of Connie. She's only joking, even though I know I'm rubbish at drawing. But of course I'll still come to your class,' she assured him casually. 'I enjoy it. It's better than embroidery or basket-making and the nurses will make me go to one of those if I don't come to your class. They like us to do something.'

'So I'm the lesser of the evils then, am I?' he said with a half smile.

She gave him a look. 'In the nicest possible way, yes you are,' she replied.

Having spotted what could be construed as fraternisation, a nurse swept on to the scene. 'Come along, Mr Sands, back to your own neck of the woods, if you please.'

'Righto, nurse,' he said, giving her a salute.

'Enough of your cheek,' she came back at him.

Although the discipline here was very strict, the nurses weren't without humour and long-term patients like May got to know them quite well. She thought they did a magnificent job for little pay and she respected every one of them, even the few who overdid the authority of their position. It wasn't an easy job and it took dedication as well as a lot of hard work. She took her hat off to them all.

'What was all that about with Doug just now?' Connie wanted to know when May got back to the ward, a long, sparsely furnished room containing thirty closely spaced beds with a locker beside each one.

'He was asking me if I would be going to his class again,' May told her.

'Well well,' said Connie. 'He didn't ask me or anyone else for that matter. Do I detect a spark?'

'Of course not,' denied May. 'He's too old for me. He only wondered if I would be going again because I'm so hopeless at drawing.'

'What was all that about you being a genius with colour?' asked Connie.

'To make me feel better at being so bad at art, I should think.'

'That isn't what they call it where I come from,' said Connie. 'We call it lust.'

'You would,' said one of the other women, whose name was Vi. 'He was just being nice to make May feel better. She's only sixteen. He must be well into his twenties.'

'Just right for me, then,' said Connie.

'You're only sixteen too.'

'Yes, but I'm very mature for my age.'

'You're man-mad.'

'Of course I am. We all are, being shut away from them like this,' said Connie. 'It isn't natural.'

'Some people don't let the rules stop them,' said Vi. 'Maybe you should arrange to meet our art teacher after dark.'

'I would do if it was me he was interested in,' she said, turning her gaze on May. 'But it isn't.'

'Don't look at me,' May objected mildly. 'I haven't even had a proper boyfriend yet. Don't start trying to pair me off with an older man.'

'Older man my foot, he can't be more than about twenty-four or-five,' said Connie.

'And I'm only sixteen. Anyway, he's a different type to us altogether,' said May. 'He seems quite classy.'

'And we're rough, I suppose.'

'You know what I mean,' said May. 'He's got a posh accent and he seems sort of, er . . . cultured.'

'Mm, he does,' Connie agreed, 'but I find that really attractive in a man.'

'He's an interesting type, I agree,' said May.

'He's different to run-of-the-mill blokes, that's for sure,' stated Connie. 'But he can't be rich or he'd be in a sanatorium in Switzerland, not a council-funded one in Surrey.'

'Yeah, there is that,' May agreed. 'He's obviously well educated, though, even if he isn't rolling in dough.'

'We'll have to try to find out some more about him,' suggested Connie.

'If you like,' agreed May. 'But now it's time for dinner, so let's head for the canteen.' She looked at Connie. 'And don't embarrass us by making eyes at him all through the meal. If too much of that sort of thing goes on, they might start making men and women eat at different times.'

'And we can't have that, can we,' laughed Connie.

'Come on, Betty, get off your fat arse and help Mum with the washing-up,' demanded Sheila of her sister-in-law one evening in late November when they had finished their evening meal.

'I'm tired,' said Betty.

'God knows why, since you do nothing all day except sit around,' said Sheila.

'I'm pregnant,' said Betty.

'I don't think any of us is in any doubt about that since you remind us every time you might be in danger of lifting a finger,' said Sheila. 'It isn't an illness, so you ought to do your share around here.'

'Why can't you do it?' asked Betty.

'Because I'm going to the pictures and I do it every night as well as being at work all day,' said Sheila. 'But that isn't the point. You're living here so you must start to pull your weight.'

'It doesn't matter,' said Dot nervously. 'I can manage all right on my own.'

'Don't be such a doormat, Mum,' Sheila admonished. 'We need some ground rules around here.' She turned to Betty. 'Look, if you start to muck in, I'm sure we'll all get along famously, but you're not a visitor in this house; you're part of the family now, so act like it.'

Enraged, Betty turned to her husband. 'Are you going to let her speak to me like that?'

'Go easy on her, sis,' George said dutifully.

Sheila gave him a scathing look. 'Come on, George, I know she's your wife but surely you don't want her to treat us all like slaves.'

'Don't talk about me as if I'm not here,' Betty objected.

'Stop quarrelling, all of you,' said Dot, becoming tearful. 'You know how it upsets me.'

'Oh no,' said Sheila. 'Don't start blubbing again, Mum, for Gawd's sake.'

'Leave Mum alone,' admonished George instinctively, protective of his mother.

'Oh, so you can stick up for your mother but not your wife,' Betty complained.

George heaved a sigh. The tension in this house had been terrible since Betty had moved in, and he was still trying to get to grips with his new circumstances. He knew that, as his wife, Betty should be his first consideration, but it didn't come naturally; he had to constantly remind himself.

'Sheila, will you stop picking on Betty,' he said with a sigh. 'She is my wife, remember.'

'Oh, I've had enough of this,' declared Sheila. 'You do what you like, Betty, but don't expect us to like you, you lazy cow.' She turned to her mother. 'Come on, Mum, let's get these dishes done pronto and leave her to rot.'

She proceeded to clear the table, the loud clatter of the crockery and cutlery indicative of the heat of her temper.

Later that night, George decided to have a quiet word with Betty in the privacy of their bedroom.

'It might not be a bad idea for you to give a bit of a hand around the house,' he suggested warily. 'At least it would keep everybody happy.'

'Oh, so you *are* taking their side over me,' she scowled.

'I'm just trying to keep the peace,' he sighed.

'I'm pregnant.'

'Yes, I know you are, but I don't think it means that you can't do anything at all, does it?' I don't know much about it, but I think most women carry on as normal, at the beginning anyway.'

'How would you like it if you felt sick all the time?' she asked.

'I would hate it,' he admitted frankly. 'But I thought it was just in the mornings. They do call it morning sickness.'

'It's worse in the mornings but I feel queasy all day,' she informed him, her voice rising. 'I don't know if that is the normal thing but that's how it is for me.'

'I can see how miserable that must be for you.' He really was at a loss to know the right thing to do. 'Perhaps it will ease off later in the pregnancy and when you're feeling better you can muck in with the others.'

Her face fell and he noticed suddenly how young and insecure she looked. She was very pale and her mid-brown hair was straight, lank and falling greasily around her face, making her look rather plain. The radiant glow of pregnancy he'd heard about was nowhere to be seen on Betty. For all her bolshie talk she was probably feeing just as trapped as he was.

'Look, Bet,' he began in a warmer tone, 'we are a couple of kids in an unexpected situation that we aren't ready for. Neither of us knows how best to cope with it. But we have a nipper on the way, so somehow we have to make it work. And seeing as we live here, it would make life easier for us both if you could get along with my family, because they are your family too now.'

'Your sister is so bossy.'

'She is a bit, but it's just her way,' he said. 'She speaks her mind but at least she does it to your face. I can promise you she won't go behind your back.'

'The truth is, I don't really like living here,' she said forlornly. 'I miss my own people.'

Reminded of her youth and immaturity he said, 'That's only natural, I suppose, you being a girl. But we can't live with your folks because they've turned their backs on you, so we'll have to stay here, for the time being anyway.'

'I know,' she said, starting to weep.

'Don't cry,' he said awkwardly, handing her his handkerchief.

'I don't really like being pregnant either,' she confessed.

'It doesn't sound like much fun, I must admit,' he said sympathetically, 'but at least it doesn't last for ever.'

'S'pose not,' she said thickly.

'Look, Bet, let's give this marriage thing our best shot,

for the sake of our child when it comes,' he suggested. 'There will have to be give and take on both sides, and I'll try to be more supportive of you, but you'll have to do your part too.'

'By helping in the house you mean, I suppose,' she said grumpily.

'By entering into the family spirit generally and trying to get to know Mum and Sheila,' he said. 'Apart from anything else you will be happier if they are your friends. We don't want our baby being born into a home full of arguments, do we?'

'I suppose not,' she finally agreed. 'I will try and get along with them.'

'Good girl,' he said, putting an affectionate arm around her and trying to crush his longing for escape. He'd made a commitment when he'd got Betty pregnant and he couldn't back out now.

The staff at Ashburn did their very best to give the patients a happy time at Christmas. For just one day of the year the segregation rule was waived and male and female patients were allowed to socialise at the party that was held in the canteen straight after lunch on Christmas Day.

One of the nurses brought in a wind-up gramophone and they listened to the new American swing music. The favourite song of the day was 'The Lambeth Walk' from the hit musical of the year, *Me and My Girl*. They played it over and over again. May wasn't feeling on top form today but she joined in with the dance that accompanied the song and enjoyed it as much as she could while feeling so horribly off colour. Bad days were part and parcel of this illness. She'd learned to accept that.

'Feeling homesick?' asked Doug Sands, sitting beside her when she took a break. 'It's that time of year.'

'Is it that obvious?' she asked, looking at him.

'You do seem a bit sad,' he replied. He was looking rather flamboyant in light-coloured trousers with a brightly patterned cravat worn at his neck. 'At least when you are not putting on a smile.'

'I am missing family and friends,' she confessed. 'I was also thinking that it's coming up to a year since I was diagnosed. It was last New Year's Eve that I knew for certain that I was ill. I remember thinking it was the end for me.'

'And here you are still around and ready to fight another day and many more after that,' he reminded her.

'Yes, there is that.'

'I've been here for more than eighteen months,' he told her, and she noticed what very nice eyes he had, a hint of green colouring the grey. Beneath his distinctive blond hair he had an angular sort of face with an aquiline nose and nicely shaped mouth. He really was rather handsome in an unusual sort of way. 'Unfortunately there isn't a short-term fix for this illness.'

'Have they given you any idea when you might be going home?' she asked.

'No, they keep quiet about that until they are absolutely certain, apparently,' he said. 'But I really believe that I'm on the road to recovery. You can feel it yourself, can't you? When you're on the mend.'

'I suppose that must be how it works' she said dismally.

'You're not feeling better, then?'

'Sometimes I feel all right,' she said. 'But I've had a few off days lately.'

'We all get those,' he said. 'You'll probably be as right as rain tomorrow.'

'We'll miss you when you leave,' she said, changing the subject. She didn't want to think about her own health at the moment. 'Thursdays just won't be the same without our art class.'

'I'm sure the staff will soon find another patient with a skill to pass on,' he said.

'With a bit of luck it will be something I can do next time,' she said drily.

'That's better,' he approved. 'You look so pretty when you smile properly.'

She narrowed her eyes at him quizzically.

Doug shook his head. 'No, I'm not flirting with you, because I'm not a cradle-snatcher,' he said, answering her unspoken question. 'Just stating a fact.'

'Thank you for the compliment,' she said graciously.

He asked her about herself and she told him about the area where she lived and the Pavilion, about her job at the department store and her family and friends.

'What about you?' she asked. 'You must come from in or around the London area to be in this hospital.'

'Yeah, that's right.'

He went on to tell her that he was twenty-four, had

left home a few years before and lived in a houseboat moored on the Thames at Richmond.

'That's different, anyway,' she said. She realised that she wasn't really surprised because she'd always had the idea that he was out of the ordinary. 'Very bohemian.'

'I don't know about that, but it suits me,' he said. 'I like the simple life.'

'It doesn't sound very simple to me,' she said. 'It sounds positively intriguing.'

'It's simple in that it's small and cosy and close to nature,' he explained.

'Yeah, I see what you mean.' She paused thoughtfully. 'Are you married, Doug?' she asked.

'No. I've had a few near misses but I'm still single,' he said. 'It's probably just as well. It would be awful if I had a wife and children relying on me. I'd be worried to death about not being able to provide for them.'

'Yes I can see that,' May agreed.

'None of the patients in my ward are married,' he told her.

'Nor mine. Probably because they are all quite young,' she said. 'Romance doesn't stand much of a chance against this illness, does it?'

'So I've heard.' He looked at her. 'Are you speaking from experience?'

She thought about how she had lost George to Betty while she was here, but as there hadn't actually been a romance it didn't really count. 'Only in a very loose kind of way.'

'You're young,' he remarked, giving her a studious look. 'You'll have lots of other chances.'

She shrugged and changed the subject. 'Have you painted the river at all? I know that artists usually do like to paint the Thames.'

'You bet,' he said. 'In many of its different moods.'

'Are you a full-time artist?' she asked. 'Or do you just do it in your spare time?'

'I'm involved in art full time but I don't sell enough work to earn a living painting,' he explained.

'So how do you make up the difference?'

'Before I got sick I subsidised my income from sales of my pictures by teaching art at a night school, but I don't know if I'll be able to do that when I get out of here.'

'Oh?'

'Consumption and the classroom; not a very healthy combination, is it? They say it can be hard to get a job of any sort when you're tainted by the TB stigma.'

'I've heard a bit about that too,' she said. 'But you'll be cured when you leave here. You won't be infectious so you can't be a threat.'

'We know that, but employers are still wary, so they say,' he said. 'A chap from here that I was friendly with and who writes to me still can't get fixed up with work, and he left here six months ago.'

'That's terrible.'

'Sorry,' he said. 'I shouldn't depress you with reality. Not on Christmas Day.'

'You haven't depressed me,' she said. 'I'd heard similar stories from the others.'

'I shall just have to sell more work somehow, won't I?' he suggested lightly.

'That would seem to be the answer,' she agreed. 'But art is unknown territory to me.'

'Anyway, I think I shall worry about that particular challenge when it arises,' he said cheerfully. 'Just being better and back home will be enough to start with.'

'I'm sure it will,' she said. 'Lucky you.'

'Your turn will come,' he told her.

'I hope so.'

'Meanwhile, let's drink a toast to loved ones at home.' He looked across the room, where there was a lot of hilarity as patients got together to do the Lambeth Walk. 'And then if you feel up to it we could join the others before we are all dismissed and sent back to our own wards like school kids.'

'Yes, this place does have the feel of school about it at times,' she said. 'Inevitable, given the large numbers.'

They drank a toast in lemonade, then went to join in the fun. Ostensibly May entered into the spirit of things, but her heart wasn't in it. She felt as though she had made a new friend in Doug, and that pleased her because he was a nice bloke and excitingly different to anyone she had ever met before. But she didn't feel well and she knew that something was very wrong.

Chapter Four

For the second time in her short life May had to face up to the possibility of an early death. The first occasion had been when she was diagnosed with tuberculosis; the second happened one bleak day in January 1938 when she was told by the doctor at Ashburn that she wasn't improving as they had hoped, despite their having collapsed her lung for a period of time. A major operation to remove the diseased lung was recommended.

'Me and your dad have had a long chat with the doctor about it and we really think it will be the best thing for you,' said her mother, who had come with her husband from London to Ashburn on a special visiting arrangement to meet with the doctor and sign the consent form, because May was still underage. 'An operation could get you properly better.'

'Do you really think so, Mum?'

'Yes, we do,' she confirmed. 'It's your decision though, love. You don't have to have it done if you don't want to. No one is going to force you into it.'

'What's the alternative?' asked May.

Flo and Dick exchanged glances.

'It doesn't seem as though I have much choice then, does it?' she said.

'Apparently he's a very good surgeon,' said Flo. She was shocked and dismayed by the idea of surgery but was trying desperately not to pass her anxiety on to her daughter.

'The top man in his field,' added Dick. 'And he obviously thinks it will be worth it in your case or he wouldn't have suggested it. They don't do operations lightly.'

'They don't often do them for this illness at all,' May pointed out with a puzzled expression. 'Rest, fresh air and good nutritious food is the standard treatment.'

'Apparently surgery is becoming more common these days and the surgeon who will be doing your operation is a bit of a pioneer in this field,' Flo explained. 'He really believes that this is the way forward for you and he has a high success rate. Until they find a definite cure for the disease, this is probably the best we can hope for. You could go on to have a normal healthy life if all goes well, though they can't guarantee anything, of course.'

'I'm not sure how I'll breathe with only one lung,' May mentioned nervously.

'The doctor explained that to us,' her mother told her. 'The other, healthy lung will be strong enough to do the work of two.'

'That's a relief, I suppose,' May said doubtfully. 'It all seems a bit scary to me, though.'

'I'm sure it must do, love,' said the terrified Flo, struggling to put on a brave face.

They were in the doctor's office at Ashburn; he had left them alone for a while to discuss the proposed surgery. This was an emotional occasion for May, as it was a year since she had last seen her parents. She and her mother had both wept openly at the sight of each other; her father had seemed a little wet eyed but had managed to maintain his male dignity.

'Still, I'm willing to give anything a try if it will get me better and back home,' said May.

'That's my girl,' approved Flo.

May looked from one parent to the other in a questioning manner. 'I know I'm out of touch, but I'm not so far gone as to not know that it's Saturday. So if you two are here, who's looking after the Pavilion?'

'George is standing in for us,' Flo explained. 'It's his Saturday off. He's got someone to help him.'

'Betty?'

'No. The baby is due next month so she's taking things easy,' said Flo.

'Who's helping George, then?' asked May.

'Percy, one of our regular elderly gents,' replied Dick.

'Bless him,' she said. 'It's good of them both.'

'They are a decent crowd, our regulars,' said Flo. 'Most of them anyway.'

May was overwhelmed with longing for home, which seemed even more distant now that she was to have surgery. The sounds and smells of the Pavilion, the playground, the house and all the people she associated with those places seemed agonisingly dear to her. She couldn't even think about Tiddles, strutting about the place demanding food and fuss, without wanting to cry. Goodness knows how long it would take her to recover from the operation. *If* she recovered, she thought gloomily.

Anxiety was making her feel nauseous and her sense of vulnerability was total. She took herself in hand; if it had to be done, the sooner the better, and no fuss about it. Negative thoughts must not be allowed to creep in. The doctor had made it clear that it was her only hope, so she had to be brave and let them do what they had to.

'Remember me to everybody at home, won't you,' she said, choking back the tears.

'We certainly will,' said Flo, sniffing into her handkerchief.

Betty always found news of May's illness hard to take. It was far too serious and frightening for her one-dimensional approach to life, especially as she couldn't face the fact that May might die. So she tried to change the subject whenever it arose, which it did when George got home from the Pavilion that evening, full of the latest development and very concerned indeed about May.

'She's only having a flamin' operation,' Betty said airily after he related what the Stubbses had told him. 'It isn't as though she's having her head chopped off. There's no need to make such a big drama of it, George.'

'Is that all you can say?' he admonished fiercely. 'She's your best friend, for goodness' sake.'

'Surely you must care about May to some extent,' Sheila said to Betty.

Dot made a timely intervention. 'Come and give me a hand in the kitchen please, Sheila,' she said, heading out of the room. 'Let's leave those two to sort their differences out on their own.'

'I don't like illness,' Betty explained to George after the others had left the room. 'I never have.'

'I don't suppose May is keen on it either,' he pointed out. 'Stuck down there in Surrey miles away from us all and feeling rotten, the poor girl. And now they are going to cut her open.'

'What am I supposed to do about it?' Betty demanded. 'I can't make her better.'

'You could at least take an interest,' he suggested. 'Instead of trying to make me shut up every time I mention her name.'

'Well I . . . Oh, you don't understand,' she began in a trembling voice and then burst into tears.

'Betty,' he said, giving her a rather awkward hug. 'I didn't mean to upset you, but May is our friend. It hurts me when you are so offhand about her. She is very sick.'

'I know that and I wish she wasn't because then I wouldn't have to care,' she snivelled. 'All these awful things are happening that I'm no good at. May getting ill, me getting pregnant . . . I can't cope with any of it.

All I wanted was to enjoy myself while I'm still young and all of that has been taken away from me. And yes I know that sounds selfish, but that's what I am. I don't want bad stuff in my life. Not yet. I don't feel grown up enough for everything that's happening and I wish it would all stop.'

George didn't feel particularly mature either, but he could see that there was no point in reminding her that May really had drawn the short straw, and that Betty was the lucky one. He himself had already tasted tragedy when his father had died in such terrible circumstances, but growing up had come as a real shock to Betty, who obviously didn't have much in the way of courage or spirit. But people were what they were and Betty was his wife, so he said, 'Look, why don't we go to the pictures tonight. A good film might cheer you up. Mr and Mrs Stubbs insisted on giving me a few bob for looking after the Pavilion for them today, so I've got a bit of spare cash.'

'I don't think I'll be able to get into the seat,' she said miserably, looking down at her enormous bump.

'Mm,' he said, observing her impressive protuberance, but knowing how much she enjoyed the cinema he added, 'Well let's give it a try and if you're uncomfortable we'll come home.'

'All right then,' she said, smiling now. 'I'd really like that, George. Thanks.'

He smiled, but it wasn't heartfelt. He was still feeling desperate about May, who was about to endure a huge ordeal. Also, he had no idea how Betty was going to face up to motherhood next month. She didn't seem able to come to grips with life as an adult at all.

For a while after the operation May's life consisted of pain interspersed with sleep with very little comfort in between. But then came moments of peace which gradually grew longer and more frequent. Her shoulder was slightly crooked now as a result of the surgery and she had a large scar, but the doctors seemed pleased with her condition and she was feeling reasonably optimistic about her chances of survival.

'Thank Gawd you're back,' said Connie when she finally arrived back on her own ward. 'It's been really quiet and miserable in here without you.'

'I'll take that as a compliment,' she said.

Connie looked more serious. 'Which is how it was meant,' she confirmed. 'I've missed you. I really have.'

'Where's Vi?' May asked, looking around.

'She's gone.'

'Home?'

'She died last week.'

'Oh.' It was like a body blow to May as the fine line between life and death hit home with more power than usual, probably because of her own current delicate state. 'She seemed to be all right when I left.'

'Mm. That was what we thought, but she took bad suddenly and they carted her off to another ward and the next thing we knew she was a goner.'

'That's so sad,' said May. 'She was such a good sort too.'

'Mm, she was,' Connie agreed. 'There have been all sorts of changes. Doug Sands has gone as well.'

'Dead? Oh no!' May's hand flew to her throat.

'No, he was discharged.'

'Thank God for that,' said May.

'It's the end of the art classes, though,' Connie informed her. 'There's whist instead, which isn't nearly so much fun.'

'Let's hope I do better at that than I did at art,' said May. 'I couldn't really do much worse.'

'One thing is for sure, the teacher isn't as much fun as Doug was,' Connie mentioned.

'Doug is a nice bloke,' said May. 'I hope he keeps well and makes a full recovery.'

'We're back to bread and bread for whist,' Connie informed her. 'As it's run by a woman.'

'Oh, it's so good to be back,' said May warmly. 'I've missed you like mad, especially your sense of humour.'

'If you haven't got one of those in here you won't last long at all,' said Connie. 'You'd probably end up being transferred to the loony bin.'

'That's a fact,' agreed May.

In this environment you were constantly reminded of the fragility of life and how powerless you were over your own destiny. But there was a lot of humour and hopefulness too, as well as warmth and humanity. A positive attitude was essential, and May had that in abundance now that the operation was over. If optimism was the key to recovery, she reckoned she stood a good chance.

'Let me get you up to date on all the rest of the gossip,' said Connie.

'Yes please,' said May, and they settled down on the porch in the bitter weather, ready for a good chat.

George had a new love in his life. He weighed in at eight pounds six ounces, had a belting pair of lungs, and they named him Joe after George's father. He arrived at the end of February, and for George it was love at first sight.

Betty was much less smitten. 'It's all right for you, you're out at work all day while he's screaming his head off. And it's me who has to get up to him in the night,' she could be heard to say in the early weeks of Joe's life.

'With the best will in the world, I don't have a pair of tits to feed him with,' George pointed out, grinning. 'And I have to go out to work to feed us all.'

'I know,' Betty was forced to agree, 'but babies are hard work. You men don't know the half of it.'

'You'd never get a more devoted dad than George,' his sister would chip in. 'You don't see many men taking their kid out like he does. Walks down the street with the pram as proud as Punch at the weekends.'

Light-hearted mockery from his mates about him having turned into a girl and doing woman's work didn't worry George one iota. This child was his pride and joy, the best thing that had ever happened to him, and he enjoyed every moment he spent with him. He showed him off to all and sundry. On a Saturday afternoon he would walk him down to the Pavilion in his pram for the paper. He'd stay for a cup of tea and a chat with the regulars, talking about his baby to anyone who would listen. If Joe started to get a bit noisy, George simply took him out of his pram and cuddled and rocked him until he stopped. On the odd occasion that the baby needed something George couldn't give him, he was forced to take him home, but it didn't often happen because he took him out between feeding times.

As spring and then summer came and Joe thrived and became more interesting, George was even more besotted. He would play with him and make him chuckle and had endless patience when the child was fretful.

Even Betty had to admit that he was much more involved as a parent than other husbands she knew of. She had become acquainted with some young mums who had told her that their husbands didn't take any part at all in the upbringing of their child. The other women thought she was very lucky, and she agreed with them.

'You're a better dad than I am a mum,' she said to him one day when Joe was coming up to six months old and they were out walking with him, sitting up in the pram in the park one Sunday afternoon.

'Don't do yourself down, Bet.' George had been amazed at how well she had taken to motherhood. She complained all the time but she did that about everything; it was in her nature. 'You only have to look at the boy to know that you're doing a really good job. Anyone can see that he's well looked after and the picture of health.'

'You've got more patience with him than I have, though.'

'That's probably because you have him all day so it's

only natural that your patience wears a bit thin now and again.'

'Maybe.'

But Betty knew in her heart that she didn't get the same enjoyment from being a parent as George did. She loved her child, of course, and had coped with motherhood better than she had expected, but she felt very trapped in her situation. It seemed as though her youth had ended before she'd had a chance to taste adult enjoyment and glamour. In rare moments of honesty she could admit to herself that she had got her comeuppance. She'd gone after George because she hadn't wanted to be alone and she'd thought marriage would be glamorous. Now she felt as though she was in a prison.

Little Joe was dear to her and she was very glad she had him but she still had a persistent yearning to be free and out having fun with no responsibilities. Her mother had always told her that she was one of those people for whom the grass was always greener, and she was beginning to think it must be true. After all, she'd had no one to have fun with after May went away and she would be on her own again if she wasn't married to George. But no matter how much she reasoned with herself, this other sort of life still beckoned.

They had reached the pond and George took the baby out of the pram to give him a close look at the ducks. There was a great deal of joyful squealing.

'I don't know who is enjoying the ducks most, you or Joe,' Betty said. 'You're a big kid, George Bailey.'

'Joe's given me a second childhood,' he said.

He and Betty smiled at each other in a rare moment of unity. Betty never would be the love of his life but she had given him his beautiful son, and for that he would be forever grateful.

May's much-longed-for homecoming in the late summer of that year was a huge anticlimax. After the first few glorious days of being back in her own home with her parents and beloved Tiddles, she missed the camaraderie she'd had at Ashburn. This was probably because she still had to rest for a lot of the time and was only allowed to walk a few yards each day. It had, after all, been a major operation.

Another factor that she found difficult to deal with was the guilt of having to be looked after by her parents. Mum had quite enough to do with the Pavilion as well as the home to run. The last thing she needed was an invalid on her hands as well.

'How can you possibly think that I mind looking after my own daughter?' Flo said emotionally when May mentioned her concerns to her. 'It's an honour and your dad and I are so pleased to have you back. We'd have had you at home all along if the doctors hadn't thought it best that you go away.'

'They did well by me at Ashburn and I'll always be grateful, but I thought when I came home I'd be back to normal, not stuck in bed for a lot of the day, cluttering up the front room.'

'We thought you might be lonely upstairs, that's why we brought your bed down.'

'It's lovely to be back home anyway, Mum,' she said. 'As soon as I get the all-clear, I'll start pulling my weight again.'

'Don't put your progress back by worrying about that,' said Flo. 'The doctor will soon tell you when you can go back to normal.' She paused, frowning. 'The only thing is, I shall have to be at the Pavilion for part of the day. I can't leave your dad all day on his own. I won't do my usual hours, though, and I'll be back and forth. Lucky it's only round the corner. I'll leave everything to hand for you.'

'Don't worry about me,' May assured her. 'I'll be fine.'

The days were long and tedious. One or two neighbours dropped by, but most people wouldn't come within a mile of someone who'd had what she'd had, even though she was no longer infectious. She rested in bed and spent some time in the back garden, well wrapped up, as fresh air was still considered to be important to her recovery.

Her mother kept her supplied with magazines from the shop and books from the public library, and she enjoyed the crossword in the paper every day. She and Flo had plenty of cosy chats in the course of the day when her father wasn't there, but she missed Connie and yearned for company of her own age.

Then one evening she had a very special visitor.

'George,' she said, welling up at the sight of him and noticing how much he had changed. His face had broadened and firmed into manhood and he was so much taller now. 'It's good to see you.'

'I thought I'd leave it a couple of weeks before visiting to give you time to settle in.'

'I would have understood if you hadn't come at all,' she said. 'Some people prefer to stay away.'

'Not me,' he said, sitting by the bed and taking her hand. She looked absolutely beautiful, he thought. He'd wondered if she might be pale and consumptive in appearance, but she had a good colour, probably because of all the fresh air she'd been getting, her blond hair was shiny and her blue eyes were more vivid than ever. She seemed very fragile, though, and he was overwhelmed by a longing to love and look after her. 'Betty will come along another time. She's busy with the baby at the moment.'

May knew exactly why Betty hadn't come, but she just said, 'How is the baby? I'm dying to see him . . . er, later on when I'm out and about again, of course.'

'Oh May, he's gorgeous, I can't wait for you to meet him,' he said proudly.

'I can imagine,' she said. 'You a dad. It seems strange, and as for Betty being a mum . . .'

'She's doing all right, as it happens.'

'Of course, I only meant that I still think of her as a kid.'

'I know. I wasn't leaping to her defence or anything,' he explained quickly. 'I think even she's surprised herself that she's coping. You know Betty; she always was a bit scatty.'

'I'm glad she's doing all right, anyway,' she said.

'May,' he began, sounding awkward. 'About Betty and me. It wasn't anything . . . I mean, there was nothing between us before. It was just one night but she got pregnant so I had to do the decent thing.'

She took his hand in both of hers. 'You don't have to explain anything to me, George,' she said.

'But I . . .' How could he tell her that he loved her more than ever now that he had seen her again when he had nothing to offer her apart from friendship? He was a married man with a responsibility to his wife and child. He had lost May the night he'd allowed himself to be seduced by Betty and there was no going back. 'No, you're right, of course. Sorry. It's just me talking too much as usual.'

'We'll always be friends, no matter what happens,' she said, though her heart was breaking.

'I hope so.'

'So tell me what's been happening around here.' She smiled, teasing him to ease the sudden tension. 'Apart from the birth of the wonder child Bailey.'

He laughed. 'Nothing else comes close to that in terms of importance,' he said jokingly.

'Of course not,' she replied, entering into the spirit.

'I suppose you've been hearing all the talk about war while you were away.'

'We did get to see the newspapers,' she said. 'So I know there are rumours about it.'

'Not many people are taking it seriously. Most think the papers are making too much of it, but it seems serious to me what's happening in Europe. This Hitler bloke is a determined bugger,' he said. 'Closer to home, I noticed the other day that they are digging trenches in the park. I asked one of the blokes about them and he said they're for people to take refuge in during air raids. It made it seem very real. That and all the posters asking for volunteers to join the ARP. It means air-raid patrol apparently.'

'I suppose the government have to make sure we are prepared just in case,' she suggested. 'It doesn't mean that anything is going to happen.'

'Mm, you're right,' he agreed. 'Anyway, I'm sure you must be more concerned with getting better than the possibility of war.'

'Good health is everything to me now,' she told him. 'I took it for granted before. Being ill soon cures you of that.'

'Have they given you any idea when you'll be out and about again?' he asked.

'Not yet. I have to go for a major examination and X-ray in January and I'm hoping they will give me the all-clear then. I'm keeping my fingers crossed.'

'I'll be rooting for you.'

Her mother brought in a tray of tea and biscuits and after a few minutes of social chat she made a diplomatic exit, realising that her daughter needed to be alone with her friend. When George left he promised to come again soon, and May knew that he would and was enormously cheered by the prospect.

★ ★ ★

'So how is she?' asked Betty when George got home.

'Pretty good considering,' he replied. 'She looks surprisingly well, actually.'

'Did she ask why I wasn't with you?'

'I didn't give her the chance. I told her right away that you were busy with the baby and she accepted it, but I could tell that she didn't believe me,' he said. 'May is a bright girl. She will know that you stayed away for the same reason as everyone else. I think she's used to it but she's bound to be very hurt.'

'I can't take any chances,' she told him. 'Not with a baby to look after.'

'Come off it,' he said. 'If you were going to catch anything you'd have done so two years ago when she was first ill and you were always together. Not now that she's better.'

'It isn't only that,' she said. 'It's the thought of being with someone who's had TB.'

'Not much of a friend, are you?' chipped in the forthright Sheila. 'First you pinch her bloke while she's away in hospital and now you won't even go to see her when she's back home. If I was May I'd tell you to get lost.'

'Yes. Well May isn't like you, Sheila,' George told her. 'She isn't such a loudmouth.'

'Who are you calling a loudmouth?' Sheila objected. 'Tell him, Mum. Tell him to watch what he's saying when he's speaking to me.'

'I can't tell him what to do,' said his mother. 'Not now that he's a married man. That's Betty's job.'

'He doesn't take any notice of me,' Betty was quick

to point out. 'If he did, he wouldn't have gone to see May.'

There was a shocked silence.

'Surely you wouldn't try to stop him from seeing May just because you don't want to?' said Sheila accusingly.

'It does seem rather heartless, Betty,' added Dot.

'Downright cruel if you ask me,' Sheila declared.

'I would rather he didn't see her,' Betty told them defiantly. 'There, now you know and I don't care what you think.'

'Right, that's enough, all of you,' George intervened sternly. 'This is a private matter between Betty and me and we will discuss it when we're on our own. We don't need you two putting your oar in.'

There was a tense silence followed by a timely intervention from upstairs.

'The baby's crying,' said Betty, glad to escape. 'I'll go and see to him.'

'I'll put the kettle on,' said Dot.

George sat down in an armchair and picked up the newspaper, but he was far too preoccupied to take much of it in. It had been an emotional evening one way and another and the ructions weren't over yet.

Living with the family meant that George and Betty had very little privacy. Their bedroom was about the only place they were ever alone, and here they were always worried about waking Joe. But tonight George had something to say and he was determined not to put it off.

'The fact is, Betty – and I want to be straight with you about this – I intend to visit May regularly while she needs it, no matter how much you go on at me about it. I really don't want to upset you, but in this particular instance I don't feel as though I have a choice.'

'That's a nice way to treat your wife, I must say,' Betty said, sounding peeved.

'Look, Bet, when I married you, I promised to look after you and be faithful and I intend to be true to everything I promised. But as far as I know I didn't sign away all my rights as a human being,' he said, keeping his voice down because of the baby. 'May needs her friends more than ever just at the moment and I am not going to let her down, because it would be very wrong. If you choose to stay away that is your decision and I'll respect it, but I must be allowed to do what I think is right without you giving me constant earache about it.'

Betty had already accepted the fact that she could only go so far with George. Annoyingly, he was very much his own man and she knew he wouldn't change his mind about this. 'Fair enough,' she said. 'I'll say no more about it.'

'Hooray for that,' he said.

Lying beside him later while he slept, Betty had a familiar ache inside that she tried to deny. But it was suddenly so overwhelming it brought tears to her eyes. The fact was, she missed May. She knew she would never have another

103

friend like her; someone who knew all her faults and still wanted to be her pal, though maybe not now after everything that had happened. Betty had thought that having managed to nab George and get herself hitched she wouldn't need a close woman friend, but she realised now that she did; more than ever before oddly enough.

An unfamiliar feeling of shame crept over her at the way she often behaved. She wished she could be different, but somehow she never was. She just kept on being horrid. She supposed that some people were just made that way, because it came naturally to her. She couldn't seem to find the empathy that other people had. It was always about herself; as though she was sliding through life on the surface, getting from day to day in pursuit of her own needs. She couldn't seem to let go of herself.

On the odd occasion when May had been really sick and Betty had imagined her in a hospital bed, she had drawn back from the image almost immediately because she hadn't enjoyed the feeling. She didn't like how she felt now either; this awful hollowness that could only be filled by one person.

The following afternoon May and her mother were having a cup of tea together while Flo was taking a break from the shop when there was a knock at the door.

'Someone to see you, May,' said Flo, coming back into the room.

'Well, well,' said May, seeing Betty looking somewhat shamefaced. 'You certainly took your time.'

Betty bit her lip. 'Sorry, May,' she said. 'You know me; not the stuff that heroes are made of.'

Patting the bed, May said, 'Come and sit down.' She paused, looking at Betty. 'If that's too close for your comfort, have a chair instead.'

'Oh May . . . don't be like that.'

Flo made a diplomatic exit, saying she had to get back to the shop. After she left, the silence was almost unbearable.

'Look,' began May to break the ice. 'I know that you have a problem with my illness – lots of people feel the same way – but you're here so you must have got over it to a certain extent. The fact is that I don't have TB any more, so can we move on from it and forget it? I'm looking to the future. The illness is in the past and pity humiliates me, so don't even try it.'

'Fair enough,' said Betty, sitting down somewhat gingerly on the edge of the bed.

'We have a lot to catch up on,' said May at last. 'You a married lady and a mum.'

Betty nodded.

'Where is your boy? I'm dying to see him.'

Betty bit her lip.

'You couldn't quite chance it for him, could you?' guessed May. 'Not with all the supposed germs flying about.'

'I thought we needed to talk, and that's nigh on impossible with Joe around. I left him with my mother-in-law.'

'Oh, I see,' said May.

'Look, I know I'm not much of a friend,' admitted

Betty. 'But I didn't invent the attitude people have towards that illness. No one wants to catch it, and I'm only human.'

'So how come you are here?'

'I've finally accepted that it's safe, I suppose,' she said. 'And I've missed you something terrible.'

'Same here,' said May.

'What was it like at that place?' asked Betty.

'*That place* is called Ashburn, and it was my home for more than a year and a half, so I grew quite fond of it,' May told her. 'I made some lovely friends there and I miss them a lot.'

'Oh,' said Betty, sounding surprised and not best pleased. 'Well, you're back with your real friends now.'

May knew that Betty would never understand the bond she had had with her fellow patients, so there was no point in trying to explain. She also knew that there was something huge standing between them, and while it remained tacit the awkwardness would remain. She decided to bring it out into the open. 'Did you go after George deliberately to get one over on me?'

Betty turned scarlet. 'May, how can you say such a thing?' she demanded.

'You knew how I felt about him,' May reminded her. 'You've always known. You flirted with him enough times when I was around and he always made it clear that he wasn't interested. Then I get news that you are in the family way and getting married. Naturally I wondered.'

'What's he been saying?'

'Nothing at all,' May assured her. 'You know George better than that.'

'Well . . . it wasn't as though you were engaged to him or anything, was it?' said Betty sheepishly.

'I was only fifteen when I went away, for heaven's sake,' May reminded her.

'Look, you weren't around and I was lonely . . . Anyway, George and I are married now, so you'll have to accept it.'

'Don't patronise me, Betty. I've been ill. I haven't gone soft in the head,' retorted May. 'Of course I've accepted it. I sent you a letter to that effect.'

'What's all this about, then?'

'It's about being truthful with each other,' she replied. 'It's what friends do.'

'All right, I'll tell you . . . There was a coronation party and there was booze around, which neither of us is used to, and it just sort of happened,' Betty said guiltily. 'So can we drop the subject now, please?'

'By all means. You won't hear another word from me about it.' May had made her point, which was all she had wanted. She wouldn't question Betty any further. In the past she had always let Betty have her own way, but not any more. She had realised that she was going to have to stand up for herself if she wanted to move forward with any scrap of dignity. She had been physically weakened by tuberculosis, but her spirit had grown stronger and she wanted people to know that she wasn't prepared to be patronised for the rest of her life. It wasn't easy, though, when you felt so isolated from the outside world. Loneliness was very damaging to the confidence.

'Good, then perhaps we can move on to more current subjects,' said Betty. 'Like Joe's christening.'

'Oh?'

'I was wondering if you might consider the idea of being his godmother,' Betty heard herself say.

May stared at her in surprise; it was the very last thing she had expected.

'When you are out and about again, of course,' Betty added quickly. 'We won't have the christening until then.'

'Do you really mean it?'

'Of course I do,' she confirmed. 'Who else would we ask but our oldest friend?'

An inner warmth spread through May. The fact that someone trusted her and thought she would be around for long enough to take on such an important and responsible job was the most uplifting thing that had happened to her since she'd been taken ill.

'I'd be very honoured, Betty,' she said, smiling. 'Very honoured indeed. Thank you.'

'It's a pleasure,' grinned Betty.

Walking home through the streets, where strange things were appearing – piles of sandbags outside buildings and a notice on a public hall stating that it was now an ARP centre – Betty felt happier than she had in a long time. She had her friend back and that was a really good feeling. The godmother thing had been a spur-of-the-moment idea but she was very glad she'd suggested it, firstly because it had got her back into May's favour and also because she knew that her friend would do a good job.

It was a peculiar thing, though, how May still had that

something special that caused Betty to envy and admire her in equal measures. Betty was now the one who had what all girls wanted, the man, the marriage and the baby and therefore some security and status in society. In comparison May had nothing. She had the stigma of illness hanging over her and not even a boyfriend to call her own. But she still had a touch of class that set her apart and eluded Betty. It was strange.

Oh well, they were friends again, that was the important thing. She would be in George's good books too, for going to visit, and he would be absolutely delighted about the godmother idea. So things had taken a real turn for the better.

Chapter Five

It was January 1939 and May and her parents were in a Lyons tea shop in the West End having a celebration lunch. As it was a Wednesday and half-day closing in Ealing, the three of them had hopped on to the tube into central London as soon as the Pavilion had shut for the day.

Dick ordered their favourite roast beef meal when the Nippy swept neatly up to their table in her smart black and white uniform with white starched apron and cap treating them with the cordiality that people had come to expect of Lyons waitresses.

May looked affectionately from one parent to the other. 'I'm having such a nice time,' she told them. 'Thank you both for giving me this lovely treat.'

'You deserve it, love, after the rough couple of years you've had,' her mother assured her. 'It isn't every week your daughter gets a clean bill of health from the doctor. Me and your dad couldn't let it pass without doing something a bit special.'

'That's right,' added her husband.

'We can have a look round the shops afterwards if you like, May,' suggested Flo. 'If you see something you fancy to wear, I'll treat you to it.'

'I'll go for a walk in the park while you do that,' said Dick with good-humoured male disapproval. 'You won't catch me traipsing round women's shops.'

'Oh, it feels so good to be out again,' May said effusively, enjoying the feel of London, the bustle created by humanity at large hurrying in all directions. Some women were wearing fashionable fur, the men in overcoats. Both sexes wore hats, women in a variety of styles, men mostly in trilbies. The buzz of the West End seemed like a riotous adventure to May after so long away from crowds of any sort. 'It's very exciting.'

'It's only a Lyons tea shop, love,' her dad reminded her.

'It wouldn't matter to me if it was a scruffy old greasy-spoon café,' she said. 'I feel as though I have finally rejoined the human race.' She looked at them earnestly. 'Honestly, nothing in my life before has ever been as good as knowing that I am not ill any more and I can have a normal life again.'

'You have to go for regular check-ups for a while, though,' reminded her cautious mother, who had been with her at the hospital when the specialist had given her the good news. 'And you must keep the appointments just to be on the safe side.'

'I will, don't worry.' May had also been told not to overdo things at first; that normal life would initially tire her and she was to have plenty of good food, rest and fresh air. Other than that she could live her life as she wanted, including working. Her post-operative crooked shoulder had proved to be permanent and it made her seem a little awkward at times, but she was so used to it, it wasn't a problem for her. 'There's no way I'll put my health at risk.'

They ate their main course, had one of Lyons famous round ice creams for dessert, followed by coffee, then headed off into the crowds outside. The overwhelming emotion for May in all of this was the joy of feeling like a normal human being again; a part of things with a right to be here. She didn't have to be ashamed any more and it was such an uplifting feeling.

She and her mother headed off to investigate the contents of the dress shops, arranging to meet her father at Oxford Circus station in about an hour.

Dick headed towards Hyde Park through the crowds in Oxford Street, lost in thought. This was a very joyful time for him and his family. Having lost one child, it had seemed for a while as though May was going to be taken from them as well. But by some miracle she had been spared and he thanked God for it. His wife had been devastated by the whole thing, and for the first time in two years she now had cause to be happy again. This was why he had such a dilemma on his hands, because something had come up that he needed to speak to her about and he didn't have the heart because he knew she wouldn't be pleased with what he had to say.

Oh well, he thought, heading into the park, the trees

stripped for winter, the sky a deep, relentless grey, making the Serpentine look dark and chilly, he didn't need to do it just yet. He wouldn't spoil her happy day.

May was in high spirits when she went into Bright Brothers store a week or so later, still flushed with the joy of knowing that she had returned to good health. Noticing that the lingerie counter was without customers, she went over to pay a social call.

'Hello, Miss Matt,' she said brightly.

'Miss Stubbs,' responded the older woman with what could only be described as a gasp of surprise followed by a look of utter horror, while a junior assistant looked on with interest. 'What brings you here?'

'I'm on my way upstairs to the personnel department to see about a job,' May explained.

'A job *here*?' she said incredulously.

'Well, yes, of course,' replied May, finding the remark odd since she would hardly come here looking for a job anywhere else.

'Oh, I see,' said Miss Matt with barely veiled disapproval. With an effort she managed to arrange her face into a more sympathetic expression. 'How are you feeling now, my dear?'

'Very well, thank you,' replied May. 'I'm better. I have been given the all-clear by the doctor.'

'You look healthy enough, I must say,' said Miss Matt as though astounded, 'but . . . er, they do say that you never truly get better from *that* illness.'

'I don't know who told you that, but I'm sure they must have been misinformed,' said May, her spirits dampened by the woman's cold and pessimistic attitude. 'People do sometimes have a permanent recovery.'

'Mm, perhaps they do. But a word to the wise, my dear,' began Miss Matt, leaning forward and speaking with an air of confidentiality. 'Why not save yourself the humiliation of going to the office upstairs? They won't give you a job here.'

'But I'm an experienced counter assistant,' May pointed out. 'I'd be an asset.'

Miss Matt twisted her face as though what she was about to say pained her. 'Here at Bright Brothers we work in close contact with the public, as you very well know,' she stated unnecessarily. 'They wouldn't dare to put their customers at risk by having you work here, especially not on the counter.'

It was as much as May could do to keep her hands off the woman; she actually wanted to physically attack her and erase that smug look from her face. But she merely said, 'I'm not a risk to anyone. As I have just told you, I am better.'

'You haven't just had a touch of flu, my dear,' the other woman pointed out in a condescending manner. 'What you've had could linger.'

Furious now, but clinging to her damaged self-confidence, May said, 'It did linger but now it has gone, thanks to the skill of the medical profession. With respect, Miss Matt, I suggest that you check your facts

114

before holding forth on that particular subject. It's bigots like you who take the humanity out of the human race.'

'How dare you speak to me like that,' objected the older woman, turning scarlet with rage, while the junior, a girl of about fifteen, watched closely, enjoying the proceedings enormously. Very little in the way of entertainment ever happened around here, and there was nothing like a good old barney to liven things up.

'I dare quite easily as it happens,' said May with a defiance she hadn't known she possessed. 'Fortunately I am not intimidated by people like you, so I will make my way upstairs. Goodbye.'

With that she marched towards the stairs, angry, hurt and absolutely determined not to be beaten by this terrible prejudice.

'So you are fully recovered then, Miss Stubbs?' said the man in the personnel department at Bright Brothers, looking at her employee file.

'Yes, completely better, thank you,' she confirmed. 'The doctor has told me that I can return to work.'

'Mm.' A thin, balding man in a dark suit and white starched collar, he had his elbows on his desk and his pyramided fingers supporting his chin. 'Don't you think you would be better suited now to work that is less physically demanding? A sitting-down job of some sort; in an office, perhaps.'

'But shop work is what I know,' she explained. 'As my file will show you, I have been fully trained by Bright Brothers and I did very well in the job.'

'But the nature of the work here demands that you are on your feet all day,' he pointed out.

'Yes, but as I have just told you,' she began, increasingly frustrated, 'I am fit and healthy now, so the job won't be a problem.'

'The thing is, my dear,' he began, peering at her over his spectacles, 'here at Bright Brothers we insist on our staff being totally reliable, and with the type of illness that unfortunately struck you down, you wouldn't meet our requirements as far as that's concerned.'

'Can you tell me why, please, since I am no longer ill?' she asked determinedly.

He stroked his chin meditatively. 'Because an illness like the one you have had could very well leave you vulnerable to other conditions, which would mean you taking sick leave. That would be very inconvenient for us.'

'So Miss Matt thinks I am still infectious, and you are convinced that I'll let you down, when I have assured you both that neither of these things are the case,' she told him.

'I'm very sorry, Miss Stubbs, but we have nothing suitable for you at the moment,' he informed her, rising sharply to indicate that the interview was at an end. 'I wish you well and hope that your recovery continues.' He walked to the door and opened it for her. 'Goodbye, my dear.'

May marched out of the store fuming. She had heard rumours of this sort of thing when she'd been at Ashburn but hadn't realised they were so devastatingly true. Well, this wasn't over by a long chalk. She would keep trying until she did get a job, and prove that she was worth employing.

The morning rush was over at the Pavilion and Flo and Dick were busy filling shelves and catching up with administration. All the tables in the café were taken but nobody needed serving, so Dick decided that he could put it off no longer. He would speak to his wife about what was on his mind.

'The thing is, Flo, something has come up that I need to talk to you about,' he began.

'Yes, dear,' she said absently, checking the paperwork related to a cigarette order from the wholesaler.

'With all the talk of war that's around at the moment, there is work for skilled men at the docks,' he said. 'They are building and repairing ships and they need men like me.'

She paused in what she was doing and looked at him. 'I'm glad there are jobs about, dear, but it doesn't affect you because you work here,' she said.

'Mm.' He scratched his head worriedly. 'Look, I know how much this place means to you, and us working here together, and I enjoy it too. But you are the heart and soul of the Pavilion and—'

'What are you trying to tell me, Dick?'

'Thanks to you, I was saved from the misery of unemployment, but the truth is, I miss my trade, Flo,' he blurted out. 'I want to go back to it.'

'But I need you here.'

'You could employ someone to take my place and pay them what the business pays me,' he suggested. 'I'll be earning good money down the docks, so we'll be better off financially.'

She gave him a studious look. 'You've already looked into it, haven't you?' she guessed.

He nodded, looking sheepish. 'Some blokes down the pub were talking about it, so I called in at the Labour Exchange to find out about it.'

'Mm, well I can't say I'm not disappointed, because we've built this business together.'

'No, Flo, you built it and I helped,' he corrected. 'And you've done a really good job.'

'Well, the idea of working with a stranger doesn't appeal to me at all, but I won't hold you back, Dick,' she told him. 'If you could give me time to find someone suitable, then you can go and see about getting back into your trade with my blessing.'

He gave her an affectionate hug, then they went back to what they were doing, both lost in their own thoughts.

May was so full of her dismal experience at Bright Brothers that evening, her parents didn't have a chance to tell her their own news for a while.

'People are so misinformed,' she said, having recounted the experience. 'But I am not going to give up. I shall keep my eye on the local paper, and if I continue to get turned down, I shall make a complaint at the Labour Exchange.'

Flo and Dick listened sympathetically, making encouraging comments, then eventually told her of their plans.

'Blimey,' she exclaimed. 'That's a shock. You'll be very much missed at the Pavilion, Dad. The customers really like you.'

'Maybe they do,' he said. 'But I can help out on a Saturday afternoon to keep in touch.'

'So you'll have to find a replacement for him then, Mum,' May remarked.

Flo nodded. 'I shall put an advert in the *Gazette* as soon as I can,' she said.

An odd silence fell as they were all struck by the same thought.

May spoke up quickly before the idea had time to develop. 'As much as I would like to take Dad's place at the Pavilion, it would be too easy for me. I have to prove that I can get a job outside of the family,' she told them. 'It's really important to me.'

'Of course, love,' said Flo, obviously disappointed. 'I can understand that.'

'I can help out, though, while I'm waiting to get fixed up, if you would like,' she offered.

'I would love that,' Flo enthused. 'We'll pay you a proper wage, of course.'

'The only thing is, you might lose customers when people see me there, given the lack of knowledge among the public in general over TB.'

'They'll get used to it,' said her mother, 'and anyway, I'll take a chance on it.'

'I'll still be applying for other jobs, though, Mum, so

it won't be a permanent arrangement.' May thought it wise to mention the fact. 'A family job will be lovely but I still have something to prove. I can't give up without a fight.'

'Of course not, dear,' Flo agreed.

'So can I go ahead and get myself fixed up with work at the docks, then?' said Dick.

'Yeah, I should think so, Dad,' said May. 'It will probably take me quite a while to get a job. If my experience so far is anything to go by, I doubt I'll be inundated with offers.'

'Employers' stupidity is our gain,' said Flo, who was delighted at the prospect of working with her daughter. She wanted her to find employment independently, of course, but she would enjoy having her around in the meantime.

Working at the Pavilion was a joy for May. She had helped out at odd times before so knew the ropes, and there was such a warm and friendly atmosphere. She had a few disapproving looks at first, but when people realised that nothing awful happened to them as a result of being in contact with her, they relaxed and accepted her.

Because she wanted to do the job as well as her father had, she even volunteered to take her turn rising early to prepare the newspapers for the rounds. When her mother suggested that it might be too much for her, May reminded her that that was exactly the sort of attitude she was fighting against.

She continued to apply for jobs. When she had no success, she decided that she had to do something more about it than just fuming inwardly.

'Our job is to supply candidates to employers who need staff,' said the male clerk at the Labour Exchange, a dark and dismal place mostly inhabited by men. 'We can't force them to take anybody on. That's their choice. So I'm afraid there isn't anything we can do about your problem, Miss Stubbs.'

'But not only is it unfair, it's also very silly not to take on a fit person just because they've been ill in the past,' she told him, having already explained about the prejudice she was experiencing.

A middle-aged man with greased hair and a bored expression, he emitted an irritated sigh. 'I can't be held responsible for the attitude of employers,' he told her. 'They pay the wages so that entitles them to hire whoever they want.'

'Maybe I shouldn't mention my illness to them,' she suggested heatedly. 'After all, I am only looking for a job as a shop assistant, not the position of managing director.'

He shrugged his shoulders disinterestedly.

'But I would feel dishonest if I didn't say anything about it,' she continued, trying not to be destroyed by his attitude. 'Anyway, illness is nothing to be ashamed of.'

'Indeed not,' he confirmed in an even tone. 'But as I have said, there is nothing I can do about it.'

'What do you suggest I do, then?'

'Keep trying, I suppose,' he advised her.

'That isn't very helpful.'

'Look, I can't change the way things are,' he said, his temper rising. 'I just work here. I don't make the rules.'

'I suppose not.'

'Anyway, as I have said, we have nothing suitable for you at the moment, and there are a lot of people waiting to see me. So if you don't mind . . .'

Angry and disheartened, she left. As she walked home in the cold and bright February weather, she became calmer, noticing some early signs of spring in green shoots in the front gardens and grass verges. She reminded herself that she had much to be grateful for. She had come through a terrible ordeal and was now healthy. That was worth everything and a lot more than many consumption victims had to look forward to. Because of her illness she had grown as a person, she was certain of that. She took nothing for granted now and appreciated her parents' support more than ever.

She also had a job she enjoyed, working with her mother. Yes, she did still have a point to make for herself and others like her, and she would make it in any way she could in the course of her daily life, because there were plenty of misinformed people about wherever you were. Hopefully one day she would win on the question of prejudice in the workplace, but in the meantime she had other plans. She quickened her step, eager to get back to the Pavilion.

There was a queue in the shop when she arrived, so she slipped behind the counter beside her mother to help speed things up.

'You can stop worrying about working with a stranger, because you won't have to,' she said to Flo when things had quietened down. 'I'm staying here on a permanent basis.'

Her mother's smile warmed May's heart and she knew that she had made the right decision.

'Oh May, I'm so pleased.'

'Me too, Mum,' she said. 'Me too.'

One of the benefits of having been seriously ill was the enhanced appreciation of everything when you were better. Senses were sharper; emotions stronger. Food had more flavour, the first smell of spring was so intense it brought tears to May's eyes and the freedom to walk among people was something she would value for the rest of her life.

The love of fresh air she had inherited from the treatment had stayed with her, and she got her bike out of the shed and began to ride it again, reminded of how much she had enjoyed it in the past. Of course, her former cycling companion George was no longer available; visiting her when she was ill was one thing, a cycle ride when she was better quite another for a married man, and Betty would have every right to be peeved. But she was happy to go alone and even went as far as Runnymede one Sunday afternoon and had a picnic by the river. The March weather was still quite chilly, but she wrapped up well and enjoyed herself.

A new pleasure for May was baby Joe, who was now a year old, the image of his father and the cutest little boy May had ever seen. She'd fallen for him as soon as she'd set eyes on him last year after she and Betty had got together again. Most Wednesday afternoons, when the Pavilion was closed, she spent time with Betty and Joe. Sometimes they went to the park, other times they stayed at home, depending on the weather and usually at the Stubbses' as a change of scene for Betty, who still often felt confined by motherhood. But wherever they were, May always spent most of her time amusing Joe.

'I didn't know you were so good with children,' Betty remarked one day.

'Neither did I till this little sweetie came into my life,' May told her. 'And he really is special.'

'You're marvellous with him.'

'Glad you're pleased.'

'We've decided on the Easter weekend for the christening, by the way,' Betty mentioned.

'That will be nice.'

'As his godmother, you'll be a sort of a relation to him,' Betty pointed out.

'I suppose I will in a way,' said May happily. 'And I just can't wait.'

One day in March, people coming to the Pavilion for their daily newspaper were shocked by the headlines, and the café resounded with voices discussing the news that Hitler and his army had marched into Prague.

'What a shocking thing,' said someone.

'Hitler wants stopping,' said another.

'He won't give up without a fight.'

'And that really will mean war.'

'Surely it won't come to that,' said one hopeful. 'The government won't let it go that far.'

'Let's hope not,' said May, moving through the tables with a tray to clear some crockery.

'I dunno,' said one doom-monger. 'They let it happen in nineteen fourteen.'

'The war to end all wars, they said.'

'They didn't reckon with Hitler when they said that.'

'That's true.'

'There's nothing us ordinary people can do about it and that's for sure.'

Having had so much to cope with in her own life, May hadn't paid a great deal of attention to the possibility of war. But things did seem to be getting serious now, which was rather frightening. As the idea of their country at war was so unimaginable, she dismissed it from her mind and concentrated on what she should get as a christening present for Joe. Definitely something that could be kept for him for later on, and probably something silver.

Standing at the font, struggling to hold a wriggling, snivelling little boy, May was very proud of her new responsibilities, even if Joe was being an absolute monster. He struggled noisily to get down throughout the part of the service when she was required to make solemn promises as laid down by the church.

Finally the vicar managed to splash the holy water on to Joe's head and the whole thing was over. 'Well he wasn't exactly an angel in the church, was he?' George remarked when they were back at the house for the christening tea. He picked his son up and kissed him. 'In fact you were a proper little horror, Joe Bailey. All that screaming and shouting. It's a wonder your Auntie May didn't decide to resign from the job.'

'It would take a lot more than that to put me off,' May told him.

'It's best to get kids christened when they are little and don't know what's going on, I reckon,' suggested George's mother.

'Yeah,' agreed one of his aunts. 'Once they can walk, it's only natural they want to run about and make a noise.'

'I wouldn't have been able to be his godmother if they'd had the christening when he was very little,' May pointed out.

'There is that,' agreed Dot.

'I'm so touched that you chose me, both of you,' May said impulsively to Betty and George. 'Thank you for waiting until I was better to have the christening.'

In actual fact the late christening was down to laziness on Betty's part. She hadn't wanted the bother of organising it and May had been the last person on her mind.

But when she'd seen her again and had wanted to get back into her favour, the godmother idea had been the perfect tactic. As it happened, she was very glad now with the way things had turned out, because there was no one else but May she would want for the job.

'What else would we do but wait for you?' she said. 'You're our dearest friend.' She looked at her husband, who was wise to her deviousness, warning him not to let the cat out of the bag. 'Isn't that right, George?'

'Absolutely,' he confirmed. He took the view that the end result had been perfect, with May having a part in Joe's life, and he had no intention of hurting her by telling her the truth.

May, Betty and George all had their eighteenth birthdays within two weeks of each other in the summer, so they decided to celebrate together. George arranged for his mother and sister to look after Joe on the nearest Saturday night and the three of them headed into the West End, which was thronged with people as usual at a weekend, everyone seeming undeterred by the threat of war evident in notices on buildings and trees all over London, appealing for volunteers to train as air-raid wardens.

The trio strolled through Leicester Square and Piccadilly, where they could hardly move for the crowds.

'Are we going to the pictures?' asked May.

'Nah, we can do that in Ealing,' said Betty.

'What about trying for a show, then?' suggested May. 'You can sometimes get tickets at the theatre on the night. *Me and My Girl* is still on, or there's *The Dancing Years.*'

'Why don't we go into a pub while we decide,' suggested Betty. 'Just for the hell of being old enough to get served.'

The others thought that might be fun, so they trooped into a pub in Leicester Square which was thick with cigarette smoke, packed to the doors and deafeningly noisy with the sound of talking and laughing. George ordered a half of bitter and the girls, wanting to be daring, had gin and orange.

'This is the life,' approved Betty, gulping hers.

'I think you're meant to drink it slowly,' suggested George. He lifted his glass. 'But cheers, you two. Happy birthday to us all.'

May chinked her glass and took a sip of the bitter liquid while Betty emptied her glass and asked for another.

'It's strong stuff,' warned George. 'I don't want to have to carry you home.'

'Don't be such an old misery,' she came back at him. 'This is supposed to be a celebration.'

'Oh all right then, just one more before we move on and try to get into a show or the pictures,' he agreed. 'May, how about you? Would you like another?'

'Not for me, thanks,' she said. 'It will take me ages to finish this, it's so bitter.'

While George ordered another for Betty, May had to admit to enjoying the warm feeling the drink gave her. It didn't taste nearly so sharp when you got used to it either. In fact she rather liked it. It certainly had a cheering effect.

★　★　★

'You really should try to have more confidence in yourself, Mum,' said Sheila in a tone of mild admonition. 'You've brought up two kids of your own, so why are you so worried about looking after Joe for a few hours?'

'I'm not the same woman as I was when you and George were little,' explained Dot. 'Anyway, I'm out of practice with children of that age. You can't reason with them.'

'Surely you've looked after Joe before.'

'Only for the odd short period during the day,' she said. 'I'm not so scared if Betty isn't out for long.'

'But Joe lives here, so he's used to you.'

'He isn't used to being on his own with me,' she said. 'He'll run rings around me.'

'He's your grandson, for heaven's sake; surely looking after him comes natural.'

'It probably does to other grannies, but things aren't as cut and dried as you might think.'

'Sorry, Mum, but I can't be expected to stay in with you,' Sheila declared.

'You said you would when George asked us to look after Joe tonight,' Dot reminded her.

'Mm, maybe I did, but I want to go out now,' Sheila explained. 'I won't be long. I just want to go round to my friend's house. She's going to lend me some *Filmgoer* magazines. She collects them and she's got a pile I can borrow.'

'Can't you do it tomorrow?'

'I could do but I want to look at them tonight,' Sheila

said. 'You're lucky I'm not out dancing like I sometimes am on a Saturday night. I would be gone for a long time then.'

'You agreed to stay in to help me look after Joe, so you should stand by that,' Dot said again.

'He's sound asleep in his cot upstairs,' Sheila pointed out. 'It doesn't need two of us to sit here. Put the wireless on, that'll keep you company. I won't be more than an hour or so.'

'An hour, just to collect some magazines?' queried her mother worriedly.

'Well I expect we'll have a bit of a natter as well,' Sheila said airily. 'I'm sixteen, Mum. I don't want to be stuck indoors every night. It's only natural I want to go out.'

'But Joe might wake up,' said Dot.

'Well then you'll have to get him back to sleep again, won't you?' She gave her mother an affectionate hug. 'You'll be fine. You must start to have more faith in yourself.'

Although Sheila was sometimes hard on her mother, she was actually very fond of her. She felt bad about leaving her tonight, but the reality was that Mum would never get her confidence back if she and George pandered to her all the time, and George was far too soft with her in Sheila's opinion. Before Dad died she was a perky and competent woman and there was no reason why she couldn't be again with a gentle shove in the right direction.

'If you're determined to go, don't be long,' said Dot miserably.

'An hour at the most,' Sheila assured her, and headed for the door. Turning, she added, 'If he does happen to wake up, just give him a cuddle and put him back down.'

'I know what to do,' said Dot. 'It's making it work that's the problem.'

When the door closed behind Sheila, Dot sat stiffly on the edge of an armchair, then got up and went over to the wireless set and turned it on. When the sound came through, she twisted the knob to adjust the volume so that she could barely hear it, in case Joe cried and she didn't hear him. Every nerve in her body was raw.

May wasn't sure when the evening began to go downhill, but she thought it was probably sometime after Betty's fourth or fifth drink. She'd insisted on having one after another while George and May still hadn't finished their first.

'I don't often get a night out,' she told them. 'I want to make the most of it.'

'We all want to enjoy ourselves,' said May. 'Let's decide what we are going to do, or we'll end up wandering about all evening or just doing a pub crawl.'

'We don't wanna do anything ordinary like going to the pictures,' Betty said in a slow, slurred tone. 'We can do that any time. This is supposed to be a special occasion. Us three are all grown up.' She burst out laughing. 'Whoopee.'

'We are not staying here in this pub all night,' said George firmly.

'Why not, Georgie boy?' Betty said, giggling. 'I like it here.'

'But you're not the only one involved in this celebration, are you?' he reminded her. 'May and I have had a birthday as well, and we don't want to sit in a pub all night. There'll be time enough for that when we're old.'

'What do you wanna do, then?' asked Betty.

'I think we'll be too late for a show now,' suggested May. 'Probably the pictures too. Maybe we could go for something to eat. A special meal would be nice. We could go to the Corner House.'

'Good idea,' agreed George.

'Later on,' drawled Betty loudly. 'It's good 'ere. It'll be even better when I've had another drink.'

'You are not having another,' George stated categorically.

'Who says?'

'I do, and as I'm paying that rather settles it, I reckon,' he told her.

'Why, you bloody skinflint,' she shouted.

'Keep your voice down,' he said, glancing around. 'You're making a fool of yourself.'

'I never get a night out, and the first time I do you try and spoil it for me.'

'It isn't spoilt,' said May persuasively. 'It will be fun to have a meal together, the three of us.'

'Except that it isn't the three of us, is it?' said Betty in a belligerent manner. 'It's you two and me. That's how

132

it's always been and how it still is, even though I'm married to George. I'm always the outsider, the odd one out.'

May and George looked at each other.

'That just isn't true,' said May.

'Of course it isn't,' added George firmly. 'The sooner you sober up the better. Drink apparently doesn't suit you, so you'd best leave it alone in future.'

'If anyone is the odd one out tonight it's me,' stated May.

'That's how it ought to be, but it never is,' said Betty drunkenly. 'I don't get a look-in with him when you're around.'

'What do I do that brings you to that conclusion?' asked May. She realised that her friend was under the influence, but she'd heard that people spoke the truth when they were drunk.

'You don't have to actually do anything,' said Betty. 'You just have to be there to cast a shadow over me.'

May was very hurt. 'I'm sorry,' she said. 'If that's the case then I should stay away from you both.'

'Don't you dare,' said George. 'She doesn't know what she's saying.'

'I do, mate,' said Betty blearily.

'Well anyway, we don't want to stay here all night,' said May, feeling awkward. 'Shall we be on our way?'

'Yeah, I think they'll be glad to see us go, the way you've been carrying on, Betty,' said George. 'Come on, girls, let's get out of here.'

Just as they were about to leave, Betty turned pale. 'Ooh, I don't feel well. I want to be sick.'

May grabbed her arm and guided her forcefully towards the ladies' room, managing to get her to the lavatory before she was violently sick.

'Ooh,' wailed Betty, sitting on the lid of the toilet. 'I feel so ill. I wanna go to bed.'

'We've a long way to go before you can do that,' said May, wondering how they were going to get her home.

'I want some water,' Betty said.

Having ascertained that she didn't want to be sick again, May dragged her to her feet and helped her back into the bar.

'God knows how we're going to get her home,' she said to George. 'She can barely stand up, let alone walk to the station.'

'We'll have to get a taxi,' he said.

'Blimey, George, that will cost a fortune,' May pointed out.

'I'll use the money I was going to spend on a meal,' he said. 'That's the answer.'

'I'll pay my share,' she offered.

'No you won't,' he said. 'It isn't your fault we can't go home on the train.'

'Yours neither.'

'My wife, my responsibility,' he said. 'Don't even think of getting your purse out.'

Between them they managed to get Betty out into the street so that they could flag down a taxi. What a horribly disappointing evening it had been, thought May, and she still couldn't get used to the idea of George and Betty being a married couple.

When George and Betty got home, having dropped May off on the way, they found Dot in tears and little Joe sitting on the floor grizzling and looking very sorry for himself.

'Don't you ever leave me on my own with that child again,' Dot sobbed. 'It's been an absolute nightmare. I just couldn't settle him. Sheila went out after promising to stay in and help me.'

'Oh Mum,' said George, dismayed. 'Surely you can look after a one-year-old child. You've had two of your own.'

'I can't do it,' she said. 'He just doesn't respond to me at all. If I pick him up, he screams.'

'Babies sense fear, so they say, Mum,' he said. 'Maybe that has something to do with it.'

George sat Betty in an armchair and she promptly went to sleep. He picked up his son, who immediately stopped crying. 'Come on, little man,' he said gently. 'Let's get you back into your cot and settled, then I'll see about getting your mother to bed.'

'And you'll need to change his nappy,' said his mother crossly. 'He screamed blue murder when I tried to do it, so I just had to give up trying.'

'Oh well, happy birthday, George,' he said to himself as he carried his pungent son up the stairs. 'So much for a birthday celebration.'

★ ★ ★

The next morning May received a visit from an ashen-faced Betty, who was bug eyed and complaining of a shocking headache.

'George said I have to come round to apologise for ruining our night out last night.'

'It was a shame but it's over and done with now.'

'He also tells me that I said some mean things to you,' she said. 'I'm sorry about that too.'

'Forget it,' said May.

'Blimey, I feel as though I've been hit by a bus,' said Betty. 'I don't know what happened.'

'You wouldn't lay off the booze, that's what happened,' May reminded her.

'I suppose so,' she agreed. 'It made me feel so nice at first I couldn't get enough of it. I don't feel at all nice now, though, so that'll teach me.'

'Mm.'

'Anyway, the three of us will have to have a night out again some other time and I'll promise not to experiment with the gin,' suggested Betty.

May muttered something vague. She knew in her heart that the three of them together didn't work any more. She also believed that Betty had meant every word last night when she'd said that May overshadowed her with George. It was something that just seemed to happen unintentionally that neither May nor George could do anything about.

Chapter Six

Because she was seeing him out of context, May didn't instantly recognise the colourful character who swept into the Pavilion a few days later wearing a blazer with a bright blue bow tie and fashionable baggy trousers. His blond hair was worn slightly longer than most men of May's acquaintance, and flopped on to his brow.

'Doug from Ashburn,' she said when recognition finally dawned. 'How lovely to see you again. What brings you to this neck of the woods?'

'I'm looking for you, as it happens,' he replied casually. 'And it wasn't difficult to track you down, as you told me about your area and the Green Street Pavilion during the chat we had at that Christmas party at Ashburn.'

'Ooh, that seems a long time ago. Fancy you remembering.' She paused, looking at him. 'Is there any particular reason why you want to see me?' she enquired, hoping he wasn't the bearer of bad news about his health.

'No, not really. I was thinking about Ashburn and remembered that you didn't live too far from me. I thought you would have left by now. It's a bit cheeky of me to turn up out of the blue, but I thought you could soon send me packing if I was a nuisance, so I hopped on a bus and here I am,' he explained. 'I just wondered how you were getting on.'

'I'm doing fine now,' she told him, 'but it hasn't been all plain sailing.'

Overhearing their conversation, Flo suggested that they continue their chat in the café and said she would bring some tea over. May introduced the two of them and led Doug out on to the veranda, where the geraniums were in full colour, a glorious mixture of red, orange and pink.

As it was quite a while since May had last seen Doug, they had a lot of catching up to do. She told him about the success of her operation, and her job-hunting and the prejudice she'd encountered with the latter; he said he'd experienced similar discrimination when he tried to join the ARP.

'So are you managing to sell enough paintings to earn a living these days?' she enquired in a friendly manner.

'Just about,' he told her. 'I have an occasional exhibition and get shopkeepers to have my paintings on display on a commission-only basis. Just when I think I'm about to be on my uppers, I sell enough work to keep me going for a while longer. It isn't the most secure of professions but I don't do too badly.'

He asked her if she'd kept in touch with anyone else that he knew from Ashburn.

'Yes, Connie and I write to each other,' she told him. 'She's also left Ashburn and we intend to get round to meeting up at some point, which will be nice. She's managed to get a job in a sewing factory, apparently. She wormed her way in by not telling them about her medical history.'

'I don't blame her for keeping it dark, but she shouldn't have to hide it.'

'I quite agree.'

They had been talking for a while and May noticed that her mother was very busy at the counter, so she felt obliged to go back to work.

'Perhaps we could continue our chat another time as you can't stop now,' suggested Doug.

'That's a good idea,' she agreed. 'I'd like that.'

'When would it be convenient for me to come back?' he asked.

'We could meet in central London to save you coming all the way over here,' she suggested quickly. She wasn't sure what he had in mind and wanted to avoid a whole lot of parental speculation at this stage.

'Whichever is best for you. I don't mind how we work it,' he told her. 'But I would like to see you again.'

They made arrangements to meet at Marble Ach the following Sunday afternoon, then Doug bade Flo a polite farewell and sauntered off down the street, leaving May feeling rather excited. The age gap seemed to have disappeared now that she was grown up. She wasn't sure if their meeting was a date as such, or just a friendly get-together of two fellow sufferers, but it should be fun whatever the purpose. She'd never had a proper boyfriend; maybe Doug would change that.

Predictably there was an inquisition that evening over their meal.

'So who is this bloke who came to see you, May?' asked her father. 'Your mother tells me he's a bit flash.'

'I know him from Ashburn,' she replied. 'And he isn't flash, not really. He just looks a bit different to the men round here, that's all, probably because he's an artist.'

'An artist. Oh my Gawd,' exclaimed her father. 'What does that mean exactly?'

'He paints.'

'Pictures?'

'I suppose they are pictures but I've never seen any of his work,' she said. 'Some artists do abstract stuff, I think. I've no idea what he specialises in.'

'And does he make a living at it?'

'It varies apparently, but he does all right.'

'It varies: well that isn't very promising, is it?' said Dick. 'That won't put food on the table.'

'For goodness' sake, Dad,' she began in a strong tone of admonition. 'I'm meeting him for a chat. Not to marry him.'

'Meeting him?' he queried, sounding outraged. 'Why isn't he coming to call for you like any decent man would?'

'Because I don't want him to be cross-questioned by you,' she explained. 'I'm a big girl now. Quite old enough to go out without being collected.'

'When I was courting your mother I always used to go and call for her,' he insisted. 'It's only good manners.'

'But he isn't courting me,' May pointed out.

'Sounds to me as though he'd like to be.'

'I hardly know the man,' she said.

'He's a lot older than her too,' her mother piped up.

'Seven years, that's all,' May informed them.

'This is getting worse by the minute,' exclaimed Dick. 'Why on earth can't you go out with a boy of your own age?'

Because the only one of those I want to be with is taken, she thought, but said, 'I probably will at some point, but on Sunday I'm meeting up with Doug.'

'You are a young girl who has been very ill,' her father lectured. 'I don't want you traipsing about on your own.'

'Doug has been very ill too,' she said.

'All the more reason to steer clear,' he retorted.

That remark infuriated May. 'That's a terrible thing to say and just the sort of attitude people like Doug and me are fighting against,' she said sharply.

'Look, I'm your father,' began Dick in a reasoning manner. 'It's only natural I want you to have someone who can look after you. This man is ill so obviously can't do the job properly.'

'*Was* ill, Dad,' she emphasised. 'In the past tense, like me. He's fine now.'

'If you say so.' He didn't seem convinced.

'Look, I appreciate your concern, but I want to go on Sunday and I won't come to any harm,' his daughter assured him. 'If I go out with him again after that, I'll make sure he comes to call for me so that you can give him the once-over. But this first time I'd rather meet him in London.'

'Where does he live?'

'Richmond.'

'Ooh, posh,' said Dick.

'On the river in a houseboat,' she added.

'Cor blimey,' her father blurted out. 'What sort of a way is that to live?'

'I think a boat is quite respectable, dear,' put in her mother mildly. 'It isn't as if it's a caravan.'

'As near as,' he grunted.

'I've always thought houseboats were supposed to be quite posh,' May mentioned.

'They are when they are moored at the end of the garden of a big house to go off on at weekends, not when you are living on one all the time,' her father said.

'Well I still think it's exciting,' said May. 'I'd love to see it.'

'Don't you dare,' he ordered, holding his head in despair. 'Who knows what might happen if he takes you there?'

'Don't you trust me, Dad?'

'Of course I do. It's him that's the problem. I know what young fellas are like.'

'Give him a chance, dear,' suggested Flo somewhat forcibly. 'He seemed a nice enough chap to me. Very well spoken and polite anyway.'

'You said he was dressed like a theatrical, Flo,' he reminded her.

'Well he was, sort of, but I don't think that really matters, does it?'

'I don't want my daughter going out with an actor type,' said Dick.

'He's an artist, Dad.'

'Artist, actor, they're all the same to me,' he retorted. 'An immoral lot from what I've heard.'

'Oh really,' exploded May, irritated now by her father's overprotectiveness. 'What does it matter what he does for a living as long as he's a decent man?'

'You be careful on Sunday and I want you home by nine o'clock,' he said.

'Come off it, Dick, that's a bit much,' Flo objected. 'She *is* eighteen, you know.'

'Look,' May cut in. 'I'm meeting him in the afternoon so we'll probably have had enough of each other by about four o'clock and I'll be back early anyway.'

'Nine o'clock, madam,' he insisted.

'She used to get home later than that when she was younger and went out of an evening with Betty,' Flo reminded him.

'She wasn't going out with some boat person who is years too old for her then, was she?'

May knew that many fathers were strict with their daughters about this sort of thing, and accepted that her dad wanted the best for her, but she guessed that her parents were exceptionally protective because of the loss of their son and her own subsequent illness. They were terrified something bad would happen to her. But whilst she understood the reason, she couldn't allow them to cast a shadow over her adult life by restricting her to this extent.

'I must be allowed some freedom, Dad,' she pointed out firmly. 'I'm not a child any more, or an invalid.'

The silence echoed around them and the tension in the atmosphere pulled tight. 'Well that's a fine way to speak to your parents, I must say,' her father complained eventually.

'Sorry, Dad, but I have to be allowed to live as a grown-up.' She looked from one to the other. 'But as it's the first time I've been out with Doug, I'll get back early to put your minds at rest.'

'That sounds fair enough to me, Dick,' said her mother. 'Can we leave it at that and wish her well?'

'Mm, I suppose so,' grunted Dick with reluctance.

May and Doug were sitting by the Serpentine eating ice cream cones they had bought from a street seller on their way into Hyde Park. Their first topic of conversation had been their mutual interest, Ashburn and their illness, but they soon moved on to exchanging personal details. She hadn't been sure if it was a meeting of friends or a date, but as soon as she'd seen him waiting for her outside the station and they'd smiled at each other she knew it was a date. She liked the idea. It was new, exciting and fun.

'So how come you live on a boat?' she enquired in a friendly manner. 'I presume you didn't grow up on one.'

'Oh no,' he confirmed. 'I grew up in an ordinary house in Twickenham with Mum and Dad, an only child. My father is a solicitor and the boat belonged to my parents. They used it for family holidays and weekends away, Sunday afternoon trips along the Thames, that sort of thing. It was great fun. I loved it, the three of us together when I was a kid. Much later, when they moved out of London to Sussex because of Dad's job, I didn't want to go with them, so they gave me the boat as a twenty-first-birthday present. They had more or less lost interest in boating by that time anyway.'

'Quite a gift,' she commented lightly. 'Most people get a wristwatch.'

'Dad has quite a well-paid job but he isn't filthy rich or anything,' Doug explained. 'I did all sorts of jobs to pay my way while I was at art school.'

'Art school?' she gasped.

'Don't sound so shocked,' he said.

'I'm not,' she told him. 'It's such a different world to the one I'm used to, that's all.'

'Anyway, I got the boat put on to a permanent mooring in Richmond with water and electricity laid on and made it my home.'

'Sounds lovely,' she said.

'It has its drawbacks; it is a little confined, but it has many advantages too, like seeing the water in all its different moods and colours and feeling so close to nature; and nowhere is cosier with the stove on in cold weather. One thing I appreciate a lot since my illness is the fresh air. I spend a lot of time on the deck and have all my meals outside in good weather.'

'All that fresh air sounds wonderful.'

'You must come and see it sometime,' he suggested in a friendly manner.

She laughed heartily. 'I think my father would

probably have a nervous breakdown if he thought I was going to do that,' she explained.

He grinned. 'Fathers and daughters, eh?' he remarked. 'And you are still quite young. It isn't really done for a girl like you to be alone with a man, not inside some-where anyway. I'd be worried about that sort of thing if you were my daughter.'

'Maybe all men are like that over their daughters. But I think the illness has made both Mum and Dad overly cautious.' She went on to tell him about her brother's death and how that had affected her relationship with her parents. 'I was in a sheltered environment for so long at Ashburn and I haven't long been going out and about again on my own. So I suppose it's only natural.'

'In that case you'll have to bring them with you if you want to see the boat.'

'Or I could take the view that what the eye doesn't see . . .' she said lightly.

'May Stubbs,' he said, pretending to be shocked. 'I'm surprised at you.'

'I don't think you are,' she said, flirting with him and enjoying it immensely.

'Don't worry, you'll be quite safe with me,' he said.

'Really?' she responded playfully. She was finding this whole process of getting to know someone new different and very exciting.

'Yes, really,' he chuckled. 'So behave yourself.'

They talked and flirted the afternoon away, and when they walked towards Hyde Park Corner for tea they were holding hands. Their attention was distracted by some noisy activity around Speakers' Corner, where several anti-war protesters were holding forth.

He took her for tea at the Corner House, and almost inevitably, given the abundance of sandbags and the subject of the speakers, the conversation turned to current events.

'Have you got your gas mask yet?' May asked lightly.

'I have, as a matter of fact,' he replied. 'I got fixed up during the week when they started distributing them in our area.'

'We went to the church hall the other night to get ours fitted,' she told him. 'It turned out to be quite a lark as it happened, because we all looked so weird in them. One poor woman there nearly had hysterics, though, because she felt as though she couldn't breathe. She rushed outside screaming blue murder and saying she'd rather take her chances than wear one of those things.' She sipped her tea and spread butter on a scone. 'Anyway, let's not talk about gas masks and the blackout and all the rest of the paraphernalia that's crept into daily conversation lately. We've come out to enjoy ourselves.'

'Yes, of course.'

She smiled at him and he almost melted. 'I'm having such a lovely time, Doug,' she said.

'Me too.' He took a mouthful of tea. 'Do you feel that you lost some of your youth because of the illness?' he asked.

'I'm far too busy being grateful to be alive to spend time with regret,' she said. 'But I would like to have some fun now that I'm on top form again. Nothing very daring; just to go to dances sometimes, the sort of things that young people usually enjoy. I suppose I want to make up for lost time.'

'We'll have to see what we can do then, won't we?' he said, smiling at her.

Everything was utterly perfect, and then he spoiled it by saying, 'When it's time for us to go, I'll take you home then get the bus back to Richmond.'

'There's no need,' she said, anticipating the embarrassing third degree her father would put him through. 'I'll be fine on my own, honestly.'

'So . . . you didn't want me to call for you,' he said in a more serious manner. 'If you don't let me see you home to put your parents' minds at rest, I shall think you are ashamed of me.'

'That's the last thing . . .'

'Why then?'

'It's just that my dad . . .'

'Will want to check me out,' he finished for her.

'Something like that, yeah.'

'I would expect him to, and it won't worry me, not in the least,' he assured her.

'Is that because you're used to it?' she asked lightly. 'You've been out with lots of girls, I expect.'

'A few,' he told her. 'I have turned twenty-five, so it'd be a bit odd if I hadn't, wouldn't it?'

'Indeed.'

'What about you?'

'I've never had a proper boyfriend,' she confessed. 'The boy I've always been sweet on married my best friend while I was away at Ashburn.'

'That must have been a blow,' he said.

'It certainly didn't do much for my self-esteem,' she said. 'But at least it made me realise that I have to look forward and not keep harking back to childhood.'

'Sensible girl.'

They finished their tea in a leisurely manner, then headed to the station to get the train to Ealing Broadway.

Despite all May's efforts to persuade Doug just to see her to the gate and then leave, he insisted on going with her to the door, which meant that her mother invited him in for a cup of tea.

'We've had tea, thanks,' said May quickly. 'And Doug is in a hurry to get home.'

'No I'm not,' he corrected annoyingly. 'I've got time to come in for a few minutes, and I can always manage a cuppa.'

'Lovely,' said Flo, and ushered him into the living room, where Dick was sitting in an armchair looking at the newspaper.

Her father wasted no time and didn't bother with subtlety. Out came all the questions about Doug's circumstances; everything from his age and his work to his living accommodation. By the time Doug finally made a move, May had abandoned all hope of ever seeing him again. But much to her surprise, he did suggest another meeting the following Saturday evening.

'I could cycle over,' he suggested. 'It'll be better than relying on the bus service. We could go dancing if you like. It will be a chance for you to catch up on all that fun you feel you've missed.'

'That would be lovely.'

'See you Saturday then,' he said, and swung off down the street without so much as a handshake, which was no wonder as he probably thought her father would have his beady eyes on his every move from behind the net curtains.

'I've never been so embarrassed in my life,' May raged when she stormed back inside and confronted her father. 'It's a wonder you didn't ask him what he has for breakfast every morning and what time he goes to bed at night.'

'Your dad is only looking out for you, love,' said her mother, hoping to appease her. 'It's only natural.'

'That sort of interrogation isn't necessary, surely,' May came back at her. 'It's enough to put any man off.'

'A decent man wouldn't be put off,' said her father. 'He isn't our sort, May.'

'Just because he happens to be a bit more refined . . .'

'You should stick to your own kind,' he said.

'Like George, you mean? We never had any sort of interrogation if I was going to be with George, did we?' she reminded him. 'Well in case you haven't noticed, George is married to someone else and I'm trying to get on with my life, and that means spreading my wings and getting to know new people.'

'We're bound to be a bit wary for you after you've been so ill,' said her mother, still trying to smooth things over.

'Am I never to be able to forget that I've been ill?' said May, her voice rising emotionally. 'You can't wrap me in cotton wool for the rest of my life.'

'I don't like your tone and I think you'd better apologise to your mother for that remark since all she does is care and worry about you,' said her father sternly.

May looked from one to the other. She knew that she meant the world to them both, and vice versa. But they were suffocating her and she couldn't bear it. She had to be firm if she was to have any degree of independence.

'I am sorry for being rude to you both,' she said in a conciliatory manner. 'I know how much you suffered when we lost Geoffrey and again when I was ill and you were so afraid that you were going to lose me too. But I got better and I need to experience the world outside of this house and the Pavilion. And that includes men you might not think are right for me. I have to make my own mistakes and not be protected from every single thing beyond these four walls.'

She saw her remark hit home and felt terrible.

'Look,' she began, hoping to make them understand and not be hurt by the stand she felt compelled to take, 'no one could have more caring parents than I have and I'm very grateful to you for everything you've done for me, but I want to live my life a little now. Doug is taking me out dancing on Saturday night and I don't want him to have to suffer in-depth questioning when he comes to call for me. If it happens again I shall meet him somewhere else in the future.'

151

'Are you telling us what to do?' demanded her father, not best pleased.

'Not really, but I do want to make my position clear.'

'Why not invite him to tea on Sunday?' suggested Flo out of the blue.

'And have him subjected to another cross-examination, no fear,' said May.

'There will be nothing like that,' said Flo, flashing a warning look at her husband. 'You have my word.'

'Oh,' May responded, surprised at her mother's definite tone but more confident because of it. 'Well, if it goes well on Saturday night, I'll consider asking him.'

'It might help to clear the air,' said Flo.

Dick looked at one then the other but he didn't say another word.

Saturday night at the Hammersmith Palais was absolute magic to May; the coloured lights, the music and the general air of excitement and glamour. Everyone had made an effort with their appearance, the women in dresses or smart blouses and skirts, the men mostly in suits. Until she'd been ill, May hadn't been particularly keen to try anything like this, even though Betty had craved it; now she was glad to be here and was having the time of her life. Maybe because of her new lease of life since her recovery, or perhaps because of the increasing threat of war, she had a hunger for fun.

Doug proved to be a good dancer and together they waltzed, quickstepped and foxtrotted around the floor.

She even attempted the tango and rumba under his guidance.

'It's funny how things work out,' she said to him when they went upstairs to the cafeteria in the interval and sat by the balcony overlooking the ballroom drinking orange squash because alcoholic drinks weren't on sale here. 'My best friend longed to come here when we were younger and I wasn't bothered, but now she's married with a child and I'm the one out on the town – so to speak.'

'Is that the friend who stole your boy?'

'Well he wasn't mine exactly – we were just kids – but yes, that is the friend. I think she regrets having got married so young now.'

'So what goes round comes round,' he suggested.

'I don't think about it that way,' she said.

The band struck up with 'Moonlight Serenade', made popular by Glenn Miller.

'Shall we dance?' he asked.

'Yes please,' she replied, and he took her hand and led her down the stairs to the ballroom.

By the time they played 'Who's Taking You Home Tonight?' for the last waltz, May was completely intoxicated by the atmosphere as well as her partner and enjoyed the fact that he held her closer towards the end. Their first kiss came near her front gate, out of the light of the lamp-post on the corner. This was her first grown-up romance and she was enjoying every moment.

'Would you like to come to tea tomorrow?' she asked, keeping her promise to her mother and also wanting to put their relationship on a respectable footing.

'I would like that very much,' he said.

'Good,' she said, and he kissed her again, then took her to her door and saw her safely inside before putting on his cycle clips ready for the ride home.

Cycling through Ealing and then Brentford en route for Richmond, Doug was in high spirits following the evening with May. It was still very early days but he had high hopes that things would go from strength to strength between them. He'd been smitten from the day she had first walked into his art class, but hadn't seen any chance of moving things forward, given the segregation of the sexes at Ashburn and the fact that she was so much younger than he was. The latter seemed to have been solved by the passing of time and her having left her girlhood behind and become a young woman.

The Ashburn Christmas party had given him a chance to speak to her, but then she had disappeared to have surgery and he had been discharged. It had seemed their paths would never cross again and he had dismissed her from his mind.

Then, in Richmond one day, the sight of a bus going to Ealing Broadway reminded him of her suddenly and registered with new significance. He remembered her telling him about her home district and the Green Street Pavilion, which couldn't be that hard to find. He hadn't kept in touch with anyone from Ashburn so had had no idea if she had come through the operation or was alive or dead, but he'd become determined to find out. How glad he was now that he'd made that decision, because she was lovely and he adored her.

A shadow darkened his mood as he reflected on the reality of his personal situation. The fact was that he ruined everything good in his life and had lost everyone he really cared for, even his parents. This time it would be different, he would make sure of it, because May was very special.

His buoyant mood returned as he pedalled over Kew Bridge and onwards to Richmond, through the town and along the towpath to his beloved boat nestled there in the shadows; his home, his sanctuary and his favourite place ever. It was full of memories of happier times, of childhood with his parents, when life had been simple and he had been an uncomplicated little boy.

The atmosphere in the Stubbses' living room when they sat down at the tea table the next day was so uncomfortable that May longed for it to be over. Her father had been ordered by his wife not to ask Doug any questions so he was being sulkily silent, her mother was overcompensating by talking too much and May was squirming with embarrassment.

'So you enjoyed the dance last night then, Doug?' said Flo in a speedy, nervous tone.

'Yes, it was very good,' he replied, seeming quite relaxed considering the circumstances. 'I like to trip the light fantastic every now and again.'

'I used to enjoy dancing, though it was the Lancers in our day,' Flo told him.

'Oh,' said Doug in surprise. 'Didn't they have things like the Charleston back then?'

'Our dancing days were over by the time that came in,' she said. 'Isn't that right, Dick?'

No response.

'Dick, I'm talking about when we used to go dancing at the town hall, remember?'

'Humph.'

'Dad,' said May, glaring at her father.

The ensuing silence was agonising. Dick was showing his awkward side at its very worst and May was almost beside herself. Then Doug saved the day, having spotted something in the back garden through the window.

'I see that you've had your Anderson shelter delivered, Mr Stubbs,' he remarked, looking determinedly at the older man.

There was a long, uncomfortable pause. Then, as four female eyes stared at him, daring him to ignore Doug at his peril, Dick said, 'Yes, it came the other day.'

'I've heard that they're not all that easy to erect,' said Doug chattily.

'They've given me some instructions, so it shouldn't be too bad,' the other man replied.

'How far down will it have to go?' Doug enquired, sounding interested.

'Four foot deep, seven foot six long and six foot wide,' Dick informed him.

'Quite a job digging it out then, before you even start fixing the corrugated-iron sheets into place.'

'Oh yeah, it'll keep me busy all right.'

'I can give you a hand if you like,' Doug offered.

'I'm not thinking of doing it today,' Dick responded.

'How about next weekend?' suggested Doug with enthusiasm. 'I could come over and we can do it together.'

Dick narrowed his eyes. 'Are you up to that sort of physical work?' he asked. Doug was very lean, with a look of frailty about him.

'I'm a lot stronger than I look,' he replied. 'We weedy types often are.'

'Mm, oh well, if you're sure, let's do it next weekend,' said Dick with the beginnings of a smile. 'It will be good practice for you for when you do your own.'

'I shall have to rely on the public shelters in the event that we ever need them,' Doug explained. 'The nearest thing I have to a back garden is the towpath.'

'Yes, I suppose it would be,' said Dick.

The ice was broken. Dick relaxed and things went swimmingly after that, especially when he discovered that he and Doug both supported the same football team, Brentford.

'I thought it was rather a drastic measure, offering to build an air-raid shelter just to get into your girlfriend's father's good books. But it worked, so well done,' May said later when she and Doug were out for a walk.

'I don't really mind helping out, and it was well worth it to see him smile.'

'I wonder if you'll be smiling next weekend when you have to do all that digging.'

'I'm not a weakling, you know,' he pointed out, 'and I'm good with my hands.'

'Using a paintbrush rather than a heavy garden fork, though,' she teased him.

'You just wait and see,' he said laughingly.

As it happened, the following weekend turned out to be a very happy occasion, as Doug became at ease with her parents. The weather was fine so May and her mother spent the time outside in the garden doing some weeding and tidying while the men worked on the shelter, the whole thing interspersed with breaks for tea and Flo's home-made jam sponge and scones.

When the shelter was finished, they each climbed in to try it out. To May it was like being entombed in a chilly and damp understairs cupboard that smelled earthy and slightly sour.

'We won't actually have to use the shelters, will we?' she said when they were all back in the garden. 'It is just a precaution, don't you think?'

'Depends on Mr Hitler,' said Flo.

'Surely the government won't let war happen,' said May.

'They are spending enough money to protect us all from it,' said Dick. 'So they must think it's a definite possibility.'

'Oh well, let's hope it doesn't happen, but what comes comes, I suppose,' said May chirpily. 'We've got our shelter so we'll be ready for it.'

'Thanks for helping me, mate,' said her father to Doug. 'I'm much obliged.'

'A pleasure,' said Doug.

May's heart soared. Having Doug involved with her family meant a lot to her.

As week followed week, May's life was increasingly enhanced by Doug's presence in it. He spared no effort or expense to entertain her. They went dancing and to the cinema; out for tea and for dinner in the West End. When she queried the money he was spending on her and offered to make a contribution, he wouldn't hear of it.

'I've sold a good few paintings lately,' he explained, 'so don't worry about it. We might as well enjoy ourselves if we are all going to be either blown to bits by bombs or invaded by the Germans.'

There was some of this feeling around in general, May had noticed. The cinemas, dance halls and pubs always seemed to be packed as the signs of war grew ever more evident and people looked for escape.

One person who wasn't out enjoying herself was Betty.

'You lucky thing,' she said to May one Wednesday afternoon when they were together in the playground with Joe. 'Out nearly every night of the week, being taken to lovely places, while I never go anywhere.'

'You were the one who wanted excitement, not me,'

said May. 'But I'm enjoying every moment. I might as well while I have the opportunity.'

'All my craving for excitement got me was pregnancy,' mourned Betty. 'I got married far too young.'

'You're all right, though, aren't you?' queried May. 'You've got his nibs here, and George seems good to you.'

'George is all right and I wouldn't be without Joe, of course,' said Betty. 'But I did get married too young and I resent having missed the fun and excitement I could have had.'

'We're ordinary working-class girls, Betty,' May pointed out. 'The social whirl you think you missed doesn't happen to people like us. That sort of thing is for the upper classes.'

'How come you're having it, then, tell me that?' Betty wanted to know.

'Mine is an unusual case,' May told her. 'I just happened to meet someone from a different background, but I'd never have met him if I hadn't been ill and out of my normal environment for a while. So I suppose you could say that it's God's way of making it up to me for giving me TB.'

'I don't think it works like that,' Betty said lightly. 'But honestly, May, I really think that all the pleasure and excitement is wasted on you because you never really wanted it.'

'No, I didn't especially, and it wouldn't worry me if I didn't have it now. But as I do have it, I'm not afraid to enjoy myself.'

May had a sudden and unexpected realisation that shocked her. She had thought that her emotions were on an even keel now and that she was completely content. Yes, she was having a great time with Doug, but she knew in that moment that she would willingly trade it for what Betty had: marriage to George.

'Mm, anyway, what about this boat of his?' Betty was saying, which recalled May back to the present. 'What's it like?'

'I don't know. I haven't been there.'

'Blimey, girl, you're slipping, aren't you?' said Betty. 'If it was me, I'd be dying to have a nose around. You want to get yourself over to Richmond sharpish.'

'He always comes over this way to call for me,' May explained. 'So it's never really come up.' She gave a wry grin. 'Except from Mum and Dad, who are terrified he'll take me there and have his way with me.'

Betty laughed. 'That's normal for parents, but there's no need to tell them you're going there,' she said. 'Get him to take you so you can see what he's worth. Then you can tell me so I'll know exactly what I'm missing.'

'Don't be horrible, Betty. You've got a hell of a lot to be thankful for.'

'Just being myself.'

'Let's give Joe a go on the swings,' May suggested quickly, upset by her realisation of her feelings for George. She took hold of the pushchair containing her adored godson. 'Be content with what you have and stop yearning for more.'

May did follow Betty's advice and arrange to visit Doug's boat. Not because she wanted to see what he was worth but so that she could picture him in his own environment when they weren't together. Despite Betty's advice she did tell her parents where she was going and nothing much was said, either because they had learned to trust Doug or because they had finally accepted the fact that their daughter was an adult.

Doug met her off the bus in Richmond on Sunday afternoon and they headed for the river hand in hand. The weather had been glorious this summer and today was no exception. It was sunny and warm, with a light breeze. Since it was the weekend, the riverside was crowded with people and there were plenty of pleasure boats on the water.

'Here she is,' he said, stopping by an elegant blue and white craft called *Sands Nest* which was moored near some willow trees on a stretch of the river away from the town.

'Oh, it's beautiful,' said May, impressed. 'I've never been on a houseboat before.'

He helped her on board and led the way down into the cabin, which had lots of polished wood and two small fitted sofas in red. It smelled pleasantly of oil and paint, and there were pictures around the walls.

'Are they your work?' she asked.

'Some but not all,' he said. 'The river ones are mostly mine but I enjoy collecting work by other artists.'

She knew next to nothing about art but they looked good to her and she said so before they returned to talking about the boat and her admiration of it.

'It suits me, though it isn't huge,' he said. 'I have

everything I need here. The sofa pulls out into a bed, the table folds away if I want more space. The coal stove keeps me warm in winter and I have the usual conveniences through the sliding door.'

'I think it's wonderful,' she said.

'Glad you like it,' he responded, looking pleased. 'I'll make us some tea and we can have it on deck as the weather is so nice. I bought some cakes, too. They won't come anywhere near the standard of your mum's home-made ones, but although I can make myself a fairly decent meal, my skills don't run to baking.'

May smiled, feeling warm towards him and very glad that she had come.

'I have most of my meals up here when the weather is good,' he told her later when they were having tea in the sunshine. 'Even in winter if it's fine I wrap up well and come up here. I've always been a bit of a fresh-air fiend, but Ashburn gave me a real passion for it.'

'It's a wonder it didn't put us all off for life, the amount we had there.'

'Sometimes so cold, too,' he said.

'Oh yes, I still shiver when I think of Ashburn,' she said. 'I think being cold is my strongest memory of the place.'

'I must say I choose only nice weather now that I can decide for myself.'

'We have a lot to thank the place for, though.'

'Indeed,' he said.

'Do you still have to go to the chest clinic to get checked over?'

He nodded. 'Only once a year now.'

'Me too. But apart from that, and the wonky shoulder the operation left me with, I'm fine.'

'No off days?' he asked.

'I know if I've been overdoing things,' she said. 'But my breathing is fine. Amazing how you can manage with only one lung, don't you think?'

'Yes, it is.'

May burst out laughing. 'Just listen to us. We sound like a couple of old codgers sitting here discussing our ailments.'

He laughed too and they moved on to other things, carefully avoiding any talk of war. May was slightly conscious of their illness being their main connection. Still, Doug was a lovely bloke and she enjoyed being with him, so she supposed it didn't really matter.

They stayed on the deck all afternoon, drinking tea and chatting. This really was the most romantic setting, with the sun shining on the water, the birds singing and a handsome man by her side. She smiled suddenly.

'Come on, share the joke,' he said.

'No joke,' she assured him. 'I was just thinking how perfect all of this is.'

'My thoughts exactly,' he agreed.

What she didn't mention was how enthralled Betty would be when she related this scenario to her. This would truly be the movie-style romantic scene her friend had always dreamed of.

Chapter Seven

When it was announced on the wireless in August that Russia had entered into a non-aggression pact with Germany, most people reluctantly accepted that war was now inevitable. The Pavilion was buzzing with it.

'Gawd knows what will become of us all,' said one woman who had called to buy a pound of sugar.

'War hasn't been declared yet,' pointed out May, clinging stubbornly to her optimistic streak. 'They still might be able to stop it. Let's look on the bright side.'

'No chance of them stopping it now,' said another customer to murmurs of agreement. 'Things have gone too far for that.'

'We'll just have to hope it doesn't last long then, won't we?' suggested, May determinedly.

'The papers seem to think it won't drag on like the last war,' said a man who had come in for a newspaper.

'Well if the Germans are going to bomb us, we won't be around to care,' said someone, laughing nervously. 'So there's no point in worrying about it.'

'I'll take a couple of extra tins of peas please, just in case we're still around,' requested May's customer.

'They reckon there'll be terrible shortages, Flo,' said someone in the queue. 'I hope you'll look after your regulars.'

'We're not sure how it'll work yet,' said Flo. 'There will be some sort of regulation, and even rationing if the worst happens. But we'll look after our regulars if we can.'

'Shall we wait and see if war does actually come before we start panicking?' suggested May.

'Nobody is panicking, dear,' said the customer. 'We are all very calm.'

'You speak for yourself,' said a woman who was known as a bit of a comic. 'I nearly wet myself with fright every time I think of the dratted war.'

Everybody laughed and the atmosphere lightened.

When the news that the country was at war with Germany was finally delivered on the first Sunday morning in September by the Prime Minister speaking from 10 Downing Street, May amazed herself by bursting into tears. It had been an emotional broadcast. She and her parents stood up for the National Anthem, and then engaged in a communal hug, an almost unprecedented event for her father, who wasn't a demonstrative man.

'So what do we do now, I wonder?' enquired May, who was feeling quite shaky with reaction but instinctively protective towards her parents.

'What we were doing before the broadcast, I suppose,'

suggested Flo, trying to hide her anxiety. 'You were peeling the spuds for dinner, I was getting the last of the blackout curtains up and your dad was in the garden tending to his plants.'

'So let's get on then,' said May, heading for the kitchen.

But no sooner had they resumed their activities than a high-pitched wailing sound filled the house.

'Bloody hell, it's the siren. The Germans are here already,' said Dick, and the three of them grabbed their gas masks from the hall stand and scuttled off to the back garden. May tried to grab Tiddles, who was lazing in the sun on top of the wooden coal store, but he shot away from her and disappeared over the back fence, so she followed her parents into the sour-smelling shelter without him.

When they emerged after the all-clear to find everything as it was before and not an enemy bomber or an invader in sight, the heavens empty except for the silver barrage balloons that now floated in large numbers in the sky over London, the trio headed into the street to find out what was going on. Neighbours were hurrying out of their houses and a warden came by on his bike with the news that it had been a false alarm.

With her gas mask slung over her shoulder and leaving her parents chatting to the people next door, May jumped on her bike and pedalled furiously towards the home of another family who were very much on her mind on this dramatic day.

★   ★   ★

Betty and George were talking to some neighbours at the front gate when May arrived, George holding Joe, who beamed at the sight of May and leaned towards her.

'You're all in one piece then,' May observed with her godson now ensconced happily in her arms. 'I thought I'd better come round to check.'

'It's a wonder we didn't all die of fright,' complained Betty. 'The siren scared the living daylights out of me. Fancy having a false alarm so early in the war.'

'How's everything round your place, May?' asked George. 'Are your mum and dad all right?'

'A bit bewildered like everyone else. It's still a shock even though we've been expecting it for ages. But we just have to get on with it as best as we can, I suppose.'

'His mother has gone to pieces completely,' said Betty, making a face and glancing disapprovingly towards George. 'She's sobbing her heart out indoors. Sheila is in there trying to calm her down.'

'I must go back in and see if I can comfort her in some way,' said George. 'She gets very upset about things these days. She never used to be like it when Dad was alive.'

'I think she's entitled to be upset on the day war breaks out,' suggested May. 'She won't be the only one shedding tears today. It's a huge thing that's happened.'

'It seems to be the idea of my going away that's upsetting Mum so much,' explained George. 'But there's nothing I can do about it. I will be one of the first to be called up, it's obvious. I'm eighteen and fit and healthy. Just the sort of man the services want.'

May felt a dull thud of reality as the truth of his words

hit home. Up until now it had been *might be* and *possibly*. Now war was here and it was *definite t*hat the young men would be sent away to fight for their country.

'Is there anything I can do to make your mum feel better?' she offered. 'I could remind her that I live close by if she wants a bit more moral support while you're away.'

'It's kind of you to offer but I don't think it will help much at the moment. She's too upset,' he explained. 'Sheila is with her and I'll go back indoors in a minute.'

'It's downright ridiculous the way she's carrying on. She's saying that George can't go away because he's got us lot to look after,' announced Betty with utter disdain. 'I mean, have you ever heard anything so stupid? Who is going to care about something like that? All the young healthy men will have to go.'

'Don't be nasty about my mother please, Betty,' requested George in a firm tone, giving his wife a cold look. 'You know how much it upsets me.'

'Well, as long as you're all right, I'd better get back home,' intervened May quickly, not wishing to stay to witness a private argument. She handed Joe to George and got back on her bike. 'Give my best to your mum and let me know if there's anything I can do to help. See you soon.'

Smacking a farewell kiss on Joe's cheek, she headed for home. Was it her imagination or had Betty not seemed particularly bothered about the prospect of George going away to war? She'd almost seemed to relish the idea.

★　　★　　★

Being an avid follower of the news and having taken a keen interest in events in Europe this past year or so, Doug wasn't in the least surprised by what the Prime Minister had had to say on the wireless. It was a historical event even so, and a shock to actually hear the words, the occasion made even more dramatic by the air-raid siren a few minutes after.

His first thought had been to get on his bike and go to May's, but when the warning sounded he hurried to the public shelter and didn't get on his way to Ealing until after the all-clear.

A sense of urgency to see May consumed him; as though death and destruction was about to strike and he had to reach her before it started. But much to his surprise, all seemed the same as ever on the streets, though there were groups of people chatting outside, which was unusual for the residents of this neighbourhood where privacy was of the essence. Naturally he was a little afraid, though having cheated death once, when he'd had TB, he was something of a fatalist. But this was something beyond himself; it was a threat to people the world over.

Seeing a telephone box, he slowed down. May hadn't been the only woman in his thoughts when Mr Chamberlain had declared that 'this country is now at war with Germany'. Someone else had immediately come into his mind. He stopped and propped his bike on the kerb. A man came along and went into the box. Doug got back on his bike and started to pedal away. But the compulsion was too strong, and he came back. A woman was waiting to make a call now. He stood behind her, forming a queue.

His legs were shaking and he could feel sweat on his brow which had nothing to do with the declaration of war.

It was warm and clammy inside the kiosk when his turn finally came, and it smelled of sweat and stale cigarette smoke. He got through to the operator and asked to place a long-distance call, whereupon he was instructed to put his money into the slot. After much hissing and crackling he was finally told that the number was ringing.

When he heard the familiar voice, Doug found he couldn't utter a word. It had been four years since he had last spoken to her and the emotion was overpowering.

'Hello,' she said.

He went to replace the receiver but couldn't do it.

'Hello,' the woman was saying, sounding anxious now. 'Who is it? Who's there?'

'Hello, Mum,' he said at last, his voice thick and distorted by tears. 'It's me, Doug.'

There was an empty, echoing silence as the person at the other end recovered from the shock.

Doug was trembling with emotion as he got on his bike after the phone call. The sound of joy and relief in his mother's voice brought tears to his eyes and compounded his feeling of guilt. He shouldn't have stayed out of touch for so long. It was unforgiveable. The sad fact was that because of his moodiness he often hurt his mother when they were in contact so he'd thought it best to stay away; he knew now that he was wrong, and in future he would ring his parents regularly and go to see them as much as he could.

His dear Mum, they'd been so close when he was a child. On the phone she'd made a pointed remark about his lack of communication. That wasn't usually her way, bless her. She deserved more from her son. He headed for the Stubbses' thinking of his happy childhood and resolving to take proper care of his filial duties from now on.

'Will you have to go into the services, Doug?' enquired Flo chattily later on when he was having tea at the Stubbses' house.

'Yeah, I suppose so,' he replied. 'All young men will be called up, won't they?'

'Most will, but you've had TB,' she replied as though it was a blessing. 'I should think you'd be excused because of that.'

'I've *had* TB, Mrs Stubbs,' he said with more than a hint of irritation. 'I don't have it now.'

'Even so . . .'

'Flat feet is a valid reason for exclusion from the military,' put in Dick. 'So I'm damned sure TB is.'

'I'm sure it would be if I had it,' said Doug. 'But I don't.'

'You've had it, though, that's the important thing,' declared Dick. He didn't seem to have noticed Doug's edginess. 'You'll get out of the services with no trouble. You'll be the envy of all your mates.'

'I don't want to get out of it,' explained Doug tartly. 'I am quite prepared to go and fight for my country.'

'Oh,' said Dick in surprise. 'That's very patriotic of you, mate.' He pondered for a moment. 'There was a lot of that sort of feeling around when the last war broke out. I'm not sure if they'll be queuing up to enlist this time after what happened to the poor devils on the front line back then.'

'Dick will be too old to be called up, thank God,' Flo mentioned. 'It isn't often we welcome the passing of the years, but it's a blessing when it comes to going away to war.'

'I'm in a reserved occupation, the same as I was last time,' Dick pointed out. 'So I wouldn't have to go to war anyway, which is a bit of luck.'

Doug flushed and May could tell that he was angered by her father's attitude. He had been in a strange mood ever since he arrived, which she assumed must be because of the events of the day.

'More seed cake, Doug?' offered Flo.

'Not for me thanks,' he said, then, catching a look from May, forced a smile and added, 'I'd love another piece of your delicious apple tart, though, Mrs Stubbs.'

The tension seemed to ease slightly, but May didn't feel comfortable. So much so that she was rather relieved when Doug suggested that he leave early.

'Just until we're used to the blackout I'd like to get home before it's dark,' he said.

'Good idea,' Flo approved. 'You get off home and watch what you're doing on the way.'

After kissing May at the front door and telling her he would be over on Wednesday as usual, he pedalled off down the street and May went back indoors.

That evening May and her mother amused themselves by listening to the author J.B. Priestley reading an instalment from his book *Let the People Sing* on the wireless. Her father went in search of male company at the pub, only to return with the news that it was closed until further notice because of the current emergency and he had grazed his knee having missed the kerb in the blackout and fallen over into the road.

'If this is what the war is going to be like, Gawd help us all,' he cursed.

'If the blackout and the pub being closed is the worst that happens, you won't hear me complaining,' said Flo. 'And neither should you.'

'All right, all right,' he sighed. 'Don't go on about it.'

It was a night for being at home, but May found herself longing for young company so went to bed early to escape the tedium of adult conversation. Before she got into bed she turned off the light and went over to the window. She pulled back the corner of the blackout curtains to see nothing but darkness apart from the searchlights criss-crossing the navy blue sky and looking oddly beautiful.

What a strange day it had been. It was no wonder

Doug had been in such a peculiar mood. Although she had been going out with him for more than four months and usually enjoyed his company, sometimes it seemed as though she didn't know him at all, and today she had felt distanced from him completely; it was as though chemistry had deserted them and all connection was lost. He had obviously had other things on his mind apart from her and the war, though being Doug, she didn't enquire so had no idea what they might be. Something she did know for sure was that he had a giant chip on his shoulder about having had TB.

Oh well, everything would probably settle down once they all got used to this strange new world they found themselves in, she thought, as she replaced the curtain and got into bed.

'So your social life has taken a battering then?' said Betty the following Wednesday afternoon when the two of them were in the playground adjacent to the Pavilion with Joe.

'For the moment, yeah,' May said, sitting with Joe on her lap on the roundabout. When May was around Betty took a break from her parental duties because May loved to look after Joe, who adored her. 'The government have closed all public places of entertainment by law.'

'How long for, I wonder.'

'There's a notice outside the Odeon saying to look out for reopening, so they can't be expecting to stay closed for the rest of the war.'

'There would be a rebellion if they did that,' Betty opined. 'Though most people reckon the war will be over by Christmas anyway, don't they?'

May nodded. 'I have heard that,' she said.

'So what will you and lover boy do with nowhere to go?' asked Betty.

'Go for walks and stay at home, I suppose,' she said. 'I haven't seen him since Sunday, but he's coming over tonight.'

'Twice a week, weekends and Wednesdays, is that when you see him?'

'Yeah.'

'You'd be better off spending your time together at his place,' suggested Betty. 'At least you'd get some privacy there.'

'I shall have to let things settle first,' explained May. 'At the moment Mum and Dad are terrified every time I leave the house in case there's an air raid while I'm out. It's still very early days.'

'Mm. It said on the wireless that petrol, coal, electricity and gas are all rationed, so it's going to be a bleak winter.'

'People will need the cinemas to escape to even more,' said May, slowing the roundabout as Joe had had enough and wanted to get off. 'Shall I get Joe some lemonade from the Pavilion?' she suggested. 'We might as well make the most of it if everything is going to be short.'

'Let's all have a glass,' said Betty.

'Good idea,' agreed May. 'Don't let anyone see us in there or they'll think the place is open and will want to be served.'

Holding Joe's hand and with her gas mask slung over

her shoulder, May led them into the wooden building that smelled of liquorice, aniseed balls and fresh tobacco. She got the large jar of lemonade powder off the shelf and began to spoon it into a jug while Joe looked on excitedly.

By the end of the month – when there had been no sign of the much-feared air raids – many of the cinemas and dance halls had reopened. But the cinema queues were very long and slow moving. Some picture houses even started to open on Sundays to meet the demand. May and Doug queued for two hours one Saturday night to see *The Wizard of Oz*.

The waiting time was a much jollier experience than before the war, though, with everyone chatting and the cinema manager coming out at regular intervals to talk to the crowds. No one really minded which film was showing; it was enough to be inside the dimly lit auditorium where everything outside was forgotten for a couple of hours.

The return to a kind of normality gave May confidence – a sense that life would go on regardless – and she found the queuing rather fun. She had noticed a new friendliness everywhere; in the street, on the bus, in shops and especially in the Pavilion. It was a pleasure to go to work, though food rationing was expected any time soon, which would mean a lot more paperwork for her and her mother. Still, they were prepared for the extra work, which seemed a minor inconvenience compared to the men who were losing their liberty to the military.

Even the blackout didn't seem so bad once you got used to it, though May did find it frightening at times. She was reduced to tears one night on her way back from seeing Betty when she lost her bearings in the dark and had no idea where she was. An air-raid warden on his way home had finally come to her rescue.

Doug had something unexpected to tell her one night as they walked home from a local dance.

'I've got a job in an ordnance depot,' he said. 'I start work next week.'

'Well done, but what about your art?'

'Shelved until after the war,' he explained. 'All the paintings that haven't been sold I'm having sent to my parents' place to be stored for safety.'

'But being an artist is your line of work,' she pointed out.

'Not in wartime.' He paused and she could feel the tension in him even though she couldn't see his face clearly in the dark. 'We are needed for more important things. Just because we haven't had any air raids doesn't mean there isn't a war on, you know.'

'I'm not a complete idiot, I know that,' she made clear. 'Will you paint in your spare time then?'

'I might if I'm in the mood,' he replied, and there was no mistaking the sharpness in his tone.

'All right, there's no need to bite my head off.'

'Well I don't know if I'll do any painting,' he explained. 'I haven't even started the new job yet. I might not feel like it after being at work all day.'

'I thought you creative types felt compelled to follow your inspiration under any circumstances,' she said. 'But anyway, I was making conversation, not asking for a declaration of intent.'

'Sorry.'

'Apology accepted,' she said. 'Why are you in such a bad mood tonight?'

'I'm not,' he denied.

'Yes you are,' she said. 'In fact you've been like a bear with a sore head ever since war was declared.'

'No I haven't.'

'Yes you have,' she insisted. 'I remember it distinctly. You came over on that first Sunday afternoon and were irritable and peculiar.'

'Was I?'

'Yes, and you've been moody ever since.'

'Really?'

'None of us like the fact that there's a war but we have to make the best of things and you should try doing the same.'

There was a silence, then Doug said, 'I'll consider myself well and truly told off.'

'So you should.'

'I didn't realise I'd been moody, but if I have, it has nothing to do with the war,' he said.

'What is it all about then?'

'There isn't anything,' he said.

She halted in her step and turned to him, even though she couldn't see him very well in the dark. 'Look, Doug, if you want to stop seeing me, you only have to say.'

'Stop seeing you?' he said as though astonished by the suggestion. 'That's the last thing I want.'

'You could have fooled me,' she said, not convinced. 'But as I've been taking the brunt of your bad temper, don't you think that entitles me to some sort of an explanation? Something is obviously bothering you.'

'Yes, you're right.' He explained briefly the problem with his parents, and added, 'Something else has upset me too.'

'What exactly?'

'I've been told that I am unfit for military service because I've had TB,' he explained. 'Which is why I decided to get a useful job.'

'Mm, I see,' she said, slipping her arm through his as they moved on slowly. 'Well, I suppose you can see their point about the services.'

'You've changed your tune,' he retorted. 'I thought you were against prejudice.'

'I am, but when it comes to the services in wartime it's about common sense, not prejudice,' she said. 'Working in a shop is one thing, being a soldier quite another. You could put your mates' lives at risk as well as your own if you are not on top form; if you can't run as fast as the others for instance.'

'Who said I can't?' he asked. 'Anyone would think I still had the wretched illness.'

'Be reasonable, Doug,' she said. 'It probably will have left its mark on us somewhere and made us a little weaker than other people; it was a serious illness, so it stands to reason.'

'Maybe,' he agreed unconvincingly.

'So can we have a little less gloom and moodiness please?' she suggested. 'Anger is a pointless exercise.'

'I suppose you're right.'

'Thank you,' she said. 'We've enough to put up with with this ruddy blackout, we don't need you putting the dampers on things even more.'

'Sorry,' he said, stopping and drawing her into his arms. 'I don't deserve you.'

'I won't argue with you about that,' she said, teasing him.

There was a sudden jolt and Doug was pushed away from her.

'What the hell's going on?' said a man's voice. 'I didn't see you there.'

'Are you all right?' May asked the stranger.

'You should have been more careful,' objected Doug. 'You could have hurt my girlfriend.'

'I'm fine,' May assured them both.

'You shouldn't be doing your courting in the middle of the pavement,' said the man gruffly. 'That's what back alleys were invented for.'

'Sorry,' said May with an embarrassed giggle.

'Yeah, sorry, mate,' added Doug.

The diversion had eased the tension between May and Doug and they were companionable for the rest of the journey.

'Oh, by the way, May,' said Doug as they reached the end of her road, 'I won't be able to see you at the weekend. I'm going away.'

'Really?' she said, curious but careful not to be presumptuous by asking more about his plans.

He offered the information anyway. 'I'm going to see my parents in Sussex. I might not have much time to travel once I start the new job next week, so I'd better do it before I start. Duty calls and all that.'

'Good idea,' said May, trying not to feel hurt because he hadn't asked her to go with him.

'Sorry to spring it on you like this.'

'That's all right,' she said.

'What will you do with yourself?'

'I'll find something to do, don't worry,' she assured him. 'My friend Betty could do with a night out, so if her husband will babysit maybe I'll go to the pictures with her.'

'That's good,' he said. 'I'm glad you won't be lonely.'

'Don't you worry about me,' she urged him. 'You enjoy your weekend away.'

'I will,' he said.

'Cor, am I glad to get out of the house,' said Betty as she and May walked to the cinema on Saturday night, a clear sky and the moonlight helping them to see their way. 'It's like a ruddy asylum in there.'

'Why?'

'Mrs Bailey is in tears again because George's call-up papers have come and Sheila is threatening to join the ATS, probably to get away from her mother's weeping and wailing.'

'George has been called up?' said May, sounding worried.

'That's right. He's going next week.'

'Why didn't you say?'

'I just did.'

'I mean straight away and bursting with it.' May was surprised that they hadn't been the first words her friend had uttered, such was the magnitude of the news. 'You seem very calm about it,' she said.

'We were expecting it, so it's no surprise,' Betty explained airily. 'All the boys will be going so there's no point in getting into a state about it, is there? Joe will miss his dad, though.'

'So will you, won't you?' said May.

'It hasn't happened yet so I don't know how I'll feel, but I'm sure to I suppose,' she said, sounding almost casual. 'But like everything else that's happening lately, including the blackout, we just have to put up with it, don't we?' They were approaching the cinema and even in the dark they could see the queue. 'Like long queues at the pictures as well; it has to be done. And I'd sooner be here waiting in the cold than in that house tonight.'

'Mm.'

May couldn't understand her friend's offhand manner about her husband's imminent departure to terrible danger. If she herself was married to George she'd be worried sick. In fact she was anyway.

George came round to the Stubbses' to say his goodbyes. When May went to the door with him to see him out he said, 'It was you I came to see actually, May. As well as saying goodbye, I need a favour.'

'Anything at all, George, you know that,' she said.

'I wonder if you could keep an eye on them round at my place while I'm away,' he explained. 'Mum's practically a nervous wreck, Sheila's got no patience with her and wants to join the services as soon as she can anyway, and Betty, as we both know, tends to look after number one. They rely on me to keep the peace and I'd feel a bit easier in my mind if I knew you were around every now and again as a stabilising influence.'

'Of course I will,' she assured him at once. 'I'll be looking out for little Joe anyway.'

His brows knitted into a frown and she knew how painful being away from his son would be for him. 'Thanks, May. You'll be the voice of sanity in that madhouse, and knowing that means I can get on with whatever is asked of me by the army.'

'We'll miss you, George,' she said.

'Same here, but the job has to be done, whatever that job might entail.'

There was a curious sense sometimes for May of wondering what the war was all about. New restrictions appeared almost daily and men were being called up in their thousands. But there was a feeling of going through the motions and not getting on with the actual war.

'I shall keep up to date with news of you from Betty,' she said, feeling emotional.

'You make sure that boyfriend of yours takes good care of you,' said George, who had met Doug briefly. 'The lucky devil doesn't have to go.'

'Come off it, George,' she said lightly. 'You'd hate it if you couldn't go.'

He gave a wry grin. 'Maybe,' he admitted.

'There's no maybe about it,' she declared.

'All right. There is a slight sense of adventure about it, I admit,' he said. 'Sailing off to foreign shores, that sort of thing.'

'Well I wish you the best of luck,' she said, feeling a burning sensation at the back of her eyes.

'Come here, you,' he said, wrapping his arms around her and kissing the top of her head. 'You take good care of yourself. You are my dearest friend.'

She was sniffing into her handkerchief as he headed off down the street and she knew he would be too if it was acceptable for a man to cry. But George's male pride wouldn't allow him to indulge in such a feminine activity.

'Personally I think it's a damned cheek,' said Doug after May had happened to mention George's request when they were walking by the river at Richmond the following Sunday afternoon. 'You shouldn't have to worry about his family.'

Shocked by his interpretation of what George had asked her to do, she said, 'And I won't have to.'

'But you just said he wants you to keep an eye on them,' he reminded her.

'Well yes, he does; just to sort of be there every now and again, which I would be anyway because of my godson and because the family are my friends,' she explained. 'I don't have to move in and look after them or anything.'

'I still think he's got a nerve,' he persisted.

'How can you say such things?' she began, her voice rising emotionally. 'George was going away to face who knows what, so of course he would be worried about his family, especially as his mother is a very nervous woman. There's a war on; we are meant to be looking out for each other.'

'My concern is you in all this.'

'I'm not so sure you'd be behaving like this if it wasn't George who'd asked me.'

'Well, he's going away covered in glory and he expects you to do his job for him, and him a married man too.'

'Doug,' she almost screeched in an effort to stop him ranting. 'George has been called up and there's nothing he can do about it. He has a mother with bad nerves and a wife and young child. Of course he's worried about them. It's only natural he would ask me to keep an eye on them. I am his friend.'

'Humph. I sometimes wonder about that.'

She threw him a cold look. 'What do you mean?'

'You seem a bit too pally with him for my liking,' he declared. 'It's always George this and George that. Of course I am going to wonder what's going on.'

'So, are you suggesting that I would have an affair with a married man, especially one who is married to my best friend?'

'If the cap fits . . .'

Her hand hit his cheek with a resounding slap and she

turned and marched towards the town in a fury to get the bus home. He came chasing after her, holding his face.

'May, please let me explain.'

'There's nothing to explain,' she said angrily. 'You've made it clear what you think of me, so now just leave me alone.'

He grabbed her arm. 'Please come back to the boat,' he begged. 'I didn't mean it. I was jealous. Just give me half an hour. I'll make you a cuppa and try to explain.'

'Half an hour then,' she said. 'Not a minute longer.'

'Thank you, May,' he said with ardour. 'Thank you.'

'It was the green-eyed monster, I'm ashamed to admit,' he told her as they drank tea in the cabin of the boat, where the stove was glowing warmly.

'That's no excuse for such a horrible accusation.'

'I know, and I really am sorry.'

'All right, apology accepted.' She narrowed her eyes at him. 'You don't really think I would carry on with a married man, do you?'

'Of course not. I was just hitting out.'

She gave him a searching look. 'It wasn't only about my friendship with George, was it?'

His grim look gave her an answer.

'This is all about you not being able to join the services, isn't it?' she guessed.

He nodded, looking sheepish.

She sipped her tea, looking at him over the rim of her cup. 'Do you actually want to go away to war?'

'Of course not. No sane man would.'

'So why make such a fuss?'

'Because I feel I *should* go,' he replied. 'I am fit and healthy so it feels wrong being on Civvy Street, and I know people around me think that too.'

'I can understand why you might feel that way,' she told him. 'But I don't think you should waste your time and energy. Anyway, what it's really all about is your manhood and male vanity.'

He shrugged. 'Probably,' he admitted.

'So swallow your pride and behave like a grown-up,' she said. 'You are doing war work and therefore your bit for the war effort, so just be grateful that you don't have to go into battle.'

'Easier said than done, but I'll try.'

'Good. As for my feelings for George,' she went on briskly. 'He is very, very dear to me, I won't deny it, as is Betty, and that won't ever change no matter who else is in my life. So if you want us to carry on, you'll have to accept that.'

'Yes, I realise that, May, and I'm sorry for my childishness earlier,' he said sheepishly.

'Let's forget it.' She paused thoughtfully. 'I've never heard you mention friends. I assume you have some.'

'No one close, not since I've been an adult. I had friends when I was a kid.'

'You didn't stay in touch?'

'No.'

'And you don't miss the company?'

'I'm a bit of a loner,' he said.

'You seemed sociable enough when we were at Ashburn and you took the class.'

'A class is different,' he said. 'The teacher is set apart so can keep their distance.'

'Don't you want the responsibility of close friends?' she asked, trying to understand him. 'Close friends do need to be given time and attention.'

'It's probably more to do with the fact that I'm not always easy to get along with, as you will have noticed lately.'

She gave a wry grin. It was true, he wasn't the easiest of men to have as a boyfriend. He could be so charming as to dazzle her, but his glum and distant moods left her reeling because she tended to think she was the cause.

'Yeah, your moodiness is upsetting,' she admitted, glad of the chance to bring this out into the open.

'It's nothing personal to you,' he assured her. 'You just happen to be there when the gloom descends. I'm surprised you've lasted this long, actually. All my other girlfriends have given me the elbow after a few low moods.'

'I presume if you could stop them from happening you would,' she suggested.

'Exactly.'

'If you can't snap out of them, can you not act your way through them?' she suggested. 'Then no one else is upset.'

'I do try but it doesn't always work,' he admitted. 'Sometimes all I want to do is stay here on the boat and shut myself away from the world.'

'Oh dear,' said May. 'That doesn't sound very healthy.'

'I'm sure it isn't,' he said, looking round the cabin. 'But

here is where I'm happiest. I love this place; it soothes me like nowhere else. It's full of sunny memories.'

'They say that childhood memories are always sunny, don't they?' she said. 'Even if things weren't that good in reality.'

'Maybe they do say that, but mine really were good.' He looked at her. 'So now that you know what an odd bod you're going out with, do you want to call it a day?'

'Of course not,' she said. 'You don't give up on someone just because they can be a bit peculiar at times.'

'Who are you calling peculiar?' he said jokingly.

'You,' she said. 'You are very peculiar indeed and I shall try to make you less so.'

'I don't know how.'

'Nor do I. It could be that you just need someone to listen to you,' she suggested.

'Could be,' he said. 'And if that someone is you, all the better as far as I'm concerned.'

All the bad feeling following their argument had dissolved and Doug seemed happy again, which led her to believe that he needed to talk his problems through more often.

'Let me get you another cup of tea,' he offered, giving her one of his most gorgeous smiles then coming over and kissing her before taking her cup for a refill. 'We might as well make the most of it before tea goes on ration.'

She smiled. When he was like this he was irresistible and the moodiness didn't seem to matter one little bit. He really was a very attractive man, even if he was rather strange.

Chapter Eight

Joe was having a whale of a time at the tea party to celebrate his second birthday in February 1940. It didn't matter to him that the cake his grandmother had managed to cobble together had only a fraction of the sugar ingredient required since it was now on ration along with butter, eggs and many other essential food items. He was at the centre of attention and had gathered a whole collection of new toys, so life was good and his countenance, a miniature of his father's, was glowing with excitement.

'Methinks it's time the visitors departed,' Betty said to May confidentially. The tots were growing tired and fretful and Joe had got so overexcited that he was running round the room in circles, finally falling over and erupting loudly into tears.

'I'll see to him,' said May, picking him up and sitting down with him on her lap at the kitchen table, cuddling and fussing him. 'You go and say goodbye to the guests.'

Betty did as she suggested, fetching coats for the young

mums she had got to know since having Joe, and their offspring.

'You're very good with him, May,' remarked Dot, who was making an after-party cuppa to revive them.

'I simply adore him, Mrs Bailey,' May told her.

'So do I, but I'm not good with little kids now,' she confessed sadly. 'I seem to have lost the knack since mine were small. Joe plays up something terrible on the odd occasion that I have to look after him, and it isn't often for that reason.'

'I'm sure you'll get it back at some point,' suggested May, who always felt rather sorry for George's mother. Sheila and Betty were openly irritated by her nervous disposition, which seemed cruel as she obviously couldn't help it. When she wasn't in one of her states she was pleasant company. 'I don't suppose you lose that sort of thing for ever.'

'Maybe not.' Dot observed how comfortable May was with Joe. 'Would you like a kiddie of your own, dear?'

'Oh yes, at some point,' said May without hesitation.

'You'll have to have a word with that young man of yours about it then, won't you?' she suggested lightly, pouring hot water into the pot and swilling it round.

May grinned but didn't say anything. She was busy wiping Joe's nose.

'You've been going out with him for a while now, haven't you?' persisted Dot.

'Only since last summer.'

'It must be fairly serious to have lasted that long.'

'We do get on very well,' responded May.

This was true. She and Doug enjoyed each other's company enormously. Since last autumn, when his moods had come out into the open, they'd had a great time, give or take one or two of his downers. He'd been more charming and affectionate than ever, had taken her out and about to dances and the cinema and had been very attentive. He had even told her that he loved her. But he never mentioned a future for them or even hinted at anything in the long term. Each date was made from one to the next, as if they had just met.

'Perhaps he'll have something special to ask you before long,' said Dot.

'It's still quite early days, Mrs Bailey,' May said. 'You can't rush these things, can you?'

'I dunno about that,' she said, chortling. 'Your pal Betty didn't waste any time, did she?'

May grinned at Dot's directness. 'That was a bit different, wasn't it?' she said.

Fortunately for May, who didn't want to get drawn into a discussion about her friend's personal life, Betty came into the kitchen.

'Phew, thank Gawd those kids have gone home,' she said. 'It's a good job you only have a birthday once a year, Joey boy, 'cause I couldn't put up with that lot of monsters invading us more often than that.' She sat down at the table. 'Can I smell tea, Mrs B?'

'Coming up,' said Dot.

'Can you pour one for me please, Mum?' said Sheila, entering the room and sitting down at the table. 'I was wondering if it would be safe to come back into the house yet, but I can see the little treasures have gone.' She looked towards Joe, who was eating a biscuit rather messily. 'Did you like having your mates round, darlin'?'

'Yeth,' he replied.

'How come you are here, May, and not behind the counter at the Pavilion?' asked Sheila.

'Dad stands in on a Saturday afternoon and Mum and I take it in turns to have the afternoon off,' she explained.

'Good for him,' said Sheila. 'How are you getting on with ration books to cope with?'

'All right now that we're getting used to them,' she replied. 'It's extra work, though; what with that and going out delivering the papers in the morning we certainly feel as though we've done a day's work at the end of it.'

'Why are you delivering the papers?' asked Sheila.

'To cut the cost of paying the paper boys,' she replied. 'Our takings are down because of rationing and shortages of things that aren't on ration, so we need to cut our outgoings.'

'Blimey, the war, eh?' she commiserated. 'What a pain.'

'Still at least we haven't had any air raids,' said May.

'Mm, it's all a bit peculiar if you ask me,' said Betty. 'Rationing has started, we're all kitted out with gas masks and air-raid shelters, but where is the war?'

'Don't say that,' said Dot nervously. 'I hope the air raids never happen.'

'At least you've had your man come home for a couple of weekends since he was called up,' said Sheila. George had had two forty-eight-hour passes. 'There'll be none of that if he's sent overseas.'

'True,' said Betty casually. 'He doesn't seem to know what will be happening, though, when he writes.'

'They're not allowed to say much in their letters,' said Sheila.

'From what I've heard they aren't told much either,' May put in. 'Just in case they let anything slip.'

'There are German spies all over the place apparently, passing themselves off as ordinary people,' remarked Sheila. 'Careless talk costs lives, as the slogan goes.'

'Creepy,' said Betty. 'I think they should stop the war right away, and I'm not the only one who thinks that. I've heard lots of people say the same thing.'

'Mm. It does seem a bit pointless. We went into it to defend Poland and now they've been crushed,' said May, who was an avid follower of war news and talked a lot about it. 'I sometimes wonder why we are continuing.'

'I think the point is to stop Hitler taking over the world,' declared Sheila.

'Yeah, there is that,' agreed May.

'Anyway, folks, I've got some news,' began Sheila. She'd chosen her moment carefully because May was here and would be a calming influence in the outrage that was bound to follow her announcement. 'I've been to the recruitment centre and joined the ATS.'

The silence was so powerful it made May's cheeks burn. 'Well done,' she said at last.

'You can't go away and leave me all alone,' said Dot shakily. 'That's a cruel thing to do.'

Sheila bit her lip, feeling guilty. 'But you won't be on

your own, Mum,' she said at last. 'Betty and Joe will be here with you. You'll be all right.'

'But you're my daughter, you should be here with me in these troubled times,' she said. 'George was made to go away by law, but you don't have to.'

'She wants to do her bit,' said Betty supportively. 'You should be proud of her. It's no picnic in the ATS, so I've heard. They have to scrub the barrack-room floors and all sorts of horrible jobs.'

'They have a damned good time from what I've heard,' Dot declared. 'They are thoroughly disreputable, the lot of them. Out in the pubs every night getting blind drunk and making up to the men.'

'Sounds good to me,' said Betty, making a joke of it. 'If I wasn't tied up I might think of joining myself.'

'It's disgusting,' ranted Dot.

'How do you know all this, Mum?' Sheila enquired.

'The women's services have got a bad name, everyone knows that,' she replied.

'It's just talk,' said Sheila. At seventeen she was hungry for adventure and independence, and the ATS seemed to be her best chance of getting both. 'I'll be able to let you know from experience when I come home on leave. I will be home, Mum. I'm not going away for ever.'

'Please don't go,' begged Dot feebly.

Sheila looked sheepish. 'It's something I really want to do,' she said. 'Please don't make it hard for me, Mum.'

'I'll be around, Mrs Bailey,' May put in helpfully. 'I'll call in regular to see how you are getting on.'

'There you are,' said Sheila. 'You'll have plenty of

company and support. You'll enjoy not having me here going on at you all the time, once you get used to it.'

Joe was growing restless and started to whimper. 'He's tired,' said Betty, affectionately ruffling his hair. 'It's all the birthday excitement, isn't it, darlin'?'

'Shall I get him ready for bed?' offered May. She loved to do things for Joe and she also felt she needed to exit this increasingly heated and emotional discussion between mother and daughter.

'Yeah, if you like,' said Betty, who was always glad of a break from mothering. 'I'll come upstairs with you.'

'Come on then, pickle,' said May, standing up and carrying Joe towards the door.

As soon as they were out of earshot, Betty said, 'That's a turn-up for the flippin' books, Sheila joining the forces. She said she was thinking about it but I didn't think she'd actually do it. I shall miss her something awful.'

'Really?' said May in surprise. 'I thought you weren't all that fond of her.'

'We don't always see eye to eye, it's true, but I don't fancy the idea of it being just me and old Droopy Drawers.'

'Betty, you really shouldn't say such awful things about Mrs Bailey,' admonished May. 'She's George's mum and she deserves some respect.'

'But she's such a flamin' misery.'

'So would you be if you'd been through what she has. Anyway, you are living in her house so you ought to be grateful and show it by being nice to her,' lectured May.

'As far as I can see, George is the only one in the family who has any patience with her at all. Now that he isn't around, as his wife it wouldn't hurt you to try a bit harder with her.'

'Oh May, you don't half go on,' Betty complained.

'Well if I don't tell you, who will now that George isn't around?'

'Nobody, and that would suit me just fine.' They had reached the bedroom and Betty fetched Joe's pyjamas while May laid him on the bed to undress him but started playing with him instead, tickling him and making him squeal with laughter.

'I bet it would, but you don't get off that easily, not when I'm around,' she told Betty.

Betty decided a change of subject was needed. 'I suppose you'll be off out dancing tonight,' she suggested.

'This being a Saturday, yeah, very probably,' said May casually.

'Lucky thing.'

'I'm not complaining.'

'I'd love a night out.'

'Well I'll look after Joe if you want to go to the pictures one night,' May offered.

'Thanks, I'll bear that in mind, though if you are babysitting, who would I go with?'

'One of your new mum friends perhaps?' May suggested.

'Maybe, sometime.' She didn't seem all that keen.

'Just let me know if you fancy it,' said May, turning

her attention back to her godson. 'Meanwhile, we have a little boy to get washed and into his jim-jams.'

Joe thought this was very funny and chuckled like mad.

May and Doug did go dancing that night. The Palais was crowded, smoky and vibrant with the heady ambience of people enjoying themselves to the music of Lou Preager. There were servicemen of many nationalities: Dutch, Norwegian, Canadian. Soldiers, sailors and airmen were all here to have a good time and forget the war for a few hours in this palace of pleasure.

Although May was enjoying herself, she was beginning to think that dance halls weren't such a good idea just now. The abundance of men in uniform and their huge popularity meant that Doug was in a minority, and she knew that he felt it even though he tried to hide it.

Things came to a head when a girl pushed past him and said, 'Out of the way, civvy, you ought to be in uniform.'

May suggested to Doug that they leave.

'I won't be driven out by the ignorant few,' he said.

So they stayed but May wasn't comfortable. When they were smooching around the floor to 'Apple Blossom Time', a woman dancing nearby with a soldier called out to May, 'Why are you dancing with someone in civvies when there are plenty of uniforms about? You should be ashamed of yourself.'

'You're the one who should be ashamed,' retorted May, leaving Doug and confronting the woman close up. 'You want to watch your mouth. You know nothing about my boyfriend or anyone else who isn't in uniform, so keep your trap shut.'

'Why, you cheeky cow,' said the woman, leaving her partner and taking a swing at May, who dodged her punch and grabbed hold of the other woman by the arms.

'You're ignorant,' said May, shaking her, then losing her grip and screaming when her attacker pulled her hair violently.

A crowd gathered and the two women were dragged away from each other by their partners.

'What did you do that for?' May demanded of Doug, who was trying to carry on dancing as if nothing had happened.

'You were making a fool of yourself, and if you'd kept on we'd have been thrown out.'

'She had no right to say those things.'

'Maybe not, but we mustn't rise to it or we're going to be arguing with people for the rest of the war.'

'How can you just stand back and let them say such things?' she wanted to know.

'Easily,' he replied. 'I just let it go over my head.'

'Well I'm not as calm as you.'

'So I noticed. I thought you were going to knock her out cold.'

'And I thought she was going to pull my hair out by every last root,' May said, laughing nervously in the aftermath. 'She damn near did as well.'

'And you such a lady too.' Doug was trying to make a joke of it, though he didn't find it funny in the least. 'I didn't think I'd live to see the day when you were involved in a dance hall-brawl.'

'No one is more surprised than I am, but she was saying such awful things about you, and I couldn't let her get away with it,' she told him.

'Thanks for trying to defend me,' he said. 'But I'd rather you didn't. Just ignore it if it happens again.'

'I can't promise anything as regards that sort of thing,' she said. They continued with the dance but the fun had gone out of the evening completely for her. She had obviously embarrassed him and that made her feel even worse than hearing him being insulted. Instinct had driven her to defend someone she cared about and it was too late before she'd realised what she was doing. She'd probably seriously damaged his pride.

Cycling home from May's with his light facing downwards to comply with blackout regulations, Doug was mulling over the events of the evening. Not the happiest of nights as it happened. May was a great girl, but what sort of a man let a woman get into a fight over him? A pathetic one was the answer to that. He'd never had much in the way of self-esteem but he truly hated himself for being a civilian in a world of servicemen.

Every day he beat himself up about it, but what could he do? If he were to pin a notice on himself saying 'Medical Reasons For Not Being in the Services', he'd turn himself into a laughing stock and it wouldn't make him like himself any more.

He hit a stone in the road and came off his bike with a painful thump. Serves you right for not paying attention, he told himself as he scrambled to his feet rubbing his bruised knees. What a rotten night this had turned out to be.

It was the month of May, the weather was glorious and low public morale had been boosted by the new coalition government headed by Prime Minister Churchill. The news from abroad had been grim all spring and warnings of an imminent German invasion had been stepped up. So someone strong and positive in charge of the country was exactly what people needed.

The Pavilion was full of talk about Mr Churchill and his confidence-building speeches. Café, shop and veranda, the discussion was general.

'I reckon we might get this war going now that he's in charge,' said one of the elderly gents who came to the Pavilion for a cup of tea in the morning when he got his paper. Tea still hadn't gone on ration.

'Yeah, it's given us all some strength and hope,' said a woman at the counter who was handing her ration books over to May.

'You want to be supportive to a man like that, don't you?' said a female customer wearing a turban over her curlers. 'Strong and clever. His speech the other day brought tears to my eyes.'

'Me too,' said Flo.

'It was very inspiring,' agreed May, carefully crossing off the items the customer had bought in the allocated spaces in the ration books and handing them back to her. 'It makes you want to do your bit, even if it's only putting up with things like rationing and the blackout.'

There was a general murmur of agreement and the conversation moved on to what was on at the pictures and on the wireless. The Pavilion had always been a meeting place, but people seemed to need it more than ever in these troubled times. May was very glad they were able to provide a spot of company for the locals, even if it was only for a few minutes while they did their shopping.

It often occurred to May that she should be doing war work, but she knew that she was needed here with her mother at the moment. She guessed anyway that she wouldn't be accepted for the services because of her medical history, but thought it must be a good experience. Since Sheila had joined the ATS she had entertained them with anecdotes about service life when she came home on leave.

Sheila admitted that it was a hard life but there was companionship and laughter too. Privately she told Betty and May that the best part was being out from under the watchful parental eye, and May could understand that. Although she herself was a home-loving girl and adored her parents, there were times when she wanted more independence and privacy, which she thought was probably natural for a woman of her age.

She was brought back to the present by roars of laughter as the customers discussed the popular comedy wireless programme *ITMA*, the initials standing for 'It's That Man Again'.

'I nearly split my sides laughing at their antics last night,' said one woman.

'So did I,' added another. 'The whole family was in fits. He's a real caution, that Tommy Handley.'

May found herself smiling. No matter what danger and hardships Hitler and his cronies inflicted on the people of this country, she thought, he would never destroy their spirit or sense of humour.

Was she being chucked, or was there something wrong? May asked herself one evening a day or two later when Doug didn't turn up as arranged. How was a girl to know? He was such a strange sort of a bloke. Although there was usually a real spark between them, sometimes she felt as though there was nothing and he seemed like a stranger.

He'd been particularly moody recently, something she'd put down to the war news from abroad, which always seemed to affect him personally, probably because he was so sensitive about what he saw as his lack of a role in the war. But maybe his absence had nothing to do with that at all and it was simply that he was bored with her. After all, he had never mentioned his intentions towards her and they had been seeing each other for almost a year now. You heard about this sort of thing all the time;

a chap not turning up for a date and the girl never seeing him again.

'Is Doug not coming over for you this evening?' enquired her mother.

'Apparently not,' she replied, her emotions confused between a feeling of personal rejection and concern for Doug. 'But I was expecting him.'

'He's probably had to work late,' guessed her mother.

'Maybe he's stopped off for a quick one,' suggested her father. 'And I don't blame him either. It's thirsty work cycling all the way from Richmond after a day's work.'

'You would say that,' said Flo with mock disapproval. 'Since a quick one or three at the pub is your answer to everything.'

'Can't beat it,' said Dick.

Her parents entered into some good-humoured bickering but May wasn't listening. As time ticked by and darkness fell, she knew he wasn't coming and she had a horrible knot in the pit of her stomach. Surely a decent man like Doug wouldn't end things between them this way, would he? And if not, where was he?

After a sleepless night May decided that there was only one way to find out what was going on. After the shop closed for the afternoon, this being half-day closing, she got on her bike and headed for Richmond in the glorious sunshine with just enough of a breeze to keep her cool.

She was nervous as she approached the riverside and was mulling over what she would say to him if she found him safe and well. 'The least you could have done was tell me to my face,' she was rehearsing silently. 'Not just stay away. That's cowardly.'

Riding along the towpath towards the boat, she stared and stared again. *Sands Nest* wasn't there! She blinked hard. She must have come to the wrong stretch of the river, she thought, looking around. But no, this was definitely Doug's mooring, away from the town and the other boats; she recognised the willow trees and the boatyard nearby. The boat was Doug's home; how could it have disappeared completely? He must have moved lock, stock and barrel, without a word to her. She'd known that Doug was deep, but this was downright devious and she didn't believe he was that.

Not prepared to leave without finding out more, she headed for the boatyard in search of information.

'I know nothing about it, miss,' said the boatyard owner, a tanned, muscular man who looked to be around sixty.

'Surely he must have told you that he was moving away,' she said. Doug knew all the river people and he was on friendly terms with this man.

'No,' said the man, looking decidedly evasive but grim too somehow. 'He didn't say anything to me.'

May didn't believe a word of it. She knew that there were times when men ganged up in defence of each other against the opposite sex. 'Look, I am not chasing him,' she made clear. 'I just want to know if he's all right.'

The man shrugged, looking shifty. 'People come and go as they please on this river,' he said defensively. 'They don't have to account to me for their movements.'

'I realise that, but he was friendly with you; surely he must have said something.'

'No. Nothing at all.'

'I can understand you wanting to cover for him if I was planning on making a nuisance of myself, but I'm not, I promise you. Can you just tell me if he's all right and I'll be on my way.'

'I don't see any reason why he wouldn't be all right – he was fine when I last saw him – but as I've told you, I know nothing about his whereabouts,' the man said again, and May thought he seemed extremely tense. 'If his boat has gone, it's gone. There's nothing I can do about it. I suggest you go home because I can't help you and I have work to get on with. Mind how you go on that bike of yours, miss.'

May fixed her eyes on him, certain he knew more than he was letting on. But finally accepting that she wasn't going to get another word out of him she said, 'Thanks for your time,' and wheeled her bike back the way she had come, stopping to look at the empty space where Doug's boat had been. What was going on, and where was Doug?

So this was the reality of war, thought Doug, as the scene registered through the smoke. Hundreds of thousands of exhausted, dispirited men soaked to the skin as they

207

waded off the Dunkirk beaches under heavy German strafing, in the hope of getting a place on a boat back to England. In the water floated the bodies of those men for whom it was already too late.

Sands Nest was being manned by the navy, some experienced volunteers and Doug himself, who, having convinced the authorities who came to commandeer the boat that he was an experienced sailor and was keen to help in the rescue mission, had been allowed to stay on board provided he didn't make a nuisance of himself. The boat was too large for the very shallow waters, so they were collecting men from the little rowing boats and taking them back to England. Many were going on the big warships waiting further out.

The noise of the bombs and the guns blasted his eardrums and the smoke, which was being used as a screen to confuse the German bombers, was so strong he thought he would choke.

Doug and the other volunteers and sailors hauled the exhausted troops on board, some English, some French, and all very wet, smelly and glad to have got a place on one of the many civilian vessels. All Doug's personal belongings had been taken off the boat to make space and put in store to be returned at a later date. Then *Sands Nest* had been towed to Ramsgate, from where the armada of little boats had departed, everyone involved in the rescue operation sworn to secrecy by law.

Now that the boat was full, with no space for another soul, they headed for home, and would return again and again until every serviceman was away from those deadly beaches. Doug was humbled by the courage of these men, and for the first time in his life he felt truly useful.

Like most people in wartime, May and her parents listened to the news on the wireless avidly. Towards the end of May they heard the BBC newsreader on the six o'clock news say that the undefeated British troops had been coming home from France with their morale as high as ever.

'That's a bit queer, isn't it?' said Dick, who had come home early to make up for working some Sundays. 'If they are undefeated, why have they come home?'

'Dunno, love,' said Flo, who was busy peeling potatoes and had only come into the living room to listen to the news. 'As long as they're back safe, that's what matters.'

'They're keen to go back to have another crack at Jerry, the newsreader has just said so,' Dick mentioned thoughtfully. 'It seems mighty peculiar to me. But the government are very cagey about what they allow us to know.'

'It isn't for the likes of us to worry about,' she said. 'We have to trust the government to run the war.'

'And if they've already been coming home,' Dick went on, 'why weren't we told about it before?'

'I've no idea,' said Flo. 'My job is to keep this family going with everything getting so short, yours is to build ships and Mr Churchill's is to look after the war. I'm happy to leave him to it.'

'We'll have to keep a close eye on the news to find out what it's all about,' said Dick.

★   ★   ★

Sands Nest chugged across the Channel for the final time, crowded with weary soldiers who were to be put on trains and taken to hospitals and army camps. Doug had been told that he was no longer needed as the mission was all but completed.

Mercifully the crossing was smooth, the sky clear, the waters calm and the sun shining. Everyone knew that bad weather would have made a failure of the rescue operation. Doug was well aware that his boat probably wouldn't have survived a storm at sea. Until now she had only been used for pottering about on the Thames, with only an occasional trip along the coast.

But she had served him well, and with nature on their side they had managed to rescue a great many soldiers. No one had said much about it, but it was obvious to him that many more had been left behind; those who couldn't reach Dunkirk in time to get on the boats. With German supremacy as it was at the moment in France, Doug didn't reckon much to their chances such was the brutality of war.

He himself had been away for nine days and would be glad to be home. The troops on this boat and those abroad would have a long time to wait before they could return home for good, with Hitler's army currently having the upper hand. He turned his mind to happier thoughts of May.

His departure had occurred at such a speed he hadn't had time to let her know he was going away. He had thought it might happen at some point, because he had sent the details of *Sands Nest* to the Admiralty when they'd made it known that they were looking for boats of all types, including pleasure craft. Even at that early stage he had been sworn to secrecy. Then a couple of weeks ago a chap had arrived out of the blue to tow *Sands Nest* away. It had happened so quickly he hadn't had time to catch his breath, let alone notify May.

He had to hope she would understand, because he was still bound by confidentiality.

'Have you heard from your bloke yet?' asked Betty on Wednesday afternoon as they were walking to the park with Joe in the pushchair.

'No.'

'You'd better get your dancing shoes on and get out there looking for someone else.'

'Why would I do that?'

'Surely you're not still hoping he'll turn up?'

'He might.'

'Don't make me laugh,' her friend said cynically. 'Honestly, May, you can be so naive at times.'

'And you can be so hard.'

'Realistic is what I am.'

'Call me stupid if you like, but I honestly don't think Doug would disappear without a very good reason.'

'The good reason being that he wants out.'

'Trample on my feelings why don't you?' said May sarcastically. 'You can be such a cow at times, Betty.'

'Just trying to make you face up to it,' she said.

'You're not exactly an expert on men, seeing as you got yourself pregnant at fifteen.'

'That's plain bitchy.'

'You asked for it,' May retorted. 'You're quick to speak your mind to me but you don't like it when I do it to you.'

'Look, I don't want you to mope about at home waiting for a man who obviously isn't going to turn up.'

'I am not moping about, as you put it, but I am certainly not going out looking for someone else at this stage.'

'You'll have to be an old maid then,' said Betty.

'I'm only nineteen; I don't think I need to worry about that at the moment.'

'Time soon passes, and there are plenty of blokes around in London at the moment. Soldiers, sailors and airmen.'

'I don't care if the entire armies of the world are at the Hammersmith Palais every night of the week. I'm not going,' said May. 'For all I know Doug might be involved in this Dunkirk rescue thing. They say civilian boats have been helping to get the troops off the beaches.'

Betty emitted a cynical laugh. 'You've been seeing too many films,' she said.

'It could happen,' argued May.

'Nah. Not in a million years,' disagreed Betty. 'That's the most far-fetched thing I've ever heard in my life. You're just making excuses for him because you don't want to face up to the truth.'

'You can believe what you like,' said May. 'I'm not giving up on him yet.'

'Oh well, that's up to you,' said Betty. 'But if you don't want to go to the Palais, why don't you look after Joe while I go? One of us might as well make the most of all the servicemen who are around at the moment.'

'Why would you want to do that when you have George?' May was curious to know.

'For a laugh, of course,' Betty replied. 'Just a bit of fun. You must have heard of it. It's that stuff you are supposed to have when you are young.'

'There's no need to be sarky.'

'Well you can be so serious sometimes, May, honestly.'

'Yes, I can, and I'm being very serious when I say that I will never look after Joe for you while you go out looking for men,' she stated categorically. 'The pictures, yes, the Palais absolutely not. Not ever!'

'All right, there's no need to make such a flamin' drama out of it,' Betty objected. 'Honestly, you are such a prude at times.'

'Not a prude; just a good friend of your husband.'

'Keep your hair on, girl,' objected Betty. 'I haven't even asked you yet.'

'Just making my position clear in advance, so make sure you remember it.'

'I won't forget, don't worry.'

They arrived at the park and unstrapped Joe, who was off like a shot, his little legs moving like pistons as he ran around on the grass. Betty and May played ball with him for a while, then sat down on a bench watching him while he tore about on his own.

The two women moved on to other topics of conversation, amicable with each other. They had known each other far too long for any sort of umbrage to have lingered from their previous heated exchange.

★　★　★

A few days later May was stacking a pile of *Evening News* on the counter when she looked up to see Doug walking towards the Pavilion. She wasn't particularly surprised. She had known in her heart he would turn up eventually, if only to say goodbye. He wasn't the stuff rotters were made of.

'Hello, stranger,' she said.

'Hello, May.'

She waited for an explanation.

'Can you get ten minutes off?' he asked.

'Go on, dear,' put in her mother, who was putting cigarette packets out on the shelf. 'Go and sit on the veranda and I'll bring you some tea.'

'Thanks, Mrs Stubbs,' said Doug.

It was another glorious afternoon and the veranda was gently shaded by the tree across the road.

'Where the hell have you been?' asked May. 'You just disappear without a word . . .'

He made a face. 'I know. It was unforgivable of me. Something came up and I had to go away. I'm really sorry. You'll have to trust me on this one, May,' he said, 'because I'm afraid I can't give you an explanation.'

'Oh, really?'

'I haven't been doing anything you would disapprove of, I promise you,' he assured her. 'I'm really sorry I let you down and disappeared like that. I'm hoping you can forgive me.'

She looked at him, mulling it over. A man breaks a date, disappears without warning and has no explanation for his absence when he turns up. He is prone to depressing dark moods and never mentions any serious intentions. A lot of women would tell him to get lost. But May thought more of him than to do something like that. Also, despite Betty's crushing disagreement, she still believed that he might have been involved in the rescue at Dunkirk, even more so now that she had seen him and heard what he had to say. He'd probably been told not to speak to anyone about it, such was the secrecy of anything connected to the military.

'I'm hoping we can carry on as we were before,' he was saying, his expression becoming grave. 'Though with quite a significant change, I hope.'

'That sounds ominous. What sort of a change might that be?' she wanted to know. 'Nothing too dramatic, I hope. I've had enough shocks with you disappearing, boat and all. No more of that sort of thing please.'

'Dramatic in a good way; at least that's how it would be for me,' he said.

'Tell me what it is then, for goodness' sake,' she urged him. 'Don't keep me in suspense any longer.'

'I want to marry you, May,' he said, reaching over for her hand and looking into her eyes.

'Oh.' It was the last thing she was expecting at this particular moment.

'Will you do me the honour of becoming my wife?' He was very tense.

'You don't have to go that far to persuade me to forgive you for disappearing,' she said with a wry grin.

'I'm not . . . that isn't why,' he began, looking worried.

'Just teasing,' she assured him.

'Sorry to spring it on you,' he said.

'Spring it on me?' she said, smiling into his eyes. 'Far from it. I thought you would never ask, and of course the answer is yes.'

He leaned over and kissed her.

Flo saw this as she approached with the tea and smiled, delighted that it seemed to be all on again. Doug would never be her first choice for her daughter, but as she couldn't have George he was the next best thing.

'We are engaged, Mrs Stubbs,' announced Doug with a broad smile, adding quickly, 'though I know I have to get Mr Stubbs' official permission first, of course.'

'Oh that's wonderful news,' said Flo, thoroughly approving. 'And as you're going to be one of the family, Doug, can you please drop the Mrs Stubbs and just call me Flo.'

'I'd be honoured.' He smiled.

One good thing about his brief brush with the war, and the death he had seen in the waters around Dunkirk, was that it had made him realise just how short life could be, and that time wasn't to be wasted in hesitation.

Chapter Nine

As the summer of 1940 progressed, hostilities became increasingly menacing on the home front, with the siren sounding day and night though a bomb had yet to fall in west London. The gloriously blue skies were alive with activity, as Allied and enemy aircraft battled it out overhead, leaving a maze of vapour trails. Warnings of imminent invasion were so frequent now, people were half expecting the German army to march up the street at any moment.

But for the most part, the general public still went determinedly about its business as normal, albeit interspersed with periods in the nearest shelter. Determined to carry on regardless, May caught up with an old friend from Ashburn. They met one Saturday afternoon in a Lyons tea shop near Marble Arch, which was a central point for them both.

'You and Doug Sands, eh?' remarked Connie, having been brought up to date and shown the diamond ring on May's finger. 'I always thought he had his eye on you.'

'Yeah, I remember you used to tease me about it,' said May. 'I didn't give it a thought at the time and could hardly believe my eyes when he turned up out of the blue one day at the Pavilion.'

'He was a real dish as I remember him,' said Connie. 'Very much so.'

'He seemed to be out of the ordinary in a suave sort of way, which made him attractive,' recalled Connie. 'What's he like when you get to know him?'

'He's a lovely man . . .'

'But?' queried Connie, detecting a note of uncertainty in May's tone.

'He tends to be moody,' she replied. 'He was devastated when they turned him down for the services because he's had TB. He took it personally.'

'Male pride, I suppose.'

'Mm.'

'Mind you, I know how he feels to a certain extent,' Connie mentioned. 'I volunteered for the Land Army but was turned down for the same reason and I was very disappointed. The idea of working in the outdoors really appealed to me.'

'That's probably a legacy from Ashburn,' said May. 'Both Doug and I are fresh-air fiends.'

Connie sipped her tea. 'I think you'd either come away from there wanting to avoid fresh air forever or not be able to get enough of it,' she suggested.

'We are so lucky to be alive, the three of us,' said May in a more serious tone. 'Not all that many people live to tell the tale after having that disease.'

Connie shook her head. 'I still get nervous when I go for my check-up in case it's come back,' she said.

'I know the feeling.'

'So when's the wedding?'

'We haven't actually got around to setting the date just yet,' May told her.

'You'd better get a move on, girl, before we're taken over by the Germans. Lord only know what will happen to us then.'

'It might not come to that, but anyway, Doug and I will take our chances.'

'Apart from anything else, I fancy a bit of a knees-up,' confessed Connie. 'A wedding would be just the thing.'

'You'll get a wedding, don't worry,' May assured her. 'We won't be leaving it long.'

'Will you live on his boat after you're married?' Connie enquired.

'I suppose we could, though we haven't really discussed that side of it yet,' said May thoughtfully. 'It would be one way of having our own place and it might be fun.'

'So this moodiness of his, is it much of a problem?' asked Connie. 'I can imagine it might put a damper on things.'

'It isn't much fun.' May leaned towards her friend and spoke in a confidential manner. 'But as it happens, he's been quite a lot better just lately.'

'That's good.'

'And I think I know the reason for it,' said May, speaking in a low voice so that she was only just audible above the babble of noise in the crowded tea rooms. 'He disappeared a while ago, his boat as well, and he wouldn't tell me where he'd been, but he proposed to me as soon as he saw me after he got back.'

'So what's the significance?'

'I suspect that he was involved in the Dunkirk evacuation and that's made him feel better about himself,' she said. 'They say there were lots of civilian boats taking part. It would all be top secret, which is why he wasn't able to tell me where he'd been.'

'It's possible, I suppose,' said Connie thoughtfully.

'Anyway, since then he's been much less moody and easier to get on with altogether.'

'So you think that taking part in the war changed his personality,' said Connie.

'I know it seems a bit unrealistic,' she said 'And if a person is moody by nature they probably will be for life, but something happened while he was away, wherever he was.'

'I should just enjoy it while it lasts.'

'I will,' agreed May.

'What happened to the boy who broke your heart when we were at Ashburn?' asked Connie. 'The one who married your best friend.'

'He's away in the army, the Middle East somewhere, though we don't know where exactly because they are not allowed to give any clue as to their location in their letters.'

'He doesn't write to you, does he?'

'Of course not, but his wife keeps me up to date with news of him,' she explained.

'So you've got over him then?'

May made a face. 'Sort of,' she said. 'He'll always be very special to me, but I've accepted that he'll never be mine.'

'And you have the gorgeous Mr Sands to console you,' smiled Connie.

'Exactly. But that's enough about me,' said May. 'Let's have your news now. Is there a man in your life?'

Before Connie had a chance to reply, the wail of the air-raid siren filled the tea shop and everyone headed for the doors. May and Connie hurried towards Marble Arch tube station and joined the orderly queue to go down to the platform to take shelter, their conversation forgotten.

Corporal George Bailey was stationed near the Suez Canal. Their job here was to guard this vital stretch of water, but the men had recently been told that Italy was now at war with the Allies so they could expect to be in combat with the Italian troops sometime soon.

Their fiercest adversary at the moment was the stifling heat, which didn't seem to abate much even at night. George longed for one of those grey, chilly English days when everyone grumbled about the weather.

His thoughts never strayed far from home and he was thinking about it now, as he and his mates took a break from duty, wondering how they were all getting along without him. He'd learned in a letter from Betty that his sister had joined the services, which had probably been a blow for their mother. On the other hand, if Sheila wasn't around she couldn't be hateful to their mother at the slightest opportunity. Poor old Mum, she used to be such a lively soul when Dad had been alive. His heart twisted at the thought of her managing without him. He doubted if Betty would offer her much comfort, because his wife had less patience than Sheila if that was possible.

His thoughts turned to Joe and he welled up. Every day away from him felt like a physical wound. May would be the saving grace at home; she would call in and keep the peace. Dear May, she also brought a tear to his eye.

Although he didn't enjoy being away from home, George had adapted well to army life from the start and had been honoured when he was made up to corporal. He liked the physicality of the life and the camaraderie. He was one of the few men who had actually enjoyed the punishing basic training and thought it was probably the would-be boxer in him, a love of physical fitness that he had inherited from his father.

Even here in the suffocating heat he still found the energy to be sad about his dad's death and angry with the killer who had ruined his mother's life and health.

'Fancy a game of cards, Corp?' said one of his pals.

'Yeah, all right, mate,' he said amiably and turned his mind to the game as the desert sun burned down.

Soon after the German incendiary attack on the London docks in September, which devastated the East End, turned miles of dockside warehouses into an inferno and lit the sky so brightly the orange glow could be seen even from Ealing, bombs began to fall in other parts of London, including the west.

Every night the siren sounded and evenings spent in the shelter became the norm for May and her parents. Sometimes Doug joined them and used their spare room for a few hours' sleep after the all-clear before cycling to work the next morning. No one got much rest but almost everyone carried on as normal. People were absolutely determined not to let Hitler disrupt their way of life any more than was absolutely unavoidable.

In the mornings, after she had done her paper round, May cycled to the Baileys' house to see if they were all right, the air always heavily spiced with smoke and the smell of cordite. Sometimes she would pass the sad sight of a pile of smoking debris where a house had been the day before.

'You're all still here then?' she said cheerfully one morning, standing at the Baileys' front door.

'Just about,' said Betty, in pyjamas and with curlers in her hair. 'Though the explosions were so loud last night I really thought we'd had it. The ground shook so violently it felt as though the shelter was going to cave in.'

'I've heard that the Germans are after Northolt airfield,' said May. 'That's why the bombing is so close.'

'There are a lot of factories around and about as well,' said Dot. 'They'll be wanting to wipe those out.'

'How are you coping with it all, Mrs Bailey?' asked May in a kindly manner.

'Not so bad. We just have to get on with it, don't we, dear,' she replied.

Oddly enough, George's mother had been better than expected since the start of the bombing. May had thought she would have a nervous breakdown at the first wail of the siren. Naturally she was very frightened of the bombs, as they all were, but Betty said she was quite calm in the shelter. May wondered if that might be because there was nothing anyone could do about this kind of danger. Dot's nervousness in the past had always been about a lack of confidence in her own ability; looking after Joe and running the house and so on. The air raids just had to be endured, and whether you lived or died was out of your hands.

May herself felt a kind of resignation about the situation. Having survived the first week or so of the air raids, she had begun to think that perhaps it was possible to live through this. Though when an air raid was actually in progress she didn't feel so brave.

'Are you staying for a cuppa?' asked Dot.

'And have you use your tea ration on me? Not likely,' said May, doing the decent thing and knowing that they wouldn't insist that she stayed. Of all the shortages, the introduction of tea rationing was the hardest to bear for many people.

A small figure appeared, rubbing his eyes, his hair tousled from bed. As soon as Joe clapped eyes on May, his face lit up and he ran to her.

'Hello, big boy,' she said, picking him up and plonking a kiss on his brow. 'Are you still sleepy?'

'He shouldn't be,' said his mother. 'He slept through

the whole thing last night. He didn't even stir when I carried him up from the shelter and put him into bed.'

'It's just as well he can sleep through all the noise,' said May. 'I wish I could.'

'Kids can only stay awake for so long when they are little, can't they?' said Betty. 'And yes, it is a blessing.'

'Anyway, so long as you're all right, I must be on my way,' said May, putting Joe down. 'Be seeing you.'

'Ta-ta,' said Betty.

As May cycled home, she was conscious of a feeling of exhilaration that she had noticed before in the mornings since the bombing had started. The air felt sharper and everything seemed to register with more clarity, the little houses and the trees shedding their leaves for winter. Things were shabbier but brighter somehow. She supposed it might be because death was such a definite possibility now and everything seemed more precious.

Let's hope that cat has come home, she thought. Tiddles always disappeared as soon as the siren sounded and didn't reappear until all was quiet, which she guessed must be in a cat's self-sufficient nature.

Oh well, another day and work to be done, she told herself as she passed the Pavilion, flowerless at this time of year but still managing to exude a welcome, the lightness of the colour standing out among the brick-built houses around.

May's buoyant mood was enhanced by the appearance of Tiddles when she got home, but dispelled later that morning when sad news reached the Pavilion. One of their regular customers had been killed last night on his way to work on the night shift in a factory. A man in his forties with a family. The war really hit home for May now that someone she knew had been killed. She felt as vulnerable as she had during the very first air raid.

People were less chatty while they did their shopping today. Voices in the café were lowered. Everybody was aware of how close the war had suddenly come.

'Could I have a cup of tea please?' said the elderly man who came regularly for his newspaper; it was a lot thinner than pre-war editions because of the paper shortage.

'Course you can,' said May, glad that they had been able to keep the café open thanks to a special ration allowance for businesses catering for the public. 'I'll bring it over to you.'

'Thank you, dear,' he said. 'Thank God for this place. You need company at a time like this.'

'That's why the pubs are packed of an evening I suppose,' she said. 'Despite the raids.'

'Definitely,' he agreed wholeheartedly. 'People get fed up with being in the shelter every night, so some of them take a chance and go out for a pint.'

'One of the pubs over Greenford way was demolished by a bomb the other night and people were killed,' May mentioned.

'Mm, I heard about that and I was shocked to the core,' he said, shaking his head and pursing his lips as he breathed in. 'But I take the view that if your name is on it, the bomb will get you wherever you are, so you might as well get some pleasure while you still can. I can't abide the shelter. It just ain't natural being six foot under when you're not dead.'

'No it isn't,' agreed May, pouring his tea while he went to find a table.

May remembered his words that night in the Anderson with her parents and Doug, sitting there in the cold, sour air waiting for the all-clear and hoping they would make it through until then. In one way the war offered advantages for courting couples in that there was plenty of scope for canoodling in the blackout, but there was less privacy if you couldn't go out so were holed up with the older generation for hours on end.

May and her mother were both knitting pullovers for the troops, her father was reading the paper by candlelight and Doug was sitting next to May under a blanket doing nothing until a spider crawling up the corrugated iron made her squeal. He picked it up and put it outside through the hole at the end.

'Funny how a harmless spider can still make you scream when there are bombs around,' he remarked. 'I would have thought one would have cancelled out the other.'

'I would have thought so too, but it hasn't worked for me,' May told him.

'We're missing *ITMA*,' complained Dick. 'The highlight of the flippin' week.'

'Oh that's a shame,' said Flo. 'I think I'll chance it and go up to the house and make a cup of tea.'

'I'll do it,' offered Doug, keen to escape from the claustrophobic atmosphere and mundane conversation. 'May will come and give me a hand, won't you?'

'Course I will,' she agreed.

'Make sure you come back down as soon as you hear the first rumble of an enemy plane,' warned Flo.

'Will do, Mum,' said May, making her way over to the opening at the back of the shelter to climb out.

As soon as they were in the garden and out of earshot, Doug took May in his arms and kissed her passionately.

'Hey, steady on, Doug,' she said. 'We need to get that tea made before another Jerry plane comes over.'

'Bugger the Jerry plane,' he said. 'I need a break, time alone with you. All this staying in with the family is driving me nuts. As much as I love them, we need to be on our own sometimes.'

'What else can we do but stay home? The air raids seem to be on every night.'

'We'll go to the West End on Sunday before the blackout and see if we can get in to see *Gone With the Wind*.' He knew how much she wanted to see that film. 'It will be a break for us and take our minds of the bombing for a little while.'

'Especially if we can get some seats in the back row,' she said laughing.

'May Stubbs, I do think you are trying to lead me astray,' he said jokingly.

'Back row or not, it will be lovely, Doug,' she approved heartily. 'I'll look forward to that.'

'Good, let's get that tea made then.'

But May could hear the hated drone of an enemy plane, which started as not much more than a distant murmur and grew to a terrifying crescendo overhead. This was the worst part of the air raids, the first throb of an engine, then the horrifying increase in sound as the plane came nearer, turning her insides to water and sucking the air from her chest. 'There's a flaming plane coming,' she said, hiding her terror.

'I can't hear anything.'

'I've got extra-sensitive hearing when it comes to bomber planes. Trust me, there is one on the way,' she said.

By the time they were back in the shelter, the aircraft could be heard loud and clear.

'What, no tea?' said Dick.

'Sorry, we'll try again later,' said May. 'There wasn't enough time to make it.'

'They've been having a kiss and a cuddle, I expect,' said Flo, chuckling.

'Mum, that is *so* embarrassing,' objected May.

'There are worse things in life than embarrassment, my girl,' said Flo wisely.

May took her point as they all waited with bated breath. The plane seemed to be directly overhead. There was a silence, then a loud crash before the plane moved away.

'Phew,' said May, puffing out her cheeks as she exhaled. 'That was a close one.'

They all started to laugh shakily, light hearted with relief. It seemed nothing short of a miracle that they were all still alive when the aircraft had sounded so close as to be almost on the roof. Sometimes after such incidents they would hear the next day that the bomb had actually dropped several miles away.

'Maybe we can have that tea now,' said May as the skies seemed quieter.

'Get on and make it this time, and less of your courting,' said her mother.

'All right, Mum, don't go on about it,' said May, giggling. She always felt shaky and emotional after a near miss, and prone to inappropriate laughter.

There were masses of people in the West End on Sunday afternoon and the queue for *Gone With the Wind* encircled the cinema in Leicester Square. There was bomb damage all around; parts of buildings reduced to rubble, dust floating in the air and plenty of official danger signs. But if this dampened the mood of the cinema-goers they certainly didn't show it. They seemed to take the view that if they waited long enough, maybe they would get in to see the most talked-about film of the year, and they were determined to enjoy it, chatting to people around.

May and Doug waited for two hours. When they finally sank into the plush seats, they revelled in the sheer escapism that Hollywood created so well. They didn't manage the back row but held hands throughout the performance, the usual pall of cigarette smoke hanging over the auditorium. An air-raid warning flashed on to the screen, but only a few people left the building. The majority, including May and Doug, preferred to take their chances and stay. They hadn't queued for so long to miss the film.

'I feel almost human again,' May said to Doug as they emerged from the cinema and walked towards the station arm in arm. 'Being out doing something nice has really cheered me up. I can put up with the shelter tonight having had such a lovely treat.'

'Yes, I thought it might cheer us up.'

'Thanks for suggesting it.'

'A pleasure,' he said graciously. 'I'm going to suggest something else now.'

'Another outing?'

'More serious than that.'

'Another one of your surprises, eh?' she said. 'Out with it. Don't keep me in suspense.'

'I think we should get married right away,' he declared. 'Or as soon as possible.'

'Well it's a lovely idea, but nothing has been organised,' she said, managing to stay realistic even though she was thrilled by the suggestion. 'Weddings take time to arrange.'

'The last thing I want to do is deprive you of your big day with a white dress and all the trimmings,' he said. 'But the way things are with the war, we have to live for the moment, and it's more important to me to be your husband than to have a great big wedding reception, which wouldn't be possible anyway now because of the shortages. We need to be together in these dangerous times, May, don't you agree?'

'Yes, of course, but it isn't quite as easy as that,' she said. 'For one thing, where would we live?'

'On the boat,' he suggested. 'Or if you feel that's too dangerous, with Jerry making a beeline for the Thames and there being no underground shelter immediately accessible, maybe we could stay at your place temporarily, just until we find somewhere of our own. I sleep in the spare room several nights a week anyway, and I would insist on paying your parents rent of course, that would be only right and proper.'

'So when did you have in mind for this wedding?' she enquired.

'Tomorrow wouldn't be soon enough for me, but obviously we have to be realistic.'

'Mmm.'

He ushered her into the crowded station and dug into his pocket for their return tickets. 'This is something we both have to want,' he said. 'If you would rather wait until a big do can be arranged, don't be afraid to say.'

'Naturally I would like some of the trimmings,' she said. 'The same as any girl would.'

'I understand,' he said.

She looked at him, seeing the love in his eyes and feeling torn. The ominous wail of the siren sent crowds hurrying into the station as May and Doug headed for the platform.

As the train rumbled noisily into the station, May

turned to him. 'Let's do it, Doug,' she said. 'Provided Mum and Dad are happy, I'm all for it.'

His beaming smile was all she needed to convince her that she had made the right decision.

'Next week?' said Betty in astonishment a few days later. 'You're getting married next week?'

'That's right,' confirmed May. She had received her parents' blessing and Doug had got a special licence.

'Blimey,' said Betty. 'Are you up the spout, then?'

'No I'm not,' May said, raising her eyes in disapproval. 'Trust you to come out with something like that.'

'It's usually the reason weddings happen suddenly.'

'Not in this case,' said May emphatically. 'Anyway, lots of people are getting married quickly because of the war.'

'Yeah, I suppose so,' Betty conceded.

'It will be a very small do as it's such short notice, and it will have to be registry office because there isn't time to get a church.'

'Not too small for me to be invited, I hope,' said Betty. 'My non-existent social life could do with a boost.'

'Of course you're invited,' May assured her. 'You and Joe and Dot and my friend Connie from Ashburn, and just close relatives apart from that. Doug's parents will come if they can get there with the bombing and the train service being so badly disrupted. We're having the reception at the Leopold Hotel and Doug and I will stay there for our first night,' she said. 'We're going to close the Pavilion for the afternoon.'

'First night in a hotel, eh?' said Betty. 'Very romantic.'

'Yes, isn't it?'

'You'll have to let me know what you'd like for a wedding present,' said Betty.

'I'll think about that,' said May excitedly. It wasn't going to be the wedding of her dreams, but she was very thrilled indeed at the prospect of becoming Mrs Doug Sands.

It was the night before the wedding and May had a pleasant gathering of butterflies in her stomach. Because it was bad luck for the bride to see the groom the night before the nuptials, Doug was staying on the boat tonight but meeting her father in a pub in Ealing for a few drinks as a kind of stag night. The few younger men of his acquaintance were away in the services so Dick was stepping into the breach to keep up with tradition.

May and her mother were preparing to look their best for the big day. Both had washed their hair and taken it in turns to lie on the floor with their head by the fire to dry it. Now they both had their hair wound into curlers.

'I'm off to meet Doug now,' announced Dick, appearing in his outdoor clothes. 'Make sure you both go down the shelter if you hear the siren.'

'And you make sure that you go to the nearest shelter or into the pub cellar.'

'Will do.'

May was really hoping there wouldn't be an air raid

tonight. She wanted to get a good night's sleep before tomorrow. There had been an occasional bomb-free night recently, so with a bit of luck it would be quiet.

Her hopes were dashed when Moaning Minnie, as some people referred to the siren, went off while she and Flo were listening to *Band Wagon* on the wireless.

'Here we go again,' said May, putting on her coat and collecting her gas mask and all the other essentials that went with them to the shelter.

When the siren was heard in the pub, some people left in a hurry; others stayed and carried on talking and drinking as though nothing out of the ordinary was happening. Dick and Doug were in the latter category, deciding to go to the shelter later if the bombing got too close.

'I admit that I couldn't decide what to make of you when May first brought you home,' Dick was saying, the two of them standing at the bar with their beer. 'But now that I've got to know you better, I'm as pleased as Punch to be having you as a son-in-law. With a bit of luck, you and I will have a good few nights out in the pub like this. It will be nice for me to have some male company in the family.'

'I'm glad you're pleased,' said Doug, on his second pint and feeling nicely relaxed.

'I'm outnumbered by two to one at the moment,' said Dick with mock disapproval.

'Glad to be making things a bit more equal for you,' Doug responded.

'Of course if we hadn't lost Geoffrey,' said Dick, becoming melancholy as the beer took effect, 'he'd have been grown up by now, so we would have been mates.'

'Yeah, that was very sad,' said Doug sympathetically.

'That's probably why the missus and I dote on May so much,' Dick went on chattily. 'Not that we didn't before, you understand, but when you've lost a child . . .'

'Of course. I understand.'

'Anyway, here we are, you and I, out having a drink together, as matey as can be,' Dick went on. 'But if you step out of line with my daughter, then you'll soon find out that I'm not such a nice bloke after all.'

'You won't have any cause for complaint with me,' said Doug, just about making himself heard above the noise outside; bangs, crashes and the reassuring rattle of anti-aircraft guns. 'I won't do anything to hurt May, I promise. But right now I think we should head for the shelter. It's getting a bit naughty out there.'

'Yeah, you're right,' the other man agreed, emptying his glass with a few swift swallows.

On their way to the door there was an almighty crash and the building crumbled around them. Ears ringing from the blast, Doug watched in horror as his future father-in-law disappeared beneath the rubble.

There was dust and smoke everywhere and people screaming and crying. The smoke made it impossible for Doug to see more than a few feet around him but he knew roughly the spot where Dick had been buried.

'It's all right, Dick,' he shouted. 'I'll get you out of there. Hang on, I'm coming.'

But as he tried to move, he was rooted to the spot. Fear had him in its grip and he was paralysed. This was the most shameful moment of his life. A man he was about to be related to was in terrible danger and he was powerless to do a thing to help him. Now Doug really knew what cowardice felt like.

'Where has your father got to, I wonder?' said Flo later that evening. There'd been a lull in the bombing and she and May were back in the house. 'Even if they had stayed until closing time he should be back by now.'

'They've probably taken shelter somewhere and are waiting until things quieten down before they head for home,' suggested May, hoping to ease her mother's fears.

'But things quietened down a while ago,' her mother pointed out.

'Mm, well they probably got talking, the way people do when they've had a few drinks.'

'Your father has no business doing that and having me worried half to death.'

'He'll be here in a minute,' said May hopefully.

Just then they heard the key turn in the lock. 'Thank Gawd for that,' said Flo with relief.

When the living room door opened, both women gasped as Dick came in, ashen faced, his head swathed in bandages, one arm in a sling.

'Oh my Lord,' said Flo, half crying as she went over to him. 'Come and sit down. Are you badly hurt?'

Together, Flo and May helped the quivering man into

an armchair. It took a while before he was able to speak. 'The pub took a hit and I got buried underneath the rubble. I thought my end had come,' he told them shakily, 'But Doug got me out; he crawled in and rescued me. The emergency services took a while to get there because they'd had so many calls in the area. What a hero! I owe my life to him.'

'Is he all right, Dad?' asked May.

Her father stared at the floor.

'Dick,' put in Flo quickly. 'What's happened to Doug? Is he hurt?'

Panic stricken, May said in a fast staccato tone, 'Dad, what's happened to him? For God's sake, tell me.'

'Sorry, love . . .' Dick bowed his head, his shoulders trembling, tears streaming down his face.

'What . . . You don't mean . . . He can't be . . .'

'He got me out and the whole lot crashed down on him; he didn't stand a chance. The rescue people did what they could but he was killed instantly. They reckon he wouldn't have suffered,' said Dick, his voice breaking. 'If it wasn't for me he'd be alive now. It should have been me. Not him. At least I've had a good few more years.'

'That sort of talk won't help,' said Flo.

'I'm very sorry, May,' said her father thickly. 'I shall regret what happened for the rest of my life.'

'Don't be silly, Dick,' said his wife. 'That isn't the way to look at it at all.'

'No, it isn't.' May was so numb with shock, the awful news hadn't registered properly, but she could vaguely comprehend that her father was suffering. 'Doug would have loved the idea that he died a hero,' she said through parched lips. 'He hated the fact that he couldn't join the services and do his bit.'

'He's done his bit good and proper now all right; did more than his bit for us,' said Flo.

The wail of the siren filled the room. 'I'll take my chances in the house for this one, if you don't mind,' said May as her parents prepared to leave. 'I can't face the shelter, not now. I'll come down later if it gets too bad.'

Her parents looked worried but she saw them exchange glances and knew they wouldn't insist. Flo came over and put her arms around her. 'I'm so sorry, love,' she said, her voice breaking. 'I know it won't be much comfort for you, but me and your dad will do what we can to help.'

'I know you will, Mum,' she said. 'I know you will.'

Breaking all the rules of safety and common sense, May went upstairs and got into bed, fully dressed, pulling the covers over her head while planes roared overhead and bombs fell. So instead of getting married tomorrow she would have a funeral to attend instead. She would need to let Doug's parents know; they were his next of kin. She never did get to reach that status.

It seemed unreal. Then she thought of Doug, that poor troubled man, dying in that bombed building without her by his side, and she wept, oblivious to the noise or the danger all around her.

Chapter Ten

Doug's mother was a pleasant, softly spoken woman with a nervous smile and a look of defeat about her, his father was tall and white haired with a booming voice which he used unrestrainedly. They had arranged for the funeral to take place in Richmond because that was where Doug had lived.

At the wake after the burial, which was held in a private room in a local pub, Mrs Sands told May how sorry she was that they had met in such sad circumstances, but that she was very glad Doug had found someone to love him.

'Unfortunately our son was not an easy person to get along with,' interrupted her husband loudly.

'He must have got along with May, dear,' his wife pointed out bravely. 'Or she wouldn't have agreed to marry him.'

'Moodiness makes you bad company,' put in Mr Sands as though his wife hadn't spoken. 'I was always telling him about it when he was growing up.'

'You do know that your son died saving my father's life, don't you?' said May, fiercely defensive of Doug because Mr Sands seemed to be so critical.

'Yes, I am well aware of that, and very courageous it was too,' he confirmed. 'I was not suggesting that my son wasn't a good man; just not an easy one.'

'So you must be very proud of him for his bravery,' said May pointedly.

'Yes, yes, of course. I was always proud of him. He didn't have to get himself killed to prove what a decent chap he was.'

'You could have tried showing your pride in him when he was alive,' said Mrs Sands, close to tears. 'Maybe we might have seen more of him if you had.'

Now May understood why Doug had gone to see his parents so rarely and hadn't seemed keen for her to meet them. No one in their right mind would want to spend time with his father.

'The train service has been all over the place because of the war, and you know how time flies by,' she said. She felt rather sorry for Mrs Sands and wanted to give her some sort of comfort. 'Doug probably meant to come to see you more often but just didn't get around to it.'

'Yes, I expect that was it,' said Mrs Sands unconvincingly, probably finding it easier to agree because she didn't want a full-blown quarrel with her husband at her son's funeral. She sighed. 'Anyway, it makes no difference now, does it?'

Seeing how desperately sad the other woman was, May instinctively gave her a hug.

'Thank you for that little show of affection, my dear,' said Mrs Sands as May drew back. 'I'm sure I would have very much enjoyed having you as my daughter-in-law.'

May's pain was hardly bearable at this reminder of how much she had lost. 'Likewise, Mrs Sands,' she said thickly.

When May received a letter from a firm of solicitors in Richmond, a few days after the funeral, asking her to call at their office at her earliest opportunity, she was rather apprehensive. Solicitors didn't normally feature in her life. But she did as they asked on her afternoon off.

'*Sands Nest*?' she said, astounded, when the bespectacled man sitting behind the leather-topped desk had finished telling her the reason why she had been summoned. 'Are you saying that Doug has left me his boat?'

'Yes, that's right.'

'But that was his most treasured possession, and his biggest asset,' she said.

'He must have held you in very high regard.'

'I can't believe it.'

The man nodded but didn't seem to want to engage in any further discussion. Instead he moved on briskly, explaining certain relevant legalities. 'Here are all the necessary papers to prove your ownership, and the keys,' he said eventually, pushing a large envelope across the desk along with a form. 'If you could just sign as proof of receipt, please. Any queries, feel free to contact me. Otherwise I hope you enjoy your inheritance.'

'Thank you,' she said numbly, writing her signature. Then, clutching the envelope, she walked out of the office into the cold November day.

'That will be worth a good few quid,' announced her father over their evening meal . 'A motor boat in good condition. Oh yes, that will fetch a pretty penny, though you'd do well to wait until after the war before you put it up for sale.'

May looked at him in astonishment. 'How can you even suggest that I sell it, Dad?' she asked emotionally.

'Well I didn't think you'd want to live on it or take up boating,' he said drily.

'I don't, but that isn't the point,' she told him. 'It was Doug's most prized possession and he chose to leave it to me.'

'Which shows how much he thought of you,' Dick said. 'He was looking after you, making sure you had a few quid. If he'd died a day later you would have got everything else as well, as his wife.'

'That's a terrible thing to say, Dad.' She was shocked at what seemed such a callous attitude. 'As if I would look at it in material terms.'

'It is a bit insensitive, Dick,' chided Flo.

'I'm sorry to have upset you, May.' Her father wasn't an unfeeling man, just a bit tactless. Having experienced poverty at first hand, he couldn't help thinking in financial terms when potential presented itself. 'Just forget that I said anything and enjoy your inheritance.'

That didn't go down well either. 'Enjoy something that has come into my possession because the man I was about to marry has died?' she said incredulously. 'Of course I won't enjoy it.'

Flo tutted, shaking her head and glaring at her husband. 'Dick, honestly, you can be so thoughtless at times. Can't you see how upset she is?'

'I'm upset too, we're all upset,' he objected. 'All I said was enjoy your—'

'Well keep your trap shut in future.' Flo turned her attention to her daughter, who seemed about to rush from the room in floods of tears without finishing her portion of shepherd's pie. 'And don't you even think about leaving one morsel of that meal, my girl. It's got a large part of this week's meat ration in it. It's a sin to waste food in these hard times, as you well know.'

'All right, Mum,' said May, forcing herself to eat. She knew that her mother was right.

May wasn't quite sure why she was so uneasy about her inheritance, but she did know that she wasn't going to sell the boat. The following Sunday afternoon she caught the bus to Richmond and went aboard and into the main cabin, which was achingly poignant without Doug. When she'd been here with him the stove had been glowing, the polished wood shining and the atmosphere warm and welcoming.

Now it was cold and uninviting. The air was stale and there were dishes in the sink, which she washed with cold water after she had let in some fresh air. There were various other items lying around too: newspapers, books, a few items of outer clothing. Doug had left here that fateful night to meet her father for a few drinks, not knowing that he would never return.

Leaving her this boat was the highest compliment anyone had ever paid her. *Sands Nest* had meant everything to Doug. Not in any material sense, but because it was full of memories of a time in his life when he'd been happy, and he had trusted her to be its guardian.

She sat on the upholstered leather bench for a long time, lost in thought, remembering Doug here where he had seemed so comfortable and right. He would have hated living with Mum and Dad after they were married, as they had planned. But he would have done it for her. She had a mental image of his crooked smile and the worried look that he had worn too often.

Realising that she was shivering with the cold, she closed up and left, now knowing exactly what she was going to do about the boat.

A couple of weeks later, on a Wednesday afternoon, May walked into Lyons Corner House in the West End, looked around for a few moments, then went over to a table where a woman was waiting for her.

'Hello, my dear,' greeted Mrs Sands. 'Thank you so much for coming.'

'No trouble at all,' May assured her, sitting down. 'It doesn't take long on the tube.'

She looked around the crowded café, at the many people in uniform, the Nippy waitresses weaving in and out of the tables. As a conversation starter she said, 'I see that the Corner Houses are managing to keep the service going despite food rationing, though there isn't so much to choose from these days.'

'The war is bound to have an effect.'

'The Nippy waitresses have gone from all the tea shops, though,' said May. 'It's self-service now. They couldn't get enough staff with so many women doing men's jobs, apparently. One of the women in our local tea shop was telling me about it.'

'That's a pity. It won't be the same without them,' said the older woman. 'Still, change is inevitable in wartime, I suppose.' She sighed, shrugging her shoulders. 'I noticed that the John Lewis store near here has some bomb damage.'

'Yes, it was bombed a couple of months ago,' confirmed May. 'The West End is looking quite battered.'

A waitress came over and Mrs Sands ordered tea and buns for them both.

'Is your husband not coming?' enquired May.

'No, I asked you to meet me because I wanted us to have a chat on our own,' she explained. 'He has come to London with me but I left him in the room at the hotel having a nap.'

'Are you just here for tonight?' asked May.

Mrs Sands nodded. 'I wanted to see you to thank you personally for your wonderful generosity in giving us the boat and it's too far to come just for the day,' she said. 'It means so much to us to have *Sands Nest* back in the family again. I was very moved when we heard from the solicitor of your intentions. We are so grateful to you, my dear.'

'Yes, I guessed you would be pleased,' May told her. 'Doug had such wonderful memories of his childhood there with you and Mr Sands.' She paused, not sure if she should continue, but decided to take a chance. 'I think his childhood was the last time Doug was truly happy.'

The older woman looked desperately sad. 'Yes, he was a very happy child; always laughing and full of fun. But when he reached adolescence he changed. He started to have dark moods and withdrew into himself. He shut himself away from his father and me mentally.'

'All the time?'

'No, there were times when he seemed like his old self, but the darkness would always come back,' she explained. 'We did think of getting medical advice but he was grown up by then and refused to see a doctor.' Her eyes were full of tears. 'I don't think there's anything they can do about that sort of thing anyway.'

'So do you know what caused it?'

'No, because he refused to talk about it,' she said. 'I don't think he realised the extent to which it affected other people. His father had no patience with it at all.'

'Was he a strict father?'

'Very. He wanted Doug to go away to boarding school, but I refused to allow it.'

'How did Mr Sands take that?'

'We argued about it for months,' she confided. 'He thought if we'd sent Doug away to school he would have been tougher; had more confidence in himself.'

'Does he think he wouldn't have had the psychological problems?' she asked.

'He does sometimes try to pin the whole thing on me for not letting him be sent away, yes,' she admitted. 'And who knows, he could be right.'

'It was in his make-up, I think. Part of his personality,' said May. 'He had been a lot better lately as it happens. Ironic really.'

'Yes, it is,' Mrs Sands agreed tearfully.

'I don't see anything of Doug in his father,' May mentioned.

'No, he was more like me in every way.' Mrs Sands paused thoughtfully as though guessing May's thoughts. 'My husband is not a bad man, you know,' she said as the waitress brought the tea. 'He is just very set in his ideas and impatient with people who don't think along the same lines. He used to get so angry with Doug over the moods. He thought he had no right to inflict them on other people and make them miserable.'

'They did take some tolerating, I must admit,' said May. 'I only knew your son for a short time, but I found that side of him quite upsetting. It's a shame, because he was such a lovely man in other ways. I wish now I'd been more patient with him.'

'You stayed with him, that's the important thing,' said the other woman, pouring the tea.

'I suppose so, but I can see why some people may have been put off,' she said. 'He gave me the impression that he'd had girlfriends before who got fed up with it.'

'Yes, he did have a few, but once he didn't live with

us any more I didn't know what he was doing. We lost touch for a while.'

'One good thing you did for him was to give him the boat,' said May. 'That was where he was happiest. He found some sort of peace there.'

'Yes, I know,' she said. 'He loved it as a boy and that's why I'm so pleased we can keep it in the family now that he's gone.'

May sipped her tea. 'What will you do with her?' she wondered. 'I expect it will cost a bit to keep her moored where she is now if you're never going to use her. Will you take her to a stretch of water near you?'

'Oh no,' Mrs Sands said at once. 'She has to be on the Thames; that was the essence of the whole thing. We'll have her stored in a boatyard somewhere until after the war, then we'll put her back on the river and use her as accommodation when we come to London. We might even have boating holidays again one day.'

'Yes, why not,' said May.

'It's somewhere that I can revive some happy memories,' she said. 'We moved away from the family home because of my husband's job, so all the memories are in the boat.' She fixed May with her gaze. 'Thank you so much, my dear.'

'It's a pleasure,' said May, and she really meant it.

It was such a weight off her mind having handed the boat back to its rightful owners that she was positively light hearted when she got home, where Betty and Joe were waiting for her.

'I sometimes fear for your sanity, May Stubbs,' said Betty when May had finished telling her and Flo about her business with Mrs Sands. 'Fancy giving the boat away. Anyone would think you had money, the way you carry on.'

'I didn't give it away,' she told her. 'I returned it to its rightful owners.'

'Rightful owners my Aunt Fanny,' protested Betty. 'That boat was yours. Doug wanted you to have it or he wouldn't have left it to you. If you didn't want to keep it you could have sold it and had a decent bit of dough in your purse.'

'You are as bad as my father about this,' protested May. 'Why can't the two of you understand that some things can't be measured in financial terms?'

'When you're in the moneyed classes maybe that's true, but when you're in the lower ranks like us you have to grab anything that comes your way. Isn't that right, Mrs Stubbs?'

'Don't drag me into it,' protested Flo. 'My daughter has a mind of her own and when she gets an idea into her head no one will alter it, not you, nor her father, and believe me he has tried. It was her inheritance so her decision.'

'So let that be an end to it please,' said May.

There was an interruption from below. 'Swings please, Auntie May,' said Joe, staring up at her with his gorgeous pale brown eyes.

'Yes, of course I'll take you to the swings, darlin',' she said, picking him up and kissing him. 'Come on, Betty, get your coat. And hurry up or the kids will be out of school and we won't be able to get Joe on anything.'

'It's bloomin' cold out there,' Betty said. 'I think I'll wait for you here, if that's all right, Mrs Stubbs.'

Flo exchanged a glance with Betty, then said, 'Course it is, love; you can talk to me while I get the meal ready for tonight.'

For once in her life Betty wasn't thinking of herself. She knew that Doug's death had devastated May, even though she didn't make a performance of it, and the only real comfort she seemed to get came from being with Joe. May's love for him exuded from every pore and Betty thought she would let her have a little time on her own with him. Besides, it really was cold out and it would be nice and warm in the Stubbses' kitchen.

May and Joe had the small recreation ground to themselves on this grey November afternoon and May sat with her arm around him on the roundabout, feeling him close to her and cherishing the moment. Doug's death had traumatised her, but because he had always been so much outside of her normal circle, it sometimes felt as though he had never been in her life at all now that he had gone. She had resumed her old routine as though she hadn't left it.

But everything was different for her now emotionally. She had been part of a couple; now she was on her own again and had to adjust to the loneliness of it. As the damp, smoky scent of incipient evening rose around her, she was transported back to earlier times spent under the lamp-post on the corner of the street when the air had smelled just like this; the three of them, her, Betty and George. An ache of longing rose inside her for simpler times when life had been safe and carefree.

'May loves young Joe, doesn't she?' said Flo as she rolled out pastry on the kitchen table with Betty sitting opposite.

'Yeah, she's a brilliant godmother, as George and I knew she would be when we chose her.'

'Have you heard from George lately?' Flo enquired.

'I get a letter every now and again,' she said.

'Where is he now?'

'His letters are censored so I'm not sure, but it's some-where warm.'

'We could do with a bit of that round here,' said Flo lightly, putting cooked meat and gravy into a pie dish and covering it with pastry.

'Not half.' Betty had switched back to her normal self-seeking ways as an idea to brighten up her life came into her mind. 'I was thinking, Mrs Stubbs, as May seems to draw such comfort from being with Joe, might it be a good idea for her to have him here one evening and let him stay over for the night?'

Flo narrowed her eyes. 'You want to go out, do you?' she said.

'I wouldn't mind a night out at the flicks, but that

isn't why I'm suggesting it,' Betty fibbed. 'I thought it might do May good; give her something else to think about other than her bereavement and do me a favour at the same time. I never get to go out of an evening. My mother-in-law won't look after Joe for me because she can't cope with him on her own.'

'I suppose if the raids ease up it might be an idea,' said Flo. 'Anything that cheers May up is all right by me.'

'People do go out despite the raids now that we are all used to them,' said Betty.

'And look what happened to poor Doug,' Flo reminded her.

'Mm, there is that,' she said. 'But some people say if a bomb is meant to get you it will wherever you are.'

'That's rubbish,' declared Flo. 'If it were true you might as well not have air-raid shelters and we'd all carry on as though bombs aren't dropping out of the sky.'

'Of course nobody means we should take it to that extreme,' said Betty.

'I should hope not.'

'But they have longer programmes and entertainment at some of the cinemas if there's a raid on, so I've heard,' said Betty. 'The organist comes up and they have a sing-song after the big film. It helps to take people's minds off the bombs.'

'That's just asking for trouble,' said Flo. 'They wouldn't stand a chance if a bomb hit the cinema.'

'I suppose they hope it won't,' said Betty, disappointed to find opposition to what had originally been an altruistic gesture. 'Anyway, it was only an idea. May can have

Joe for a night and I'll stay in if it will make everyone happy. I was only trying to help.'

Flo had known Betty all her life and she knew that May was the giver in that friendship. Betty always wanted what was best for Betty, but Flo was quite fond of her just the same. Probably because she was so transparent she could be comical at times.

'You need to speak to May about it,' she suggested. 'It's nothing to do with me.'

'Right you are,' agreed Betty.

The idea of having her godson for a whole night really appealed to May and she was confident that he would be happy to stay with her because she had built an excellent rapport with him.

'You go off to the pictures and Joe and I will have a nice time together,' she said later when she and Betty were on their own with Joe in the living room. 'Let's do it when we get a couple of quiet nights.'

'Your mum seems to think that I am only offering for my own ends,' said Betty.

'Knowing you, you probably are,' said May without animosity. 'But that's fine with me; you never get to go to the flicks, so why not take the opportunity and please me as well.'

'Why does everybody always suspect my motives?' asked Betty, looking peeved.

'Probably because we know you so well,' replied May.

'I really did have the idea for your sake,' Betty insisted.

'At first, anyway. It was only afterwards I thought I might as well make the most of it and go out.'

'I believe you, thousands wouldn't,' laughed May. 'Look, I'll be enjoying myself with Joe, so why shouldn't you go to see a film, organist and all if they have one.'

And so it was arranged for the next time there was a lull in the raids.

Flo and Dick embraced the idea of having Joe to stay and Flo put the geyser on so that May could have hot water to bath him.

'Might as well make the most of it before the government puts hot water on ration,' said Flo lightly.

May gave a wry grin. Every week it seemed something else either disappeared altogether or went on ration. People were urged to grow their own food and keep chickens. Anyone coming to stay either provided their own food or brought their ration books. Betty had decided on the former for Joe and sent along milk and orange juice, which his child's green ration book entitled her to, as well as bread and cheese for his tea and porridge for breakfast.

The little boy enjoyed his bath, especially as May let him splash about and played with him. Afterwards she took him downstairs, where her father got down on the floor and let him ride on his back, then May gave him some warm milk, read him several stories and tucked him into bed.

It was a blissfully silent night. Hitler had given London

a break this past week, and long may it continue, she thought, though she guessed it wouldn't. There was a long way to go before this awful war was over. Because Joe was in unfamiliar surroundings, May sat with him until he dozed off, feeling enormously privileged to have this time with him on her own. She hoped Betty was enjoying the film as much as she herself was enjoying looking after her son.

This was more like it, thought Betty, looking around at the crowds of people lining the dance floor at the Hammersmith Palais, a pall of smoke hovering over everything and the smell of Evening in Paris perfume creating a delicious hint of sin. This was where all the fun was. Blow the flicks. She wasn't going to waste a night out sitting in some cinema and not speaking to a soul. She'd planned this all along but knew that May wouldn't look after Joe if she'd told her the truth, so a little creativity had been needed.

It was the music and the dancing she wanted; the sheer glamour of it that she'd missed by getting pregnant at such a young age. If this involved a little harmless flirtation along the way, so what; she was entitled to let her hair down once in a while as a change from the boredom of looking after a child all day.

How she had changed, she thought. At one time she wouldn't have dared to come to a place like this on her own. Now she positively revelled in her freedom. There was enough competition here already without her bringing more along with her.

The women she'd seen so far all seemed to look far more glamorous than she did. As a mother living on army pay, she couldn't afford much in the way of new clothes or make-up. But she thought she looked quite presentable in a white blouse and dark skirt and a smidgen of lipstick she had left in a tube she'd bought from Woolworth's ages ago. Her biggest asset was her figure, which she knew was good.

All those gorgeous men in uniform; how smart they looked and how ardently she hoped one of them would ask her to dance when the music started. The band struck up with 'In the Mood' and her stomach lurched nervously. Supposing no one came over to her and she was a wallflower? Oh why had she put herself through this?

But then a deep voice said, 'May I have this dance please?' and she found herself looking into the smiling face of a soldier with dark brown eyes.

'Certainly,' she said with a polite grin and allowed herself to be whisked off for a quickstep, excited by the sheer fun of this new adventure.

'So how was he?' asked Betty when she collected Joe the next morning after breakfast.

'Good as gold, no problems at all,' replied May. 'I thoroughly enjoyed having him and he seemed happy enough to be here. How did you enjoy your night off?'

'Well . . . I missed Joe, of course,' she said carefully. 'But it felt good to get out of the house.'

'What was the film like?' enquired May.

'Not bad,' she replied.

'Did they have the organ?'

'Oh yes.'

'No sing-song, though, I suppose, as there wasn't a raid,' assumed May.

Betty shook her head, thanking her lucky stars that May had inadvertently shown her the way through her web of lies. 'No, no sing-song,' she said.

'I'm glad you enjoyed yourself,' said May warmly. 'The break will have done you good.'

'As it was such a success, maybe we can do it again,' suggested Betty eagerly.

'Yeah, why not,' said May, seeing no harm in a night at the pictures for her friend.

'Next week maybe?'

'Fine with me,' said May. She had been finding that the days seemed depressingly long and gave her too much time to be sad now that Doug wasn't around. Looking after Joe was something to look forward to. 'I'd love to have him.'

'Good, that's settled then,' said Betty, beaming and putting her son's outdoor clothes on him. 'I'll get off home now and leave you to go to work.'

The air raids continued, though not every night. Sometimes they came, other times they didn't. There was no reliable way of predicting except perhaps that the bombers favoured clear nights. Whilst it wasn't possible for everyone to take the raids in their stride, most people did learn to accept them and try to carry on regardless, which continued to be something of a national obsession.

Wednesday half-day closing became the highlight of May's week, because that was when she had Joe to stay. If there was a raid, they took him into the shelter and he usually slept through the whole thing, sometimes waking when they carried him back into the house. He was too little to realise the seriousness of what was going on around him, and was so used to the noise of the air raids that it was normal to him.

Betty didn't seem to mind being out during a raid, so the arrangement became regular. May did worry about her, of course, but being afraid was such a part of life now that she lived from day to day, glad to have survived each raid as it came and trying not to worry about the next one.

One thing that did concern most women, though, especially married ones, as the festive season approached, was how on earth they were going to provide a happy Christmas with food being in such short supply.

Ideas and recipes were keenly exchanged at the Pavilion. Someone had made a Christmas pudding with grated apple, chopped prunes and carrot to replace the missing dried fruit, someone else had a way of making icing for the Christmas cake using dried milk among other unusual ingredients, and most people had been putting tinned fruit away since the autumn.

'It's the kiddies I feel sorry for,' said one customer. 'What isn't rationed is hard to come by or very expensive.'

'You're telling me,' said a woman in a turban. 'I queued

up for two hours the other day for some Dinky cars for my little boy but they only let me have one car and one lorry after all that waiting.'

'Well I'm going to the West End looking for toys and sweets and I'm not coming home till I've got some of each,' said another customer. 'I'll queue for as long as it takes.'

'John Lewis have only a fraction of the toys that they used to have,' mentioned someone. 'Their toy department is tiny compared to the size it used to be before the war.'

'I think the government should put sweets on ration,' declared the woman in the turban.

'It would certainly be fairer,' agreed another. 'And much better than not being able to get any at all because as soon as the shops get them in they sell out.'

There was general agreement about that.

'One thing is for sure,' said one woman. 'The kids might not have as much stuff as usual but they will have something to unwrap on Christmas morning and a full stocking even if we have to make everything ourselves. The war isn't going to wreck Christmas for the little ones.'

There was an enthusiastic roar of agreement.

Behind the counter, weighing up a customer's cheese ration, May was cheered by the positive attitude of people in general. She herself had already managed to get a clockwork tank from the range of military toys on sale and was knitting a teddy bear with the wool from one of her old jumpers. Joe was one little boy who would be smiling on Christmas Day.

★   ★   ★

A few days later, out doing her paper round in the early morning, all thoughts of the preparations for Christmas were pushed to the back of May's mind by the brutal reality of war. A couple of houses in a row of terraces on her round had been completely demolished during last night's raid and the rubble was still smoking. It wasn't yet light but she could see enough to know that it would have been fatal for anyone inside, and hoped desperately that the occupants had been in the shelter.

Her hopes were shattered when one of the men working to make the site safe told her that the building had been hit by a parachute mine and several people had been killed and others injured. She was trembling inside as she went on her way.

This incident, as bombings and any other air-raid event were known, was only a mile or so from her home. This was real, not just a rumour, and these streets were dangerous at night. However much people tried to carry on as normal to defy Hitler, they couldn't afford to be careless, and for that reason May decided she must have a serious chat with Betty.

Much to May's surprise, Betty seemed to be in agreement with her suggestion that she forgo her night out on Wednesdays while the raids were so close to home.

'I think you need to be indoors with Joe at night for the time being,' she said.

'Mm,' nodded Betty casually.

'As much as I love having him, it just isn't sensible for

you to be coming home late at the moment, not while the streets are so dangerous,' May continued, still thinking persuasion was necessary. 'I know that lots of people take a chance and the cinemas and pubs are packed out every night, but when you've got a kiddie you have to be more careful. You don't want him to be an orphan, do you?'

'Course not,' Betty assured her.

'Oh, so you don't mind, then?'

'Not at all. We'll leave it until things quieten down a bit,' she said. 'That's fine by me.'

'Oh,' said May, giving her a searching look. 'I was expecting you to argue.'

'Why should I? I've had a good few nights out,' she said. 'That was all I wanted. My son comes first and my place is at home with him of an evening.'

Knowing her friend as well as she did, this unexpected acquiescence didn't quite ring true with May. She didn't know what they could possibly be, but she suspected that Betty had her own reasons for agreeing so readily.

Chapter Eleven

The Stubbses and the Baileys decided to team up at the Stubbs house on the afternoon of Christmas Day to pool resources and share the joy of having a little one around. Sheila was on leave from the ATS and full of amusing barrack-room tales, so it was a jolly gathering.

Dot had made some wartime sausage rolls – with only a taster amount of filling – and brought along various other goodies including a tin of peaches and pineapple and some evaporated milk. Naturally she also brought some of their precious tea ration, and a bottle of sherry that Sheila had managed to obtain.

'I see I'm in the minority again,' said Dick good-humouredly, referring to the lack of male company, which was a little insensitive considering recent events.

Everyone maintained a diplomatic silence, for fear of hurting May, but she was already painfully aware of the fact that Doug would have been one of the family this Christmas.

'You've got Joe, Mr Stubbs,' said Sheila quickly to

gloss the moment over. 'He can be your pal for the day.'

'Yeah, that's right,' said Dick, smiling down at the boy. 'We'll have to stick together against this lot, young man.'

Joe didn't have a clue what they were talking about, but he was old enough to sense a good atmosphere and chuckled loudly, whereupon Dick picked him up and threw him in the air.

'Good grief, son, you're getting a bit too heavy for me,' he groaned. 'You'll soon be able to lift me up.'

'He'll be three in a couple of months, Dad,' said May. 'So he'll be buying you a pint before long.'

'He's got a good while to go yet,' said Dick, lifting him on high again.

Joe reacted enthusiastically, but he did have something else on his mind today: a clockwork tank that had appeared mysteriously by his bed this morning along with other new toys.

'You made a good choice there, May,' remarked Dot as the boy ran the toy along the floor. 'He's hardly put it down since he clapped eyes on it this morning. The only problem is it needs to be wound up every few minutes and he can't do it himself.'

'So we'll do it for him, won't we, darlin'?' said May, turning the key in the side of the toy and watching it scuttle across the lino.

'After the first three hundred times the novelty begins to wear off,' said Betty drily.

'Come on, everyone,' urged Flo. 'Take your coats off and we'll get stuck into the Christmas cake, though Lord knows what it'll be like with the alternative ingredients I've had to use.'

'I'm sure it'll taste nice, dear,' encouraged Dot. 'Our Christmas pudding wasn't too bad, even though it had a taste of sawdust about it. We can't be choosy these days.'

They all piled into the front room, which was only used on special occasions. Today there was a fire glowing in the hearth, paper chains they had had since before the war looped across the ceiling and little bowls of sweets placed around.

Tea was made and Christmas cake devoured with glee. Watching Joe play with the new toys he had brought with him was the main entertainment, but as evening came and he got sleepy, they put him to bed in May's room and moved on to more adult pastimes. Out came the sherry and beer and they drank a toast to lost loved ones – Geoffrey and Doug – and absent friends – George – then they listened to the wireless, sang carols and songs and played cards whilst making short work of the savoury snacks. Fortunately Hitler's bombers stayed away and May was proud of the way they had managed to have a happy Christmas despite everything.

When May went into the kitchen to get some drinks for the guests, Betty followed her.

'I need to speak you,' she said conspiratorially.

'Go ahead,' urged May, unscrewing the top of a beer bottle and filling a glass for her father. 'I'm listening.'

'Not here,' she said in a low voice. 'It's a very private matter. Someone might come in. Let's go for a walk when you've finished doing the drinks. We'll tell the others we want a breath of fresh air.'

'It must be serious for you to want to go out in the cold,' remarked May.

'It is,' said Betty. 'Very serious.'

Not in her wildest dreams could May have suspected what Betty had to tell her, and she was both shocked and angry.

'Pregnant?' she gasped, her voice rising in astonishment. 'You're telling me that you are pregnant?'

'All right. There's no need to shout about it,' warned Betty as their voices echoed in the stillness of the deserted streets. 'I don't want the whole town to know.'

'But how . . . I mean, George is away.' They'd been walking past the Pavilion but this news had brought May to a standstill and she stood facing her friend in the blackout darkness. 'So who . . . I mean, you haven't been seeing anyone.'

'A soldier,' said Betty sheepishly.

'Oh, I get it,' said May. 'Wednesday nights. You met him at the pictures.'

There was a brief hiatus. 'Er . . . not exactly,' said Betty.

'Where then?'

'Hammersmith Palais.'

'When did you go there?'

Betty paused only briefly. She was in such trouble anyway, she decided she might as well tell May the truth. 'Every Wednesday night when Joe was with you,' she informed her.

'You lied to me from the start, then.'

'Well yeah, but only because I knew you wouldn't approve of the Palais.'

'I've no objection to the Palais as such. It's a smashing place,' May said sharply. 'It's you going there looking for men when you already have a husband that I don't like and I made that very clear to you. Knowing that you still went there, deliberately deceiving me . . .'

'I just wanted a bit of fun,' Betty said feebly. 'I wasn't looking for men so much as glamour and enjoyment.'

'And what you got was pregnancy, oh very glamorous,' May said with withering sarcasm.

'I knew you'd be cross.'

'Cross?' exploded May. 'I'm absolutely furious. You've betrayed George in the worst possible way and taken me for a fool. How dare you, Betty? How dare you treat people this way?'

'As I've told you before, you can be so flippin' strait-laced at times, May.'

'That isn't true and you know it,' roared May. 'How other people live their lives is no concern of mine. Live and let live has always been my motto. If you want to go out dropping your drawers for any man who wants you to, that is your business. But when you involve me and cheat on a dear friend of mine, then it becomes mine too.'

'It is pretty bad, I know,' admitted Betty.

'Bad? It's downright disgraceful, as well as selfish,' seethed May. 'What more do you want from life, Betty? You made sure you caught George by getting yourself pregnant and forcing him to do the decent thing, you have a beautiful child, and that still isn't enough for you.'

'I suppose I heard about all the fun people are having at dance halls and I thought I'd like to try it.'

'You didn't just try it, did you? You positively threw yourself into it,' fumed May. 'Well I don't know how you're going to explain a brother or sister for Joe when George comes home, but I want nothing more to do with you.'

'But May, you can't desert me.'

'Just watch me,' challenged May rashly. 'After today, you needn't bother coming round again, because I won't want to see you. You've gone too far this time.'

'May, please,' Betty begged.

'I'm going back to the house now,' May declared. 'It's freezing out here.'

'I need you, May.'

'I needed you when I was ill but you were too busy looking after yourself to bother about me.'

'Sorry.'

'It's too late for that,' she said, and turned and marched back up the street, leaving an astounded Betty looking after her.

Of course May had known she wouldn't be able to keep to her threat, because her sense of duty towards the friendship was too strong. So the next morning when Betty came to collect Joe, who had stayed the night as he'd been sleeping when the others had left, she said, 'Let's take him over to the swings, shall we?'

'Yeah, he'd like that,' said Betty with a hopeful smile.

As soon as Joe was settled on a swing and out of earshot, May said, 'So what are you going to do? Will you write and tell George to warn him of the situation before he comes home?'

'I can't have the baby, May,' Betty told her.

'Oh . . . well what does the father have to say about it?'

'He doesn't want any part of it,' she explained. 'He's given me some money to get it attended to and I won't see him again because he's being posted, or that's what he says. He couldn't get away from me quick enough once I'd told him.'

So that was it. Betty hadn't been bothered about staying home on Wednesday evenings recently because her boyfriend had cooled off and she was in trouble. It was surprising she'd waited this long to tell May; perhaps it had taken her a while to pluck up the courage.

'So you don't even have an address for him.'

Betty shook her head. 'We didn't get around to exchanging personal details. I know he was stationed somewhere just outside London temporarily and that's about it.'

May sighed in frustration at her friend's careless attitude. 'A complete stranger, then,' she said.

Betty made a face. 'I suppose you could say that, but it didn't seem like it because I used to see him every Wednesday,' she explained.

'But you know nothing about him.'

'I know he's a good dancer and a handsome fella and

that was all I needed to know,' she said. 'It was just a bit of fun, May, an adventure.'

'Not much fun now, though, is it?'

'No it blinkin' well isn't,' Betty confirmed. 'But it'll be all right once I get it sorted. No one need know except you and me.'

May went back to the swing with Joe on it and pushed it, thinking how her friend sailed through life in pursuit of her own pleasure, never seeming to think seriously about anything. 'Betty, you can't do that,' she said. 'It's illegal as well as barbaric.'

'What choice do I have?' she asked. 'I can't have another bloke's kid running around when George comes home, can I? Besides, there's his mum and Sheila to think about. They would throw me out and Joe and I would have nowhere to go. My own family turned their backs on me when I got pregnant the first time. Can you imagine what they'd be like if they knew I was in the family way again with a baby that isn't my husband's?'

'It doesn't bear thinking about.'

'So I shall have to get rid.'

'But how? Who do we know who does anything like that?'

'We don't, but one of the young mums I know got pregnant too soon after the first and she got it seen to. I'll ask her.'

'Oh well, it's your life, your decision, I suppose,' said May worriedly. 'I'll stay out of it and keep my opinions to myself.'

'The thing is, May,' Betty began in the wheedling tone

she used when she wanted something, 'I wondered if you would consider going with me if I can get it arranged. I don't want to go on my own.'

May emitted an eloquent sigh. She hated what Betty had done and was about to do, but whatever her faults, she was a friend and needed her support. May couldn't turn her back on her.

'All right,' she agreed. 'As much as I hate the whole thing, I'll go with you.'

It was a bitter January night as May and Betty waited in the queue for the trolley bus back to Ealing from Acton. May's mother, who was looking after Joe, had been told that they were going to see an old school friend who hadn't been well. The deceit upset May terribly, but she had to go along with it for her mother's sake as well as Betty's. Mum would be horrified to know the true purpose of their outing.

Her friend was standing beside her shivering and weeping. It had been a very traumatic experience for her. It was strange how such an ordinary house in an unremarkable street could be doing a roaring trade in illegal practices. May had expected it to be in a sleazy area, but it was respectable and normal just like the street she lived in. Even the woman seemed like any other middle-aged mother in an apron and carpet slippers. The only clue to anything untoward was in her furtiveness. She looked up and down the street before ushering them inside when they arrived, and when they left she asked for complete secrecy about their visit. May had sat on a hard wooden chair in the hall while a petrified Betty was taken upstairs.

Now May put her arm around her. 'Are you all right?' she asked in a warm tone.

'Yeah, I suppose so,' Betty sniffed. 'I'm glad it's over but I hope I get home before things start to happen. She said it will be all over by the morning. I've got a terrible stomach ache now, so it's probably the beginnings.'

'The bus will be along in a minute,' said May encouragingly. 'We'll soon be home.'

But she hadn't reckoned with the Luftwaffe. The wail of the siren echoed into the night, sending people heading for shelter. May followed them, dragging Betty with her.

'I'd sooner wait for the bus,' said Betty, pulling back. 'The raid probably won't come anywhere near here anyway. You know how they sound the siren for miles around.'

'They wouldn't have sounded it in this area if it wasn't fairly near,' said May.

'You can go for cover,' said Betty. 'I'm staying here. I've got to get home.'

'We'll go home after the all-clear,' said May.

'I can't wait, May,' said Betty, bending over and holding her stomach. 'The pain is getting really bad.'

'Hang on to me,' said May, half carrying her towards the other side of the street where the shelter was, the roar of the enemy planes becoming louder. 'We'll have to get to the shelter. It's only a bit further.'

'I can't get there, May.'

'Lie flat on the ground on your tummy then,' said May urgently as the planes came ever nearer. 'That's what we're supposed to do if we can't reach a shelter.'

'Don't leave me,' said Betty feebly as she got down on to the ground.

'Of course I won't leave you,' May assured her. 'But I wish you would come to the shelter.'

'Stop going on about the flamin' shelter,' shrieked Betty. 'I'm in terrible pain here. I want to go home. I don't want to lose my baby here in the street.'

'When the all-clear has sounded we'll find somewhere to go if you don't think you can make it home. We might be able to find a church,' said May, now prostrate on her stomach on the pavement, almost too worried about Betty to care about the deafening explosions which shook the ground.

'Oh, my luck is in,' said Betty. 'The bus is coming.'

'Betty, no . . .'

'If the driver has got the guts to drive his bus through an air raid, I'm damned sure I'm brave enough to get on it,' she said, scrambling to her feet and running towards the bus stop.

May got up and went after her. As the trolley bus approached the stop, she heard the terrifying whistle of a bomb, which sounded as if it was heading straight for them.

'I hope May and Betty are all right,' said Flo as she and Dick settled in the Anderson shelter with Joe. 'I really hate it when May is out during a raid.'

'She's a sensible girl,' he said. 'She'll take shelter. Where are they anyway?'

'Over Acton way somewhere,' replied Flo. 'One of their friends from school moved there and they've gone to see her, apparently.'

'They might not have a raid there,' he suggested, hoping to ease Flo's mind.

'It isn't far from here.'

Joe stirred in his makeshift bed. 'Mummy,' he said, sounding fretful. 'I want Mummy.'

'Mummy will be back soon, love,' said Flo, stroking his brow. 'Shush now and go back to sleep.'

But Joe had other ideas. He sat up and looked round. 'Where's Auntie May?' he said, rubbing his eyes.

'She's out with Mummy. They'll both be back soon,' she said gently.

'I want to see them,' he said, his eyes filling with tears.

'You can't until they get back. Hey, how about I tell you a story?'

'No story,' he said, starting to cry loudly. 'I want my Mummy . . . Mum-ee.'

'Now come on, son,' said Dick, trying to be firm and failing. 'You're not usually one to make a fuss.'

'Course he isn't,' said Flo, trying to soothe him.

'Oh Joe, mate,' said Dick as the boy's wailing filled the shelter. 'Have a heart. That noise is hard on our eardrums.'

But the child had worked himself up into such a state he couldn't stop, and was sobbing with intermittent hiccups.

'Unusual for him to carry on like this,' remarked Flo. 'He's always been as good as gold before.'

'It isn't surprising he's woken up with all the noise going on outside,' said Dick.

'Poor little thing,' sympathised Flo. 'Kiddies shouldn't have to put up with wars, should they?'

'No, love, they shouldn't,' her husband agreed.

Together they tried to soothe him while the enemy planes dropped their lethal cargo all around, causing earth-shattering explosions.

It all happened so fast, May was dazed. One minute she had been running after Betty, the next there was a terrific crash and she landed on the ground some distance away, grazing her knees and elbows.

Scrambling to her feet, coughing, her nose and throat stinging from the smoke, she was aware of an eerie, suffocating silence. She could hardly see through the dust clouds, and the harsh, raw smell of dissolved brickwork made her nauseous. Eyes streaming, throat smarting, she stumbled through the debris in search of her friend. Suddenly the silence was broken by the sound of voices and screaming. She called Betty's name, peering frantically through the smoke, and guessed that the shops near the bus stop must have been hit.

Then she saw what looked like a bundle of clothes on the ground and her heart pumped horribly.

'Betty,' she called. 'Betty, is that you?'

There was a groan and May got down on her knees.

'I've copped it good and proper,' said Betty. May was shocked at the sight. In the dim light she could just make out an ugly wound on her head from which blood was gushing. 'I'm bleeding at both ends. The bomb certainly speeded things up. It would probably have done the whole job and saved me paying that woman.'

May was heartened by the fact that Betty had managed to hang on to her sense of humour. Surely it must mean that she wasn't too badly injured if she had the savvy to make a joke.

The sound of the planes receded into the distance and the welcome all-clear replaced it.

'We need to get your head seen to,' said May. 'The rescue people will be here in a minute.'

'I don't think I'm gonna make it,' said Betty, sounding weak suddenly.

'Of course you are,' encouraged May. 'You just hang on and I'll shout for help.' She stood up and called at the top of her voice. 'Help over here, help please!'

Back on her knees on the ground, she cradled Betty's head in her arms, trying to stop the flow of blood with her handkerchief.

'I know I've always been a bit of a nightmare,' Betty said, her strength seeming to fade. 'Always wanting more than I've got. I never loved George as a wife should – we just made the best of a bad job 'cause I was pregnant – but I do love my boy Joe. Maybe I like to get away from him now and then to have some grown-up fun, but he means the world to me.'

'I know, Betty, I know,' May assured her. 'Don't talk, save your strength until the first-aid people get here.'

'You will look out for my Joe if I don't make it, won't you, May?' she said weakly.

'Of course I will, but you'll be here to look out for him yourself, so no more of that sort of talk,' said May. She was trying her utmost to stay calm, but panic was beginning to rise, especially when blood started to trickle on to the ground near Betty's legs. 'Once they get your head stitched up you'll be fine.'

Hearing voices and managing to see further afield as the dust began to settle, she shouted again, 'Help please, over here.'

'Soon as we can,' said a voice. 'There are a lot of people hurt in this lot.'

May concentrated on keeping Betty awake as she drifted in and out of consciousness, her head on May's lap as she sat on the ground. 'Come on, Betty. Don't go to sleep on me.'

'All right, stop bossing me about, May Stubbs,' Betty said, opening her eyes. 'You always have been a bossy cow.'

May smiled through her tears. It was so good to hear her friend sounding normal. 'I've always had to be, with you as my friend.'

'Yeah, because I always get into a mess. This latest one being the worst of the lot.'

'Don't worry about that now,' urged May. 'You need to save your strength.'

'Look out for Joe, May,' said Betty.

The first-aid people arrived. 'Thank God for that,' said

May with relief. 'She's bleeding heavily from a head wound. She must have been hit by flying debris.'

'All right, love; you leave her to us,' said one of the men.

She was just wondering if she should mention the other source of the bleeding when Betty went limp and her head fell to one side.

'No,' May screamed. 'Do something, please.'

'Out of the way please, miss,' said the man. 'Let's get her on a stretcher.'

Trembling from head to toe, May got up and stood to one side while the first-aid man went down on his knees to Betty.

'Sorry, miss,' he said after a while. 'She's gone.'

'She can't have done,' May said. 'She was talking to me just now, making a joke.'

'I really am very sorry,' he said, as two men moved in with a stretcher. 'We need to take her away to clear the area. I think you should go home now.'

Having forcibly to stifle her rising hysteria, May watched as they covered Betty's body and carried her away. This was the reality of war: people becoming objects to be moved off the streets along with all the other debris and rubbish. With tears streaming down her face, she started walking home. There would be no buses as the road was blocked by wreckage.

It was as though a huge chunk of her life had been stripped away and she could barely take it in. Anger rose at these terrible things that kept happening; they seemed so unjust and pointless. But uppermost in her mind was Joe. With his mother dead, his father away at the war, maternal grandparents who had never acknowledged him and a paternal grandmother who couldn't cope with young children, what was going to happen to him?

He slept in her bed beside her that night while she lay awake grieving and worrying. Mum and Dad had been frantic when she'd eventually got home, quite late because it was a long walk. They'd been shocked at the news, of course, and had told her that Joe had been unusually difficult at around the time Betty had died.

Pure coincidence, of course, but May couldn't help thinking that there would be more fretting to do for the poor little thing. But he would have her support through it all. Even if she hadn't made the promise to Betty she would have looked out for him. She was his godmother and she adored him.

Dot Bailey was visibly shaking after May told her the news.

'I can't believe it,' she said in a trembling voice. 'She'd only gone to Acton to see an old friend, hadn't she?'

The deceit had outlived the perpetrator, thought May, as she said, 'That's right, Mrs Bailey.' No one must ever know the real reason they were out last night. That was one secret that should be kept for the greater good.

'Ooh, I shall have to make some tea and bugger the rationing,' said the older woman, taking the kettle from the hob and filling it. 'I feel shaky and weak from the shock. I expect you could do with one as well.'

'Thank you.' May waited until they were sitting at the kitchen table with their tea before broaching the subject. 'Of course we shall have to decide what's going to happen about Joe, won't we, Mrs Bailey, with George being away,' she said. 'He's with my mum at the shop at the moment. I thought it best to break the news to you while you were on your own.'

'Yes, thank you, dear,' she said nervously.

'His other grandparents won't want to know,' May pointed out. 'So I am quite happy to look after him at home with us until his dad gets back. Mum and I would do it between us as we both work.'

Dot seemed a bit vague about this for a moment, stirring her tea and looking bewildered. Then she said, 'Thank you for offering, dear, but I'm his grandmother and his place is here with me.'

May was astonished and not at all happy with the idea. Dot was nervous and Joe was a boisterous little boy who needed a strong hand as well as love. 'But I thought you found looking after him too much for you,' she said.

'Yes, I always have in the past,' she confirmed. 'But I shall have to toughen up now that he needs me, won't I?'

'Well, yes . . . if you think you're up to it.'

'You don't think I can do it, do you?'

'It isn't that,' said May. 'It's just that you've always said he's too much for you, and Joe would sense any reluctance on your part and be upset.'

'I know he means the world to you and you're worried about him,' said the older woman. 'But I promise you that I will do everything I can to make sure my grandson has the best life I can give him until George gets back.'

May stared at her, noticing the resolution in her voice and perceiving something she had never seen in Mrs Bailey before: strength.

'I know I've been a bag of nerves since I lost my husband in such a terrible way and everybody thinks I'm a feeble old bat,' Dot went on. 'But I have been given a challenge now and I intend to rise to it.'

'Good for you,' said May.

'Of course, if Joe's adoring godmother wants to help me out now and again and offer some moral support, it will be very much appreciated.'

'I'll call round every day in my lunch hour to see how you're getting on,' said May. 'And I'll have him on my afternoon off or on Sundays to give you a break if you would like.'

'Thank you, dear,' said Dot, reaching over and putting her hand on May's. 'Together we'll get through this.'

May's eyes filled with tears. Suddenly she trusted Mrs Bailey. 'Yeah,' she said thickly. 'We will.'

There was only a small gathering for Betty's funeral. It had been arranged by her parents, who May didn't know well because Betty had never been allowed to have friends home as a child.

When May had delivered the news of their daughter's death to them, it was the first time she had ever had a conversation with them. They had just been the shadowy figures inside the house when she and Betty were children, as indeed most parents were. They must have recognised their duty in arranging this one last thing for their daughter, but there was no wake back at the house because of the rationing.

'That wasn't much of a send-off, was it?' said Sheila to May as they walked home together. Dot had stayed home with Joe, who they had considered to be too young to attend the funeral. 'I wasn't a particular fan of Betty's but surely they could have done better than that.'

'You can't put on a spread with rationing being as it is,' May pointed out. 'Anyway, they'd been estranged for years.'

'Mm, I suppose so,' said Sheila, who was on compassionate leave because of a death in the family. 'It's a shame George didn't make it. We did let the army know his wife had died but I suppose he's too far away to be able to get back.'

'Probably,' said May. 'He'll be worried about Joe, though, wondering who's looking after him.'

'Mm . . . and that's the biggest surprise I've had in years, Mum getting stuck in and making such a good job of it.'

'I was amazed when she said she would do it,' said May. 'I was quite prepared to have him but she insisted. I do take him off her hands on a regular basis, but I do that for me because I love to have him.'

'You'll be keeping your beady eye on her, I expect,' suggested Sheila.

'Not really,' said May. 'I thought I would need to, but she's doing really well.'

'It's taken something like this to get her back to her old self,' said Sheila. 'I knew she still had it in her. That's why I was always so impatient with her, because I knew it was possible for her to get back to how she'd been before.'

'Poor little Joe, though,' said May. 'It's heartbreaking when he cries for his mother.'

'Yeah, but because he's so little he'll soon forget, and he's got a good back-up team in you and Mum,' said Sheila. 'I'm sorry I'm not around to help.'

'Are you glad you joined up?' asked May.

'Yes and no. I miss the home comforts, of course, and it's a very hard life, but there's great comradeship and lots and lots of laughs,' she said.

'I thought about it myself but I know I wouldn't pass the medical,' said May.

'I've learned to drive and to weld and to use a type-writer. Chances I'd never have had before the war.'

'Yeah, that's one positive thing the war has done for women: given them jobs other than working in a shop and cleaning up after other people.'

'I think we would all rather not have had it, especially poor old Betty, but it's here and we have to put up with it.' Sheila thought for a while. 'Of course you've had a double blow, haven't you? First your intended, then your best friend.'

'It has been hard,' May told her. 'Of the two it's Betty I shall miss the most because we'd known each other all our lives and shared so many experiences. I don't quite know how I'm going to get through it, to tell you the truth.'

Sheila linked her arm through May's companionably. 'You'll do it,' she said warmly. 'You're the sort of person who will get through anything and come out smiling.'

'Really?' said May. 'How do you make that out?'

'TB, the loss of your brother, even before the latest disasters, and you're still game to fight another day.'

'I'd never thought about it in that way.'

'Well you can give yourself a pat on the back and that's definite,' Sheila said with a smile in her voice.

Those few words of encouragement raised May's spirits and renewed her strength. Betty's death had all but floored her, but now she felt as though she could carry on and win through.

'Thanks, Sheila,' she said, and they went on their way chatting pleasantly. May thought how far Sheila had come from that petulant child who was forever being horrid to her mother. Now she was remarkably mature for her eighteen years, which probably had something to do with being in the services.

The air raids eased off towards the end of the month and into February, something Londoners attributed to bad flying weather and the fact that the Luftwaffe were concentrating on provincial cities. Missing Betty and badly in need of a friend now that Sheila had gone back to camp, May took advantage of the lull in the bombing to get together with Connie again. They met on a Sunday at Marble Arch and had a walk through Hyde Park, which was awash with people in uniform.

'Betty wasn't what you could call the most loyal friend,' May confided as they walked at a steady pace, the weather cold but bright and clear, the silver barrage balloons gleaming in the pale sunshine. 'In fact she was a taker and out for herself and could drive me mad at times, but I miss her something awful and think I always will. We shared so much history, and for all her faults – and she knew she had them – she made me laugh.'

'That's what friendship is all about, isn't it?' said Connie. 'Liking someone warts and all.'

'Exactly,' said May. 'I probably got on her nerves at times.'

'None of us is perfect.'

May laughed. 'You were supposed to say that you were sure I didn't.'

'Ha ha, sorry,' she said. 'I'm not best known for my sense of diplomacy.'

'No you're not. I remember that from Ashburn. You always did say it like it was, especially with your predictions about Doug and me.'

'I was right too,' said Connie, adding more seriously, 'poor old Doug. He survived TB then fell victim to a bomb. Staying alive is such a matter of luck these days.'

'Not half,' said May and changed the subject quickly to raise the mood. 'Anyway, what have you been doing since we last met?'

'I've gone into war work.'

'Have you really?' said May in surprise. 'No problem with your medical history then?'

'No, probably because I'm not in munitions,' she explained. 'Anyway, they are so desperate for people now they can't afford to be too strict.'

'Where is the job?'

'In a parachute factory.'

'And you actually told them you'd had TB?'

She nodded. 'I was quite honest about it and expected the bloke to turn me down flat, but he thought about it for a while then said they wanted people to make parachutes and he thought I should be all right with that, especially as I'm very experienced with sewing machines.'

'A different attitude to before the war, then.'

'Absolutely,' she agreed. 'With so many men away at the war they have to cut a few corners, I think. You don't get a choice about where you work either. I'm based in Acton, which is fine for me, but I know people who have quite a journey to work. Some even have to leave their area and find lodgings.'

'Dad has to go a long way every day to the docks,' said May. 'It's right across London on the tube.'

It wasn't warm enough to sit by the lake, so they made their way back to Oxford Street and went into Lyons and had a cup of tea and a wartime bun.

'So you're single again then,' remarked Connie casually.

May nodded. 'Sadly, yes. How about you in the love-life department?' she asked.

'I met a really nice chap at a dance but he's a soldier and away at the war,' she said. 'I write to him regularly and we have a sort of understanding, but he isn't around so I'm free if you'd like company at any time. We could go to the pictures one night if you fancy it. Nearer to home than the West End might be better. Ealing Broadway is only a few stops on the train for me.'

'I'd like that,' said May.

No one would ever replace Betty, but having some female company of her own age did help to ease the aching loneliness of life without her long-term friend.

Chapter Twelve

It was generally thought that children were surprisingly resilient, and May saw proof of this when Joe's bewildered cries for his mother began to abate quite soon. He was, of course, very young, with a short memory span, which meant he might have very little recollection of Betty as he grew up. So once things had settled down after the death and she felt the time was right, May made a conscious effort to keep his mother's memory alive in a cheerful way by mentioning her in happy circumstances every now and again.

'Mummy would be so *proud* of you,' she would say if he did some praiseworthy little thing like standing still while she put his coat on, or not yelling when she washed his hair as she sometimes did to help his grandmother.

'Would she?'

'Oh yes; she'd want to know that her boy is being good,' she would assure him.

Such was the dialogue between them one blustery Wednesday afternoon in March when they were at the playground and he'd been down the slide for the first time sitting on her lap.

'I've broken all the playground rules by going on the slide with you, since I'm well over the age limit,' she told him chattily. 'But wasn't it fun, and your mummy would think you were such a brave boy.'

'Again,' was his beaming response.

She looked around furtively.

'I'll turn a blind eye,' said a young woman pushing a child on a swing.

'Thanks a lot,' said May, running after Joe, who was tearing towards the slide.

'Wheee,' she cried as they slid down together, both laughing with exhilaration at the bottom.

'Again,' said Joe.

'You'll have me at this all afternoon, you little perisher,' May said, grinning, completely engrossed in him. 'Once more, then, and it really will be the last one, I mean it.'

It was only then that she realised that they were not alone. She saw a pair of shiny black boots, and as her gaze moved upwards it rested on a tanned and smiling soldier.

'You always did like the slide,' he said. 'You've been down it a time or two on my lap.'

'George,' she gasped, welling up with emotion. 'How did you get here?'

'In the usual way, I walked in through the gates.' He threw his arms around her. 'Oh it's so good to see you, May.'

'Likewise.' She turned to see Joe about to climb the

slide steps on his own. 'Oh my Lord. Joe, no, come back.' She tore after him. 'Joe, Daddy is home. Come and see Daddy.'

But the child had only one thing on his mind, so she had to go down the slide with him again.

'Hello, Joe,' said George thickly when they got to the bottom, holding his arms out to his son.

Joe fixed him with a long, studious stare, then opened his mouth and emitted a scream of epic proportions, clinging on to May as though his life depended on it.

'He wasn't much more than a baby when you went away,' May reminded George when the child had finally calmed down and Flo had taken him into the Pavilion so that May and George could have a chat on their own, sitting on a bench near the swings. 'Children of that age have short memories, so it's only natural he wouldn't remember you.'

'I know,' sighed George. 'But I've been longing to see him and I wasn't planning on making him yell his head off.' He paused and she could see that he was desperately disappointed. 'I was so proud to see him, May. He's a proper little boy now.'

'Yes,' she said, wanting to howl with a mixture of joy at seeing George and sadness at Joe's reaction to him. 'He's a proper little boy all right and a very fine one too. He'll be three tomorrow.'

'I hadn't forgotten.'

'How long are you home for?'

'Ten days' compassionate leave. I should have been back for the funeral, but that's the war for you. By the time the news reached me, then the leave was arranged and they got me on to a boat, the whole thing was over and done with.'

'Thing aren't straightforward in wartime,' she said. 'But I'm sure you were there in spirit.'

'Of course,' he said in a serious tone. 'Poor Betty. It's such a shock and so dreadfully sad. It seems really odd to think that she isn't here any more. She was so young and had always been around, a part of our lives.' He paused thoughtfully. 'It must have hit you hard, May, having been best friends all your life.'

'Yes, it has been tough.'

He cleared his throat. 'Seeing you with Joe in the playground where we spent so much of our childhood was so . . . so comforting,' he said. 'Mum said you are an absolute godsend to her, so thanks for that. I've been worried sick about him, wondering who would look after him. But then I saw Mum and I couldn't believe the change in her.'

'So you can go back with an easy mind, though you've only just got here so you won't want to think about going back.'

'You're right about that.'

There was a silence, and tension drew tight. They each knew what was on the other's mind.

'Mum said you were with Betty when it . . . er, happened,' George said at last.

'That's right.'

'Did she suffer?'

May had a vivid flashback to that terrible night, the blood and the grimness of Betty's death and the events preceding it. 'Not for very long,' she said, managing to keep her voice steady. 'It was all over quite quickly.'

'Hit by debris, Mum said.'

'That's right.' He would never hear from her of what else had ailed Betty at the time of her passing. 'It hit her head.' She swallowed hard. 'A very deep wound.'

He reached across and put his hand on hers in a gesture of comfort. Neither of them spoke; there was no need.

Joe flatly refused to go home with his father on his own, so May went with them, the boy clutching her hand.

'He'll come round,' she said to George encouragingly. 'When he's had time to get used to having you home.'

'By that time I'll be due to go back.'

'Don't talk daft,' she said. 'You're George Bailey. You could persuade Hitler himself to surrender if you could get near enough to him. I'm sure you can make your charm work on a three-year-old boy.'

'If I don't, it won't be for want of trying.'

They walked on in silence for a while, then May said, 'What's it like being at the war?'

'Hot,' he replied.

'I know that, but is it terrible, the fighting I mean?'

'We manage,' he said, and moved on swiftly. He didn't want to think about the fierce, inescapable sandstorm that had howled around them for days in the desert and penetrated the nose, mouth, eyes and ears of men on both sides in the battle against the Italians for Tobruk. He didn't want to remember the noise of the guns or the deafening explosions or the dead soldiers on the barbed wire and strewn around on the ground. 'So what's been happening around here, apart from the air raids and the rationing and people getting killed long before their time?'

She realised that he was telling her he wasn't going to talk about his life as a soldier and would rather she didn't ask, so she brought him up to date with local news.

As they approached the Bailey home, Joe let go of May's hand and tore towards the house. 'Gran!' he shrieked, banging on the door with his fists because he couldn't reach the knocker. 'There's a soldier out here. Come quick.'

May couldn't help but laugh, and fortunately George saw the funny side too.

'You'd better start working your charm on him right away, I think,' she advised.

'It does look that way,' he agreed.

George had been watching May and Joe in the playground for a while before he'd made his presence known; just feasting his eyes on the pleasurable sight of a young woman and a small boy totally engrossed in each other, comfortable and happy together, all the more poignant as the boy had just lost his mother. Thank God for May, who seemed to get the balance of fun and authority just right. She played with him, but the boy knew he could only go so far. You could see the bond between them and it touched his heart. Seeing May coming down the slide with her blond hair flying had made him smile and swept away the years to those golden carefree days now gone for ever.

After the things he'd seen this last year or so, he knew there was no going back to more innocent times. The world had changed. Even here at home the evidence of brutality was all around in shattered buildings and bomb craters. But one thing that shone through the violence and hatred of war was human spirit. He'd experienced it first hand in his comrades in battle and he could see it here at home. People carried on against all the odds.

Catering for a children's party in wartime required a great deal of imagination. But between them Dot Bailey and May managed to provide a spread of sorts for Joe's third birthday that included low-on-points pilchard sandwiches, banana spread made from parsnips and banana essence and a birthday sponge cake produced without eggs and iced with some precious melted chocolate mixed with dried milk.

'Give little kids other little kids to play with and a few toys to fight over and they're happy whatever you give them to eat,' observed May after tea, when the children, all little boys, started rushing around, play-fighting boisterously and filling the house with more noise than a schoolyard at playtime.

'That's true,' agreed Dot. 'But they're getting a bit too wild now. We'll have to organise a game to calm them down before somebody gets hurt.'

'Right, you lot,' said George commandingly, stepping into the centre of the room. 'Stop.'

No one took any notice.

'Shut up. Now,' he said, increasing the volume to a shout. Silence fell.

'Good. That's better,' he approved. 'Now, hands up all those who would like to play a game.'

A forest of hands went up.

'Right, that's the stuff. We'll have musical chairs,' he said with his sister's wind-up gramophone in mind. 'Nobody move until we've put the chairs out.'

They all stood reverently still while the adults got the game organised. Then a little voice said proudly and with a proprietorial air, 'That's my dad.'

Standing back while May and George organised the game, Dot was treasuring the joy of having her son home and being involved in Joe's party. Not so long ago she'd thought she would never feel part of anything again, or enjoy life even to a small degree. But here she was in the midst of it and happy.

To this day she didn't know how she had done it. It had just sort of happened. When Betty died, she'd felt duty-bound to look after Joe but had been terrified at the idea to the point of feeling physically incapable. Even after she'd taken on the job it had still seemed beyond her until she had realised that she was actually doing it, despite her lack of confidence. Maybe she didn't get it right all the time, and sometimes she did still feel very nervous, but Joe seemed to thrive and her involvement had turned out to be her release from the prison she'd been in since her husband's murder.

She had become a useful member of the human race again and it felt good. Of course she did have a great deal of outside help from May, and she really valued that. Together they would bring up Joe while he needed them.

'Have we got anything we can give the winner as a prize, Mum?' George was saying.

'Yes, I've got a few jelly babies,' she replied.

There were shrieks of delight, but the real highlight of the party came a bit later when George took all the boys into the street with an old football of his. They all loved this.

'I think George has probably won Joe over now, don't you?' Dot said to May.

'Yeah, it certainly looks like it.'

'It's a shame he has to disappear again so soon.'

'It certainly is,' said May, feeling a shadow fall over the afternoon.

'It will be harder for him to bond with the boy as Joe gets older if he's away for long periods,' said Dot.

'We'll just have to hope and pray that this war comes to an end before too long,' said May.

But they both knew these were just empty words, because there was no sign of an end to the hostilities.

Both May and Dot were hoping that there wouldn't be an air raid during George's leave, because it would only enhance his worries about going back and leaving them if he actually experienced a raid first hand. But on the penultimate night of his leave the siren wailed its miserable message and Dot went through the usual procedure of collecting gas masks, coats, blankets, pillows and ration books, heading off into the Anderson and making up a bed for Joe.

'You're very organised and matter-of-fact about it all, Mum,' George remarked as they settled down in the candlelight.

'Not really,' said Dot. 'But we are used to the raids now, so it's an automatic procedure.'

'Bangs in a minute,' said Joe. 'Will there be shrapnel, Gran? The big boys like that.'

'I expect so, darlin',' said Dot. 'Let's get you settled down, then you can have a story.'

'I want my daddy to read the story,' said the boy.

'All right, son,' agreed George, picking up the book of fairy tales. 'Which one do you want?'

'Riding Hood,' said Joe, settling down under the blanket.

'Riding Hood it is then,' said George.

The planes came over with all the usual heart-stopping thumps and explosions. Dot assured her grandson that

297

nothing bad was going to happen to them and the boy accepted it without question. George thought his mother was probably terrified, but there was no outward sign of this; just a grim kind of acceptance. George had seen bravery on the battlefield but he knew he was witnessing courage here tonight. Mum didn't even have Sheila as support now, so when he wasn't here it was just her and a small child in the shelter. It was a very upsetting thought.

By the time the all-clear went, Joe was fast asleep. The trio made their way back to the house and George put his son into bed with barely a whimper from the boy.

'Fancy a cup of cocoa, love?' asked his mother when he came back downstairs.

Hesitating for only a moment, he said, 'Yes please, Mum, that would be grand.' He would much rather have gone to the pub for a pint and some male company, but his mother needed him in the short time he was home. He couldn't offer her much in the way of support, things being as they were, but he could give her his company when he was around.

On Saturday afternoon George called at the Pavilion with Joe to say goodbye to May and her parents.

'It's been good to see you again, son,' said Dick, who had the afternoon off from his job at the docks. 'You take care of yourself out there and come back soon.'

Customers wished him well — anyone in uniform was

warmly treated – then May's father took over from her at the counter so she could say her goodbyes.

'So you're off again,' she sighed as they ambled almost automatically towards the playground with Joe running on ahead.

'Yeah, the leave has flown by, but at least it gave me a chance to see everyone and make sure all was well with Mum and Joe,' he said. 'Thanks for being so good with him.'

'I'm his godmother; what else would I do?' she said. 'Anyway, I adore him so I love to be with him.'

'Yeah, I can see that,' he said. 'So what do you in your spare time apart from helping look after my son?'

'I do my bit for the war effort, knitting for the troops, fire-watching and so on.'

'Mm.' He looked at her. 'But now that both Doug and Betty have gone, what do you do for fun?'

'Not a lot,' she replied. 'I do go to the pictures some-times of an evening with a friend I met in the sanatorium. She's the same age as me.'

'At least you have some young company, then.'

She nodded. 'Oh yes. Don't worry about me. You've got enough on your mind with a war to fight.'

A swing became free, so George put Joe on it and gave him a gentle push, whereupon the boy squealed with delight.

'He's great, isn't he?' said George.

'Absolutely.'

'I wonder how old he'll be when I see him again.'

'Maybe you'll get another leave before too long.'

'It will be a while, I expect,' he told her. 'I only got home this time because poor Betty died.' He sighed heavily and shook his head. 'I still can't get used to the idea.'

'Me neither. Still, let's hope that next time you're on leave it isn't in such sad circumstances,' she said hopefully.

'Mm.' He pushed the swing, looking around. 'This place . . . the swings and the Pavilion, it's ingrained in my mind. When I think of home, I think of here.'

'Probably because we spent so much time here when we were growing up.' May smiled. 'In fact we were probably here for more of our childhood than we were at home.'

Yeah,' he said, smiling. 'Happy times.' Then he frowned, remembering the trauma of his father's death. 'Most of it, anyway.'

'Good grief! Neither of us is even twenty-one yet; we shouldn't be looking back,' May pointed out. 'That's something people do when they get older.'

'You're right; nostalgia is further down the line for us. Young people usually look to the future and the adult adventure ahead of them.' He gave a wry grin. 'I suppose we didn't bargain on an adventure like the war. It's being away from home, I think. It makes you reflective before your time.'

May wanted to weep at the sadness of parting, both at a personal level and for little Joe. But she just said, 'You're probably right. Still, at least now you can rest assured that your Mum and I will take very good care of Joe. I'll drop you a line every so often to let you know how he is. I'll get the address from your mum.'

'Thanks, May. I'd like that.' The truth was, he wanted to make love to her whenever he was around her now. All the innocent schoolboy hugs had to stop; it was just too tormenting. They were adults and both newly bereaved, and anything like that was out of the question. He'd lost his chance with her when he betrayed her with Betty, so just friends they must remain. 'I'd better be on my way, if I can get that son of mine off the swing.'

They collected a reluctant Joe and May walked to the end of the street with them. Then, after a brief peck on the cheek from George, she watched until they were out of sight. Joe was too young to understand why people he loved disappeared out of his life. He would learn to get used to it, but he would miss his father for a while.

Feeling dreadfully sad, she walked back to work at the Pavilion, telling herself to snap out of it.

One day in April, May said to her mother, 'I shall have to sign on for war work now. All young women without dependent children have to by law.'

'Yeah, I heard about the new law, but it won't apply to you because of your medical history.'

'I shall still have to register so that my case can be considered,' May explained. 'I wanted to tell you just in case they do send me on to essential war work. We shouldn't have a problem finding someone to take my place at the Pavilion if that were to happen. Older women aren't obliged to register at the moment, so there should be a few who might want to work with you.'

'I hope it doesn't come to that,' said Flo. 'You and I are such a good team.'

'Yes, Mum, we are, but we have to do what we're told in wartime,' said May.

The Labour Exchange was filled with women waiting to register for war work.

'Best thing that's happened to me in years,' said a woman in the queue in front of May. 'My husband can't stop me going out to work now that Mr Bevin has made it law. Thank Gawd for that. It will be lovely to get out of the house and have a bit of dosh in my purse again.'

This was the general mood among the women, some of whom had been forced to resign from their jobs on getting married. Until now it simply wasn't done for a decent married woman to go out to work. Now they could be put in prison for not having a job if they were eligible, and the age range for compulsory war work was expected to widen if the war continued.

When May's turn came, she was told by the clerk that her details would be put on record but she was unlikely to be called up for work in a factory because of her medical history.

She felt relieved in a way because she knew that work in the munitions factories was punishing, but disappointed too, because she wanted to do her bit and the idea of working with younger women appealed to her. Oh well, she'd done her duty and registered, that was the important thing.

Although the air raids had eased off in London by the spring of 1941, they hadn't finished completely. One night in April was so bad the Stubbses stayed in the Anderson until the early hours, hearing through the grapevine the next day that ten local people had been killed. There was also a rumour about St Paul's Cathedral being hit.

But somehow life went on and people did their best to keep their spirits up. May still called at the Bailey home regularly and made sure she took an active part in Joe's life.

The Pavilion continued to be a favourite meeting place for locals, and May found the company a great comfort. When the shop and the café were full of people chatting, she felt almost invincible. After a night spent in the shelter with nerves stretched to breaking point, the everyday dialogue – sometimes spiced with gossip involving a spot of adultery in the neighbourhood – was a tonic. Its ordinariness in the midst of these extraordinary and dramatic times had a therapeutic effect.

'At least the weather is getting better now that we are into May,' said one cheerful soul. 'It isn't quite so perishin' cold in the shelter and we've got the summer to look forward to.'

'On the other hand, clear skies mean good flying weather for the bombers,' said a pessimist.

'Ooh, cheer us up why don't you?' retorted the optimist drily.

Everyone laughed and the conversation turned to food and how to make it go further. Someone said they'd queued for two hours the other day for a piece of fish, which wasn't rationed, and another mentioned that a friend of a friend had managed to obtain that most precious of edibles, an onion. They also discussed what was on at the pictures and on the wireless, running through their favourite bits of *ITMA*, which was popular with the nation in general.

'I don't know what we'd do without this place,' said one of the customers in the queue. 'Coming in here of a morning after a bad night makes me feel human again.'

'Hear, hear,' said someone else. 'Bless you, Flo and May, for being here.'

People murmured in agreement, then someone brought them all back down to earth by saying in a jokey manner, 'Give over, it's our money they're after.'

There was a general chuckle, which saved the company from sinking into sentimentality.

'Who's next, ladies?' said May, because she and her mother had to keep working as well as take part in the conversation. 'Come on, let's get this queue moving.'

One night in May there was a full moon and the bombing was relentless. The Stubbses were settled in the shelter with a pot of tea and some wartime biscuits, which tasted a bit like dust and dried-up porridge. May and her mother knitted in the candlelight while her father tried to read the paper in the flickering candle glow.

The noise was deafening and the explosions sounded very close indeed.

'It's a bomber's moon tonight all right,' said Dick. 'And they are making the most of it.'

'They do sound very near,' said May.

'Probably a few miles away,' suggested Flo. 'You know how deceiving the noise can be.'

'Someone local is getting it, that's for sure,' said May. 'And human nature being what it is, we are all praying it won't be us . . . or Dot and Joe.'

The night wore on and May was stiff and chilly and longing for the all-clear. Surely it must come soon. Suddenly there was the most tremendous crash and she said, 'That really was close. I'm going up to see if the house is still standing.'

Waiting a few minutes for the noise of the plane to grow fainter, they all climbed out of the shelter to see with relief that the house was indeed still there, as were those around it. No sooner had they got back into the shelter, however, than the voice of the air-raid warden, who lived nearby, drifted down to them.

'Flo, Dick!' he shouted. 'The Pavilion has copped it.'

'Oh bloody hell,' said Dick. He started to climb up to ground level, followed by his wife and daughter. After hearing that news, none of them were prepared to wait for the all-clear.

★　★　★

It was the middle of the night, but news still travelled fast and there were quite a few people hurrying towards what had once been the Pavilion. The street was littered with the remains of the stock – broken biscuits, battered tinned goods – and May spotted someone picking up a packet of cigarettes. People would grab what they could; it was only human nature in hard times, and she tried not to be upset by it.

In the brilliant light of the moon May and her parents could see that the Pavilion and the playground had both been completely demolished. All that was left was a smoking bomb crater. Being of a wooden construction, the Pavilion had been burned to a cinder. People just stood looking at the firemen working with their hoses, then, having offered their regrets to the Stubbses, they began to drift away. No one even noticed the all-clear.

'Heartbreaking, isn't it?' said Flo early the next morning as she and May stood looking at the bombsite, still smoking slightly, mangled pieces of wood and iron from the playground lying around along with broken chairs and tables from the café, dust everywhere. 'All that work, for nothing.'

'We'll rebuild it, Mum,' said May, determinedly positive. 'The government give people compensation for war damage. We'll use that to pay for it.'

'We won't be allowed to rebuild it because of the wartime regulations,' Flo reminded her.

'Not now, but eventually we will,' said May encouragingly.

'After the war, when the ban on building is lifted, we'll build a better Pavilion than ever, I promise you. As soon as it's possible, we'll have another café here on this exact same spot.'

'In the meantime, people won't half miss it,' said Flo tearfully.

'They will and all.'

'It was more than just a building,' said Flo.

'I know it was, Mum,' said May, putting her arm around her mother. 'But at least there was no loss of life; we have to be very thankful for that.'

'Yeah, I know,' said Flo. 'It was just that I absolutely loved running that place.'

'And you will do again. One day after the war, you and I will be working together again in a place as much like the Pavilion as we can get it.'

'The playground's gone as well,' said Flo. 'Where will the kids play now?'

'In the street, on the bombsite when it's cleared, anywhere,' said May. 'They won't have swings but they'll still find somewhere to play. Kids always do.'

'Yeah, I suppose so,' Flo agreed tearfully, linking arms with her daughter. 'Let's go home and have a cup of tea and work out what to do next.'

Together they walked home.

As it happened, they soon had a diversion that took their minds off their own problems. Shortly after they got home, they had an unexpected visitor.

'Connie,' said May, answering the door and seeing a dishevelled figure standing there. 'What are you doing here?'

'We've been bombed out,' she explained. 'Mum and Dad and the others have gone to various relatives, but they're very overcrowded, so I wondered if I could stay with you until they find us somewhere to live. I remember you saying you had a spare room that Doug used to have when he stayed over.'

'Stay for as long as you like, dear,' welcomed Flo, who had come up behind May.

'I'll pay rent,' said Connie.

'No you will not,' said Flo, ushering her inside. 'You can pay for your keep like May does, but no more than that.' She looked at Connie. 'As long as you've got your ration book.'

'That was in the shelter with me,' she assured her. 'Mum always takes them down with us.'

'Lucky you were all in the shelter when your house was bombed,' Flo remarked.

'We weren't all down there,' Connie said, her voice breaking. 'My grandad hates the shelter so he stays in the house when there's a raid.'

'Oh, so . . . ?'

'Grandad was . . . he was killed,' said Connie, and dissolved into tears.

Losing the Pavilion didn't seem nearly so bad suddenly, thought May as she comforted her friend. Material things could be replaced; people couldn't.

★　★　★

'I'll have to get to work soon,' said Connie when she had calmed down and had something to eat.

'What! Even when you've been bombed out and lost your grandad?' queried Flo.

'Oh yes, production has to go on no matter what when you're on war work. The country would grind to a halt if everyone who's been bombed out stayed at home,' she told them. 'I had a bit of a wash at the rest centre, but my clothes are dusty and I've only got what I'm wearing. Everything inside the house has gone.'

'I'll fix you up with something to wear,' May offered. 'You and I are about the same size.'

'They give extra clothing coupons to people who have been bombed out, I believe,' Flo mentioned.

'Yeah, the WVS woman at the rest centre said something about that,' said Connie. 'I'll look into it when I get a chance.'

'And I shall have to get off down to the Labour Exchange now that I don't have a job,' said May.

'Mm, I suppose you will,' agreed Connie. 'It's a real shame about the Pavilion.'

The other two women nodded, though compared to Connie, who had no home, no clothes and no grandfather, their loss seemed minimal.

'They often need people where I work,' Connie remarked thoughtfully.

'I don't know one end of a sewing machine from the other,' said May.

'You could learn,' suggested Connie.

'Sewing is one thing I really hate,' said May. 'I never have been any good at it.'

'Personal taste isn't a consideration,' Connie reminded her. 'We all have to do what we're told for the war effort.'

'I know,' said May, feeling guilty for mentioning it. 'I'll see what they have to say at the Labour Exchange. But first I'll find you something to wear.'

'And I'll make the bed up for you, Connie,' added Flo. 'You must look on the place as your home.'

Connie became tearful again, but this time it was caused by appreciation of their kindness.

'So you're twenty years old, have only ever done shop work and have a history of illness,' said the man at the Labour Exchange when he finally found May's details in a huge metal filing cabinet.

'I've had TB, which left me with a crooked shoulder, but that's no problem to me at all,' she said, though her upper arm did occasionally ache. 'Nothing else of a serious nature, so I don't think that can be described as a history of illness.'

'It means you're not suitable for work in a munitions factory, though,' said the man, who had greased hair parted in the middle and spectacles.

'What about the Websters parachute factory at Acton?' she suggested bravely. 'They often want people there, so I've heard. My friend works there and she's had TB.'

'Handy with a sewing machine, are you?'

310

'No.'

'You won't be much use to them then, will you?' he said.

'I could learn.'

'They are not looking for trainees at the moment,' he informed her. 'They wouldn't be prepared to teach you.'

That was actually a huge relief, because May knew her limitations when it came to sewing. 'I would like to do some sort of war work,' she said.

He looked at her over his spectacles. 'I'd like to do a lot of things but I'm stuck with this job,' he said.

'I just meant that I'd like to do something useful,' she said. 'I don't mind what it is.'

'Most jobs are useful in wartime, miss; we all have our part to play, even me.'

'Besides which, I need to earn some money, as my income was another casualty of war.'

'Yes, yes,' he said, flicking through some cards in a box file and pulling one out. 'Mm, there is something here that might suit you. As a matter of fact it's at the parachute factory that you mentioned, but in the office.'

'Oh Lor,' said May worriedly. 'I don't know anything about clerical work.'

He gave her a withering look that indicated that he thought she must be devoid of any useful assets before turning his attention back to the card. 'It's only routine office work; no shorthand or typing needed. Nothing too strenuous for someone with your health problems.'

311

'I don't have health problems,' she told him again.

He sighed dismissively. 'So you say. '

'I'm in excellent shape actually,' she persisted.

'Mm.' He clearly wasn't interested. 'Anyway, if you are found suitable you'll be taught how to do the work.' He picked up the phone and dialled, then told someone at the other end that he had a possible candidate for the office vacancy. 'They will see you at two o'clock this afternoon,' he said to May when he'd finished speaking on the phone. He wrote something down on an official-looking card. 'Take this along with you to the interview. The address and the name of the person you need to see are on here.'

'Thank you.'

'Good day to you,' he said, and even before she had got up he called out, 'Next please.'

How suddenly your life can change so completely, thought May, as she headed home. This time yesterday she had been safely installed behind the counter of the Pavilion. Now that no longer existed and she was heading off to pastures new. Oh well, it will be a challenge, she thought, determinedly optimistic despite the fact that any form of office work was a foreign country to her.

Chapter Thirteen

'So, Miss Stubbs, as you will have been told at your interview, you will be doing routine office work here at Websters. Your job will involve filing and operating the switchboard,' said the head of the department, Miss Palmer, a stout middle-aged woman with chaotic grey hair, sagging breasts and a scrubbed-clean complexion. 'A good telephone manner is essential for every caller and the filing must be kept up to date in the cabinets next to your desk. It mustn't be allowed to build up; we keep a tidy office here and everything has to be filed away so that it can be found quickly if necessary.'

Dressed in the sombre clothes she used to wear for work at the department store, May stared in bewilderment at the contraption in the corner of the large office, a board impregnated with holes in which a tangle of wires were plugged. A woman in headphones – who was apparently filling in until May took over – was manipulating the wires and saying in an affected voice things like 'Good morning, Websters' and 'Putting you through' and 'The line is engaged at the moment, would you like to hold?'

'Don't look so worried, my dear,' said Miss Palmer, who seemed friendly enough if a little stern. 'You'll soon get the hang of it.'

May wasn't so sure. It looked very complicated indeed to her.

'Phew, what a morning. I'll probably be sacked by the time we knock off tonight,' May confided to Connie in their dinner break in the canteen. They were encouraged to use it because it helped with the rationing at home. 'I'm hopeless on the switchboard. I've been pulling out the wrong plugs and cutting people off in mid conversation as well as connecting callers incorrectly. And how I'm supposed to find time for the filing I've no idea, as the switchboard never seems to stop.'

'Everything will slot into place once you get used to the job, I expect,' encouraged Connie.

'I flippin' well hope so. I really am like a fish out of water at the moment,' she said. 'I've never done this sort of work before.'

'It does sound rather complicated, I must say,' admitted Connie. 'I'm glad I'm in the factory. At least I know what I'm doing.'

'I'd be even worse in there, as I'm hopeless at sewing,' said May. 'That's what comes of working in the family business. You get used to not having anyone standing over you and telling you what to do. It's too comfortable and you lose confidence so far as other work is concerned.'

'Mm,' said Connie, finishing off some sort of wartime shepherd's pie made with lumpy mashed potato mixed with swede. 'Before the war, office girls used to be quite snooty. But all of that has changed now that people from all classes are doing their bit. We've got a couple of really posh women working with us. They're all right once you get to know them.'

May became overwhelmed with a sudden feeling resembling homesickness, a kind of dull ache in the pit of her stomach which made her eyes burn.

'What's up?' asked Connie, noticing.

'I know that there are lots of people worse off than I am; you, for instance, have lost your home and your grandad,' she said, tears meandering down her cheeks. 'But I feel so alone, Connie, in an environment I'm not used to. I know this will sound really pathetic, but I think I'm homesick for the Pavilion. It was more a way of life than a job.'

'We are still allowed to feel sorry for ourselves about small things, you know,' said Connie. 'We aren't expected to keep a stiff upper lip about everything just because there's a war on and awful things are happening. Anyway, you've had your share of losses. Your best friend, your fiancé. And you were probably too busy putting on a brave face to grieve properly back then.'

May thought there was something in that. She had never let her true feelings show about either of those traumas, maybe because she hadn't wanted people to worry about her. Or it could just have been that her illness had left her with a hatred of pity.

She blew her nose. 'Thanks for being such a pal,' she said. 'Maybe things will fall into place this afternoon.'

'That's more like the May I know,' said Connie.

By the end of the afternoon May was beginning to feel slightly less bewildered, and by the evening her spirit had returned full blast.

'I actually managed to put some calls through properly and didn't cut anyone off this afternoon,' she told her mother.

'Well done, love,' said Flo heartily. 'I've got some news of my own, actually.'

Both May and Connie waited expectantly.

'Two bits of news actually,' she said. 'I've got a part-time job on the counter in the Co-op, and I've managed to transfer our newsagent's licence from the Pavilion to home.'

'Well done, Mum,' said May. 'So we'll still be taking it in turns to get up with the lark to do the papers.'

'I can do it every day as I'm only working part-time hours if you like,' offered Flo.

'Not on your life,' May responded. 'You run the house as well as having a job outside, so you need your rest on some mornings at least. Turns each is fair.'

'If you insist, then thank you, dear,' said Flo gratefully. 'I think I'll start looking out for some paper boys to do the rounds again soon as I'll be earning, so at least we won't have to trail round the streets of a morning.'

'I'm all for that,' approved May.

The night the Pavilion was bombed – a night that caused death and destruction all over London – marked the end of the air raids for the time being, much to the relief of the population at large. No one knew for how long the respite would last, but everyone enjoyed sleeping in their own beds again.

The shortages worsened, though, with clothes going on to ration in June.

'White weddings will soon be a thing of the past, I reckon,' remarked Flo one evening after the latest restrictions had been announced on the wireless. 'Something like a traditional wedding dress would take far too many coupons. People are committed to the war effort so it would be considered too extravagant.'

'People will borrow their frocks, I expect,' suggested May. 'Women will always want to dress up on their wedding day.'

'Parachute silk makes up into lovely bridal wear,' Connie remarked. 'But it's all used for military purposes. The only way you can get hold of any, apart from paying a fortune on the black market, is if you spot a parachute mine the day after a raid. Finders keepers with that.'

'It makes nice petticoats too, so I've heard,' said Flo.

'Do they let you have any offcuts, Connie?' May enquired.

'Not on your life, and if one of the girls tries to take so much as a scrap out of the factory, there's hell to pay,' she replied. 'They keep a close eye on stealing. The temptation will be even greater now that clothes are on ration.'

There was an interruption from the man of the house. 'If you'll excuse me, ladies, I'm going out to the garden to give my vegetable patch some attention,' he said.

'Too much women's talk, eh?' said Flo.

'Not half. Three to one means I don't stand a chance,' he said in a jovial manner, adding quickly, 'but we love having you here, Connie. You're a real tonic for May.'

'Thank you, Mr Stubbs,' smiled Connie.

It was true what he said. May did enjoy having Connie around because it was company of her own age, and they often talked well into the night. Besides which, it was someone to go to the pictures with and not have to come home on your own in the blackout. Connie fitted in with the family as though born to it.

'One thing the war has done for that husband of mine is to give him a serious interest in gardening,' said Flo. 'He's done wonders with his vegetable patch.'

'It's more than a patch now, Mrs Stubbs,' said Connie. 'It's the size of a lawn.'

Flo laughed. 'It *was* the lawn until the government told us to grow our own.'

Both the the girls laughed, then they all started clearing up after the meal.

May had always wished she had a sister. Having Connie staying with them made her feel as though she had.

One positive element about fighting the war in the desert, thought George, was the fact that there were no civilians around to become accidentally involved. It was generally considered by the men to be a 'clean war'.

Having been sent to the Middle East quite soon after he'd done his basic training, and served in several different areas involved in various campaigns, George was hardened to desert life and his comrades were almost like family. Among the men there was a great deal of affection and humour, interspersed with the odd conflict and show of bad temper.

In the cool of the evening the men played cards, smoked cigarettes and wrote and read letters. Letters from home were much treasured by all of the soldiers, and George's mail had increased now that May wrote to him as well as his mother.

He read May's letters over and over again, their content usually dominated by news of Joe, which was the whole idea of their correspondence. She did mention that the Pavilion had been bombed but no one had been hurt, and in true Stubbs' style she spoke of her determination to rebuild it after the war.

Living so close to death made the fragility of life

omnipresent in his mind. Because of this he made a decision one night in the late summer of 1941. He decided to write a very important letter.

Life fell into a routine for May as she settled into the job and began to enjoy it, especially as she got to know her colleagues and stopped feeling like an outsider. Her telephonist duties entailed dealing with members of the management, who were based in offices around the factory and called on her throughout the day for their telephone needs. The phone numbers of the people they would need to call in the line of business were listed in a book close to hand near the switchboard, so May was able refer to this and connect them speedily.

All long-distance calls had to be logged, which entailed her calling the GPO after the call to find out the duration and charge, which would eventually be checked against the phone bill by the accounts department. If someone asked for an outside line it meant it was a personal call at the firm's expense, but as these people were all superior to her in rank it wasn't her place to ask questions. She was merely 'May on the switchboard'.

The management was entirely male and middle aged, and pleasant enough in their dealings with May. But there was a Mr Saxon – the head of the purchasing department – who she couldn't bear on account of his condescending attitude towards her. He was an aggravation too because he frequently made personal calls, which meant she was kept waiting for an outside line to keep up to date with her list of outgoing calls. On the whole, though, she didn't have any trouble and she enjoyed the work, even though she still missed the Pavilion.

At least once a week she and Connie went to the cinema, and having got used to the lack of air raids, sometimes Flo went to the pub with her husband on a Saturday night. Another wartime Christmas passed and Joe had his fourth birthday. May's twenty-first birthday passed quietly. She didn't want much of a celebration because it would have been Betty's twenty-first too. So her parents gave her a watch and her mother made a wartime birthday cake and they left it at that.

Then one day soon after her birthday, something magical happened to May. She received a letter from George, dated last September, explaining how he felt about her in case the worst happened and she never got to know. He asked nothing of her but spoke of how his feelings for her had changed from childish affection to deep adult love. He was in love with her.

'What's got into you?' asked Connie as they headed to the bus stop to go to work. 'You look as though you've lost a penny and found a fortune.'

'I haven't lost a penny,' she said. 'But I have been given more than a fortune.'

'It's something to do with that letter you got this morning, isn't it?' she guessed.

May nodded, her face wreathed in smiles.

'It was from your friend George, wasn't it?' guessed Connie.

'More than a friend now,' she beamed.

'Oh,' said Connie, unable to restrain a frown.

'What's the matter?' asked May. 'You don't look very happy about it.'

'Isn't he the one who married your best friend when you were ill?' she mentioned.

'That's right,' said May.

'Enough said, then.'

'That was then, this is now,' May reminded her.

'Yes, of course,' said Connie. She didn't want to spoil things for her friend. She herself was in no position to judge, since she had never even met George and could have no idea of their feelings for each other. Her only concern was that May didn't get hurt. 'Does he want the two of you to be together when he gets back, then?'

'He just wants me to know how he feels about me in case he doesn't come back,' she explained. 'That's enough for me for now, though of course I will write back and tell him how I feel. I've loved him all my life.'

'And Doug?'

'I cared for him deeply but there has never really been anyone else for me except George.'

'I hope it works out for you then,' said Connie, as the bus came and they moved with the queue towards it.

'For the moment, I'm happy knowing what I know,' May said, hopping on to the platform, feeling cherished and special. With George's love to cheer and sustain her, no problem seemed insurmountable.

★　★　★

'Grandma, come quick,' shrieked Joe one Saturday afternoon in summer, banging on the front door with his fists. 'I can do it. I can do it. Come and have a look.'

The door opened. 'What's going on out here?' asked Dot in concern. 'What's all this noise?'

'Show her, Joe,' urged May. 'Let her see what you can do.'

Cheeks glowing and shandy-coloured eyes shining with excitement, he clambered on to a small bicycle May had managed to get for him second hand and rode off without any help from May, who had been teaching him.

'Oh well done,' praised Dot.

'Isn't he clever?' enthused a delighted May. 'I've told him that now he's got his balance he'll be able to ride a bike for ever. It's something you never lose.'

'Can I ride to the end of the street?' asked Joe, keen to try out his new skill.

'Better than that,' suggested May. 'Why don't we go to the park and you can ride your bike there?' She paused, looking at Dot. 'Maybe Grandma will come too.'

'Yeah!' cried the boy. 'Will you come, Gran? I can show you proper then.'

'I was about to do some baking,' she began, then, infected by her grandson's sparkling enthusiasm, she added, 'All right then. Why not? I'll just take my pinny off.'

May was ridiculously proud of her godson's latest achievement. It was one of those golden moments she knew she would remember long after Joe had forgotten it. It was a pity that neither of his parents was around to see it. As a stab of sadness about his mother threatened to rise up and spoil the occasion, she comforted herself with the thought that she could write to George and tell him all about it.

Corresponding with him was her biggest joy in life and she couldn't wait to put pen to paper tonight. His letters took ages to reach her and were very irregular, which was understandable under the circumstances; sometimes several came all together after a long gap.

'He's coming on a treat,' Dot told May as Joe pedalled around the park, singing the wartime version of 'Under the Spreading Chestnut Tree' and showing off like mad. 'You've done a good job teaching him to ride at this early age. I never had a bike when I was a kid — we didn't in those days — so I still can't ride one to this day.'

'I'll teach you if you like, on mine,' offered May casually.

'I think I'll manage without that particular skill, dear, if you don't mind,' she said smiling. 'I'm a bit long in the tooth for that sort of carry-on.'

'You're never too old to learn, and that applies to most things,' said May. 'But I won't press you if you don't fancy it.'

Dot was watching her grandson riding round in circles with the confidence of a veteran.

'I never thought anyone could give me such joy as

Joe does,' she confessed emotionally. 'I thought my life had ended along with my husband's, but since I've been looking after Joe, I've changed my mind in a big way. He gave me back my confidence and my appetite for life.'

'I'm so glad, Mrs Bailey,' said May.

'He is so much like his dad at that age it's quite uncanny,' the other woman remarked. 'It sometimes feels as though I'm bringing George up all over again.'

'It's a pity George isn't here to see his boy growing up, and Betty too.'

The other woman sighed. 'Yeah, it's a sad old business all right,' she agreed. 'It's up to you and me to try to make it up to him. Fortunately the boy is young enough to adapt. I don't think he even remembers his mum, though I know you mention her from time to time to give him a little reminder.'

'Between us we'll get him through until his dad comes home,' said May.

'Let's hope it isn't too long before George comes back for good.' Dot turned to May. 'I'm so glad you're writing to him, dear. If the two of you get together when he comes home, you know you'll have my blessing.'

'Thank you,' said May, smiling at her. The truth was there didn't seem to be any sign of an end to hostilities; just more shortages of everything and yet more government slogans urging the British people to pull together for the war effort. The only really good news was the current lack of air raids on the home front and the fact that the Americans were now with the Allies in the war. Most people were heartened by this because of the sheer might of the United States. 'Nothing would make me happier, but there's a long way to go. We'll just have to wait and see.'

Generally speaking, at Websters parachute factory there was a good atmosphere. People had their differences, of course, but not usually anything that couldn't be put right. Not many days passed without some sort of a laugh and a joke in the office.

Then one day in the autumn of 1942 a cloud descended over the entire building when it was discovered that parachute silk was being stolen, for the black market it was thought as there was such a large amount unaccounted for. Suspicion immediately fell on the machinists because they were the ones with access to the material. Each one was summoned to the general manager's office to be questioned and urged to speak up about anything suspicious they'd seen, even if it did concern a friend. All conversations would be confidential.

Connie was distraught about the whole thing.

'I'm sure they think it's me who's stealing,' she said to May and her parents over their meal that evening. 'All the girls think the finger is pointing at them. It's causing a bit of an atmosphere at work and we're usually such a friendly bunch.'

'Have they involved the police?' Dick enquired.

'No, not yet,' replied Connie. 'They want to keep it

quiet for the sake of the firm's reputation so they are doing their own enquiries. But I ask you, Mr Stubbs, how could any one of us girls possibly get the amount of parachute silk that's unaccounted for out of the factory without anyone noticing?'

'I don't know what security precautions they have there, but I would think you couldn't,' he told her. 'Not unless they suspect that someone who knows the layout of the factory is getting in at night or something.'

'It can't be that because there's no sign of a break-in,' she explained. 'Anyway, whoever is doing it is costing the firm a lot of money.'

'They would do,' said Flo.

'I hope they don't cut our wage rate because of it,' said Connie. 'They can't get rid of us because the parachutes are in such demand.'

'They need to find out who's doing it and get it stopped sharpish so that you girls can get back to normal,' declared Flo.

'Personally, I think it's someone higher up in the company,' Connie mentioned. 'Someone with a key to the premises and contacts in the black market.'

'That's a good point,' said May. 'I wonder if they are considering that.'

'If they are, we won't get to hear about it,' proclaimed Connie. 'Not unless they actually find out who the culprit is, then we might be informed, though I expect they'll keep it quiet if one of the bosses is involved. Meanwhile we machinists feel as though we are living under a cloud.'

'Try not to let it upset you too much, dear,' urged Flo.

'Yes, you're right, Mrs Stubbs,' said Connie resolutely. 'I've survived TB and being bombed out, so I'm damned if I'm going to let this destroy me.'

'That's the spirit,' encouraged Flo. 'And as a treat to cheer you up, you can have a few more runner beans from Mr Stubbs' vegetable garden.'

'Ooh, how lovely,' whooped Connie. Extra food was always welcome, since hunger in varying degrees was a permanent state for most people. 'But what about everybody else?'

'I've had enough,' said Flo.

'Me too,' added the others. They all wanted to cheer Connie up.

'There's enough for you to have a few more too, May,' said Flo, going to the kitchen and returning with a saucepan.

'Thanks, Mum.' She looked at her father. 'You're doing really well with the vegetables, Dad. I didn't realise you had it in you. You never did more than keep the garden tidy before the war and you weren't always very up to date with that.'

'It makes a change from working with metal all day,' he said. 'I enjoy it.'

'Tell 'em what's next on your self-sufficiency agenda, Dick,' his wife urged.

'Chickens,' he announced. 'I'm going to get some chicks and rear them for the eggs.'

'Oh how lovely,' approved May. 'Lots of people do that

round here now. London is becoming quite a smallholding.'

'Needs must when the devil drives,' said her father. 'But I am rather looking forward to it.'

'We'll take it in turns to feed them,' offered Connie.

'I might hold you to that,' said Dick.

May thought how much a part of the family Connie had become. She would miss her when she left, though she might be here for a while yet, because the housing shortage was chronic in London with so many homes being lost to the Luftwaffe.

'We'll all help, Dad, since we'll all be having the benefit of the eggs,' said May.

'We'll see. I have to find the materials to build a chicken run first,' he said.

'As long as you don't ask us to eat the chickens,' said May, looking towards the windowsill, where the cat was lazing in the evening sun. 'That would be like eating Tiddles.'

There was a questioning silence as the three women stared at him.

'I haven't even made the damned chicken run yet,' said Dick defensively. 'But there is war on and food is very short.'

May didn't like the sound of that at all, but she didn't say any more on the subject for the moment.

Life and work went on at Websters and the mystery of the stolen material remained unsolved. According to rumour, the stealing had stopped so the subject was no longer the main topic of conversation in the office or the factory.

News from abroad took precedence when they heard of an offensive in the desert involving hundreds of thousands of Allied troops. May wondered if George was involved in the battle for El Alamein.

'If he is, he's got the best possible man in charge,' said one of the clerks when they were discussing it in the office. 'General Montgomery, or Monty as they call him. They reckon he's a marvellous soldier.'

'Mm,' said May, not at all comforted. 'I suppose the worst part is not knowing what's going on. He doesn't say anything about the war in his letters.'

'I think you might worry more if you did know what was going on,' suggested someone. 'At least we are spared the gory details.'

'There is that, I suppose,' May agreed, before her part in the conversation was terminated by every line on the switchboard lighting up and buzzing at the same time.

Flo and May were still delivering the papers, as they hadn't yet found any suitable boys for the job. May's round took her past the Pavilion bomb site, which was already covered in stinging nettles and rosebay willow herb. She assumed it would stay like this for the rest of the war, because any sort of private building or redevelopment was prohibited.

The mornings were cold now as the year headed

towards winter, but May still took the time to linger awhile here, something she often did when passing, and said a silent prayer for George and Betty. The only remaining landmark was the old horse chestnut tree nearby, from where they had gathered conkers as children. Everywhere was silent at this time of the morning and the air was imbued with the damp mist of autumn.

Into the stillness of her mind came the sound of children's voices: George, Betty and herself. This small area had once been vibrant and cheerful; kids playing, adults going to the Pavilion and chatting over a cup of tea. Now it was dead and sad; just another piece of waste ground created by the bombing.

One day it would be rejuvenated and returned to its former glory, she resolved as she went on her way to deliver the rest of the newspapers before going home for breakfast, her heavy bag slung over her shoulder.

Although the gossip and speculation about the silk stealing at the factory had abated, no one had forgotten it and until the culprit was named anyone was potentially a suspect. It was a moment of carelessness on May's part that finally solved the mystery and put her in a very difficult position.

The switchboard was busy that morning and May was working flat out. A familiar voice asked for Mr Saxon, and when she enquired 'Who's calling?' – a standard part of her duties – the reply came in the usual supercilious manner, 'It's a personal call.'

May put the call through and carried on working with her plugs and wires, connecting and disconnecting, being polite to callers, some of whom liked to remark on the weather or the war or anything at all. She must have accidentally nudged a lever, because she suddenly found herself listening on her headphones to Mr Saxon's conversation, something that was absolutely forbidden.

Before she had a chance to put the matter right, the subject under discussion made such compulsive listening that she stayed on the line, freezing with horror at what she heard.

'This is a very awkward situation you've put us in, Miss Stubbs,' said Miss Palmer when May told her what she'd heard. 'You've broken the terms of your employment here at Websters by listening in to the private conversation of a senior member of management. And, even worse, repeating it.'

May stared at her in disbelief. 'But they were talking about stealing silk, so I considered it my duty to listen for the sake of the company,' she said.

'I'm not sure if members of the hierarchy will see it like that,' said Miss Palmer.

'It was Mr Saxon all along doing the thieving, so surely he must be brought to justice,' pronounced May. 'The caller is obviously his black market contact; he was asking Mr Saxon about getting more material to him.'

The older woman mulled this over. 'You'd better tell

me exactly what was said,' she said eventually. 'Verbatim if you can remember, please.'

'Mr Saxon said he couldn't risk getting more silk for him at the moment because the other stuff had been noticed. The caller asked how that could be because the silk was delivered direct to him on the way to the factory, one or two rolls per delivery. It never even went through the factory, which is why no one saw it go. It was never here.'

Miss Palmer bit her lip worriedly. 'Yes, that does add up. The thefts were only noticed because the number of finished parachutes didn't match up with the amount of silk ordered,' she explained. 'Mr Saxon must have had an accomplice in Goods Inwards, who check deliveries with orders to make sure it's all there.'

'Anyway, the caller said that wasn't good enough because they had a firm agreement and he was supposed to get a regular supply and he had customers waiting,' said May. 'He wasn't happy and he sounded a bit threatening.'

'Good Lord,' said Miss Palmer.

'Mr Saxon said there would be more as soon as he thought it was safe to get it to him and the caller said he had better not leave it too long. So there you have it. We know who the culprit is, so he can be named and all the speculation can stop.'

'Hmm, it won't be quite as easy as that,' Miss Palmer said thoughtfully. 'This is a tricky one.'

'Why?'

'Because Mr Saxon is a highly respected member of the management, and you are just the switchboard girl,' stated the older woman.

'What difference does that make?' asked May naively. 'He's a thief whatever class bracket he's in.'

'It will be your word against his, and apart from anything else, you will be in trouble for making the accusation,' Miss Palmer explained.

'I'd sooner lose my job than let him get away with it, especially as the machinists are all under suspicion,' May told her.

'That's all very well, my dear, but things could get very unpleasant indeed for you, and as the head of the department it's my job to protect you.'

'I don't want protecting, I want justice,' declared May. 'Anyway, it isn't just an accusation. It's true. I heard it loud and clear. The man is a thief and he'll do it again as soon as he thinks it's safe.'

'But it is all just hearsay,' said Miss Palmer. 'We have no evidence and Mr Saxon will deny it if challenged to save his own skin.'

'Surely you are going to report it to someone on the management, Miss Palmer,' said May.

The other woman mulled it over. 'I'm not sure what I'm going to do about it at the moment. Leave it with me.'

'If you don't tell someone at the top, I will,' said May in a determined manner.

'Don't threaten me please, my dear,' said Miss Palmer in that way she had of making a point without raising her voice; a kind of polite determination with a hint of admonition. 'And don't tell anyone else about this. No one at all for the moment.'

'Oh, but—'

'Absolutely no one, and that includes your friend from the factory who is staying with you,' she repeated. 'Now get along back to the switchboard and relieve whoever is covering for you. I'll let you know what's going to happen.'

Clearly nothing, thought May crossly as she went back to her place at the switchboard. Talk about one rule for the management and another for the workers. If that had been a machinist she had overheard, they would have been sacked instantly and probably reported to the police.

The desert moon was so brilliant it was almost like daylight. Some men chatted, others preferred to sit in quiet contemplation smoking; some prayed. Most were nervous because soon they would be forging ahead again in the battle for El Alamein, which was proving to be the most brutal experience of George's life, a graveyard for both sides.

War dehumanised people as far as George could make out. He himself had become almost immune to death, having seen so much of it. He'd seen mates drop beside him; others lose limbs and lie screaming with pain in the sand. The Allies were making headway, but at what price?

Anyone who said they weren't afraid was lying in George's opinion. He himself was paralysed with fear at times. But still he went on, because there was no choice.

In the midst of battle you stopped feeling and relied on instinct and the will to stay alive.

In this quiet time before battle commenced again, he thought of home and the bomb sites he'd seen on that last leave, and of Betty killed before she was even twenty-one, and he reminded himself that he wasn't the only one suffering.

He'd had some leave in Cairo a while ago, which had been a welcome break from the fighting. Most of the men had made a beeline for the bars; female company too had been high on many of the lads' agendas.

George had enjoyed the respite, but it was a poor substitute for home leave. He was beginning to feel completely distanced from home and a normal way of life. It seemed like another world, a world he didn't know if he would ever see again. He wasn't much of a church-goer, but these days he often prayed, and he did so now.

Chapter Fourteen

Contrary to May's suspicions, the conversation she'd had with Miss Palmer wasn't the end of the matter as regarded Mr Saxon and the silk stealing.

'I want you to call me to the switchboard when Mr Saxon's contact comes through again,' the older woman said, speaking to May in a confidential manner at her desk. 'I need to listen in.'

'He might not ring up again,' suggested May.

'If he's putting pressure on Mr Saxon for more material, as you say he is, he'll call again.'

'But I've told you what was said. Why can't you take my word for it?' asked May, impatient for the matter to progress and slightly miffed that her account of the conversation wasn't to be trusted.

'I need to hear what is said before I take things further,' Miss Palmer explained. 'It's a very serious matter and I have to make sure that the people at the top take notice. If I have actually heard it for myself, I can speak to them with more confidence.'

'You'll be breaking the rules by listening in deliberately, though,' May pointed out.

'Needs must when the devil drives, my dear.'

'Why will they believe it if you have heard it rather than me?' asked May.

'Obviously because I am a senior member of staff and an employee of very long standing,' she explained in a forthright manner. 'I was working here long before they started making parachutes, whereas you are a mere girl and a newcomer. It is no reflection on you personally, but on your word alone they might dismiss the whole thing and you along with it for eavesdropping.'

'But you could be in deep trouble if you are going to listen in,' May reminded her worriedly.

'If that happens, then so be it,' she said. 'Justice must be done, as you have said. So if that certain gentleman calls again, delay the connection until I am there. If I am not around, then find me.'

'Yes, Miss Palmer,' said May obediently.

Several weeks passed before Mr Saxon's 'friend' telephoned again and May was beginning to think they had heard the last of him. When he did finally get in touch, their plan was foiled, because although May delayed the connection until Miss Palmer was in place with the headphones on, Mr Saxon wasn't in his office and couldn't be found. The caller refused the offer of a call back and said he would telephone Mr Saxon at some other time.

'We'll just have to hope he doesn't ring him at home, won't we?' said May.

'Indeed,' the other woman agreed.

He came through again the next day, however, and this time things did go according to plan.

'Gotcha,' said Miss Palmer, returning the headphones to May when she had heard enough. 'It's time I went to visit our managing director, I think.' She paused. 'Don't worry, my dear. I will take full responsibility for our eavesdropping.'

'There's no need for that,' May assured her. 'I'm willing to shoulder the blame if things turn nasty. So long as Mr Saxon gets his due and the machinists are off the hook, I'll take my chances.'

But there were no repercussions. The matter was dealt with quietly and promptly. Mr Saxon left the company immediately and a memo was circulated to all departments to that effect. His dishonesty was mentioned but not how it was discovered. The factory was buzzing with it.

'That's a turn-up for the books, old Saxon getting the sack,' remarked Connie when she and May were waiting for the bus after work. 'It was him all along who was nicking the material; the thieving old devil.'

'Mm,' muttered May vaguely.

'I wonder how they found out,' Connie mused.

'Yeah,' said May innocently. She was still sworn to secrecy over the matter. Her part in it was crucial but the method used had been unethical to say the least, so Miss Palmer deemed it wise to keep it quiet in case of later repercussions. 'Still, as long as they've got the right person, it doesn't really matter, does it?'

'I suppose not,' said Connie as they got on the bus.

May smiled, pleased that justice had been done.

There was a big day in the Bailey home in the spring of the following year, because Joe was to start school. So important was it judged to be that May took a day's leave so that she could go with his grandmother to the school to offer some moral support. Joe was gleaming with cleanliness, every one of his curly hairs combed into place, and enthusiastic about this new adventure, though he didn't seem to have quite grasped the rules. 'I shall come home if I don't like it,' he announced chirpily.

As it was his first day, they were allowed to take him into the school and hand him over to the care of the teacher, but any tendency to linger was firmly discouraged as were any attempts to inform the teacher of a child's personal needs.

'He'll be fine,' said May to Dot as they walked across the playground on their way out.

'Course he will,' agreed Dot, wet eyed.

'He'll have a lovely time, I bet,' remarked May.

'I'm not so sure about us, though,' said Dot. 'I think we'd better have a cup o' tea at my place to keep us going. It's a long time until we can collect him.'

'I'll go along with that,' agreed May.

★   ★   ★

'He's only gone to school; he hasn't been sent out to clean chimneys or anything,' said Sheila, who was home on leave and in the kitchen in her pyjamas when Dot and May got back, both of them close to tears.

'It's a big thing, Sheila, a new era,' said Dot emotionally. 'He'll never be quite the same again.'

'We all have to grow up, Mum,' said Sheila. She was sitting at the kitchen table smoking and drinking a cup of tea.

'I hope the teacher realises that he's quite a sensitive little boy even though he seems very confident,' said Dot, too engrossed in thoughts of Joe to pay much attention to her daughter.

'Yeah,' agreed May, sounding concerned. 'He doesn't need the other kids to be too rough with him.'

'Oh for goodness' sake,' said Sheila in a tone of affectionate admonition. 'He's gone to school, not into the army cadets to be trained for the front line.'

'He's still being plunged into a new world, though, isn't he?' her mother pointed out.

'Gawd blimey, I don't remember all this drama when I started school.'

'You wouldn't have known about it because you were only five, the same as Joe is,' her mother pointed out.

'Mm, there is that, I suppose,' Sheila conceded. 'Anyway, there's tea in the pot, so have a cup and calm down, the pair of you.'

They did as she said and spoke of other things.

'So what do you do for fun these days, May?' enquired Sheila with interest.

'Not a lot,' she replied. 'Usually go to the pictures once a week with my friend who's staying with us.'

'Don't you go out dancing?'

'No, not since Doug died.'

'That's a shame,' said Sheila. 'It's terrific fun now that the Yanks are around. They're very smart, and boy can they jitterbug.'

'I haven't been to a dance since they've been over here,' said May. 'But I've seen them around in London and heard about the jitterbugging, of course.'

'How about we have a night out?' suggested Sheila. 'Bring your friend along; the more the merrier.'

'I'm not looking for a chap at the moment,' said May.

'I suggested we go out dancing for a bit of fun, not sign up at a marriage bureau.'

'She's sort of with George now, aren't you, love?' said Dot supportively.

'And you think George doesn't have any fun when he gets leave, wherever he is?'

'I haven't really thought about it,' she said.

'You're not engaged to him, are you?'

'Well, no . . .'

'George is the last person to want you to stay at home every night,' pronounced Sheila. 'He would want you to enjoy yourself. God knows we need to take our minds off the flamin' war.'

'I'll see what Connie has to say about it and let you know,' said May.

'Good.' Sheila lapsed into silence. 'So what time can we go and get Joe?' she asked eventually.

They both stared at her.

'What was all that about us making a fuss over nothing?' asked her mother with a wry grin.

'You were going on about it a bit, but . . . well, he is only little and he is my favourite nephew,' she said.

'You only have one,' her mother reminded her.

'All the more reason why I should come with you to meet him later on then,' said Sheila.

'Maybe you do have a heart after all,' said Dot. 'Even though you do your best to hide it.'

May kept a diplomatic silence. This was definitely a private moment between mother and daughter.

The Lyceum in London's West End was crowded, smoky, dimly lit and buzzing with fun and laughter. Most of the men were in uniform and they were of many nationalities.

May had no shortage of partners. She waltzed with a Polish soldier, quickstepped with a Canadian airman and learned to jitterbug with an American GI called Tom, who was polite, smart and unbelievably handsome.

Once she began to get the hang of the jive and the jitterbug she couldn't get enough of them and danced every dance after the interval with the gorgeous GI. It was fun, exciting, and she was having a wonderful time. When it came to the last waltz, however, it became obvious that he had mistaken her enthusiasm for the dance for something of a more personal nature, and she found herself fighting him off rather forcibly.

But she had enjoyed herself immensely despite this little misunderstanding. It was a tonic to see everyone looking so well turned out, the men in uniform, the women smart despite a shortage of clothes and stockings and almost non-existent cosmetics and toiletries. But they all looked nice with hair done, stocking seams painted up the back of their legs with charcoal and beetroot juice for lipstick.

It spoke volumes about the tenacity of the human spirit, she thought. No matter how hard life became, people could still go out and have fun. Hitler probably hadn't bargained on that when he set out to seek world domination.

'I didn't expect you to come home with us, May,' said Sheila when the three of them were on the train. 'I thought you'd have a much more interesting escort.'

'If you mean the American, he did ask to take me home as it happens,' she told her.

'And you said no,' Sheila said incredulously.

'That's right.'

'Have you lost your mind?'

'Not at all. I'm very sane as it happens,' she said. 'I didn't want to do what he obviously had in mind and I think I have the right to refuse even if I did dance with him a lot.'

'You could have held him off and got a good few treats out of it,' Sheila said laughingly. 'The Yanks are loaded and they can get all sorts of nice things. Think of all those lovely nylons and chocolates you could have had.'

'I couldn't be that materialistic,' May told her.

'Some women don't seem to worry about that sort of thing when it comes to the Americans and all the goodies that come with them,' Connie put in. 'Nor do they seem to care about their reputations.'

'My reputation would be the last thing I'd worry about if I had a gorgeous Yank after me,' Sheila pronounced. 'But I'm in the ATS so mine can't be much worse anyway.'

'It isn't so bad now,' May pointed out. 'I think most people realise that you do a good job.'

'It's after work that the trouble starts, when we go to the pub,' she said. 'Decent women aren't supposed to do that except on the arm of a man, so we're considered to be fast and loose.'

'Attitudes towards that sort of thing surely must be changing because of the war,' said May. 'At one time you wouldn't have seen a woman smoking, now lots do.'

'Me included,' said Sheila, who was always puffing away.

'So how come you two didn't click with anyone tonight?' said May, addressing them both.

'I didn't want to because I already have a boyfriend – Dave – my lovely brown-eyed soldier who's overseas,' said Connie.

May looked at Sheila, who had grown up into an attractive brunette with brown eyes and hair taken up at the sides. 'What about you?' she asked.

'I'm obviously not as irresistible as you are,' Sheila replied. 'I had plenty of partners but no one asked to see me home.'

'The main purpose of a dance hall is to get off with someone, so men think that's the only reason women are there,' mentioned May.

'What's wrong with that?' said Shelia. 'There has to be somewhere for people to meet.'

'Of course, but if you aren't interested in finding someone it seems a bit silly to go,' said May.

'Not if you enjoy dancing,' Sheila disagreed. 'It's a dance hall; the clue is in the title.'

'But you can't just dance, can you? You end up fighting someone off like I did.'

'I should be so lucky,' Sheila joked. 'But yes, I suppose it could send out the wrong message, though it shouldn't stop anyone going if they like to dance.'

'I don't think I'll be doing it again. When that Yank was all over me, I felt cheap. I felt as though I had led him on just by being there.'

'You shouldn't have done,' said Sheila with emphasis. 'If he chose to get the wrong impression that's his problem. Most of the fellas are decent types, though some are probably hoping for something a bit more spicy than a quickstep. It's in a man's nature.'

'Come on, you two,' said Connie as the train rumbled into Ealing Broadway station. 'We've got the blackout to contend with yet. There's no moon so it will be dodgy.'

The three of them alighted from the train and went up the stairs and out into the inky blackness of a wartime night.

Along with growing vegetables, keeping chickens became a way of life for the Stubbs family and was another thing that amazed May about the adaptability of human beings. Before the war their little garden had consisted of a scrubby area of grass that her father, to whom the job of gardening had been assigned, rarely got around to cutting.

Now, in the summer of 1943, it was cultivated into rows of carrots, potatoes, swedes, cabbages, runner beans and beetroot, a chicken run at the side next to the coal shed. Her father was very territorial about his vegetables and didn't trust anyone to help tend them in case they pulled out a plant instead of a weed.

'It's done him the world of good,' Flo could be heard to remark. 'A complete change for him from being stuck in a shipyard all day.'

For May, the most exciting part of the whole self-sufficiency project was when they were rewarded with an egg, though they had to be patient because it wasn't an everyday occurrence.

The chickens' most ardent enemy was Tiddles, their most devoted fan Joe, who thought it great fun when they were let out to peck and cluck around the garden, at which point the cat hissed and arched its back before leaping to safety on top of the coal shed. Joe adored the cat and his loyalties were seriously divided one day when an aggressive cockerel they had named Horace chased Tiddles down the garden.

Although there hadn't been any raids for a long time, neither was there any sign of the war coming to an end. Mr Churchill had warned the public some time ago, after several successful campaigns abroad, that they were only at the end of the beginning and not the beginning of the end, but everyone wanted peace with such ardour it was hard to stay patient.

People talked about something called the second front, or D–Day, which May understood to be another invasion of western Europe similar to the one that had failed earlier in the war. Everyone was expecting it at any time but still it didn't happen.

The population in general took comfort from two of the heroes of the war: Churchill, whose gravelly tones came across the airwaves every so often, and General Montgomery, nicknamed Monty, the leader of the successful El Alamein campaign in the desert. As far as May knew, George was still abroad somewhere, but she had no idea where. His letters were more heavily censored than ever and didn't give much of a clue. Home leave was never mentioned, so she assumed he wouldn't be back until the war ended.

Then, as the summer progressed, May began to have worries of a personal nature to contend with, and the war was pushed to the back of her mind.

★　★　★

While not judging herself to be any sort of a heroine, May had thought she was a person who faced up to things with a reasonable amount of courage. Until now . . .

She told herself it wasn't happening; that the exhaustion was due to long working hours and early mornings sorting the papers. She tried to convince herself that the night sweats were normal for this time of year and the general feeling of being off colour was all in her imagination. She rubbed her cheeks in front of the mirror to take away the horrible pallor. After all, she didn't have a cough, so it couldn't be TB back, could it? Well, maybe she was a bit chesty, but nothing like before.

But try as she might, she couldn't erase the fear, which was physical in its intensity, giving her knots in her stomach and nausea, which added to the horrible feeling of being unwell. Guilt at not getting herself checked out and therefore possibly passing it on to other people added to her distress.

Already feeling below par, she made things worse by expending a great deal of energy trying to hide it from her parents. She sang popular songs like 'Paper Doll' around the house and laughed a lot even though it was the last thing she was in the mood for. Mum and Dad would be worried sick if she were to tell them how she was really feeling, and she couldn't bear to put them through that again. Somehow she would have to bluff it out.

Of course, the rational part of her knew that this wasn't a permanent solution and she was only making things worse, but her emotional side recoiled from the idea of acceptance.

'So . . . what's up, May?' enquired Connie one day on their way to work.

'Nothing,' she replied.

'Oh come off it,' Connie persisted. 'You might be able to fool your mum and dad with all that jolliness, but not me. I think you might need a friend to talk to at the moment.'

'I don't know what you mean,' May lied huffily.

'I think you do.'

May had the idea that if she spoke about it, it would make it real. While she didn't say it out loud she could pretend it wasn't happening.

'Come on,' urged Connie. 'Has something happened between you and George? Is that what it is? Has he said something to upset you in one of his letters?'

'No, nothing like that.'

'What is it then?' persisted Connie. 'I know something is wrong so you might as well tell me, because I'll keep on until you do. I don't want you to be miserable on your own.'

At last May allowed herself to admit that it would be a tremendous relief to talk to someone about it. 'It's back, the unmentionable,' she blurted out. 'I've got it again.'

Connie turned pale; they both knew the seriousness of this, especially as May had already lost a lung. 'Oh God,' she said quietly. 'I thought you might not be feeling well, but I didn't dream it was anything like that. Are you sure?'

'Oh yeah. No doubt about it. I feel exactly the same as before,' she replied. 'There's no mistaking it.'

'Oh May, I'm so sorry.'

'Me too.'

'You need to go to the doctor right away.'

'No, I can't face that.'

'You'll have to. You need treatment as quickly as possible.' Connie swallowed hard, trying not to show her feeling of panic. Having experienced the illness herself, she could imagine how awful May must be feeling. She also knew that she would be tormenting herself about passing the infection on to someone else, and Connie didn't want to pile on the agony by mentioning it.

'I can't go through all that again, Connie,' May confessed. 'All that illness and being away; the stigma and feeling set apart. I'd sooner be killed by a bomb.'

'I can understand how you must be feeling and I expect I'd be exactly the same if it was me, but you can't ignore it and you don't need me to tell you that,' Connie advised sympathetically. 'You're one of the strongest people I know, May. You'll get through this.'

'But if it's in the other lung, they can't remove that one as well, can they?' she said. 'So what are my chances of getting better?'

'There are other things they can do besides surgery,' Connie reminded her, struggling to stay positive because there was still no cure for this vile disease. 'I didn't have a lung removed and I recovered.'

'Mm, there is that.' May looked worried. 'Oh Connie, how can I tell Mum and Dad? They'll be devastated.'

'They'll have to know.'

'Maybe I can leave it until I've been to see the doctor,' she suggested.

'They'll be very hurt if you deceive them,' Connie said. 'They are tough old sticks. Stronger than you think. They'll want to know. You are their child; it's only natural.'

'Everything you've said is true, but I seem to have lost my spirit,' May confessed. 'I just want to hide away somewhere and let the illness do its worst. I don't feel as though I have it in me to fight back.'

'I'll pretend I didn't hear that,' said Connie. 'The May Stubbs I know would never say a thing like that.'

'I'm tired,' said May.

'And we both know why, because we've been there before,' said Connie. 'So get down the doctor's before the flaming thing takes a hold.'

'I suppose you're right,' sighed May wearily. 'I'll have to pay up and see what the doc has to say.'

It was as May was pretending to be brave as she was giving her parents the horrible news that her courage returned, albeit temporarily.

'It'll be all right, honestly,' she tried to assure them. 'I've beaten it once and I'll do it again. I'm as strong as a horse, so you must try not to worry.'

'As if we would worry,' said her shaken mother in an attempt at humour.

'It might not take so long to shift this time,' May suggested.

'Maybe not,' said her father.

'There might be some new and better treatment available now,' added Flo.

But it was all just empty talk because none of them knew how serious the problem was. May found herself courageous and feeble in equal measures. It wasn't so much the fear of death as the misery of illness that bothered her.

The doctor examined her but didn't make a diagnosis. Instead he sent her to the hospital for an X-ray and gave her a sick note for work, telling her that she must stay away from people until she had the result. He told her to take things very easy and eat as much good food as she could, which was no easy task as rationing was biting even harder.

Here we go again, said May to herself as she came out of the doctor's surgery, which was actually the front room in his house. But she did feel better for having faced up to it; stronger somehow and more able to cope. Whatever came, she would accept it with as much fortitude as she could muster.

George could hardly contain his excitement as he got off the train at Paddington and headed for the underground, his kitbag slung over his shoulder. Because he had served for more than three years in the Middle East, the army had given him some home leave, and a change of posting. He wouldn't know where he was going until after this leave, but all he could think about now was getting home. No one knew he was coming, so he would give them a surprise.

He was dying to see Joe, and his mother of course, and absolutely longing to see May, especially now that their relationship had changed. He was a little nervous too about the latter, because it would be strange after a lifetime of being just friends and he wanted to get it right; he didn't want to disappoint her.

Heading down on the escalator, the familiar warm, acrid draught of air blowing in his face as he headed for the platform, he thought how wonderful it was to be back in London.

The first disappointment was the lukewarm reception he received from Joe, who was out playing in the street when George arrived and was called in by his grandmother after the two of them had had a chat.

'Why do I have to come in, Gran?' asked the boy. 'We're playing hopscotch and I'll miss my turn.'

'Look who's here,' she said, looking at George. 'Your daddy's come home.'

'Oh, 'ello,' said Joe casually, glancing at his father then back to his grandmother. 'Can I go out again now please?'

'No you can't,' said Dot, also disappointed at his reaction. 'Surely you want to stay in and talk to your dad?'

'Can I do it later?' asked Joe in a matter-of-fact manner. 'Everybody is out playing today and we're having a really good game.'

'Joe,' admonished Dot sternly. 'Your daddy has come a long way across the sea to see us.'

The boy looked at George with just a glimmer of recognition. 'What was it like on the boat?' he asked dutifully.

Appalling was the honest answer to that, but he couldn't tell a five-year-old boy that the ship was overcrowded with troops, and smelly and uncomfortable, and that he was seasick for part of the journey, so he said, 'It was all right.'

'I've seen boats on the river when Auntie May takes me to Richmond,' said the boy. 'Please can I go out again now that I've talked?'

'No you can't,' said Dot.

'But they'll be waiting . . .' he objected.

'Let him go,' said George. 'We can talk later on when he comes in.'

'Can I Gran?' Please can I?' asked Joe, looking towards his grandmother for confirmation.

Dot tutted and didn't look at all pleased. 'Well . . . if your father doesn't mind, then off you go,' she said.

'Thanks,' he beamed, and tore off, slamming the door behind him.

'Sorry, son,' Dot said. 'It wasn't what you could call a warm welcome, but he's just a little boy.'

'I'm glad to see that he's well and happy,' said George, 'and I can remember how I used to love playing out. The kids are in their own world out there in the street. I know I used to be.'

'I have tried to keep you alive in his memory, and so

has May,' Dot told him. 'But it obviously hasn't worked too well.'

'I've got ten days,' said George. 'Plenty of time to get to know him all over again.'

'Before you disappear again.'

'Still, as long as I come back like the proverbial bad penny, you won't hear me complaining,' he told her. 'It's better than the alternative, anyway.'

'Not half, but I want you back for good.'

'All in good time, Mum. Meanwhile, what time does May get in from work? I can't wait to see her.'

Dot bit her lip. 'I'm afraid you can't see her, son,' she said, looking worried.

His brows knitted in a frown. 'Why not? Has she gone away or something?' he asked.

'No, she's at home, but she isn't well,' she explained. 'They think she's got consumption again.'

The blood drained from his face. 'Oh no,' he said, shocked. 'How awful.'

'Yes, it's horrible,' sighed Dot. 'We're all worried sick.'

'I must get round there right away to give her some support,' he said, moving as though to leave the room.

'No, son, you can't,' said his mother, grabbing his arm. 'Because of the infection.'

'I'll take that chance,' he said. 'I have to be there with her. She'll be needing me.'

Dot restrained him more firmly. 'No, George, you can't see her because of Joe,' she said. 'You'll be putting him at risk if you have physical contact with her. If you catch it he might pick it up from you. She isn't seeing anyone at all at the moment. Not until she's had the result of the X-ray.'

He sat down and held his head. 'Oh Mum, what a blow,' he said thickly. 'And how terrible for May.'

'Yes, we are all dreadfully upset about it,' she told him sadly. 'There isn't anything we can do to help, either.'

'I can cheer her up, though,' he said. 'Have you got any writing paper?'

'Not as such because of the shortage,' she said. 'But I've got some bits of scrap paper that I've saved.'

'That'll do if you can spare me a bit,' he said. He was trying to keep cheerful, but he was shaken to the core by the news about May.

Although May had worked hard to get herself into a state of readiness for bad news, she was still paralysed with fear as she sat waiting for the result of the X-ray, painfully aware that her life hung in the balance. Her appointment with the doctor had been made for after surgery so there was no one else waiting, for reasons of possible infection.

It was a month since she'd had the chest X-ray done and during that time she had knitted socks and several pullovers for the troops, done a few make-do-and-mend jobs on her own clothes and tried not to let herself sink into a mood of negativity, which wasn't easy with such a huge issue on her mind, especially as she was alone in the house for much of the day while her parents were both at work. There was a saying about too much isolation bringing about morbidity, and she'd had to battle with that on a daily basis.

She'd been enormously cheered this past week or so by letters from George written on scrap paper and put through the letter box. Although she was desperately disappointed about missing his leave – he was going back this morning – his little epistles brightened up her life no end. Her mother posted her replies through the Baileys' letter box for her.

It was heart-warming to feel loved but she was aware of a responsibility too, because George would be as devastated as she was if she did have the illness. She didn't want to upset him, even though she knew the situation was beyond her control. She'd promised to write and let him know.

'May Stubbs,' said the doctor, opening the door of his consulting room.

Feeling as though her legs were about to buckle beneath her with nervousness, she followed him in.

May was crying when she emerged from the surgery. She paused and blew her nose, tried to compose herself, then ran as fast as she could down one street and up another, tears streaming down her cheeks. Stopping briefly because she had a stitch, she raced onwards until she reached her destination, rapping the knocker as hard as she could.

Dot Bailey opened the door.

'May, dear,' she said worriedly, seeing the tears and fearing the worst.

'Has he gone, Mrs Bailey?' May asked.

'Yeah, a few minutes ago; you've only just missed him, love.'

'Thanks, Mrs B,' she said and tore in the direction of the station, leaving Dot in a state of anxiety about the result of the X-ray.

He was sitting on a bench on the platform reading a newspaper with his kitbag on the ground beside him. She flew down the stairs and rushed up to him.

'George . . .'

'May,' he said, leaping up, his expression a mixture of joy and fear. 'What . . . what happened?'

'Oh I'm so pleased I managed to catch you. I thought I'd missed you,' she said, gasping because she was out of breath.

'So . . . tell me please, and put me out of my misery,' he begged ardently.

'I don't have it,' she said, still weeping with relief. 'I don't have TB again.'

'Oh May, really?'

'Yes, really,' she confirmed. 'The X-ray was clear. The doctor thinks I was a bit run down and that was making me feel poorly; that and my imagination running wild and making me feel sick and exhausted. He's given me a tonic and said I should be feeling better in a week or so.'

George was wet eyed too as he took her in his arms. They had both waited so long for this. It was one of those ineffably wonderful moments.

359

'I'm so pleased for you, but the timing is rotten. I'm on my way back to camp,' he said hoarsely.

'At least I was able to see you before you disappear again,' she pointed out.

'Yeah, there is that,' he agreed, 'but there isn't enough time to get married.'

'We can do that the next time you are home,' she said, grinning. 'If you ask me nicely, that is.'

'May,' he said, barely able to speak for emotion. 'Will you marry me?'

'I certainly will,' she said, her voice drowned out by the sound of the train rumbling in.

As this station was the end of the line, they had a few precious moments together before the train headed back into central London. Once George had gone, May walked home happily via the Co-op to tell her mother her double good news, then called on Mrs Bailey for the same reason. After an awful few weeks, life was very bright indeed again.

Chapter Fifteen

It was January 1944, and after another make-do wartime Christmas, people were weary of waiting for the eagerly anticipated second front. To add to the gloom, Londoners found themselves under attack from the air again at night after nearly three years of relative calm. They were out of the habit of sheltering, and it was hard to have to climb into those dark, damp holes again.

'I don't think I'll bother to go down the shelter,' said Dick Stubbs on the first night of the air raids since the lull. 'I'll take my chances up here.'

'Oh no you will not,' his wife pronounced. 'I'm not having you asking for trouble. That's just plain stupid.'

'She's right, Mr Stubbs,' added Connie, who was understandably nervous of air raids having lost her grandfather and her home to one. 'Best not to chance it.'

'Consider yourself told, Dad,' said May with feigned cheeriness. 'You don't have a hope against all us women.'

'The story of my life,' he said. Everyone was behaving with false jollity. 'I've always been short of male allies.'

'Never mind. You'll be all right when George comes home,' May reminded him. 'You'll have a son-in-law to take your side then.'

'It can't come soon enough for me,' he said.

'How do you think I feel then?' responded May, grabbing her gas mask, coat and blankets and heading out of the back door into the garden. 'But even apart from getting you some male support in the family, everyone is sick and tired of the war now and we want the boys home.'

'Surely the Allies' invasion must start soon,' muttered Flo, collecting her coat. 'Why don't they get on with it?'

'Because it's such a massive operation to organise, I suppose,' her husband suggested. 'They'll want to make absolutely certain it doesn't go wrong. Nobody wants another Dunkirk.'

'I hope Dot and Joe are all right,' fretted May. 'Joe was only a baby during the Blitz and he slept through most of it. Not so little now. He might be terrified.'

'Well don't get any ideas about going round there to check on them while the raid is on, because we won't let you out of the shelter,' declared Flo.

'I'll pop round there on the way to work in the morning,' May remarked. 'I hope Tiddles will be all right too. I wish that darned cat would come down the shelter with us instead of shooting off to God knows where as soon as the siren goes.'

'Cats are free spirits,' said her father. 'You can't keep them in like you can a dog. He'll find a place to hide.'

'Here come the bombers,' announced Connie as the

drone of enemy aircraft grew louder. 'Hold on to your stomachs.'

There was an attempt at laughter as they climbed into the shelter, but the only sort that emerged was the nervous kind. The feeling of resignation they'd developed during the Blitz was noticeably absent because they were out of practice, and they were all very frightened.

Dot was absolutely terrified when the siren sounded after being silent for so long. She was paralysed with fear, breathless and shaky, the symptoms exacerbated by the worry that she might let Joe down because of it. Somehow she got herself into action, collecting gas masks and blankets and hoping she had a candle left over from the Blitz.

'What's happening, Gran?' asked Joe, who was still up but in his pyjamas.

'It's an air raid, sweetheart, and we're going down the shelter,' she told him.

'Cor, how exciting,' he enthused. 'Can I take my toy soldiers with me?'

'Yes, as long as you're quick; you'll need something to amuse yourself with. Bring the snap cards as well if you know where they are,' she told him.

Together they went into the back garden and climbed down into the Anderson. To Dot it was a hateful prison, damp, smelly and full of spiders. To Joe it was an exciting adventure which would delay his bedtime.

The noise was terrific: planes, bombs and the crack

of anti-aircraft guns. Dot made a makeshift bed for Joe. He lay down, but there was no sleep in him and he didn't seem in the least bit bothered by the racket outside.

'Fancy a game of snap, Gran?' he asked.

It was the last thing she wanted to do, but she needed to keep them both distracted from what was going on outside.

'All right then. Give us the cards and I'll shuffle them,' she offered.

'It's good in the shelter, isn't it, Gran?' he remarked happily as she prepared the playing cards. 'You get to stay up late and play games.'

'I can see that you might like that part of it,' she said, hearing another enemy plane drawing nearer and feeling her tummy tighten. 'But as far as I'm concerned it's a flaming nuisance.'

'Well, grown-ups can stay up late whenever they like, can't they? So you don't need air raids,' he said in a matter-of-fact tone.

'I certainly don't need them,' she said, careful not to show her fear and pass it on to him.

She dealt the cards and the game began, accompanied by explosions all around them, though none sounded as though they were too close.

'Snap!' shrieked Joe.

'All right, no need to shout,' said Dot, as though these were ordinary circumstances. 'I'm not deaf.'

'Sorry, Gran,' he said.

Overwhelmed with love for him, she leaned across and hugged him. 'That's all right, darlin',' she said, with renewed strength. She knew that while she had this child to look after she could get through anything. He had proved to be her salvation and she adored him.

George was far away from the air raids, stationed in a camp in the countryside. They were undergoing special training, so all leave had been cancelled. He could endure the harsh regime, the lack of freedom and the general physical hardship of army life in wartime, but he wasn't a happy man for other reasons.

Fate had played a cruel trick on him and brought someone into his life to torment him, resurrecting all the anger and lust for revenge that he'd experienced for so long after his father's death. As he'd matured and become a father himself, he'd managed to put the murder and his feelings about it into the past. Now it was back with a vengeance, and all because of a man called Ron Bikerley who had joined the platoon a few weeks ago and who was the son of the man who had taken George's father's life.

Everyone George held dear – May, Joe and his mother – was overshadowed by the violent longing for recompense, a feeling that he must right a wrong for his father. If Ron Bikerley had made the connection he showed no sign of it. But Bailey was a common enough name so it probably hadn't occurred to him. It could even be that his family had kept the details of the killing from him when he was a boy.

But George knew who Ron was. How many Bikerleys

were there in Shepherd's Bush, or London even? It was a very unusual name. And a few seemingly casual remarks had ascertained that Ron's father had died around the time Bill Bikerley had been hanged, so there was no doubt about it in George's mind. Obviously the man wasn't going to make the circumstances of his father's death generally known, but George knew it was him.

Ron Bikerley seemed like a decent enough bloke and was popular with the rest of the men, which made George's dreadful plight even worse. Because he wanted to kill him, and that was a very powerful and frightening feeling. It took a great deal of effort to keep his emotions under control, and he wasn't sure for how long he could restrain himself.

As the air warmed towards spring, the air raids died out and the main topic of conversation, in shops, offices, pubs and on the street, was the Allied invasion, otherwise known as D-Day; when it was going to start and how much blood would be shed to get this war won.

'Will George be involved in it, do you think?' Connie asked May one day on their way to work.

'I should think so now that he's back in England. I suppose that must be what his special training is for.'

'That must be worrying for you.'

'Very, but worry is as natural as breathing to us now, isn't it? If we're not holed up in the shelter worrying about staying alive until morning, we're bothered about the men at war or when we are next going to get a decent meal.' May paused, grinning. 'Ooh, hark at me. I'll be renamed Moaning May if I carry on like that.'

'We could go to the pictures tonight and forget all about the war and flaming D-Day if you like,' suggested Connie.

'Yeah, let's do that,' agreed May. 'We might as well make the most of the fact that the raids seem to have stopped again.'

They went on their way chatting amiably and antici- pating a night out at the flicks. One thing the war had done was make them grateful for small blessings. All most ordinary people wanted was a return to normality. But peace was such a terribly long time in coming.

George's feelings finally got the better of him one night in the NAAFI when he was having a drink with his mates. Ron Bikerley was in the bar with another group of men from the platoon. The soldiers trained hard all day so some relaxation when they were off duty was much needed. Having had a couple of pints George was feeling cheerful and was actually laughing when Ron Bikerley walked past him on his way to the bar counter. Instantly George's mood changed, and on impulse he walked over to Bikerley and grabbed hold of him roughly by the arm.

'Do you know who I am?' he asked in a belligerent manner as the other man turned towards him.

'Yeah, of course I do,' said Ron, looking puzzled. 'What are you on about?'

'Say my name; go on, say it.'

The other man stared at him, perplexed. 'What's got into you?'

'Say it!'

Bikerley shrugged. 'George Bailey,' he said. 'There. Are you happy now?'

'Does the name ring any bells?' asked George.

'No. Should it?' he asked.

'Yes it bloody well should,' said George, rage scorching through him. 'Bailey, Bailey, Bailey, son of Joe Bailey, who your old man murdered in cold blood.'

There was a long silence, then Bikerley said, 'Oh, so that's what it's all about.'

'Yeah, I thought that would jog your memory,' said George.

'I think you and I have some business to sort out in private, don't you?'

George's pals were trying to intervene. 'Leave it, George,' said one of them. 'You'll get put on a charge if you start brawling. You know the army takes a dim view of that.'

'For God's sake, George, leave him alone,' said another man, trying to drag George away from Bikerley. 'You don't want to get into trouble; save your energy for the battlefield.'

Bikerley spoke up suddenly. 'George is right, lads. We do have private matters to attend to. We'll go and do it outside.'

He walked towards the door, and George followed him as though Bikerley was now in control.

Immediately the door had closed behind him, George

took charge again, grabbing the other man roughly by his battledress. 'Do you know what your father put my family through?' he snarled. 'Not only did he kill my dad, he almost finished my poor mother off; she was a nervous wreck for years after the murder. So my sister and I lost her as well as our father in a manner of speaking.'

He laid into Bikerley, aiming blow after blow, beside himself with rage, but he was taking punches too. Both men were extremely fit and strong from army training and Bikerley wasn't prepared to take this attack without retaliation.

'I lost my father too,' he reminded George breathlessly.

'He deserved to die,' said George, wrestling the other man to the ground and pinning him down by the arms. 'And all because my father was a decent man who wanted to keep boxing clean and your old man wanted a fight fixed.'

'Oh, so that's what they told you, is it?'

'Of course that's what they told me because that's how it was; that's what the fight was about.'

'The fight had nothing to do with boxing.'

'Of course it was to do with boxing,' said George, panting from exertion. 'What else would it be about? That was their line of business; their connection.'

'Yeah, that's true, but the fight wasn't about business.'

'Course it was.'

'No! It was about your father and my mother,' blurted out Bikerley, struggling against George's grip. 'Your old man had been sleeping with her. That was why my dad went after yours, and I don't blame him either. Any decent man would have done the same thing. The fight got out of hand and your old man copped it. It could easily have gone the other way.'

'Don't try and lie your way out of this,' said George.

'I don't have to lie my way out of anything. All this happened years ago when we were both just children and was nothing to do with either of us. It wasn't me who had the fight with your dad. I would have been at home in bed at the time, the same as you. But since you want to make an enemy of me because of it, you might as well have the facts. Yes, my father did start the fight, because he was angry and I can understand why. Now that you're a man yourself and have heard the truth, you can probably understand it too.'

'That's a pack of lies,' George protested. 'My mum and dad were devoted. He wouldn't have cheated on her.'

'He did, mate. It happens.'

'Stop lying.'

'No lies,' stated Bikerley. 'But it's all in the past, so let it go, for pity's sake.'

But George could neither accept what he'd heard nor move on from the terrible sense of injustice that had haunted him for so long. It was almost outside of himself, and the violence of his emotions frightened him. He feared that if he struck one more blow he wouldn't stop until he'd killed Bikerley.

The door opened and one of the soldiers said, 'The sarge has got wind of a barney and is on his way.'

George and Bikerley scrambled to their feet.

'What's going on 'ere?' demanded the platoon sergeant,

a bully of a man who relished his authority and welcomed any opportunity to inflict punishment.

'Nothing, sir,' said the two men in unison, standing to attention.

The sergeant's deep-set eyes darted from one to the other. 'That isn't what I've heard,' he said. 'Someone told me there was trouble out here, and the army doesn't tolerate fighting among our own men, as you very well know.'

'Yes, sir,' said George.

'Sir,' echoed Bikerley.

'So get back inside and don't let me hear of any more bother, or you'll both be on a charge.'

'Sir,' said both men again.

The sergeant went back inside with the two of them following. Bikerley rejoined his pals, but George went back to the barrack room.

Lying on his bed, George recalled the events of the evening and cast his mind back to the time of his father's death, trying to work out if Bikerley's version of events could possibly be true. He didn't want even to consider it but felt compelled to do so. The whole thing had been shrouded in secrecy at the time. As far as he could remember, he and his sister had been told what had happened by their mother, who had asked them never to mention it again as it was too upsetting for her. Could she have lied to them to protect them because she knew how much they had loved and looked up to their father?

Or had they just assumed the reason for the fight and she'd gone along with it because it was less painful for them that way.

If Bikerley's story was true, George's mother must have known about it, because it would all have come out at the time. She would probably have had to go to court when Bikerley senior was sentenced, though George couldn't remember anything about that part of it. It hadn't been the sort of case that had made the headlines for long; just a back-street brawl that had gone wrong.

Looking back, the whole thing was very hazy indeed, but he did remember how his mother had changed. He'd always believed it was because of the death alone. Supposing she had found out that her husband had been cheating on her as well; that was all the more reason for her heart to be broken and her nerves shattered.

In an uncomfortable corner of his mind he was beginning to realise that Ron Bikerley's story could be true and that George's beloved father had been an adulterer. Even more devastating was the thought that he himself was a chip off the old block because of what had happened with Betty. He'd always put that down to too much cider and an overload of youthful urges, but maybe he wasn't able to be faithful either.

Of course, years of army life and mixing with men of all types had made him realise that sex was less of an emotional commitment for men than it was for women. But he still had his standards and he wanted to keep it that way, despite his bad blood.

He was tempted to write to his mother and ask for

the truth, but he knew he would never do that. For one thing it would open old wounds and cause her pain; for another, he wanted her to believe that he and Sheila still looked up to their father's memory. So he would never speak about it. He would protect her as she had protected him and Sheila all these years. No wonder the poor woman had almost been broken by it.

Turning his mind to the more recent past, he was deeply ashamed of his violent behaviour and very unnerved by it. He could have killed one of his fellow soldiers, a member of his own platoon. It had been as though his actions had been guided by someone else. He'd been a man possessed, and all because of something that had not been the fault of his victim. Until now he'd never considered himself to be a violent man, but the fact that he was scared the hell out of him.

Could his behaviour be a legacy of war? After all, he had seen a lot of action in the Middle East. But he had always believed that military killing was just a job, something done under orders. What he had wanted to do to Bikerley was quite different and there was no excuse for it. He had a son of his own and should know better.

Whatever the truth of the past, he must make things right with Ron Bikerley, who hadn't deserved that onslaught. He would go and make his peace right away, although he wouldn't be surprised if the other man didn't accept his apology. George was deeply ashamed and felt as though he didn't know who he was any more. He certainly didn't feel worthy of May's love. She deserved better than him.

The tension had been building for months, but in early June, when people knew that D-Day was imminent, the air positively buzzed with the feeling that something was going on, increased by intense activity in the skies, which were rarely free of aircraft roaring overhead day and night.

When the news finally came through on the eight o'clock news on the morning of the sixth of June that Allied troops had landed in France, May had already left for work. It was only later, after the switchboard was jammed with calls – practically on fire, she said to the office in general – and she wondered what was going on that Miss Palmer said, 'It's because of D-Day, dear, everybody wants to talk about it.'

'Has it started, then?'

'Yes, our boys are over there, God bless them,' she said. 'The King is doing a special broadcast to the nation about it tonight.'

Everyone seemed excited, but May had mixed feelings. Although she knew the invasion was necessary to end the war, she was also painfully aware that somewhere among the thousands of men risking their lives would be George.

During a brief lull on the switchboard, she cast her mind back to the last time she had seen George. He'd had a brief embarkation leave, which had been a huge disappointment. He had seemed very tense and distant

374

towards her; it was almost as though the marriage proposal hadn't happened. She'd put it down to nerves about the military task he had to face, but it was hard to take after the euphoria of their last meeting. Joe had been unusually naughty and offhand with his father so the atmosphere for romance had been painfully absent. George had told her he loved her, though, and she believed him. But there had been something horribly ominous about his mood and a sense of doubt about their future together had lingered in her mind.

That evening May, her parents and Connie gathered around the wireless to listen to the King's broadcast, delivered in his achingly sincere style.

'Surely none of is too busy, too young or too old to play a part in the nationwide vigil of prayer as the great crusade sets forth.'

The words heartened and warmed May. They broadened her vision and made her feel part of a whole. So what if George had had an off mood when he was last home. There were bigger things at stake than her personal feelings. George's life for one thing and all those others with him in the dangerous mission to bring this awful war to a conclusion.

'Oh my Lord, whatever's that?' said Flo, staring up at the sky one evening a week or two later as she was taking some washing off the line. What appeared to be a damaged aircraft was hurtling noisily across the sky with flame spurting from its tail.

'Looks like a German raider on its last legs,' observed Dick, who was attending to the vegetable patch. 'Good job too. That'll be one less of the buggers to drop bombs on us.'

'Girls, come out here, quickly!' Flo shouted into the kitchen where May and Connie were washing the dishes. 'It's a Jerry bomber in trouble.'

'Ooh er,' said May, dashing into the garden with a tea towel in her hand and staring heavenwards. 'I hope it doesn't land on anyone's house.'

'Looks as though it's about to crash-land somewhere,' observed Connie.

The aircraft disappeared over the rooftops and a few minutes later they heard an explosion, which they judged from experience to be a few miles away.

'That's the end of that, and good riddance too,' said Dick. 'Let's hope it didn't do any damage.'

It did cause a lot of damage and plenty more of its kind followed, and not just at night but during the day as well. Speculation as to what the aircraft actually were ended a few days later when a member of the government announced that pilotless aircraft were now being used against the British Isles, and that when the engine of the machine was heard to go out an explosion would soon follow.

'Whatever next,' lamented Flo, when they heard the

news on the wireless. 'Just when things are going so well for the boys overseas and we were all thinking we'd got Hitler beat, he comes up with this rotten trick.'

'He's probably getting desperate and is using every means he's got,' said Dick.

'He'll soon run out of ideas,' suggested May.

'Let's hope so,' said her dad.

But the doodlebugs, as the new weapons became generally known, wreaked havoc, and coming at this late stage, when people thought the war was drawing to a conclusion, they were loathed by everyone. Being unmanned, they seemed weird and sinister, but they were lethal and caused extensive damage.

They also caused a new wave of evacuation from London. May arrived at the Bailey home one day to find Dot in tears, packing a small case.

'I shall have to send Joe away on the school evacuation scheme,' she wept. 'I always said I would never let him be evacuated; the poor little thing, having to go and live with strangers. It breaks my heart.'

May wanted to weep with her. She too hated the idea of Joe going away. 'The doodlebugs are worse in south London than around here, so I've heard, Mrs Bailey,' she mentioned hopefully.

'Maybe they are,' said Dot, 'but we are getting them here as well; all day long the perishing things come rattling over. It's too dangerous for a child.'

'But he was here during the Blitz,' May reminded her.

'He was too little to be sent away then, and we knew where we were with those raids,' she said, sniffing into her handkerchief. 'These wicked things are dropping all day and he has to go to school. I can't protect him like I did before.'

'No, I suppose it will be for the best,' May agreed sadly. 'It's what George would want for him, and the government are recommending that people send their children away.'

Dot stopped what she was doing and sat down with her head in her hands. 'Oh May,' she sobbed. 'First his dad goes away, then his mum dies, and now I've got to send him away as well; to live with people he doesn't know in the middle of the country somewhere. It's enough to damage him for life.'

'He'll be all right,' encouraged May, though she was sick at heart. 'Kids are tough little things; he'll soon adapt.'

'Some of the country people don't want us Londoners in their villages,' said Dot. 'You hear such awful stories. I remember that when the kids came back after the Blitz.'

'The stories aren't all bad. It's only occasionally you hear of an unhappy experience. Some children have a lovely time,' May pointed out. 'And it might not be for long.'

Dot seemed suddenly to pull herself together. 'Yeah, you're right, dear. I've got to be strong for him.' She blew her nose. 'I won't half miss him, though, May.'

'You and me both,' said May, wiping the tears from her eyes.

It occurred to May in that moment that it wasn't only the drama from the battlefields that touched your emotions in this war. It was the little things, like a six-year-old boy being sent away from everything he knew and loved, and a devoted grandmother trying to be strong for him, that broke your heart.

George often found himself fighting alongside or close to Ron Bikerley as they advanced from the beaches towards Caen. They hadn't become best mates after George's apology – events of the past still came between them – but neither were they enemies. They existed in a state of indifference which George didn't like but didn't know how to change. However, all the men were more interested in staying alive and winning the war than how they got along with individual members of the platoon, as important as mates were in army life, especially in action.

Since the landings it had been a hard and dangerous slog as they trudged on through constant bombardments. The morale of the men remained reasonably high despite heavy losses, probably because at last something was actually happening, and although they were experiencing resistance along the way, there was a definite sense of progress.

Along with his comrades, George was marching along a country lane with bayonet fixed, trucks coming up in the rear. Suddenly something moved out of the corner of his eye, and looking up he saw the barrel of a gun poking out through the branches aimed slightly ahead of him.

Instinctively he flung himself forward, pushing the man in front to the ground just as the bullet passed over where he had been standing.

'Blimey,' said Bikerley, scrambling to his feet. 'That one was meant for me, I reckon. Thanks.'

'Instinct, mate,' said George modestly. 'You'd have done the same for me.'

'Thanks anyway.'

This was no time for fancy speeches, just bullets and bombs to be dodged. George was certain he would have acted in the same way whoever the man ahead of him had been. But he was very glad it had happened to be Bikerley, because he now realised that the other man had been through the same pain as himself, losing his father at a young age.

Proof of his own instinct to save life was a huge relief to him, as the tendency to violence he had discovered in himself still worried him. He thought his action had probably gone some way towards having Ron as a pal in the future, if there was one. Oh well, here we go again, he thought, as a grenade exploded nearby.

May called in to see how Dot was getting along without her beloved grandson, expecting to find her in pieces.

'I miss him something awful,' Dot said, 'and he's only been gone a few days.'

'That's only natural,' said May, though the other woman seemed calmer than she had expected.

'Anyway, I won't have time to brood too much, because I've got myself a job,' she announced.

'Oh, really!'

'You can put your eyes back into their sockets,' said

Dot drily as May stared at her in astonishment. 'They're employing women of all ages these days, even old codgers like me. Now that I don't have Joe to look after, there's no reason for me to stay at home, not when they need people to go out to work to keep the country going.'

'Good for you,' approved May. 'What sort of job is it?'

'On the buses; a conductress, or clippie as they call them these days,' she replied.

'Ooh, that will be fun, but a bit tiring for you, up and down those stairs collecting the fares.'

'It'll be better than sitting at home moping,' she said.

'It certainly will,' agreed May, knowing that the other woman was fretting terribly over Joe.

'I hope I don't make a mess of it,' said Dot, looking worried. 'Still, you can only do your best, can't you?'

'Of course you won't make a mess of it.' May knew that Dot hadn't been out to work for years so would naturally be feeling nervous, but she was doing it with a willing heart and once again showing that she had mettle. 'You'll be a smashing clippie, Mrs Bailey! One of the best in London!'

Chapter Sixteen

Although bombs were still raining down on London at all hours, hopes were high that the war would end in the autumn. News from abroad of the breakout from the Normandy beachhead and then later the liberation of Paris created huge optimism at home, especially as there were also rumours about some of the blackout restrictions being lifted.

'At least there are signs that normality is on its way back,' said May to Connie one Saturday morning in Oxford Street. They both had the morning off and were shopping with what was left of their clothing coupons.

'The blackout makes no difference to the doodlebugs as they are robots, so the government might as well get rid of it altogether,' remarked Connie.

'They must be confident that there won't be any more proper piloted bombers to have mentioned lifting some of it in September,' said May.

They stood looking in a dress-shop window, rather wistfully as neither had many coupons left.

'I don't actually mind the utility clothes,' mentioned Connie. Utility garments were manufactured under restrictions as to the minimum amount of material that was used and the price was strictly controlled to make them affordable. 'I quite like wearing simple things.'

'I don't dislike them either,' said May. 'But it will be nice after the war when rationing finishes and we can buy what we like again; pretty, stylish things.'

'Oh I'll say,' agreed Connie. 'I don't think anyone can wait for that.'

They walked on, stopping to look in every dress-shop window. The siren went, but very few people took any notice. Even when the doodlebug clattered into sight, with its distinct grating roar, most people just glanced up and then went on their way.

'We are all getting a bit too casual about the darned things now,' Connie remarked.

'Mm,' agreed May. 'The siren is going so often, most people just ignore it.'

'Everything looks so shabby, doesn't it?' observed Connie, looking around. 'Even our lovely West End.'

May nodded, glancing at the bomb damage and the peeling paint on the woodwork of the buildings. 'The store owners can't even give their shops a lick of paint, as only essential repairs are allowed,' she said.

'Let's go in Lyons for a cuppa,' suggested Connie. 'That'll cheer us up. At least there are still some tea shops around, even though a lot have disappeared because of the war.'

As usual, Lyons tea shop was crowded, noisy and

fragrant with the scent of toast. The siren sounded again while May and Connie were in the queue with their tray. People paused in their chatter for a few moments then carried on regardless. A careless attitude perhaps, but there was something courageous about it to May's mind.

'What are you looking forward to most about the end of the war?' asked Connie when they were seated at a table with tea and a bun.

'Oh, there are so many things,' replied May wistfully.

Her friend looked surprised. 'I thought your answer would be George coming home,' she said.

'Obviously that is at the very top of my list,' she said. 'Same for you with Dave, I expect.'

'Not half.'

'Are you a bit nervous about it, though?'

Connie thought about this for a moment. 'I expect I will be when the time comes, because you don't know if it will be the same after so long, do you?'

'No, you don't,' said May with that last disappointing leave in mind. 'George and I go back such a long way, but we've never made it work somehow and I don't know if we ever will.'

'But he asked you to marry him.'

'Yes, he did, but we haven't had any time together to make the transition from being just friends; to get to know each other in that way,' she said. 'Besides, things change and so do people, and the boys have been through so much it's bound to have had some sort of an effect on them. You just never know.'

'That's the way life is. Nothing is ever certain even when there isn't a war on,' said Connie. 'And talking of change, Mum has found somewhere to live where all the family can be together at last, so I'll be moving out of your place soon.'

'Oh.' May was downcast. She'd got so used to Connie being around, she'd almost forgotten that it wasn't permanent. 'I'll miss you, and I know that Mum and Dad will too.'

'I feel a bit sad about leaving too. It's been fun and I've felt very much at home with your family, but Mum will be glad to have us all back together again.'

'So I lose my surrogate sister,' sighed May.

'I suppose you do, but we'll still be friends.'

'Course we will,' said May, struck with a sudden memory of another friend who was still often in her thoughts.

Having Connie around had helped to fill the emptiness of a lost friendship, but no one would ever replace Betty completely.

Expectations of an autumn victory began to fade in September when Hitler launched a new and even more deadly weapon on London. The V-2 long-range rockets just dropped and exploded, giving no warning so there was no time to shelter.

Later that month the Allies suffered a setback abroad with the failure of the airborne landing at Arnhem, and everyone accepted that they had to wait longer for peace.

May was distracted from the technicalities of the war

when Dot Bailey came to call at the Stubbses' one evening on the verge of tears and clutching a letter she'd had from the evacuation office at the Town Hall.

'They're moving Joe to different lodgings because the people he's with can't cope with his difficult behaviour,' she said, holding the letter out for May to read.

'Difficult behaviour?' echoed Flo, who was peeling potatoes at the sink. 'But Joe is the easiest little boy I've ever come across.'

'Exactly,' said Dot.

'It doesn't say what he's actually done to bring this about, does it?' said May, having read the letter.

'No it doesn't, and the office was closed when I came off my shift,' Dot said. 'But the only place he's being moved to is home. I'm going down to Wiltshire to get him. I'm not having him shifted about like a piece of luggage with no one wanting him.'

'I'll come with you,' offered May to give the other woman some support; she knew that Dot had never been far afield on her own. 'It's Saturday tomorrow. We'll go after I finish work at midday. We'll have to try and find lodgings for the night when we get there.'

'Oh May, will you really come with me?' said Dot, imbued with gratitude. 'I could certainly do with some company.'

'Of course I'll come. He's my godson, remember, and I'm as upset about this as you are,' she told her. 'We'll go together and get it sorted.'

'A good thing too,' added Flo supportively.

★   ★   ★

It was raining heavily as May and Dot got off the train at the small country station and trudged down a narrow lane, having been given directions by the man in the ticket office. The abundant puddles were deep and muddy and the women's town shoes no match for them. The wind blew their umbrellas inside out so by the time they reached their destination they were soaked to the skin and thoroughly chilled.

The house they were looking for was in a row of cottages on the outskirts of the village. With a determined air they walked up the path and rapped the knocker.

A large woman in a wrapover apron opened the door and looked at them questioningly.

'Mrs Green?' asked Dot.

The woman nodded, eyeing them suspiciously.

'I'm Mrs Bailey, Joe's grandmother, and this is a close family friend who is also Joe's godmother,' said Dot in an even tone. 'We've come to collect Joe to take him home.'

The woman's eyes widened in surprise. 'Back to London?' she said disapprovingly.

'That's right.'

'But I heard you've still got bombing there.'

'We have, but it's all over bar the shouting and I want my grandson back home,' she said. 'Evacuation is not compulsory, you know.'

Mrs Green shrugged. 'It's your business what you do about the boy,' she said. 'But I was told the evacuation people would be moving him to another billet.'

'Perhaps you were told that, but I'm telling you that

he is coming home with us now,' declared Dot. 'He isn't staying anywhere he isn't wanted.'

'You're welcome to him,' the other woman said nastily.

May put a restraining hand on Dot's arm as she looked ready to set about Mrs Green. 'Can you tell us what the trouble with Joe actually is please?' she asked, hanging on to her temper. 'He's normally the easiest of children.'

'Maybe he is by your London standards,' she said scornfully. 'But I don't tolerate that sort of behaviour in my house.'

'What behaviour are you talking about? What has he actually done wrong?' asked May, keeping a firm grip on Dot, who was on the verge of explosion.

'He don't eat the food I give him, he won't do as he's told without asking why, and the other night he presented me with wet sheets to wash.'

Both women were stunned into silence.

'What is it you ask him to do that he questions?' asked Dot eventually.

'Normal things.' She seemed evasive.

'And does he do as he's told in the end?'

'Eventually he does, yeah,' she replied. 'With a little persuasion from me.'

'If you've laid a finger on him . . .' threatened Dot.

'There are other ways of making children behave.'

Dot gave her a hard look. 'I shall find out exactly what's been going on and make sure the evacuation people know about it,' she said.

'She's probably been making him do jobs and errands for her,' suggested May.

'He has to do his bit around the place, of course,' admitted Mrs Green.

'He's six years old, for heaven's sake,' said May.

'That's quite old enough to bring the coal in from the coal shed and help around the house,' she said. 'And he does it too, I make sure of that, but it's his damned questions that I can't abide.'

'He isn't used to doing the work of an adult, that's why he asks why, and rightly so,' Dot declared.

'And as for the accident in the bed, that will have been caused by fear – of you,' May put in.

'You Londoners don't train your kids proper, that's why it happened; it had nothing to do with me. I was just the one who had to clear it up.'

'Perhaps we could wait in your porch while you get him,' suggested May as the rain poured down on them. 'We are getting soaked to the skin here, as you can see.'

The woman's brows went up in disapproval but she opened the door wider and they stepped into a tiny lobby containing shoes and coats. It struck May how quiet the house was considering there were children here; there were no young voices. It seemed strange to her; where there were infants there was usually the high-pitched sound of their voices. She knew there were other evacuees besides Joe and guessed they were too afraid of Mrs Green to make a noise. She decided not to upset Dot further by pointing this out to her.

After about five minutes a small figure appeared in his dark outdoor coat with his gas mask over his shoulder and carrying the small case he had brought with him.

He looked pale and apprehensive but May knew she would never forget the look of pure joy when he saw his grandmother. Then he noticed May and his face was wreathed in smiles.

She and Dot were crying openly as they trudged back towards the village in search of lodgings for the night with Joe walking between them. They were cold, wet and tired but they had their boy back so they could endure anything.

'From what we can make out from talking to Joe, he was obviously terrified of the woman,' May told her parents when she got home from Wiltshire the next day. 'It must have upset his whole system so that he felt sick and couldn't eat, so she shouted at him which made him feel even worse. He didn't understand how to do the jobs she told him to do around the house because he had never done adult work before, so he asked and she shouted at him some more and the whole thing led to him wetting the bed and her telling the evacuation people she wanted rid of him.'

'The poor mite,' said Flo.

'The woman wants shooting,' added Dick.

'Dot is going to the Town Hall to tell the evacuation people about the way she treats the kids, so hopefully they'll do something about it.'

'Terrible to think there are people like that taking kiddies in,' said Flo.

'We were unlucky,' said May. 'For all the stories you

hear about bad evacuation experiences, there are more good ones, though no one will know the truth of it until all the children come back for good after the war. Joe seems absolutely fine now, that's the important thing.'

'He's back where he belongs, thank goodness,' said Flo.

Winter came in with frost, ice and freezing fog. People were cold, hungry and weary of the war, especially as shortages became even more acute. When news came in that the Germans had broken through in the Ardennes, hopes of peace in the near future vanished completely.

Another wartime Christmas seemed almost too much to bear, but most people managed somehow to create a festive atmosphere. The Stubbses and the Baileys joined forces for Christmas dinner as well as tea this year to help make the rations go further. They only had meat pie with very little meat and rice pudding for afters, but they had Joe back and he created his own magic. Sheila was home on leave and Connie came over on her bike in the afternoon, so they managed to enjoy themselves, playing games, singing songs and talking.

'We may not have peace yet but at least the streets aren't quite so dark since some of the blackout restrictions were lifted,' said Flo to Dot as they were making sandwiches for supper in the kitchen. 'It'll be a bit easier for you when you go home later on. I know it's only half lighting but it's better than nothing.'

'I'll say,' agreed Dot. 'And I think we've all enjoyed the day even though the war is hanging on for grim death.'

'I agree,' said Flo.

'I've got Joe back; what I want now is his dad back too,' said Dot.

'I'm sure it won't be long,' said Flo encouragingly.

Although the freedom of peacetime gradually got under way in the new year, with various restrictions being lifted and the public tasting what life would be like after the war, still victory remained elusive.

The tension built almost to breaking point during the spring months, when it became legal to buy bunting without coupons so long as it was red, white and blue, and factory hooters were allowed to be sounded again for the first time in nearly six years, but still no end to the war.

Then things really started to happen when the Allies achieved huge successes in Germany and news came through that Hitler was dead. Peace was almost upon them.

May had never experienced anything like VE Day before; a unanimous outpouring of jubilation so strong it was overwhelming. She couldn't imagine that anything would ever be this powerful again in her lifetime. It was a new world for every man, woman and child in the country. Knowing that they were free; that they would wake up each morning to a bomb-less life after years of danger and threat. The joy was indescribable.

Everybody was out in the streets, hugging each other and laughing. The Stubbses and the Baileys decided that there was only one place for Londoners to be today, so they headed for the station and joined the crowds outside Buckingham Palace. With Joe sitting on Dick's shoulders they stared at the balcony draped with crimson and yellow with a gold fringe and cheered until they were hoarse when the royal family came out through those famous doors.

The capital throbbed with patriotism and emotion. People were singing and dancing and kissing complete strangers. Later on, May and the others went home to join in the celebrations there. London was one big party.

May experienced a sudden moment of sadness for Betty and Doug, both struck down at an early age. In the outpouring of relief and joy that peace was here at last, it was easy to temporarily forget those who hadn't lived to see it. She guessed that all over the world people would be having quiet moments just like hers.

Although nothing could diminish the joy of freedom, the shortages and shabbiness were still there when the celebrations were over, and all the signs were they would be with them for a very long time to come.

May became unemployed when the parachute factory closed its doors to war workers and prepared to return to its former purpose. Her mother's job at the Co-op would no longer be available to her when single service-women were demobbed and wanting their jobs back.

'We'll get the Pavilion rebuilt as soon as the compensation comes through,' Flo said to May. 'Then we'll both have a job.'

'It might be a while before we'll be able to do it, Mum,' warned May. She knew how much her mother wanted it, but they had to be realistic. Getting the country back to normal was going to be a huge and lengthy task. 'They might not lift the restrictions just yet and materials will probably be short for a while.'

'I know all that,' Flo sighed. 'But we'll get it up and running as soon as we can.'

'And meanwhile I'll keep looking for a job,' said May chirpily. 'Nothing will defeat us now that we have peace.'

'Nothing at all,' agreed her mother.

As the victory flags went down, so the WELCOME HOME banners went up. All over London the dusty, damaged streets were warmed and brightened by them.

WELCOME HOME GEORGE appeared outside the Bailey home one day in the late autumn. Dot and May didn't know what time he would arrive but they did know the day. It was a Friday. Now working on the switchboard at a canning factory, May went straight to the Baileys' after work, because it seemed right that she should be there when he arrived.

She was inwardly quaking with a mixture of excitement and nerves, Dot was shaky and emotional too. Joe, who wasn't old enough to understand the huge significance of the occasion but had been told that it was going to happen and he could stay up late, was looking out of the window, bored with waiting.

Then, just after they had come in for a break from their welcoming positions at the front door, there was the sound of the key being pulled through the letter box and a voice said, 'I'm home. Anyone in?' And there he was grinning and handsome as ever.

May stood aside while his mother greeted him by flinging her arms around him and sobbing for joy.

'Is that him?' asked Joe.

'Yes, that's him,' said May. 'Your daddy is home.'

'Hello, son,' said George, smiling and putting his arms out to the boy.

There was a silence while Joe stared at his father. Then he burst into tears and rushed from the room.

'He's overwhelmed, I expect,' suggested May, almost physically hurting from the look of disappointment on George's face. 'I'll go and see to him.'

'No, I'll go, May,' said Dot thickly. 'You stay here and look after George.'

May felt quite shy as she went over to him. 'Welcome home, George,' she said, slipping her arms around him.

'It's good to see you, May,' he said, kissing her, but she sensed that his heart wasn't in it.

'And you,' she said.

Dot re-entered the room looking worried. 'He doesn't want to come down and it's very naughty of him. I've given him a telling-off,' she explained. 'I think he's a bit tired. It's been a long wait. He probably worked himself up over your coming home and got overexcited.'

'Don't worry about it, Mum,' said George, putting on a brave face. 'He'll come round when he's ready.'

'It isn't like Joe to be awkward.'

Feeling unusually distanced from what was essentially a family occasion and deciding that she probably shouldn't have been at the Baileys' house for George's homecoming, May said, 'Well, I'll leave you to it then.'

'Don't go, May,' said George, but he didn't sound overly insistent.

'No, please don't,' added Dot.

'I think you need to concentrate on Joe,' May insisted. 'I'll see you later on or tomorrow.'

Convinced that she was doing the right thing, she slipped quietly from the house. The relationship between George and his son was a vital and delicate thing and George needed to deal with it himself, without the distraction of having her around.

The rift between them that she had sensed during his last leave now seemed like a reality, especially as she had felt a holding back when they had embraced. She hoped desperately that it was all in her imagination, because after all the years of loving him, rejection now would be too much to bear.

George was aware that he had ruined his homecoming for them all but felt unable to rectify it because he had been travelling for two days and was mentally and physically exhausted. The men had had to wait ages to get transported to the port, then queued for hours to get on the boat. The crossing had been choppy and a lot of the men, including George, had been seasick throughout the journey. They had gone to the barracks this side of the Channel to be officially sent on leave, and only then had been free to go. A few had decided to stay overnight before travelling home because they were tired, but George couldn't wait another night after so long.

He had been so excited about coming home for good at last. It was what he had lived for and what had kept him going for the past six years. He knew the expectation here at home would be high, and he'd let them down. His son didn't want to know him and May had been so disappointed in him she'd left.

The truth was, he wasn't some sort of a super-soldier; he was just an ordinary bloke who was subject to the same human frailties as everyone else, and at this moment he didn't have the energy to put things right.

'I'll put the kettle on for a cuppa, son,' said his mother as he sank gratefully into an armchair.

'Thanks, Mum,' he said.

When she brought the tea to him, he was fast asleep.

'Didn't George make it back, then?' asked Flo when May came home alone.

'Yeah, he arrived,' she said.

'Oh. Is he all right?'

'Yes, he seemed to be fine,' she said distantly.

'I thought he'd have come back with you to see us,' said Flo, obviously disappointed.

'He wants to be with his own family at the moment,' she said sharply.

'I was only asking,' said Flo.

'And I was only answering your question,' retorted May, still bitterly upset by the let-down of George's homecoming. 'I'm not his keeper. I can't tell him what to do. He'll come and see you when he's ready, I suppose.'

'Now then, May,' admonished her father. 'There's no need to bite your mother's head off.'

'Sorry, Mum,' she said, desperately needing to be on her own. 'I'm tired. I think I'll go to bed.'

'All right, dear.'

After she had left the room, Flo said to her husband in a low voice, 'Trouble by the sound of it. I do hope it isn't going to go wrong for them again, after all this time.'

'So do I,' said Dick. 'But there's nothing we can do about it if it does.'

'That's the difficult bit,' she agreed worriedly.

In her room, May sat on her bed feeling miserable and frustrated. As well as being upset by George's disappointing homecoming, she was also beginning to feel very restricted by living at home. She adored her parents but she had outgrown their constant nurturing and felt as though she was living under a microscope. Having to explain your every move and knowing that when you were hurt they felt it too was a strain. She was twenty-four. It was time she was out from under their feet. But as the usual way of achieving this for a girl like her was marriage, there didn't seem to be any sort of a solution at the moment.

George dominated her thoughts. What was going to happen between them? she wondered. She knew he would come to see her when he was ready and felt she must wait until the time was right for him. But what would he have to say to her? His attitude towards her definitely seemed to have changed, which probably meant he was going to tell her that it was over as a romance and he wanted to revert to being friends. But that wasn't enough for her now. She would rather not see him at all than endure that.

She smiled bitterly. Over before it had even started, she thought. He had proposed to her on the station on his way back off leave and had been oddly remote the next time she had seen him. Theirs had been the court-ship that had never happened.

Oh well, whatever the outcome of that situation, she had another matter to deal with; she must go downstairs and make amends to her mother for being so rude. It wasn't her parents' fault she had such a disastrous love life.

George woke up to see that it was daylight and two bright eyes were studying him at an unnervingly close range.

'You woke up then,' said Joe.

'Seems like it,' said George sleepily, realising that he

was in his own bed at home. He could only vaguely remember moving from the armchair downstairs. He must have slept all evening and all night and felt much rested.

'Can you play football?' asked Joe.

'Yeah,' muttered George, struggling to gather his wits after sleeping so soundly. 'I can do that. I played a few times in the army.'

'Are you any good?' he asked.

'I can handle a football, yeah.'

The boy thought about this for a while, then said, 'My friend at school; his dad used to be very good at it.'

'Did he?' said George, feeling slightly out of his depth with this child who seemed like a stranger whilst being achingly dear to him. Gone were the days when he could please him just by lifting him up in the air.

Joe nodded. 'He's dead now, though,' he said in a matter-of-fact manner. 'He was a sailor and his boat got bombed.'

'Oh,' said George, shocked to hear news of such a tragedy delivered so calmly by one so young. 'That's sad. I hope that you're kind to your friend.'

The child looked thoughtful. 'Do you mean I shouldn't fight with him?' he asked.

'I hope you don't fight with anyone,' said George.

'I do if they hit me first,' he explained. 'You have to stick up for yourself or they think you're a sissy and steal your marbles.'

George felt about a hundred years old and hopelessly out of touch with how little boys behaved. 'Mm, there is that, but you should never look for a fight.'

'All right.'

'Good boy.'

'I've got to go now,' Joe announced.

'Are you going to school?'

'It's Saturday,' he said. 'I don't have to go today. I'm going to play with my friends in the street. It isn't raining so Gran says I can go out.'

'I'll see you later, then.'

'Yeah,' said Joe and walked out of the room, leaving George feeling warmed but worried.

He felt as though he was back to square one as regarded being a father. He'd lost a lot of years. He had been very involved with Joe when he was a baby. But being a parent to a seven year old who didn't know you was a different thing altogether. It was going to take time and patience and he would give it his utmost.

But right now there was something else he had to attend to, as a matter of urgency.

'I'll do the shopping today to give you a break, Mum,' offered May that morning, seeing the weekend stretching out emptily ahead of her and needing to get out of the house.

'All right, dear,' said her mother, tactfully avoiding the subject of George. 'Here's the list, and don't forget to take the ration books.'

'Won't be long,' said May, and set off down the street with her mother's shopping bag.

It was a glorious autumn day in late October. There

was a chill in the air but a hazy sun had broken through, emphasising the shabbiness of everything but pleasurable even so. May was beginning to feel a slight worm of anger towards George. It wasn't right to propose to a girl and then behave as though you hadn't. Yes, he did have more pressing matters to attend to, but surely he could have popped round to see her last night, even if only for a few minutes.

Passing the Pavilion and playground bomb site, she paused, looking beyond the overgrown grass, the nettles and the rosebay willow herb to how it used to be and would be again. There would be laughter and conversation, a buzz in the air and community spirit. Together she and her mother would make it happen, May was absolutely determined.

To remember the Pavilion and the playground was to think about George because he'd been at the very heart of it. She thought of him now, and of Betty, just kids hanging out together with no thought of money or war or responsibility. Innocent times long gone.

She was so absorbed in her thoughts that she was startled when she heard a step behind her.

'George,' she said, swinging round. 'Well, you certainly took your time.'

'Sorry I didn't come round last night, May,' he said, looking very contrite. 'I fell asleep and didn't wake up until this morning. I was so shattered when I got back, I couldn't function properly and messed up the whole thing for all of you.'

'Oh, I see.' It was that simple. Exhaustion. She should

have realised, and hated herself for not doing so. 'Of course, you would have been tired.'

'Anyway, that was yesterday. Now I'm recovered, and I have something to say to you.'

'Oh, go on then.'

'I know that you said yes when I proposed to you, but it was all in the future then,' he began. 'Now that the war is over, we can make plans. But I need to point out the facts to you, some you already know, others you don't. I didn't know about them myself until recently.'

'I'm waiting.'

'Right, first up, I don't have a job to go to yet,' he said.

'I realise that.'

'Secondly, I have to start from scratch learning to be a dad to my seven-year-old son who doesn't know me from Adam, so I will need to commit myself to that.'

'Of course.'

'I don't have a home of my own to offer you.'

'Mm.'

'And if all of that isn't bad enough, my father, who was my idol, I now know was an adulterer, and I almost deliberately killed a man in my platoon.' He paused for breath. 'It's taken me a while to come to terms with these last things and I think I was probably a bit offhand on my last leave because of it.'

'I knew there was something bothering you,' she said. 'I thought perhaps you had fallen out of love with me.'

'Oh May, that's the last thing,' he said emotionally. 'I'm

sorry if I upset you. Later on I'll tell you the whole story, but for now I want to ask you if, knowing all these things about me, you would still consider taking me on. I love you, May, so much, and I want to share my life with you.'

Her face was a picture of delight. 'You don't really need me to answer that, do you?'

'Not now that I've seen your lovely smile,' he said, slipping his arm around her.

They stood, arms entwined, in the place where it had all begun, war torn now, but still theirs. It had been a long journey, but at last they were home – together.